In Memory

Of

Marian Agnew

Praise for *Stray Bullets*

"A cracking good story."

—*Toronto Star*

"Rotenberg really knows how to build legal suspense."

—*The Globe and Mail*

"The added frisson of a city craving justice combined with evidence that can't quite add up the way law enforcement and prosecutors want them to gives Rotenberg the extra storytelling juice he needs to propel *Stray Bullets* to its inevitable but riveting conclusion."

—*National Post*

"Rotenberg makes it his own with propulsive plotting, crisp, vivid, no-wasted-words writing, and, most importantly, distinct characters virtually all of whom make individual claims on a reader's interest and empathy. . . . In fact, the entire unfolding and resolution of a tragic, sadly semi-familiar, crime-and-punishment tale shows a real pro of a writer, just getting better and better."

—*The London Free Press*

Praise for *The Guilty Plea*

"A compulsive page-turner . . . His humanizing of seemingly obvious killers raises doubts in the reader at the same pace as it does for the jury."

—*Maclean's*

"This book's page-turning twists and relatable, personable characters are sure to thrill mystery loves and lit elitists alike."

—*Precedent*

"Rotenberg's . . . courtroom drama is terrific."

—Ian Rankin

"Not since *Anatomy of a Murder* has a novel so vividly captured the real life of criminal lawyers in the midst of a high-stakes trial."

—Edward L. Greenspan, QC

"Rotenberg juggles the many plot elements with aplomb, unveiling each new surprise with care and patience."

—*Quill & Quire*

"A great book for summer."

—*The Globe and Mail*

"Rotenberg has crafted an idealistic but gripping—and distinctly Canadian—portrait of how justice does and does not get done."

—The London Free Press

"It's a solid whodunit."

—Winnipeg Free Press

"A dock-chair novel . . . the book has local buzz galore."

—National Post

Praise for *Old City Hall*

"Loved it! Rotenberg's *Old City Hall* is a terrific look at contemporary Toronto."

—Ian Rankin

"Breathtaking . . . a tightly woven spiderweb of plot and a rich cast of characters make this a truly gripping read . . . Robert Rotenberg does for Toronto what Ian Rankin does for Edinburgh."

—Jeffery Deaver

"Robert Rotenberg knows his Toronto courts and jails, he knows his law, and he knows his way around a legal thriller. *Old City Hall* is a splendid entertainment."

—Andrew Pyper, author of *The Killing Circle*

"Clever, complex, and filled with an engaging cast of characters, *Old City Hall* captures the vibrancy and soul of Toronto."

—Kathy Reichs

"It's clear that *Old City Hall* has enough hidden motives and gumshoeing to make it a hard-boiled classic."

—The Globe and Mail

"The book has wowed pretty much everyone who's read it . . . A finely paced, intricately written plot is matched by a kaleidoscope of the multicultural city's locales and characters."

—Maclean's

"Twenty-first-century Toronto is a complicated place, rife with the kind of paradox and contradiction that lends a city depth and complexity. It's a good setting for sinuous legal machinations to unfold, steeped in that elusively desirable literary quality we call character."

—Toronto Star

"Rotenberg is Canada's John Grisham."

—Telegraph-Journal

ALSO BY ROBERT ROTENBERG

Old City Hall
The Guilty Plea
Stray Bullets

ROBERT ROTENBERG

STRANGLE-HOLD

A TOUCHSTONE BOOK
PUBLISHED BY SIMON & SCHUSTER
NEW YORK   LONDON   TORONTO   SYDNEY   NEW DELHI

Touchstone
A Division of Simon & Schuster, Inc.
1230 Avenue of the Americas
New York, NY 10020

This Touchstone export edition May 2013

TOUCHSTONE and colophon are registered trademarks of Simon & Schuster, Inc.

For information about special discounts for bulk purchases, please contact Simon & Schuster Special Sales at 1-800-268-3216 or CustomerService@simonandschuster.ca.

Designed by Akasha Archer

Manufactured in the United States of America

10   9   8   7   6   5   4   3   2

ISBN 978-1-4516-4239-1
ISBN 978-1-4516-4244-5 (ebook)

For my brothers
Lawrence, David, and Matthew,
my best friends

I have done these things,
That now give evidence against my soul.

– William Shakespeare, *Richard II, III, 4*

PART
ONE

1

THIS WAS NOT THE WAY ARI GREENE HAD EXPECTED TO BE SPENDING HIS MONDAY MORNING. No self-respecting homicide detective would be caught dead driving a motor scooter. And yet, here he was putt-putting along Kingston Road, home to a string of low-rent strip malls, tax refund specialists, tired-looking furniture stores, and cheapo motels that rented out rooms by the week, by the day, and by the half day. The type of places cops called "have-a-naps." Today's predetermined destination was the Maple Leaf Motel. Maybe it would be a step up from the in-appropriately named Luxury Motel, the tacky place where they'd met last week. Of course, this get-together was not about the decor, but about the one thing in his life that never seemed to change: *cherchez la femme.*

The silly scooter was the best way he could think of to get across town during the day, not an easy thing to do because he was one of the best-known police-men in Toronto, and his car was a distinctive '88 Oldsmobile that every cop on patrol would recognize. Buying a second car, or renting one, was out of the question. Left a paper trail. A bicycle was possible, but it was too far to ride. Plus, he didn't want to arrive all hot and sweaty for what had become over the previous five weeks their regular Monday-morning "romantic rendezvous."

It had been easy to find a scooter for sale in the newspaper – no traceable computer searches on his laptop – and buy it and a helmet for cash, no names given. He hadn't registered the ownership or gotten a motorcycle licence. If he were ever stopped he'd just show his badge and that would take care of that. He'd found a paved lot behind an abandoned garage a ten-minute walk from his home where he could park and lock it. Even the gas was simple. He'd go to a different independent station when they were busy at rush hour, buy twenty dol-lars' worth, and hand over the cash with his gloves and helmet still on. No credit cards. No trace. Invisible.

In a strange way he enjoyed the challenge of covering his tracks. He'd always thought that the many criminals he'd chased and arrested over the years had been motivated by the game, not the crime. The feeling of beating the system. Fooling everyone. Being on the outside, looking in.

Now he was playing. Not that having an affair with a married woman was a crime. Well, at least it wasn't illegal. And, thankfully, this was the last Monday he'd be doing this. Next week she was going to split with her husband, and everything was going to change.

Being on a scooter made Greene much more aware of the weather. He'd driven a patrol car along Kingston Road hundreds of times, but had never before realized how windy the street could be, thanks to its proximity to the lake, and the long, uninterrupted line it followed near the shore. Today was sunny and warm, the sky was a startling blue although the wind was strong. But the traffic was unusually slow and now it had ground to a halt.

He shot his left hand from the sleeve of his leather jacket to check his watch. Damn. He was going to be late. It was already ten-thirty. He was supposed to be there by now.

Ten-thirty on the first Monday in September after Labour Day. A time when the rest of the world was hard at work. Kids in school. People at their desks. Criminal trials in their opening stages.

As a homicide detective, Greene's time was his own, and it was easy for him to slip away for a few hours, once a week. But for Jennifer Raglan, it was more complicated. She was the head Crown attorney in Toronto. It was a job she'd had for years, had given up, then had returned to at the end of July when Ralph Armitage, the lawyer who'd taken over from her, was arrested for obstructing justice.

Her first week back, she'd got in touch with Greene and invited him out for lunch.

"I told them I'd do the job until Christmas, not a day longer," she had said. They were in a booth in the corner of the City Hall cafeteria, a place where cops and Crowns regularly ate. Underneath the table, unseen, she'd slipped off one of her shoes and was caressing his calf.

"Very loyal of you," he said.

"On one condition. That I get my Mondays off until I'm in a trial."

"Sounds fair."

She smiled at him. There was a little dimple in her cheek that showed when she was very happy. She rubbed his leg harder. "Howard has a client in Boston, and he flies down there every Monday."

Howard was her husband. A year earlier she had left him and their children and soon after that started seeing Greene. They had worked very hard to keep their relationship secret. But after a few months, the ordeal of splitting up her family had become too much for her, and she had returned home.

"You want the day off to be with the kids," he said.

"No." She tucked her toes up inside his pant leg and stroked his skin. "I want Monday mornings with you."

Then she told him how she had begun long-distance running again. How it was a brisk, half-hour jog from her house to the strip of cheap motels on Kingston Road. How they all took cash and didn't ask for ID. And that she'd already paid for a room at the Dominion Motel for the following Monday. Sixty bucks. No tax. Room 8.

He offered to pay half and that made her laugh. "Money's tight but I think I can handle it," she said. "And besides, this is all my idea."

He shrugged. "I'm not exactly unwilling."

"And you're not exactly comfortable with it either."

She stared at him with her bold brown eyes. There was no point in denying it.

Last winter, when her mother was dying and he was in a tough trial that involved the murder of a child, they'd spent a night in an out-of-town hotel. It was the only time they'd slept together while she was still living with her husband.

He had thought that was the end of it. Stress of the moment.

Over the next few months, they'd occasionally run into each other in court, say hello. He'd ask about her kids. She'd ask about his father. Her message was clear: It's over.

She pulled her foot away.

"If you don't show up," she said, getting back up to leave, "I can watch *Law and Order* reruns for two hours."

She insisted he take every possible precaution to hide his identity. He'd come up with this idea of the scooter and for the last five Mondays had walked into whatever motel room she'd booked, always number eight, at exactly 10:30. Their two hours together always went quickly. And now, thanks to the damn traffic, it was 10:39 when he finally pulled into a strip mall that had a payday loan shop, a nail salon, an out-of-business adult video store, a convenience store, and a place that sold discount goods from almost every country of the world. The motel was less than a block away.

He parked the scooter beside a bank of newspaper boxes between the Money
Mart store and the Cupid Boutique. The city had four major dailies, and all but
one of them had huge front-page pictures of Brad Pitt and Angelina Jolie getting
out of a stretch limo or walking up the red carpet to a movie theatre. It was all
part of TIFF, the Toronto International Film Festival, a September ritual that
saw top-flight movie stars parachute in each year. In his early days as a division
cop, Greene had been one of those policemen he now saw in the photo, holding
back the crowds.

He walked past a poster featuring a group of bulky high-school boys in
rugby uniforms. They were black, Asian, East Asian, and white. Typical of a
suburban Toronto school. In big type the words SCARBOROUGH SCRAPPERS NEED
YOUR SUPPORT! In smaller type there were details of how to send money to help
the team.

The sign was a typically clever move by Hap Charlton, the chief of police
and Greene's mentor for many years, who now was running for mayor. Since
becoming chief, he had got a huge amount of publicity for his work as the coach
of this team of underprivileged students. Most of it very positive, except for the
time when former U.S. president Bill Clinton was in town for a conference and
Charlton missed it because of a game.

Charlton was a master at knowing the rules, and bending them just enough
so they wouldn't break. The election rules very clearly stated that no signs could
go up until thirty-eight days before the vote. This was his way of getting his message out there, without showing face.

A month earlier, Charlton had gone on a talk-radio program and announced
he was running for mayor. His campaign pitch was that he was tough on crime,
that he was going to get rid of wasteful spending at City Hall, that he would
drive his own car, no more limo service for the mayor, and his own personal ob-
session: He'd declared war on graffiti. He'd held his first press conference in front
of a vacant suburban warehouse where he'd taken a power washer and cleaned
off a whole wall of what his critics called urban art and he called garbage. Pictures of him wielding the nozzle like a gun had been picked up by the press
across the country.

The local media pundits, who almost all lived downtown, were not impressed. But Charlton immediately jumped to an early lead in the polls, leaving
his main challenger, the left-leaning mayor, Peggy Forest, flat-footed. Since then
he'd kept gaining momentum. On Wednesday night, he was going to have his

first big rally at a hotel near the airport. Greene would be there, along with every other homicide cop on the force.

Someone had spray-painted in HAP IS A HAZARD on the sign. The poster and the graffiti pretty much summed up the radically divided sentiments about his campaign.

There was no one else on the narrow sidewalk. In the six times Greene had driven his scooter out here, he'd never seen a pedestrian or even the occasional cyclist. This was suburbia, where people drove their cars everywhere.

The exterior of the Maple Leaf Motel featured red brick with white trim. Continuing the design theme, the signage was also red type on a white backdrop. All of it was accented by a healthy dollop of metal maple leaves, fastened to the facade. A huge, green Dumpster in the front driveway squatted atop cracked concrete and a bed of weeds. There were no cars parked anywhere. The motel was two stories high. There was a passageway that went under the second floor in the middle of the side facing the street. It was the only way into the courtyard where all the rooms were located. He went to room 8.

Earlier, just as Greene was leaving his house, Jennifer had called him on his cell from a pay phone at a Coffee Time doughnut shop up the street.

"Ari, Howard just texted me," she'd said. "His meeting in Boston cancelled at the last minute."

"Oh."

"He wanted to get together for coffee."

"Okay, then –"

"No," she said. "I texted him back that I was doing a fifteen-K run."

They had talked for about another minute, both excited that their lives were soon going to come together. "Don't be late," she'd said before she hung up.

He took a last look at his watch. It was 10:40. In a few seconds he'd be with her. Jennifer always insisted on having half an hour by herself to set things up. Now the fluorescent overhead light would be off, and her usual array of white candles would be lit. There would be fresh pillowcases on the pillows and on her iPod Oscar Peterson would be tickling the piano keys. Today there'd be a small bottle of champagne chilling in the ice-filled bathroom sink. His mouth was dry in anticipation of kissing her.

She always lowered the blinds, closed the door, and left it unlocked. He always left his helmet and gloves on, until he was safely inside.

The door was slightly ajar, which was unusual. Usually she kept it closed but unlocked so he could walk right in. The overhead light was on inside. The candles were set up all around the room, but only the one on the far bedside table was lit. He could see it had burned down quite a ways. No music was playing, though her iPod was set up in its speaker dock. And even with his helmet still on, his visor still down, he could tell the smell of the room was off.

There was an ugly comforter on the bed, the kind that Jennifer always hid away, and there was a body-shaped mound under it. He took another step inside and glimpsed a strand of her brown hair. She was facing away.

How odd.

Had she fallen asleep?

He smiled. She was playing a joke on him.

He tiptoed to her side of the bed and flipped up the visor. Her head was covered by the comforter. He bent down and gently pulled it back with his gloved hand.

"Hello, Sleeping Beauty," he said. "It's time to –"

Then he saw her face.

Her brown eyes were bloodshot and bulging. Her forehead had a slick line of sweat over her eyebrows. The skin on her neck was red. Her tongue hung helplessly out of her wide mouth.

He couldn't breathe.

In five years on the homicide squad he'd seen enough death to know it instantly. He yanked off a glove and touched the carotid artery on her neck. No pulse. Her skin felt pasty. He put his hands in front of her nose and mouth. Nothing.

He had to think. Had to call 911.

How could this be?

Tears jumped into his eyes. His stomach lurched and he started to gag.

He turned away from her and felt for his phone. The bathroom door right in front of him was closed. The killer. Maybe he was in there.

He lifted his heavy boot and, anger coursing through his body, kicked in the door.

2

WHAT A BORING MONDAY, AWOTWE AMANKWAH, COURTROOM REPORTER FOR THE *Toronto Star*, thought as he flipped through the trial list on the centre hall desk at the 361 University Avenue Courthouse. For the last two months there'd been nothing decent to write about thanks to the court's annual summer break — when all the well-heeled judges were up north at their family cottages. He could barely remember the last time his byline had appeared on the front page. And now the film festival was monopolizing half the ink in the paper with paparazzi crap.

The *Star*'s new editor, Barclay Church, a British transplant who lived for stories filled with sex and scandal, would have no interest in the handful of run-of-the mill crimes on this court docket: a stabbing; two shootings; a dead body found in a ravine; a real dumb drug-importing case (a bunch of boxers from the islands who shipped the stuff up in their gym bags); and the inevitable sexual assault cases. One pitted a stepfather against his stepdaughter, another featured a drunk, minor-league hockey player versus a failed actress-turned-waitress.

All the usual suspects. Strictly six-paragraph, page-eight filler.

None of this was going to help Amankwah reboot his career. He needed the ink to earn a promotion so he could start doing feature stories. That would give him more exposure and more money to maintain his support payments so he could keep seeing his two children. For the last few years he'd been doing extra overnight shifts in the radio room to make his nut. And now, with the hotly contested election for city mayor about to start, only the biggest and sexiest crime stories had a chance of not getting buried, if not cut out altogether.

His best bet this morning was Courtroom 406, where Seaton Wainwright, the high-flying filmmaker who was charged with scamming investors out of millions, was scheduled to make an appearance. Last Wednesday things had heated up when Phil Cutter, Wainwright's aggressive, bald-headed lawyer, had tried to change the bail conditions to allow his client to go to New York for five days to "work on some deals he planned to sign during the Toronto Film Festival" before his upcoming trial.

Jennifer Raglan, the lead Crown on the case, had produced copies of Wainwright's Visa card that showed the last time he'd been in the Big Apple, he'd hired a series of high-class Manhattan hookers and charged them to his company as "promotion."

The judge, Irene Norville, no shrinking violet herself, was not impressed. She gave Wainwright forty-eight hours in New York, ordered him to be back in court this morning at ten, and rushed off the bench.

Wainwright, who was about six feet ten and weighed close to three hundred pounds, ploughed out of the courtroom. When Raglan walked into the hallway with the other lawyers and reporters, he accosted her.

"Why the fuck are you trying to ruin my life," he shouted. "Do you know how many jobs I've created in this town?"

Raglan was maybe five six and thin, but she stood her ground like a halfback confronting a charging linebacker. "Maybe you should start thinking above the shoulders," she said, "not below the waist."

Two court security guards ran over.

She waved them off and turned on Cutter. Her eyes flashed with rage. "Your clown of a client comes near me again, and I'll have him in cuffs so fast it will make his fat ass pucker up like the scared chicken he really is."

She stormed off, leaving everyone standing in stunned silence. Raglan was a well-respected prosecutor and known for keeping her cool in tough situations.

"Where'd that come from?" Amankwah asked the other reporters.

Zach Stone, the *Toronto Sun* writer who was the veteran of the crew, didn't seem surprised. "That's the old Jennie," he said.

"Meaning?" Amankwah asked.

"Not many people know this, but she started out as a cop."

"Raglan. A cop?"

"Long time ago," Stone had said in his usual cryptic tone. He had begun his career at the old *Toronto Telegraph*. When that paper closed he spent a few years at the *Star*, then moved to the *Sun* a long time ago. He had a million sources and even more secrets. It was clear he wasn't going to say anything more.

Amankwah knew there would be no fireworks this morning between Raglan and Wainwright. Last week she'd told Norville she was taking Mondays off until the trial began, next week, and she wouldn't be here today.

Five minutes before ten o'clock, Amankwah watched the junior lawyer on the case, a beautiful young woman named Jo Summers, come into court and set herself up at the Crown counsel table. There was no sign of Wainwright, who always made a grand entrance at the last moment, angering Norville more each time, but was never technically late.

Cutter scurried in just before ten. His bald pate gleamed with sweat. He strode over to Summers and whispered in her ear. She looked around the empty courtroom, frowned, and shook her head, like a vice principal frustrated yet again with a difficult pupil.

Watching Cutter wipe the perspiration from his brow, Amankwah could tell that this time there'd be no dramatic, last-second entrance by his mini-movie-mogul client.

There was a loud rap, and the oak door at the front of the courtroom swung open. Norville swooped in, followed by her robed registrar, an older gentleman named Mr. Singh. A former railway engineer in India, Singh had been a key witness in a murder trial a few years earlier and had become enamoured with the court process. Now he worked here. Courteous, efficient, and always with a smile on his face, he loved to chat with people and everyone loved to talk to him.

She ran up to her elevated dais, plunked herself down in her high-backed chair, put on a pair of plain but stylish black glasses, and scanned the empty seats in front of her. Her eyes fixed on Cutter.

"Counsel, where's your client?"

Cutter, usually a fearless advocate, bowed his head. "I haven't heard from him all morning." He pulled out his cell phone. "Mr. Wainwright always e-mails and texts me about ten times a day. But he's not responding."

"Tell me that at least he came back from his Manhattan adventure."

Cutter nodded. "Yes, Your Honour. I saw him at my office last night. But this morning, I have no explanation. This is not his usual MO."

"Hah," Norville said.

She looked like she wanted to spit at him, Amankwah thought. Now, that would be a front-page story.

"If by his usual MO you mean arrogantly striding into my court at exactly ten o'clock, not a second earlier, I have to agree with you." She turned to Summers. "The Crown's position?"

"Bench warrant," Summers said. "Time to send the accused a message that this isn't just another appointment on his busy schedule. The trial starts next Monday, let him have a week in jail to think about what it means to get to court on time."

"Your Honour, I'll admit my client regularly tests the patience of the court," Cutter said, jumping in. "Last night he assured me he'd get here early." He held up his phone. "His personal assistant hasn't heard from him either. An hour ago, I had my partner, Barb Gild, rush over to his condo. She called five minutes ago. The concierge said that Mr. Wainwright left at seven P.M. last night and didn't come back. I met with him at seven-thirty. He gave me his passport, as you requested he do when he got back from New York. He left my office at eight-thirty and that's the last anyone has heard or seen of him."

Norville yanked off her glasses and let them clatter on her desk. "Mr. Cutter, what do you want me to do?"

"Give me one day. We'll do everything we can to find him. I'm confident there will be some explanation for this."

Norville squinted at the big clock on the sidewall above the jury box. She sighed. "For the record. It is now 10:09 A.M. on September tenth. This court is adjourned until one o'clock. Mr. Cutter, if your client isn't standing right beside you this afternoon, I'm going to issue a bench warrant. And he'll sit in jail until this trial is over. Got it?"

"Yes, Your Honour."

Amankwah had never seen Cutter look so humble in court.

"And, Mr. Cutter," she said.

"Yes, Your Honour."

"If I were you, I'd pray very hard that he hasn't left the country."

Out in the hallway, Cutter marched away, tearing off the white tabs around his neck and unbuttoning the top button of his too-tight white court shirt. The slap of his black wingtip shoes echoed off the marble walls with a loud clang sound. Amankwah caught up and walked with him step for step.

"Where do you think Wainwright's gone?" he asked.

Cutter shrugged. "How the fuck should I know? This job would be a hell of a lot easier if we didn't have clients."

"What are you going to do to find him?"

"Call in Dudley Do-Right and the Mounties," Cutter said. He got to the frosted-glass door of the barristers' lounge. A prominent sign above the wood handle read: LOUNGE STRICTLY RESERVED FOR MEMBERS OF THE LAW SOCIETY OF UPPER CANADA. CLIENTS AND MEDIA ARE STRICTLY PROHIBITED.

He yanked the door open and disappeared.

Amankwah stood alone in the empty hallway. He looked down at the pathetic few lines he'd scribbled down in his reporter's notebook. Shit. A dud story on a dud Monday morning.

3

GREENE STEPPED INSIDE THE MOTEL BATHROOM. IT WAS EMPTY. IN THE SINK, A HALF BOTTLE of champagne lay in pool of icy water.

He wanted to vomit. Under his helmet, tears were streaming down his eyes. He could hardly see. He could hardly think.

How could Jennifer be dead? Murdered?

Ari, think, he yelled at himself. This is a crime scene. Everything here is evidence.

He looked back at the bed, tiptoed out, and crouched down beside Jennifer. He wanted this one last, private chance to see her, before it all began.

She was curled up under the covers. The candle burning by her side. His heart was thumping harder than he'd ever felt it.

He froze.

He didn't want to leave. Didn't want the moment to end. Time had lost all meaning. At last he got up. Careful not to disturb anything, he took a step back and reached again for his cell phone.

He heard a sound. Something scratching against the outside of the front door, which he hadn't closed behind him.

Someone was out there.

He jammed the phone back in his pocket. It was two steps to the foot of the bed and three more across to the door. He flung it open. Scanned the little courtyard. Something caught his eye at the passageway. A person fleeing. All he saw was the heel of a shoe before it disappeared around the corner.

He ran to the street, puffing hard under the helmet, the visor crashing down with his motion. There was no one in front of the motel. Out on Kingston Road, three lanes of traffic whizzed by in both directions. To his left was an empty lot. To his right was the strip mall where he'd parked his scooter. No one was there either.

He sprinted over to the mall. A few cars were parked, but nothing seemed out of place. He looked up a short alley that started between two stores and saw a garbage can that seemed to have just been overturned. He ran through the alley. At its end, just steps away, two residential streets intersected, going off in four directions. He forced himself to stand still to see if anything moved. Look, he told himself. Look. Listen.

Nothing.

Whoever it was could have gone down any of these roads.

He needed to catch his breath. Back at his scooter he looked at the motel entrance. No one was in front. Across Kingston Road was a big shopping mall. No windows faced outward. Cars kept zipping by as if nothing unusual had happened. He reached for his cell phone again.

As he was about to dial in, he heard a siren come screaming toward him. He looked down Kingston Road and saw a police cruiser flying up the street, full flashers on. Right behind it was an ambulance, lights and sirens roaring too.

He watched in amazement as they tore through the traffic, zipped past him, and cut into the motel courtyard.

He looked at the cell phone in his hand. There was no point in calling 911 now. If he did, it would just add to the confusion.

But wait.

Something about this didn't make sense.

His phone told him it was 10:44.

Response time on an emergency call like this would take about seven or eight minutes, max. He knew for sure he'd walked into the room at 10:41. Someone had called in the murder before he got there. But what if he'd been on time? What if he hadn't given chase to this suspect?

He thought of Raglan, strangled. The most intimate and angry way to kill someone. Then of her body, neatly tucked into bed. The one candle still lit. As if the killer had felt remorseful.

Jennifer's phone call. Her husband, Howard, had texted her and wanted to have coffee with her this morning. She'd said no. Said she was going running.

His shoulders slumped. Somehow, Howard must have found out about their affair. He could see it. The poor man, enraged to the point that he killed his wife. Then he called 911 and waited until Greene showed up. He wanted to set him up for his crime. Made sense. Obviously he was the person at the door who'd run away.

Greene had seen this too many times in his career, a murdering spouse turned suicidal. If he was on foot, Howard was probably on one of those streets behind the strip mall. Intent on ending it all.

Greene pocketed his phone and jumped on his scooter.

4

WALK SLOWLY, HOMICIDE DETECTIVE DANIEL KENNICOTT TOLD HIMSELF AS GOT OUT OF THE unmarked police car. He'd parked at the far corner of the cracked concrete driveway in front of the Maple Leaf Motel so he could get a view of the whole scene.

Walking or doing anything slowly didn't come naturally to Kennicott. But after five impatient years on the police force, at the end of June he'd finally made it to the homicide squad. It felt like forever, even though he'd done it in record time, thanks mostly to his mentor, Ari Greene, who was the master of the slow, deliberate homicide walk.

Greene wasn't here. Which was how it should be. Kennicott was on his own now, about to take on his first murder case.

At the entrance to the motel's courtyard, a well-dressed man in street clothes was talking on his cell phone. He nodded as Kennicott approached. Although they'd never met, Kennicott knew this would be Detective Raymond Alpine from 43 Division.

While Kennicott was rushing over here, he'd been on the phone with Alpine, who updated him on what they had so far: At 10:39, police received a 911 call about an apparent homicide in room 8 at the Maple Leaf Motel. The first squad car and the ambulance arrived at 10:44. At 10:48, PC Arthurs, the first officer on scene, reported that she had gone into the room, accompanied by an ambulance attendant, and found a white female, estimated age thirty-five to forty-five, NVA – no vital signs apparent, the victim of an apparent strangulation. Alpine arrived at 10:51, went inside the room briefly with the same attendant, and confirmed the initial findings. By 10:58, he had deployed two pairs of officers to knock on every door in the motel. It had twenty-six rooms. The identification officer who would be in charge of all forensic work was en route and would be there shortly.

Kennicott introduced himself, giving the detective a firm handshake.

"Raymond Alpine." The officer's voice was laconic, verging on bored.

Kennicott pointed into the courtyard at the squad car and ambulance parked there. "You guys got here fast," he said.

Alpine shrugged. "Slow Monday. We were hoping Gwyneth Paltrow would stop in at the station. We even got a whole box of fresh doughnuts for her. But she never showed."

Kennicott realized that for Alpine this was just another hooker-motel murder. He couldn't blame the guy for being jaded. These homicides were almost always the same: a prostitute, too old for the game, with a drug or alcohol problem, or both, was found stabbed to death, or with her head bashed in, or, as in this case, strangled. The murders were nearly always a crime of passion. The perpetrator could be counted on to be some loner, often with no criminal record, who was bad at covering his tracks. He'd claim he'd lost his head, usually after the woman had made some unflattering comment about his performance. Ninety-nine percent of these cases were settled with a quick plea to manslaughter.

Kennicott turned back to Kingston Road. Along this stretch, it was six lanes wide, with a concrete barrier in the middle. The blocks were long and the cars sped past. On the other side of the street, probably half a mile away, was an inward-facing shopping mall.

"Not much street life here for us to find witnesses," he said.

Alpine snorted. "Welcome to outer Scarberia. I don't know why they even bother building sidewalks."

Scarberia was the nickname for Scarborough, Toronto's sprawling eastern suburb. Home to bad planning, dysfunctional public transportation, horrendous high-rise housing, a mishmash immigrant population, and the city's highest murder rate. Big surprise.

Kennicott pointed to the motel office. There didn't appear to be anyone inside. "Anyone at the check-in desk see anything?"

"No such luck," Alpine said. "Handwritten sign on the door says the owner is not in mornings from nine to eleven. There's a cell number and we've called him. He'll be here in about ten minutes."

Kennicott frowned. "Okay," he said. "I'll take a look around the courtyard while I'm waiting for the ident officer."

He ducked under the yellow tape strung across the passageway and went through. He could see there was no other way in or out of the courtyard. It was a few steps to room 8, where a squad car and an ambulance were parked. A female officer stood in front of the door, her arms crossed. She was a tall woman, close to six feet, just a few inches shorter than Kennicott.

He showed her his badge.

"Morning, Detective." She unfolded her arms and shook his hand. "PC Arthurs."

"You were the first officer on scene," he said.

"Yes." She was holding a police notebook in her other hand so tightly her knuckles were white. Her voice was surprisingly high-pitched for such a big woman and Kennicott wondered if it was always this way or if it was stress.

"Your first homicide?" he asked.

"How'd you guess?"

"You went in with the ambulance attendant."

Arthurs nodded.

"He try CPR?"

"No. Said there was no pulse, no breath."

"So the scene's undisturbed."

She nodded again. "We were real careful not to touch anything."

He peeked past her into the motel room. It was dark except for a candle flickering on the far bedside table. The bathroom door was open.

"Detective Kennicott," a loud voice with a heavy East European accent called out from behind him. "Is detective now, no?"

Brygida Zeilinski, a squat Polish woman and veteran identification officer, waddled toward him at a determined pace, a black fanny-pack bouncing on her stomach. She looked like a pregnant penguin on the march, Kennicott thought as he reached out to shake her hand.

"Is Scarborough prostitute killing, no?" she said, her face a big frown. Ari Greene liked to brag that he was the only one on the force who could make Zeilinski smile. "Easy case for your first homicide, yes?"

"Let's take a look," he said.

She pulled two pairs of latex gloves and plastic shoe coverings out of her fanny pack and handed him one. Kennicott put them on then pressed the door to room 8 with his forefinger. It creaked on rusty hinges.

A queen-size bed dominated the room. He could see the back of the woman's head on a pillow, facing away from the door, her body covered neatly by a comforter. That was unusual. Most killers would have left the poor woman in a crumpled, discarded state. Kennicott pictured some future defence lawyer arguing in court that this showed his client was filled with remorse – after, that is, the man had strangled his victim to death with his bare hands.

Steps behind him, he could hear Zeilinski breathing calmly. For her, this was just another day at the office.

There was little space to get around the bed. A dresser sat to his left. On top were four thick white candles, none of them burning, though he could see recently melted wax on each. Beside them was an iPod Nano in a small speaker dock but no music was playing.

He locked eyes with Zeilinski. He knew they were both thinking the same thing: This woman must have fancied herself a high-class hooker. He tiptoed around the bed to where the woman's head was facing the bathroom door. There were traces of a tread mark under the handle of the hollow-core door where it had been dented.

Someone had kicked it in. The violence to the door was in stark contrast to this otherwise serene murder scene, he thought.

The bathroom was empty, save for a half bottle of champagne in the sink, sitting in water with a few small chips of ice still intact. An empty ice bucket was underneath.

"I check the temperature in the bathroom and the temperature of that water," Zeilinski said.

"Sure," he said.

In the main room, he spotted a red wig and a pair of oversize sunglasses on the floor beside the bed. This was even stranger. Why would a hooker go to this trouble to hide her identity?

The candle on the bedside table had burned down farther than the extinguished ones on the dresser.

"I photograph and videotape all the candles right away," she said. "Then blow this one out."

"Okay," he said.

"The iPod too. Make them all exhibits."

"Fine," he said. Good identification officers tended to be fanatical about even the most irrelevant details. Often it made for a ton of extra work, but he knew it was the price of admission.

The head of the woman on the bed was nestled neatly on a pillow. He bent his knees to look at her face at eye level.

An electric current shot up his spine and his whole body jerked. His throat contracted. His fingers twitched. "Ah," he heard himself say, unable to control his own voice.

"What?" Zeilinski said. "You feel sick?"

"I know her." Kennicott croaked out the words.

"You do? Well, it's prostitute."

"She's not a prostitute."

"No? I wondered when I saw candles and –"

"She's Jennifer Raglan. The head Crown attorney."

"Ms. Raglan? Here?"

He stood and scanned the room. He felt light-headed. His mind was racing. Zeilinski crouched down beside him to take a look.

What was Jennifer Raglan, of all people, doing here in this cheap motel room? On a Monday morning? Disguising herself with a wig and sunglasses? Celebrating with champagne and candles?

"Is unbelievable," Zeilinski said.

Is, Kennicott thought, my first homicide.

5

gone nowhere; instead of checking out any of the murder trials, he'd taken a chance on the hockey-player sexual assault trial. And he'd hit pay dirt.

Deirdre Acton, the actress-turned-waitress, was being cross-examined by Canton Carmichael, a perfectly coiffed defence lawyer with a silky-smooth voice. It had just come to light that she used the professional name TAD for certain extracurricular activities.

"What does TAD, capital *T*, capital *A*, capital *D*, stand for?" Carmichael asked, acting innocent as a lamb.

"Uh, it means 'The After Date,'" Acton muttered.

"The what?" Carmichael asked, hand to his ear, giving the jurors nearest him a sly look.

"The After Date," Acton spat out. "That's what it means."

"And what exactly is an after date?" Carmichael asked, acting naive for the jurors, who now couldn't take their eyes off Acton.

"Well," she said, "I'm the date that players have, after they've had a date with, you know, another woman."

"Players, what kind of players?"

"Well, like, hockey players."

Carmichael grinned. He'd set up a projector near the jurors, where everyone in court could see it. He picked up a remote, and a screen shot of a website page appeared. The site was titled the Penalty Box, and featured a photo of a woman in a bikini, leaning provocatively on a hockey stick. "Ms. Acton, do you recognize this?" he asked, all sweetness and light.

"It's my site," she mumbled.

"Your what?"

"My website." Her eyes were slits as she stared at Carmichael.

"And the woman we see in the picture . . ."

"That's me."

Amankwah watched the next image come up on the screen.

Now Carmichael was showing her Facebook home page, headed by a photo of Acton from the waist up. She wore a pair of shoulder pads that barely covered her breasts, and nothing more. The small inset photo was a close-up of a tattoo extremely low on her backside. It featured a hockey stick about to hit a puck with the words "Slap Me" underneath.

"And this is . . ."

"My Facebook page."

Carmichael switched back to her website.

"Would you mind reading your biographical sketch for the jury, please?"

She looked over at the Crown's table, as if the prosecutor, a bright young lawyer named Albert Fernandez, could somehow help her. He didn't make eye contact with her.

She glared back at Carmichael. "Okay, it says, 'I'm an after-hours player for players who want to play,'" she said without looking at the screen. "You happy?"

Carmichael, totally unfazed, looked up at the presiding judge, Oliver Rothbart, who had been patiently watching the proceedings, a mildly amused look on his face. "I think, Your Honour, this might be an opportune moment to take the morning break. I don't know about the jury, but I sure could use a cup of coffee."

The jurors were all grinning. A few of them laughed. Amankwah willed the judge to agree. He was dying for some java.

"Good idea," Rothbart said. "I have a few administrative duties to attend to this morning, so we'll come back after lunch. That may give you both some time to consider any relevant legal issues that might arise when we recommence."

He let his gaze settle on Fernandez, then Carmichael.

The judge's message was clear: *I can't say this in front of the jury, but obviously this case is going nowhere fast. I've got better things to do with my time. Why don't you two try to settle it.*

Rothbart looked at the witness. "Now, Ms. Acton, I must warn you. You are in the middle of your cross-examination. That means you are absolutely forbidden to discuss your testimony with anyone. Understood?"

"Yes, but can't I talk to Mr. Fernandez?"

"Not Mr. Fernandez, not the officer in charge of the case, Detective Kormos. No one."

Acton took a deep breath. "Okay."

"Good," Rothbart said. "Back at two o'clock."

Perfect, Amankwah thought. Bradley Church was going to love this story. He could just see the headline: HOCKEY PLAYER SCORES IN "AFTER DATE" OVERTIME.

6

OFFICER ZEILINSKI HAD HER HAND PRESSED TO HER MOUTH. HER ALREADY PALE SKIN HAD turned white. She was breathing hard.

Kennicott grabbed her free hand.

"Such nice woman," she said after a moment. "With children."

Kennicott was trying to think. You're the homicide detective in charge of this investigation, he told himself. Stay professional. This is a crime scene. He had to get Zeilinski focused.

"I worked on a few cases that she prosecuted." He squeezed her fingers.

"She is very good lawyer." She took her hand back. "We need do perfect job."

"Of course," he said.

"My team on the way. I get them in. Photograph, videotape everything. Blow out candle. Then iPod too, and take all."

He pointed to the wig and sunglasses on the floor. "You saw those."

"Of course. We go through everything. She must have purse. Cell phone. Will find for you."

He looked around again. For the next few months he'd be staring at photos and videos of this crime scene. But it wouldn't be the same as being here, right now. Seeing it. Smelling it. Feeling it. What story does this god-awful room tell me? Beside the obvious. She must have been having an affair with someone.

The dent in the bathroom door looked fresh. Forensics would take the door back to the lab and examine it to see if they could get a better read on the tread marks. Someone had wanted to get in that door very badly.

If it was the killer, what was he looking for?

Kennicott checked the bathroom floor. Beige vinyl tiles, worn but clean. There was a dark scuff mark near the door.

It was easy to imagine someone kicking in the door, taking a step in, and looking around. The bottle of champagne was floating in the sink. The empty ice bucket had water droplets in it. A standard-issue toilet looked untouched.

And the cheap plastic-lined shower, with a stained curtain pulled to the side, was dry inside too.

There was nothing personal here. No toiletries. And no signs of a struggle.

Did the kicker bust the door in looking for Raglan? Didn't look like it. Then who broke down the door? And why?

A shudder went through him. It was as if he could feel the murderous, sweaty anger of the killer. But also something else. What it was he wasn't sure.

In a few steps he was outside, back in the fresh air and the land of the living. The sky was impossibly blue, the wind strong. His skin tingled in the sunshine. Alpine was waiting for him, his notebook in hand.

Kennicott needed a moment to try to process that the murder victim in room 8 was the former head Crown attorney. He wanted to get some background before he told Alpine what was going on. "Do we know who called 911?" he asked.

Alpine shook his head. "Anonymous caller."

"What did they say?"

Alpine had his finger in his notebook. He flipped it open and gave Kennicott a bored look that said: *You homicide guys always ask the same questions.* He cleared his throat. "The anonymous caller said, 'Dead body, Maple Leaf Motel, Kingston Road, room 8.' That's it. I talked to the dispatcher. She said he sounded male, was very abrupt, and hung up before she could ask any questions."

"Traceable?"

He closed his notebook. "No. This isn't TV. All we know is that it was a cell phone."

Across the courtyard, Kennicott saw two officers coming toward them. "Any luck with witnesses?" he asked.

Alpine crossed his arms. "We knocked on every door. Thirty-six rooms, and three were rented out. Tough business. The owner says Mondays are always slow. That it fills up more as the week goes along. Who knew?"

"The three rooms?"

Alpine went back to his notebook. "There was a worn-out wino in room 12. They had to wake him up. Said he'd been asleep since last night and heard nothing. Name: Vincent Skinner. Forty-two years old. Status Indian. Born on a reserve up near James Bay. Room was clean. He didn't have any scratch marks on him. Minor record, all mischiefs and thefts. All recent. Nothing before that. Said he was a schoolteacher for fifteen years. Wife, kids, the whole thing. Then he hit the booze."

What a sad and lonely place to end up, Kennicott thought, looking around the desolate yard.

Alpine pointed to the room above the passageway. "We found a prostitute who works out of there."

"Good," Kennicott said. "She would have seen people come in and out."

Alpine eyed him. "If she was looking out the window, yes. But claims she was working. A young officer, Askari, tried to interview her, but she wouldn't let him in. Said essentially, 'What do you want from me, cop? How am I supposed to see anything when I'm on my knees.'"

"Great," Kennicott said.

"Name is Hilda Reynolds. Or at least that's the name she gave. Askari asked her to come in and give a video statement, and she slammed the door in his face." Alpine shook his head.

"Nice to get so much cooperation from such an upstanding citizen," Kennicott said.

"Welcome to Scarborough."

"What about the third one?"

The cynical smirk lifted from Alpine's face, replaced by an unexpected seriousness. "Room 41, the other side, second floor. A pair of young Taiwanese prostitutes who look about twelve years old. They spoke only enough English to say, 'See nothing, see nothing. Want go home. Go home.' I've already had a car take them back to the division. We'll get them a translator and take a statement, but don't expect much. I've contacted child services. I think I know who their pimp is."

Alpine's meaning was clear. These two young girls probably wouldn't help with the murder, but this was something he cared about.

"What about the owner?" Kennicott asked.

"He showed up. Greasy guy named Alistair Dodge. Said a woman came in on Sunday afternoon, red wig and sunglasses. Paid cash for the room. Insisted on having room 8."

"He see if she was driving a car or anything?" Kennicott asked.

"Said he was watching the Jays get beat by the Orioles. Didn't remember anything else. All he really cared about was how quickly he could get the room back."

The officers crossing the courtyard had arrived. Kennicott caught Alpine's eye and tilted his head, in a we-need-to-talk-alone gesture.

Alpine hesitated but Kennicott stared him down.

"What's so important you couldn't tell me in front of my men?" Alpine asked when they were a few steps away.

"The dead woman wasn't a prostitute," Kennicott said.

Alpine crossed his arms again. "Oh, you think because of the candles and the wine? So what was she, then, some yummy mummy looking for a little fun?"

Kennicott waited until Alpine met his eyes again. "She was a Crown attorney."

"What?"

"Jennifer Raglan."

Alpine shook his head. He pointed to room 8. "That's Jennie Raglan? We did a big robbery case together two years ago."

"Keep your voice down," Kennicott ordered. "As soon as the press finds out about this, it will go nuts. Zeilinski says she has kids. Do you know if she's married?"

"Shit," Alpine said, still stunned. "She was, at least two years ago when I did my last trial with her. Husband's an accountant or something. Two or three kids, I think."

"It looks like she had a boyfriend too."

"Rough trade," Alpine said. "That's what the hookers call this kind of asshole."

"The Crown's office will have a personnel file on her, with emergency contact information. We need it fast. I want your men sworn to secrecy. Three kids. Get three squad cars. Find out where those children are and get to their schools right away. Make sure they're safe. And find out everything you can about her husband."

Alpine was nodding now. "Right," he said.

"And get me everybody you can over here right away. That crummy little strip mall next door, the shopping centre across Kingston Road, the residential streets behind here. I want every damn door for half a mile knocked on in the next hour. And see if there are any video cameras, anywhere."

The latex gloves Zeilinski had given him felt hot and itchy. Kennicott yanked them off, with an authoritative snap.

7

OKAY, CHECK JUST ONE MORE BLOCK, GREENE TOLD HIMSELF. FOR THE LAST TEN OR FIFTEEN minutes at least, he'd been charging up and down the boxy side streets of the suburban subdivision on his scooter, looking in vain for Jennifer's husband, Howard.

There was no sign of anyone.

At the next stop sign he turned left. Another empty street lay before him. How do people live out here? he wondered. It seemed so barren. Small houses. Flat lawns. Short trees, few and far between.

He knew he had to end this fruitless search. He hadn't even called for backup. With good reason, he told himself. The first minutes when someone flees the scene of a crime are the most crucial. Every second counts. Waiting for backup would have wasted valuable time.

Was that the real reason he was charging around looking for Jennifer's husband?

He was rationalizing. Because in his gut he wanted to find Howard. The man who'd killed Jennifer. The man Greene had betrayed.

And what? Arrest him. Yes.

What else? Apologize?

He decided to try a few more blocks. He kept driving and turning, seeing nothing. At last he came to a dead end at a ravine and got off his scooter.

He felt faint, as if he were going to collapse. The adrenaline, the anger, the shock, the sorrow all hit him at once. He yanked off his helmet and sat on the curb. How could Jennifer be dead? Think, Ari. *Think*, he told himself.

He checked his watch. It was 11:12, much later than he thought it would be. How many homicides had he done when the witnesses lost all track of time after a murder?

He breathed in deeply and exhaled. Did it again.

By now the homicide detective assigned to the case would be on scene.

Greene knew that Daniel Kennicott was next up in the batting order. He'd been a lawyer before he joined the force, and Greene had taken him under his wing, was his so-called rabbi – an ironic title as Greene was the only Jewish detective on the homicide squad.

They'd already agreed that when Kennicott got his first murder call, he would do it alone. It was important. The other detectives would be watching, wanting to see if he could stand on his own two feet.

But Jennifer had been murdered. Strangled. Jennifer. Greene's whole life turned upside down in an instant.

This was no normal homicide.

Everyone would be surprised to learn that he and Raglan were having an affair, they'd gone to such extremes to keep it secret. But that's what happened with every murder. All sorts of hidden facts get exposed. Collateral damage, he called it, and now he was part of the fallout.

He pulled off his gloves and threw them inside the helmet. Took out his phone. He had to tell Kennicott the simple truth: I was Jennifer's lover. We were supposed to get together this morning. When I walked into room 8 she was dead. I checked to make sure she was had no vital signs. I kicked in the bathroom door, looking for the killer. Was about to call 911 when someone outside made a noise. I ran after whoever it was, but just missed him. When I saw the squad car and ambulance rush into the motel, there was no need to call in, so I got on my scooter and raced around all these side streets, hoping to find whoever had been at the door. Was pretty sure it was the husband, and thought he must be suicidal. I lost track of time, driving around so long, and now I'm calling in.

He lifted the cell phone. Hesitated.

Something was bothering him. What if Raglan's husband, Howard, wasn't the one who called 911? But who else could it be? The motel room was empty. No one could have seen Jennifer's dead body inside room 8. Except for the killer.

If he'd arrived on time, at 10:30, and not rushed out, then the ambulance and the police would have found him there alone with the dead body. Was he crazy, or was Howard or someone else trying to set him up?

The phone in his hand started to buzz. He looked at the display. It was Kennicott.

"I was about to call you," Greene said, answering it right away, on the first ring.

"Then you've heard," Kennicott said, without identifying himself. His voice was faint. There was the gusty sound of wind passing through.

"I'm not far away and on my way over," Greene said. "There's something I need to tell –"

"That's why I called," Kennicott said.

So he already knows about Jennifer and me, Greene thought. That I was in the room this morning. How did he find out so fast? Jennifer must have got careless and left something on her phone. Or maybe there is a witness. Or maybe they've already caught her husband. Anything can happen in the first half hour of a homicide investigation.

"Whatever you do, don't come here," Kennicott said.

"But," Greene said, "I've got –"

"Wait." Kennicott's voice moved away from the phone and became even fainter. "Send those officers to knock on doors in the streets behind here. I'll be with you in a minute."

Greene heard another loud rush of air through the phone. Kennicott came back on. "It will look terrible if you show up now, as if I need you to hold my hand. I want this to be my crime scene. Period. Let's meet somewhere tonight where we can talk."

Greene shook his head. Kennicott wasn't saying he'd found out about their affair. Nor was he saying that he knew Greene had been at the motel room this morning. What he was saying was don't show up and undermine my authority with the troops.

His mind was scrambling to think of a place they could meet in private. "How about the bakery where I took you once?" he said, making sure not to identify it.

Almost a year earlier, Greene had a case when a stray bullet killed a young boy. Kennicott had helped him out, and late at night when they needed a break, he'd taken Kennicott to Silverstein's Bakery. The place was run by one of Greene's old school friends and it never closed.

"Done. Five o'clock. Got to go," Kennicott said, and hung up before Greene could say another word.

8

KENNICOTT SLID HIS CELL PHONE INTO HIS JACKET AND TURNED BACK TO LOOK AT DETEC-tive Alpine. He had walked a few steps from him to call Greene.

"I got someone at the Crown's office to pull up Raglan's employment file," Alpine said. "She and her husband live in the Beach, it's about fifteen kilometres from here. I sent a car right away. The officer says it looks like no one's home. She'll stay there and keep an eye on it."

"What about her kids?"

"Three children, all at different schools. I've got cars on the way to each one. They're going to talk to the principals, make sure the kids are safe, but not tell them anything yet. I got a family photo out of Raglan's office to head-quarters. They scanned the face of the husband, name Howard Darnell, and every squad car in the city has it now with instructions to stop him if they see him."

"What do we know about the guy?" Kennicott asked.

"Works at an actuarial firm on Queen East, about a five-minute walk from their house. I got another car in front of the office. I told them not to go in. Here's the address."

"Good," Kennicott said. Going to Darnell's place of work was the obvious next move. But he still had things to cover here. "Did the Crown's office expect Raglan to be in today?"

Alpine shook his head. "No. She didn't work Mondays. Hasn't since she went back to the job six weeks ago. She's a long-distance runner. Said Monday was her training day."

Six weeks, Kennicott thought. Enough time for her husband to figure out that she was having an affair. He could tell Alpine was thinking the same thing.

He tilted his head in the direction of room 8. "We found a wig and sun-glasses and some clothes under her bed in a little backpack. Get Zeilinski to photograph them before she bags them and have a few officers go up and down the motel strip. See if anyone remembers renting out a room to a redhead in sunglasses on Mondays in the last six weeks."

"Done," Alpine said.

Kennicott had been a marathon runner himself in law school. Raglan probably started out after the kids left for school. If she ran with her disguise in her backpack, she'd have had to change somewhere close by.

"Check every restaurant and gas station for a mile or two between here and her home."

"What are we looking for?" Alpine asked.

"Video cameras. Staff that worked today. Did anyone see a women go into the washroom dressed as a jogger and come out wearing clothes and sunglasses?"

"Good thinking."

Kennicott walked back to the motel room door. Zeilinski had spread a cloth out on top of the bed and had emptied the contents of Raglan's purse onto it. She had a cell phone in one gloved hand, a pair of pillowcases in the other.

"I find in backpack, nice cotton," she said, referring to the pillowcases.

"Good," he said. "Can I see the phone?"

She put the pillowcase down. "I bring you."

She came to the door and reached into her fanny pack for a new pair of gloves. Kennicott saw her catch Alpine's eyes as she handed them over to him.

Rookie mistake, he realized. Taking his gloves off too soon. He slipped the new pair on and checked the cell's phone records first. There was one outgoing call this morning, to *Jo Summers, Crown attorney*, at 8:45.

Kennicott knew Jo Summers quite well, but not as well as he'd like to. They'd met in law school and had a one-night stand in their last year there. Then two years ago their paths had crossed again. She'd left the big law firm where she'd been an associate and became a Crown attorney, and by then he was a cop. Since then, they'd danced around each other, never quite getting involved.

They had talked on the phone one night in August. She'd heard he'd made the homicide squad and had called to congratulate him. He couldn't be sure if that was the only reason she'd called.

She was excited because she'd been assigned to be the junior lawyer on a big fraud case and would be working with Jennifer Raglan. They were prosecuting a well-known movie producer and there'd be a lot of media coverage. The trial was set to start next Monday. This murder would be horrible news for Jo. Horrible.

He tapped the text button on the cell phone. There was one chain of correspondence from this morning. It started at 9:51.

The first message was from Howard, her husband: *Jen. Trip to Beantown cancelled. Do u want to grab a coffee this a.m.?*

Then came Raglan's reply: *Too bd about trip. Can't meet a.m. Doing lng run. Crt this aft. C u 2 nite.*

This was amazing, Kennicott thought. He was holding right in his gloved hand the evidence of a spurned husband with motive and now the opportunity for murder.

Something made him jump. It took a moment for him to realize that Raglan's phone was vibrating. Someone was calling.

He looked at Alpine. What should he do? Answer it? Let it go to voice mail?

The call display came up. *Jo Summers. Crown attorney.*

Oh no, he thought. He hit the answer button. "Hello," he said slowly.

"Hello. Who's this?"

"Hi, Jo," he said.

"Who is this?" She sounded angry. Suspicious.

"It's me. Daniel."

"Daniel." He heard her exhale in relief. "Oh, sorry, I was calling Jennifer. I must have pushed the wrong button . . ."

Wrong button, Kennicott thought. Does she have me on speed dial?

"No, Jo. This is Jennifer's cell."

"What do you mean?"

He looked back to room 8, where Zeilinski was on her knees, combing the rug.

"You called Jennifer." His voice sounded dead to him. "I'm holding her cell phone."

"I don't get it," Summers said. "She always does a long run on Monday mornings. I was calling to leave her a voice mail about what happened in court."

He tried to speak but couldn't.

"My God," she said into the silence between them. He could tell by the sudden fear in her voice that she was putting it together. She knew he had made Homicide. She knew he was first in line for the next murder. He had Raglan's cell phone.

"Daniel," she asked. "Where is Jennifer?"

9

A CAR HORN BLARED. BRAKES SQUEALED.

Greene swivelled his head and saw that his scooter had drifted into the lane of a huge pickup truck. He yanked it back.

"Watch it, buddy!" the driver yelled as he zipped past Greene and gunned it down Kingston Road.

All these years as a homicide detective, and you haven't learned a thing, Greene scolded himself. Time after time he'd seen people who were in shock after coming upon a murder scene. It was always the same. They did irrational things, found easy tasks almost impossible to perform, made foolish decisions, lost track of time and space.

And here he was almost getting killed on his stupid scooter.

Concentrate, he told himself. As anxious as he was to tell Kennicott the whole story, he'd have to wait until this afternoon. What to do in the meantime?

He got to the end of Kingston Road and headed into the city, keeping to side streets.

Think like a detective. Get home. Take your clothes off and preserve them. Take a hot shower. Sit down. Use your brain.

The image of Jennifer under the sheets flooded his mind. Her bruised neck. Her dead eyes.

He pictured the room. The one candle still lit by her bed. The champagne in the bathroom sink. Something about it felt wrong. What was it?

Another horn blared at him.

Shit. He'd just gone through a stop sign.

Enough, Ari. Get home in one piece. Fortunately, traffic was light this time of the morning. He started talking to himself to make sure he didn't get in an accident. There's a stop sign. Stop. Speed limit is forty. Keep to it. Red light coming up.

But his mind wouldn't leave the motel room.

The crime scene pointed squarely to a domestic homicide. Howard had found out about the affair and that Jennifer was about to leave him. He'd killed her in a rage. Then he'd called 911 to set Greene up, before he'd run away. He'd assumed Greene would be there when the cops showed up.

Maybe, just maybe, Greene thought, it wasn't so bad that he hadn't spoken to Kennicott yet. Deep inside, a voice was warning him of danger.

"The night the Nazis came to our village," his father had told him many times, "everyone said the best thing to do was stay there. Don't try to escape. I had no choice, because of my wife and children I couldn't leave. But my little brother, Jacob, was a bachelor. He ran into the valley and hid in the woods. Two thousand Jews lived in our village and he and I were the only ones who survived."

Greene parked behind the old garage and, out of some ingrained sense of caution, took out a rag he always kept under the seat and rubbed the scooter down, making sure that none of his prints was left on it. Then he put his gloves back on and walked it out to the street, leaving the keys in the ignition. Although Hap Charlton was basing his campaign for mayor on fears that crime in Toronto was spinning out of control, in fact it was still a very safe city. But when it came to car and bike theft, the numbers were sky-high. By tomorrow morning, the scooter would be long gone.

He walked half a kilometre in the opposite direction from his house and tossed one of his gloves into a garbage bin. He made three more stops, getting rid of his second glove, his helmet, and his jacket.

By the time he got home, he was chilled and shaking like an underdressed schoolboy on a cold morning. And he had no idea if this was the smartest thing he'd ever done in his life, or the stupidest.

10

THE SPANKING-CLEAN SIGN THAT READ ANDERS, CHESNEY & JAI, ACTUARIES, WAS PROMI-
nently displayed on the outside of an old redbrick house on Queen Street East in
the upscale neighbourhood known as the Beach. The walkway cobblestone, and
the front door featured a large window covered with a white lace curtain.

"May I please speak to Mr. Howard Darnell," Daniel Kennicott said, passing his police card to the pretty receptionist who sat perched behind an antique
wood desk.

"Oh," she said. "Mr. Darnell?"

He bent closer and noticed that she had a stud in her nose. "I don't have an
appointment. But it's important police business."

"Um. Um, maybe I can get Mr. Jai to speak to you." Her forehead crinkled
in concern.

"Isn't Mr. Darnell here?"

She popped out of her chair. "I'll get Mr. Jai."

He looked at the phone console on the side of her desk. There were tags next
to six buttons giving names in alphabetical order. The top one read *Anders*, the
second *Chesney*, the third was blank. After that came *Golding, Upta*, and then
Jai.

"Yes, sir, can I help you?"

Kennicott looked up to see a young, well-dressed Asian man, wearing expensive-
looking matte-brown glasses. He clutched a sleek steel pencil in his hand.

"Daniel Kennicott, Metro Toronto Police." Ari Green had taught him never
to identify himself as a homicide detective the first time he met someone.

"Arthur Jai." The man shook his hand. "Please, come downstairs to our
boardroom. Can I get you a coffee, water, anything?"

"I'm fine," Kennicott said.

It was a windowless room, small, but tastefully furnished. Sepia photos of
rowers on the Toronto waterfront, which looked like they were taken in the

1920s, adorned the walls. Jai motioned him to a seat, took one across from him, and passed over his embossed business card. It felt brand-new. It read: *Arthur Jai, Actuary, B.Com. FCIA.*

"Anna said you were looking for Howard Darnell," he said.

"That's right," Kennicott said.

Jai sucked in his thin lips. "We were expecting the police to come."

"You were?"

"Yes. Because of the institute's investigation."

"Institute?" Kennicott asked.

Jai took off his expensive glasses and put them carefully on the table. "The actuarial institute. The missing client funds."

"Actually, that's not why I'm here," Kennicott said.

"Oh." Jai clicked the end of his pencil.

"It's quite urgent that I talk to Mr. Darnell."

"You didn't know? Howard doesn't work here anymore."

"He doesn't?"

Jai clicked his pencil twice this time. "We finally had to let him go about two months ago. I've been here for a few years and I was made partner this summer. But for B and B it was real tough."

"B and B?"

"Bob Anders and Bryce Chesney. Everyone calls them B and B. They've run this firm for twenty-four years. All three of them went into actuarial sciences together – Bob, Bryce, and Howard." He shrugged. "Howard never passed his exams. Lots of people fail. They're really tough."

Jai put his glasses back on. Clearly this ambitious young man wasn't one of the flunkies who had a problem passing.

"If he wasn't an actuary, why was he working here?" Kennicott asked.

"B and B kept him on. Gave him work, but they couldn't bill him out at anywhere near their rate."

"And two months ago they fired him?"

Jai started clicking his pencil again. "Everyone loved Howard. But then there was the missing money. Twenty thousand dollars." He shrugged again. "They didn't have any choice. The CIA is investigating."

"The CIA?"

Jai laughed. "Everyone has the same reaction. No spies here. It's the Canadian Institute of Actuaries."

"Can I talk to the other partners?" Kennicott asked

"Oh, it's Monday," Jai said. "They're in Boston every Monday for a client meeting. Been doing it for years."

Kennicott still hadn't told Jai he was investigating a murder. He didn't want to tell him until he'd got as much information from him as he could.

"Where's Howard working now?"

Jai fiddled with the edge of his glasses. "I don't think he has a job. I saw him on the subway last week. He was dressed in a suit and tie, with a briefcase, so I went up to him and said, 'Howard, how are you? Where you working?' He blushed and said that he wasn't. But he didn't want to tell his wife and kids he'd been fired. So every morning he was pretending to go to work, and he just rode the subway all day. It was weird. I felt bad for him. He made me promise not to tell anyone. You're the first one I've told. Not even B and B."

"So he could be anywhere right now," Kennicott said.

"I guess." Jai sneaked a look at his watch. Probably worried about the billable time he was using up, Kennicott thought.

"Did he ever talk to you about his relationship with his wife?"

Jai fingered his pencil again. Kennicott noticed he didn't wear a wedding ring. "We weren't really friends. I mean, I'm single and he's married and older."

Kennicott nodded. Waiting him out.

"But about a year ago, he told me that she'd moved out."

Kennicott kept his face expressionless. "Did he tell you why?" he asked.

Jai shook his head. "Not really. He said once they got married too young. I know they were high-school sweethearts from the same small town. And look, his wife's a successful lawyer. Head Crown attorney. Runs a big office. Her picture is in the newspaper all the time. And Howard, well, you know."

Jai looked at his watch again, this time less discreetly. He reminded Kennicott of so many of the lawyers he'd worked with at his law firm. Smart, ambitious. Always on the clock. Not much interested in colleagues who didn't pull their weight.

"Have you met her?" Kennicott asked.

Jai shrugged. "Just at the annual party when she showed up. She came this year because they got back together again. In July, they took a trip to Cooperstown with their oldest son. The boy had some problems and Howard is a real baseball nut. That's all I know."

"So you have no idea where he is now?" Kennicott asked.

"None," Jai said. "Howard's not in any trouble or anything, is he?"

Kennicott didn't answer the question, which for someone as smart as Jai was answer enough. "I need a recent photo of him. Do you have one?" The picture of Howard that Alpine had got from Raglan's office was dated.

"Um. Yeah." Jai looked shaken. He stood up. "We all had our photos taken for last year's company report. I'll get it for you right away."

Kennicott stood too. "Final question. Does he have a bad temper? You ever seen him get angry?"

Jai chuckled. "Howard? You kidding? It's a cliché, but he wouldn't hurt a fly."

Kennicott thought of how Jennifer Raglan's head had been carefully positioned on the pillow, her body tucked in under the comforter, the candle left burning by her bedside. He had a horrible feeling that these were true signs of remorse. And that in a few hours he'd have to tell Jennifer Raglan's children that their father had killed their mother, then killed himself.

11

AMANKWAH SPENT THE REST OF HIS MORNING WRITING AND POSTING HIS STORY, "THE Hockey Player and the After Date" to the *Star*'s website, and filming himself for a short online video. He wolfed down a horrid roast beef sandwich from the courthouse cafeteria and at one o'clock rushed up to Norville's court to see if Seaton Wainwright had shown up. There was no sign of him. Norville snarled at Wainwright's lawyer, Phil Cutter, as she issued a bench warrant for the arrest of the so-called mini–movie mogul.

Then he ran down to catch Carmichael's continuing cross-examination of Acton, or After Date Deirdre – the name he'd given her in his article. Word about the trial had spread like wildfire and the courtroom was almost full. He'd tipped off his crime-reporter friends from the city's three other newspapers, and they'd saved him a seat in the front row.

He got there just as the jurors were taking their seats. Acton was standing in the witness box, biting her nails.

Zach Stone from the *Toronto Sun* leaned over and whispered, "This is great shit. Good work, Mr. Double A."

Stone had called Amankwah "Mr. Double A" since they'd first met fifteen years earlier, claiming there was no way he could remember or pronounce such a long, African name. He had had nicknames for everyone. Carmichael he called "Charm Michael," which fit to a tee. Fernandez was "Frozen Mayonnaise," because the Crown attorney was always so proper. Judge Rothbart, who'd been a well-known child actor, he tagged "Romeo Rothbart."

Carmichael rose to his feet. "Good afternoon, Ms. Acton, I hope you had a nice lunch." Right off the bat he was in full charm mode.

"It was okay," she said. Her attitude seemed different from this morning. More relaxed. Her words slightly slurred. "I had to eat by myself."

"That's unfortunate," Carmichael said. He picked up the remote and projected another website page on the screen. It was headed *Copper Topper* and featured a close-up of a woman's mouth, and her tongue licking a police officer's badge. "Ms. Acton," he asked in his calm, confident voice, "do you recognize *this* website?"

"Well, kind of." She teetered slightly on her feet.

"'Well, kind of'? Yes, kind of you do recognize this website, or, no, kind of you don't recognize it?"

She shrugged, flicked her hair back, and looked at Fernandez again. He was turned away, in deep whispered conversation with Detective Kormos, seated next to him.

"It's your website, isn't it? Ms. Acton," Carmichael said, stating what was obvious to everyone in the courtroom.

"One of them." She gave Carmichael a big grin. "Yep, it is."

"And, not to put too fine a point on it, but the tongue we see in the photo?"

She giggled. "Yes, sir, it's mine." Her words were really slurred now.

Amankwah realized she was drunk or stoned, or maybe both.

Judge Rothbart turned his head and gave Acton a harsh look.

"And who is *this* website set up for?" Carmichael asked. Playing along with her now.

"Well." She was still looking at the Crown's desk. Still grinning. "You know, like police officers. The fuzz. Cops."

"Objection." Fernandez was on his feet.

Rothbart looked down at him. "On what basis, Mr. Crown?" he demanded.

"Well, Your Honour," Fernandez said, flipping through his notebook.

"Yes?"

Amankwah had seen Fernandez in court many times. He was always well prepared and completely organized. Unflappably cool. But now he was scrambling. He had a drunk witness on the stand and his case was falling apart.

"I didn't object to the earlier line of questioning," Fernandez said. "That involved the website for hockey players. Given that the accused is a hockey player, I let it go in."

"And?" Rothbart drawled. Not impressed.

"But any activities that this witness may have had with other members of the public –"

"You mean police officers, Mr. Fernandez?"

"Well, yes, but –"

Rothbart had a theatrical, baritone voice that boomed out, "In a sexual assault trial, when she is the complainant, the prime witness, I wonder how this could *not* be relevant."

Amankwah could see that he was royally pissed at Acton for showing up in his court drunk, and there was no way he was going to let Fernandez protect her.

"I do see your point, Your Honour." Fernandez was knocked off his usual game. Kormos tugged the sleeve of his court gown, and he bent down to listen.

"Anything more, Mr. Fernandez?" Rothbart demanded.

"Yes." He nodded at Kormos and stood back up. "Could we have a ten-minute recess please, Your Honour?"

Rothbart smirked. Shook his head. "On what grounds? This is the Crown's key witness, and the defence is in the midst of its cross-examination."

Kormos tugged Fernandez's robe again, harder this time. He jabbed his pen into his notebook as they spoke. Fernandez listened intently then straightened up.

"Perhaps I could have a word with my friend." Without asking the judge's permission, he walked over to Carmichael and began to whisper to him.

Carmichael put his arm on Fernandez's shoulder like a sympathetic coach consoling a star player who had made a bad play. He listened attentively and shook his head. Fernandez kept talking.

At last Carmichael smiled and nodded. He took his arm back and stepped in front of Fernandez. "Your Honour. I believe my friend wishes to address this court, and I'm pleased to allow him to do so."

He flapped up his robes and sat down. His client looked at him, bewildered. He put his hand over the hockey player's wrist and lifted a finger, indicating he should just wait a minute.

On the witness stand, Acton looked at Kormos, confused. She mouthed the words *What the fuck?*

"Your Honour," Fernandez said, clearing his throat. "In all of the circumstances, the Crown has decided to withdraw the charges." Without saying another word, he sat down.

"Well, I'm not totally surprised by that." Rothbart edged his chair away from the witness box and didn't even look at Acton. "The defendant will rise," he said.

Carmichael practically heaved the hockey player to his feet.

"Sir," Rothbart said. "You are free to go."

"Hey, what about me?" Acton asked, weaving from side to side in the witness box.

Rothbart scowled at her. "Ma'am, your business here is finished."

"Oh, good." Acton stumbled, and almost fell getting down.

Amankwah was amazed this had all happened so fast. He looked over at Fernandez and Kormos. They already had their briefcases packed and were hurrying out the side door reserved for lawyers, as if they couldn't get out of there fast enough.

"Looks like some of our boys in blue are having a bit of fun on the side," Zach Stone said, his ever-present smirk firmly in place.

Was that all? What had just gone on here? Amankwah wondered. What were the cops trying to hide?

12

"WELCOME TO YOUR MONDAY AFTERNOON, DETECTIVE GREENE," FRANCINE HUGHES, THE veteran receptionist at the homicide bureau, said, greeting him in the same timely manner she welcomed everyone as he strolled up to her well-ordered desk, the elevator closing behind him.

Greene watched her record his name on the attendance sheet in the middle of her desk. "Always better when I see you," he said, following the script of their daily exchange.

Hughes had a rich English accent, and an amazing ability to stay chipper no matter how horrific the news. But today, her perpetual smile was gone. "I imagine you've heard," she said.

He stopped beside her desk. Greene had never been a very good liar, and he couldn't imagine being an actor, yet here he was about to put on the performance of his life. Until it came out that he'd been having an affair with Raglan, if it ever did, he had to play the part of someone who'd just lost a friend, not a lover. He felt ill.

"It's horrible," he said. Well, that was true.

"You did a few cases with Jennifer, did you not?" Hughes asked.

He broadened his legs, steadying himself. "Two murder trials. She was a talented lawyer."

"She was so lovely," Hughes said. Her big blue eyes welled up with tears. He'd never seen her weep before.

Greene walked around the desk and put his arm over her shoulders. She grasped his hand. "What's happening to this city?" she said. "When I came here it was such a peaceful place."

It was a strange remark for someone who'd been the receptionist, and knower of all things, at the homicide bureau for the last twenty years. But Greene understood what she meant. Even though these days legal academics were touting how Toronto's overall crime rates were going down, and in wealthier and more middle-class neighbourhoods that was true, in the last decade there'd been an unprecedented rise in gun and gang violence. It seemed to erupt in random spots, and the fear of murder and mayhem had seeped into the very pores of the city.

"Kennicott is trying to find the husband," she said. "He texted Jennifer this morning and said his business trip to Boston was cancelled. Turns out that was a big lie. He'd been fired from his job because a whole bunch of money went missing. No one knew. Apparently he gets dressed as if he's going to work and rides the subway all day. We've sent his photo out to every officer we have on the street."

Greene was glad he was beside Hughes so she couldn't see the shock on his face. Raglan's husband had been fired and was keeping it from her? He probably had been following her and found about their affair. Where had he gone? This was turning darker and darker.

"He's a bright one, that Daniel." She was still holding his hand firmly, like a lonely aunt hugging her favourite nephew. "You did a good job training him, Ari. He's got Jennifer's children safely covered at their schools. Me, I think the poor man must have done himself in. I'd look below every bridge in the whole bleeding city. Lord knows there are enough of them."

Of course. The cell phone would be one of the first things Kennicott would look at, Greene thought. But if Howard were the killer, why didn't he take her phone with him when he ran? He had to know his text would be on her cell. Guy had to be suicidal.

"Daniel told me he asked you to stay away from the investigation," she said.

"It's his case," Greene said. "He'll do fine."

She swivelled her chair around and flicked her head, indicating the row of offices behind her desk. "You know how it works. He starts running to you for help, and no one here will think he's up to the task. Then again, if no one finds out you two are talking –"

It was the practice that no one on homicide ever admitted to. Everyone needed a senior detective to talk to so they could see if they were missing something obvious, or just to relieve the pressure. They all did it. But no one talked about it.

He kissed her on the cheek. "See no evil, hear no evil," he whispered in her ear before he took his hand from her grasp, squeezed her shoulder, and walked to his office. He closed the door behind him. Thank goodness for the door. He put his back into it and slid to the floor.

He looked over at his desk and focused on the sleek black lamp he'd bought at a design store on Davenport and a matching pen-and-pencil holder.

Back in July, Raglan had been in the homicide squad's offices, meeting with another officer. Greene had run into her in the hallway as he emerged from his office. At that point he hadn't seen her in months and he'd assumed whatever they'd had was over.

"So this is where the great detective works," she'd said, peeking inside.

"Want to take a look?"

She had glanced behind her. The hallway was empty. Without saying a word, she went inside. He followed her in and closed the door.

She inspected his space. The room was sparse. A wood desk, a standard-issue chair, a grey filing cabinet in the corner, and his black lamp. Beside it, pens and pencils were jammed into a chipped white mug, the words *Toronto Police* stencilled on the side above a cheesy-looking logo.

She walked over to the desk, picked the mug up, and laughed. "Ari, for a guy who is always so well put together, you can do better than this."

"Doesn't win me any style points."

"You must have watched too many episodes of *Hill Street Blues*."

They stared at each other.

"Do you think it was a coincidence that I bumped into you in the hallway?" she asked.

"I don't know," he said. "Were you stalking me?"

"You could say that."

"I thought stalking is illegal."

"Depends how the person being stalked feels about it." She put the mug down, came over, and kissed him hard. "Meet me for lunch tomorrow at our usual place, I have a proposal for you."

At lunch the next day in the cafeteria, as she rubbed his calf under the table, she had given him the matching black pen-and-pencil holder as a present. The note inside said simply, *Get rid of that mug and keep this where you can see it. Always.*

Now the only thing in the room he could see was the black pen-and-pencil holder. He couldn't get past the feeling that he hadn't appreciated the gift enough. Or Jennifer.

13

KENNICOTT SAT IN THE FRONT WINDOW SEAT OF THE BEST COFFEE HOUSE, A COZY, INDEPEN-dent coffee shop on Queen East, half a block down from Raglan and Darnell's house. His eyes were glued to the street, watching the eastbound streetcars from downtown pick up and dispense travellers right outside. He had the actuarial firm's photo of Howard Darnell on the table in front of him, tucked under his notebook. Every few seconds he lifted the book and stared at the picture, like a nervous poker player who kept checking to see if he really did have an ace in the hole. Then he looked back out the window.

Where are you, Darnell, where are you?

He looked at his watch yet again. It was 3:45. Another streetcar came to a stop and one passenger got out, a young mother with an expensive-looking stroller. He turned to the side window and looked at the iconic Garden Gate Chinese restaurant, known as "The Goof." For years the D in their 1950s-style GOOD FOOD neon sign was out, and because the two words met at a right angle, the sign had read GOO F. The place had been trendified since the last time he was in the area, and the sign had been fixed, but he was sure the old nickname had stuck.

He looked back at Queen Street and kept running through his mental checklist, trying to figure out what else he could do to find this guy.

The three children were safe. Each of them had been brought to their principal's office at the end of the day on a pretext. They hadn't been told anything. Raglan and Darnell's house was under constant surveillance by two sets of plainclothes policemen. Two police cruisers were waiting around the corner and he had two others driving the neighbourhood side streets, checking the parks. A third was checking out the beach, two blocks to the south. Two more were checking under each of the city's many bridges – the most common spots for suicides in Toronto.

And now every cop in the city had a copy of Darnell's photo and, theoretically at least, was on the lookout for him. But he knew from experience, for most officers on patrol, this would be one of many alerts they got each shift. It was all a long shot.

This morning, he and Detective Alpine had checked out Darnell's house. They'd knocked on the front door, no answer. They'd walked around back, peered in the windows. The place looked empty. They'd looked in the windows of the garage. All around what looked like the family van were bicycles, hockey sticks, and a canoe. No one was there.

Kennicott had got an emergency search warrant, and inside the house he and Alpine found a typical, cramped, downtown Toronto home. Nothing unusual. No sign of Darnell. They'd set up hidden mini-microphones throughout the house, and in the van in the driveway, just in case.

With so much police activity going on, by about noon the media had got hold of the story. He'd personally called the editors of all four major newspapers and news directors of the city's main TV and radio stations and convinced them to hold off for a few hours. He told them all that if the story went live in the middle of the day, even though Raglan's three children were in school, with their cell phones and Internet access they'd be sure to find out. Everyone agreed to wait until four o'clock.

He watched a pair of mothers in yoga gear pushing fat baby strollers down the sidewalk. He couldn't think of anything else he could do. Metropolitan Toronto had a population of more than two and a half million people and sprawled over 250 square miles. There was no point in driving around and around. Ari Greene had taught him that sometimes the hardest thing to do on a homicide investigation is to sit and think. To wait.

Patience. It had never been his virtue.

He had Detective Alpine stationed at the Remarkable Bean Café across the street half a block down. How, he wondered, did cops do surveillance before Toronto was littered with coffee shops?

Another streetcar pulled up outside the window. He kept thinking of how sad it was for a man to get dressed, pretend to go to work, and instead ride the subway all day. Then find out your wife had been unfaithful.

The doors of the streetcar opened and Kennicott's back stiffened. There he was. Howard Darnell, wearing a business suit, a briefcase in one hand and cell phone in the other.

Kennicott didn't need to look at the photo under his notebook to be sure. He grabbed the police radio he'd secreted on his seat and clicked it on.

Darnell walked casually straight toward the café, not stopping to look around at all. The buttons to his jacket were undone and it flapped in the wind.

"Alpine, I see him," Kennicott said.

"Where?"

"He just got off the streetcar and is heading here."

"My sight line's blocked," Alpine said.

Darnell was steps from the door. He tapped the screen of his cell phone and put it to his ear.

"Get some backup but stay outside," Kennicott said. "Got to go."

A moment later Darnell was in the cafe, talking on his phone and heading up to the counter. He was a thin, well-groomed man with a pair of thick glasses.

Kennicott got up and followed him in line. Darnell's clothes looked clean. His hands did too. There were no obvious scratch marks on them.

"Barry, it's Dad," he heard Darnell say. "I'm back from Boston. I've been trying to reach Aaron, but your big brother's not picking up. For a change."

Darnell looked casually behind him. Kennicott reached for his wallet and kept his eyes down.

"Howard, how was Beantown?" a female voice said behind the counter.

Kennicott looked up. A fat woman wearing a T-shirt that said THE BEST BEAN IN THE BEACH was smiling at Darnell. Her name tag identified her as Tula.

"The usual nonsense," Darnell said. "Demanding clients."

Tula had pulled out four paper cups and a cup holder. "Two large hot chocolates for the young ones, an Americano for your oldest, and your dark Columbian."

Darnell held up his phone. "I can't seem to find the kids," he said. "Just give me my coffee and I'll walk down with them when they get home."

Kennicott felt the presence of someone close at his side. A gangly, unkempt man cut in front of him in line. Before he could react, the man started to talk. His speech was forced, high-pitched, and he had a bad stutter.

"Mr. Darnell, w-w-why did you only, only, only have one drink, not f-f-f-four?" he asked.

Darnell grinned gently at the man. "Francis, my children are staying late at school," he said.

"Yes, b-b-but what about, about, about their d-d-drinks –"

"Francis," Tula said from behind the counter, "Mr. Darnell has already ordered for them. Hot chocolates for the younger two and an Americano for Aaron. Now sit down and finish your latte. Customers are waiting."

Francis beamed at Darnell. "Van-vanilla latte with so-soya milk," he said.

"I know," Darnell said. "Your favourite."

"Francis," Tula barked.

"Okay. Ok-k-k-kay," Francis said. He looked back at Kennicott. "Francis isn't only a g-g-g-girl's name. Francis Tarkenton was a quarterb-b-b-back in the National Football, Football League and he lost the S-S-S-S-Super Bowl three t-t-t-times."

"Francis!" Tula yelled.

"Ok-k-kay," he said, before retreating to a table piled high with unfolded newspapers.

Darnell put his phone in his pocket. Kennicott watched him pull out his wallet. His hands were steady.

"Watch it, dear, it's hot," Tula said, handing him his coffee.

"Thanks, Tula." He gave her a dollar tip, took his coffee, and headed for the door.

"Mr. Darnell," Kennicott said, before he got there.

Darnell turned and looked at Kennicott. He smiled. "Yes, do I know you?"

"I'm afraid not, sir, but I'd like to speak with you for a moment." Kennicott pointed to his table by the window.

"Who are you?"

"Officer Daniel Kennicott," he said. "Toronto Police."

Darnell's eyes widened. He reached in his pocket and pulled out his phone. "I've been trying to reach my kids, is something wrong?" The words tumbled out at rapid-fire speed.

"No, no," Kennicott said, shaking his head. "They're fine. It's something else."

Darnell's shoulders sagged.

He knows, Kennicott thought.

"Okay." Darnell looked resigned. He followed Kennicott to the table and set his coffee down without taking a sip. "I was expecting this," he said.

"You were?" Kennicott asked. The hairs on the back of his hands stood on end.

"Do I need a lawyer?"

"Well . . ."

"I know the firm found some irregularities in my books. They reported it all to the CIA, but I can account for every nickel."

He thinks this is about his problem at work, Kennicott thought. "It's not about your job," he said.

"Oh. Then what?"

He seemed genuinely surprised. Or maybe this guy was a great actor. Impossible for Kennicott to tell. "Let me ask you this," he said. "Where were you today?"

"Today?"

It was the first time since they'd started talking that Darnell hadn't given an immediate answer. He was stalling for time.

"Yes. Sounds like you were in Boston, perhaps?" Kennicott asked, hoping to lead him into a lie.

Darnell shook his head and chuckled, a nervous little laugh. "Not today. I didn't want to bore Tula with the details, but no. The clients cancelled the meeting."

He knows what this is all about, Kennicott thought. He knows I've seen the text he sent to his wife this morning and he's smart enough not to lie about that.

"Where were you? Your office is farther up the street, isn't it? But I just saw you get off the streetcar coming from downtown."

Darnell chuckled, a little nervous laugh. "Yeah. Well. In fact I was meeting with another client."

Good, Kennicott thought, now he knew what Darnell looked like when he lied.

"Ex-ex-excuse me," a voice behind Kennicott said. It was Francis, holding a bundle of badly folded newspapers under one arm. "I-I-I hope your children get their h-h-h-hot chocolate," he said. "A-A-A-Aron drinks Am-m-merican-no now."

Darnell gave him a sincere smile. "I'll make sure they do, Francis. You find some good articles today?"

"Real, real, real g-g-g-good ones. I'm going to c-c-c-cut them all out." Francis hugged the papers to his chest and sauntered out.

Darnell looked back at Kennicott. "He'll be up all night cutting and sorting."

Kennicott opened his notebook and brought out a pen. "Can you tell me your client's name?"

Darnell sighed. "What's this about, Officer?" he asked.

"I think you know." He knows I know he's lying, Kennicott thought.

Darnell hung his head. "I guess you found out I don't have a job. Why would the police care about that?"

"Does your wife know you were fired?"

"No."

"Do you know where she is now?"

Darnell looked at his watch. "It's four o'clock. She's starting a big trial next week. I know she's busy, so I haven't talked to her all day."

"How about this morning?"

"She's training for a marathon, so on Mondays for the last few weeks she's been doing long runs in the morning then working later in the day. Why?"

Kennicott felt a gigantic lump in his throat. He looked straight at Darnell. "I'm afraid I've got terrible news for you."

"What?" Darnell's eyes seemed to stare right through Kennicott. His hands started to shake.

"Your wife. She's dead."

Darnell's mouth gaped open. He seemed to stop breathing. Then his body collapsed onto the table, his arms flailing out in front of him, splattering scalding coffee across Kennicott's chest.

14

ARI GREENE HAD BEEN IN THE OFFICES OF DIPAULO, PARISH, BARRISTERS & SOLICITORS, CERTI-
fied Specialists in Criminal Law, many times during his investigations of various
homicides. But never as he was now: a potential client.

He took a seat in Ted DiPaulo's office in the Thomson Building, across from
both old and new city halls. DiPaulo closed the door behind him and sat beside
Greene in the other client chair facing his desk.

Twenty-five years earlier, when Greene joined the police force, DiPaulo was
an up-and-coming prosecutor in the Crown's office. They worked together on
a number of files, and as their careers progressed, so too did the seriousness
of their cases. DiPaulo's wife had died when his kids were teenagers and he'd
become a defence lawyer so he could spend more time with them. Since then
he and Greene had tangled from opposite sides of the fence. Always profes-
sionally.

DiPaulo was a big man with powerful energy. His body always seemed to be
in motion. Turning in his seat, he arched his thick eyebrows. "Ari, what's going
on? You said this was personal, not professional. You're always one of the best-
dressed men I know. But you look terrible."

Greene pulled a hundred-dollar bill out of his coat pocket and handed it
over. "I'm retaining you as counsel," he said.

"Don't be silly." DiPaulo raised his hands, palms out, refusing to touch the
money.

"Please, Ted," Greene said.

"Ari, I'd never charge you."

"That's not the point. I need to retain you. Officially."

DiPaulo nodded. He took the bill, put it on the corner of his desk, and
placed a Skier of the Year, 2005, paperweight over it. "It's going into trust and
I won't touch it. But now I'm your lawyer, meaning my lips are sealed forever."

He pointed to a framed quote on the wall beside his desk. "Whenever anyone retains me, the first thing I do is read this out loud." He cleared his throat: "'Despite all the rules and objections and soft illusions of decorum, a trial was after all a savage and primitive battle for survival itself.' This comes from the novel *Anatomy of a Murder*. It's my way of warning my new clients that there is always a rough road ahead, and that I'll do whatever it takes, within the rules, to win."

"Smart," Greene said.

"Reality."

DiPaulo meshed his fingers and rubbed his thumbs together. He smiled. "What's up?"

"This is bad." Greene knew DiPaulo had mentored Raglan for many years and that they'd been good friends. This would be devastating news for him.

"What?" DiPaulo squeezed his thumbs.

"Jennifer Raglan." Greene was having a hard time getting the words out. He could see the concern mount in DiPaulo's eyes. "She's been murdered."

"Jennifer?"

Greene nodded.

DiPaulo exhaled a huge gust of air. "How? When?"

"She was in a cheap motel out on Kingston Road. Someone strangled her to death."

"My God." DiPaulo bolted to his feet and put his hands to his forehead.

"Ted," Greene said. "She was having an affair."

DiPaulo shook his head. "Oh. I know she and Howard had some problems and she moved out for a while, but . . ." He stopped.

Greene could see DiPaulo's brain clicking into gear. The initial shock wearing off. He looked down at the hundred-dollar bill under the paperweight on his desk. "Ari. You said this was personal." He balled his hands in front of his chest. "How do you know she was having an affair?"

Greene looked up at his old friend. DiPaulo's chair was deep and comfortable. This was probably the first time he'd sat down all day. A wave of fatigue hit him.

"Tell me, Ari," DiPaulo said.

"Mondays. Six weeks ago Jennifer started taking them off. She wanted to run a marathon, and she told everyone she was using the mornings for long training runs."

"But she wasn't running, was she?" DiPaulo asked. His large, energetic body was as still as a statue.

Greene's gaze drifted out the window, across the street to the plaza in front of City Hall. Normal people were going about their normal workday. For them this was just another Monday in September. They had no idea how lucky they were.

He turned back, determined to meet DiPaulo's stare.

"When I got there today she was dead. Someone strangled her."

DiPaulo's whole body rocked forward and back, like a religious man in prayer. He frowned. "What did you do?"

"I was about to call 911, of course."

"Of course."

"But then I heard someone outside the room. I ran into the courtyard and down the street to this cheap little strip mall. I'd driven there on a scooter and had parked it there. Whoever it was got away. I took out my cell again and was going to call it in and . . ."

Again he couldn't speak.

"What?" DiPaulo demanded. The old prosecutor in him coming to the fore.

"A squad car and an ambulance came screaming past me. They turned right into the motel. I jumped on the scooter and raced around the side streets in back. I was sure the killer was Jennifer's husband and that he'd be suicidal. I wanted to find him."

He told DiPaulo how he hadn't found anyone, about how he was about to call in when Kennicott called him and insisted he not come to the scene and how they didn't have a chance to talk. "He's going to meet me later tonight."

"Okay," DiPaulo said. "Who did you tell about this back at Homicide?"

"No one."

"No one? Are you crazy? No one knows you were having this affair?

"No."

"That you were in the motel room and saw Jennifer's dead body?"

"No."

"And that you left?"

"That's right."

"Christ almighty."

"I was about to call when everything happened," Greene said.

"Instead you took off from the scene of the crime."

"I didn't take off. I chased a suspect." Greene could hear how defensive his voice had become. How bad it sounded.

"Don't split hairs," DiPaulo said. He was in full cross-examination mode now. Very effective. "Are you telling me that right at this moment" – he checked his watch – "at 4:10 P.M. on September tenth, no one knows that you were there."

"No one but you." Greene pointed at the hundred-dollar bill.

"Yes, and you shut me up by hiring me." DiPaulo shook his head. "Ari, what were you thinking?"

"I wanted to find her husband. I thought he was suicidal."

"But no one knows where he is?" DiPaulo asked.

"Not as of half an hour ago."

Greene lowered his head. "I don't know what I'm going to do. The timing. What I saw in the room. You'll think I'm crazy, but it all felt wrong. Like someone was trying to set me up."

Greene told him about where he'd parked his scooter and how he'd gotten rid of his helmet and gloves.

"In other words, you disguised yourself before you went to the motel. Took off after she'd been killed, hid your clothes and vehicle, and then went to a lawyer." DiPaulo put a hand over his eyes. "This could not be any worse."

"I'm telling you the truth."

DiPaulo moved slowly behind his desk and slumped into his leather chair. "Classic defence lawyer's nightmare," he said. "Horrible facts and an innocent client."

Neither man spoke.

Greene looked back out the window. His eyes fixed on the clock tower atop Old City Hall. He'd never noticed before that there were no numbers on the clock face, but long dashes. "You're going to want to know how long this has been going on with Jennifer and me."

"Don't want to, but I might need to," DiPaulo said.

"Started a while ago, when she left her husband. Then she went back to him and it stopped."

"But then it started again," DiPaulo said. "You better hope they find Howard and that he confesses real fast. Then they probably won't care who she was sleeping with. When are you meeting Kennicott?"

"After this. At five."

"Okay, but when you meet him you're going to tell him everything, right?"

Greene stood up. He was restless. "I've thought about it more. From every-thing she's ever told me about her husband, he doesn't sound like the type to flip out and kill her like this. And the murder scene looked too, I don't know, staged."

DiPaulo took out a pad of paper and grabbed a pen, his irrepressible nervous energy returning like it was coming out of a deep freeze. "Leaving the scene is very bad. Is there any other reason you can give me for doing that?" he asked.

"Yes," Greene said. "Somewhere along the line I realized that Howard might not be the killer. And if I told Kennicott I'd been there in that motel room, then I'd be a witness."

DiPaulo nodded. "And then you'd be off the case."

"That's right."

"Ari Greene," DiPaulo said. "Always the homicide detective. Even when you are the one in the crosshairs." He reached for the bill and waved it at Greene. "You retained me because, if you don't tell Kennicott anything and you get charged one day, you could waive solicitor–client privilege and testify that you told me about this. That you thought there was more to this murder than met the eye, and that in fact you were being set up. So, smart detective that you are, you decided to keep your role secret until you could solve the crime yourself. That sound about right?"

"And one other reason," Greene said, reaching over to shake his old friend's hand. "I needed to tell someone."

15

THE COFFEE WAS HOT. IT STUNG KENNICOTT. BUT IT DIDN'T BURN HIM. HE WAS DETERMINED to keep his eyes on Howard Darnell, who looked devastated by the news he'd just heard about his wife.

If he was the killer, he's a great actor, was Kennicott's first thought.

"What happened?" Darnell sputtered. He didn't even notice the coffee he'd sprayed all over Kennicott.

"This morning." Kennicott righted the overturned mug and wiped the table with a napkin.

"She was jogging," Darnell said. "What? A car hit her? I always worry about that. I keep telling her to wear a reflective vest."

The shock in Darnell's eyes was mixing with denial. His brain not believing the news. Or was it a magnificent performance? All of Kennicott's years of training, first as a lawyer, then as a cop, had conditioned him to be skeptical. "Never be impressed by first impressions," Ari Greene had told him, over and over again. "Don't let your heart overwhelm your head."

"Why do you think she was jogging?" Kennicott asked. He wondered if Darnell would try hide the fact of the texts he'd exchanged with his wife that morning. They clearly showed he had opportunity to kill her. And if he found out she was cheating on him, that gave him motive.

"She's training to run the half marathon here in October," Darnell said. His voice sounded defeated. "Where is she? What happened?"

"Are you sure that's what she was doing this morning?" Kennicott was determined to hold back what he knew about the murder as long as possible, see if he could catch Darnell mentioning something that only the killer would know.

Darnell put his hand down to his side and Kennicott heard something go *click*. He wasn't sure what it was until Darnell's hand emerged with a cell phone in it. He'd obviously unhooked it from his belt. Was he a nerdy mathematician who wore his phone on a clip, or a cold-blooded murderer?

He tossed the phone on the table. "Jennie and I talked. Well, I mean we texted this morning. I was hoping to have a cup of coffee with her. Here, take a look. Aren't you going to tell me what happened?"

Kennicott took the phone in his hand, pretending he was surprised that there were relevant texts to read.

Darnell pointed to the screen. "Touch the text-message icon."

Kennicott read the texts, acting as if he hadn't seen them before.

Darnell put his head in his hands. "That was the whole thing," he said. "I was fired in July and didn't have the nerve to tell her. Jennie's mom died in February and our oldest son is having problems and . . ." He started to cry.

Kennicott froze. Don't say anything, he told himself. Watch.

Darnell lifted his eyes. "She thought I had a weekly meeting in Boston. This morning I was finally going to tell her."

Kennicott looked hard at the man in front of him.

Darnell looked bereft. His reactions seemed normal. Shock. Disbelief. He hadn't lied about his fake job or tried to hide his texts with his wife.

Suddenly Darnell inhaled deeply. For a moment Kennicott thought he was going to faint. His eyes expanded in fear. "The kids," he said, almost shouting. "Do they know?" He was hyperventilating.

"No." Kennicott softened his grip. "Not yet."

"Oh God." Darnell nodded slowly. Then shook his head. His breathing was still laboured. "I don't understand. What happened?"

Kennicott pulled his arm back. "I'm sorry," he said. "She didn't die while she was running. She was murdered."

"Murdered? Jennie?"

Kennicott could only nod.

"But . . ." He stabbed at his phone. "She texted me . . ." He started to cry. "Who did this?"

Kennicott shrugged. "We don't know yet."

If Darnell didn't know that his wife was having an affair, then he had no motive to kill her. Kennicott could tell it hadn't occurred to him yet that he was a suspect.

Darnell rubbed his fingers through his hair. "Jennie's a tough Crown," he said. "She puts a lot of people in jail."

He's still speaking of his wife in the present tense, Kennicott thought. Her killer might inadvertently speak of her in the past.

"Last week that asshole Wainwright threatened her in court," Darnell said. "I told her she should get police protection. She laughed it off."

It was a logical connection for the spouse of a Crown attorney to make. A top prosecutor such as Raglan would have sent many nasty criminals away for a long time. Or maybe, Kennicott thought, Wainwright's threat to his wife was a perfect cover for Darnell to commit this murder. And he'd heard that Wainwright didn't show up in court today. Nobody knew where he was. Had this meek-looking man sitting across from him killed Wainwright too?

"If you didn't go to Boston, what did you do today?" Kennicott asked. This was the crucial question. If Darnell gave Kennicott a false alibi, he'd be suspect number one.

"What I've done every Monday since I lost my job. I left the house at eight pretending to be on my way to the island airport to catch the Porter flight to Boston. I took the 501 streetcar downtown. Today I got on the Yonge subway south, rode it around to Eglinton West. I've got a Metropass, and every day I go somewhere different."

There were cameras in every subway station and every subway car, Kennicott thought. This would be easy to check. "Then what did you do?"

"I'd never been to that part of the city before. I walked all the way over to Rogers Road. People were so friendly."

"Did you stop anywhere?"

He looked at Kennicott and almost smiled. "There's a patty shop, I don't remember the name, on the south side. I was the only white person there, that's for sure. This woman who served me kept calling me 'dear.' I ordered a vegetable patty and she said I should try the beef ones too. I told her it was too early to eat meat, but she insisted. It was spicy, but delicious."

"What did you do next?" Kennicott was amazed at how calm Darnell had become. As if he were in a trance.

"I took the bus south to St. Clair and that new dedicated streetcar line back to Yonge. There's a quiet library there, and I read the *Economist* for about an hour." He looked squarely at Kennicott for the first time. "I didn't kill my wife, Detective, I loved her. Please tell me what happened."

The transition had been swift. Somewhere in the telling of his activities during day, the penny had dropped and Darnell realized he was being questioned. The man was no fool. He knew Kennicott would check out his story, and with so much detail it was almost certainly true. He had a solid alibi.

But that didn't confirm his innocence. Perhaps the exact opposite.

Was the Howard Darnell sitting in front of him the slightly nerdy husband and good father he appeared to be? Or was he an angry, failed actuary? A man lost in his life who had crafted a conspicuous alibi while he had a surrogate murder his wife?

Everything Darnell said or did could be interpreted either way.

"I understand you and Jennie were separated for a while a year or two ago," Kennicott said.

"She left me. It was really hard on the kids, especially our oldest son, Aaron. Then she came back. We're both from a small town. Welland. We met in high school."

If Darnell was innocent, then Kennicott was about to give him the second piece of very bad news. If he was guilty, it wouldn't be news to him at all. "From what little we know," Kennicott said, "it appears she was having an affair."

Darnell closed his eyes. "What does it matter?" he said. "Don't you understand I love her? Please, tell me what happened. Take me to see my children."

Kennicott was fighting hard to remain skeptical, but right now his brain and his heart were screaming: This man is innocent.

He put his hand back on Darnell's shoulder. Softly this time. "Of course," he said.

16

IN HIGH SCHOOL, ARI GREENE HAD BEEN A BETTER-THAN-AVERAGE BASKETBALL PLAYER. NOT the best shooter, but he'd been good at passing. Because he was big for his age and strong and determined, he could always make space for himself at the top of the key, or under the net, and dish the ball off. His favourite target was Brian Silver, a beanpole-tall redhead with unnaturally long arms and a nose for the basket.

They became fast friends. The Silvers owned a bakery downtown that had been in the family for three generations, and on weekends the two of them would work the Sunday-morning shift, starting at five. They'd end at noon and gorge themselves on dim sum at one of the nearby Chinese restaurants on Baldwin Street.

After high school, Silver spent a few unenthusiastic years at university before he started working full-time at the bakery. Within a decade he and his younger brother, Abe, were running the place. Years of working from before sunrise until late in the evening had thinned his still-red hair and bulked out his once-thin frame but had not taken anything away from his rough sense of humour. It was on full display when he and Greene greeted Daniel Kennicott at the bottom of the concrete steps inside the bakery just after five o'clock.

"You ever play trivia with this guy?" he asked Kennicott after introductions were made.

"No, I haven't," Kennicott said.

"Don't," Silver said as he led them past rows of steel trays piled high with loaves ready to ship. "Mr. Smarty Brain. You know he used to always carry a book with him in his gym bag. One time we're playing Mackenzie, and they're killing us. Coach looks at the end of the bench, and there's Ari reading *Catch-22*."

Silver had a deep laugh, and he cackled to himself as he walked them into the main baking room. Loaves, fresh out of the oven, descended on a circular, two-story-high wire drying rack that made a staccato, rattling sound. The floor shook, the way it had shaken so many years ago when Greene first walked into the place.

"Watch this," Silver said to Kennicott, before he turned to Greene. "Last month we got this new driver, an old Somali history professor from Mogadishu, or something. He's doing the run down on College, and my customers are so happy because Mohammed talks to them in their own language. Guess which language?"

"Italian," Greene said. "Somalia used to be an Italian colony."

Silver raised his eyebrows at Kennicott. "See."

He led them up a narrow staircase, his laugher echoing off the thin walls. His office was a small, windowless room. An ancient wood desk took up most of the space, its surface cluttered with purchase orders, a stack of six-cup coffee holders, two huge balls of elastic bands, and an unsteady-looking column of *Sports Illustrated* magazines. A faded photo of Cheryl Tiegs in a fishnet bathing suit was taped to the wall above it. There was one chair, and both its arms were broken.

"Welcome to the executive suite. Only the best for Metro's finest." Silver looked at Kennicott. "Did you know Somalis spoke Italian?"

"No, I didn't," Kennicott said.

"No white person in Toronto did, except this guy." He smacked Greene on the chest. "Stay as long as you like, gents." He closed the door behind him on his way out.

"This factory is like a little Ellis Island." Greene put his back against the wall when they were alone. The rat-tat-tat of the drying rack downstairs could still be heard coming through the floor. "The Silver family has employed people from every immigrant group you can imagine as they come to the city."

Kennicott looked tired, the way homicide detectives always look after the first long day of a murder investigation.

Greene had gone back to the homicide bureau after he'd met with DiPaulo, and the receptionist, Francine Hughes, had filled him in on Kennicott's meeting with Howard Darnell and the man's intricate alibi. Greene couldn't wait to learn more.

"I appreciate you meeting me like this," Kennicott said. He leaned against the desk.

"You wanted a private place," Greene said, sweeping his arms in front of him. "Can't do any better than this."

"It's perfect," Kennicott said. "Look, I know what you wanted to tell me this morning."

"You do?" So he does know about Jennifer and me, Greene thought. Probably knows I was in the motel room this morning too. Greene was relieved. It saved him from having to break the news.

"This isn't just any old murder, and I knew you'd want to be involved," Kennicott said. "Let me update you right away. I'm sure you think the husband is the obvious suspect."

"Oh," Greene said, thinking his voice sounded foolish. He realized Kennicott had no idea about him and Jennifer.

"His name is Howard Darnell. You heard I found him this afternoon. He walked into the local coffee shop down the street from their house. He didn't have a mark on him. And he has a perfect alibi. Turns out he was fired a couple of months ago and hadn't told his wife, so he was pretending to go to work every day. We've got him on TTC cameras over on the west side of the city all morning. He couldn't possibly have killed her. When I told him the news, I thought he was in genuine shock. And once that wore off, all he worried about was the safety of his kids."

"Okay," Greene said. "But –"

"I know," Kennicott said. "You're always saying, don't be too impressed by first impressions, but I have to tell you I can't see it with this guy. Even when I told him it looked like Jennifer was having an affair with someone, he didn't flinch."

Greene swallowed hard. "What did he say about that?"

"He said it didn't matter. That they'd been married for a long time and that the only thing that mattered was that he loved her. He kept talking about her in the present tense. Does that sound like a guy who strangled his wife?"

Greene's head was spinning. Kennicott hadn't connected him with Raglan, and if her husband hadn't killed her, then who had? Who was outside the door of the motel? Who had he been chasing? Who called 911?

"I expect you're going to say, 'What do we do if his alibi checks out?'" Kennicott said. "He could have hired someone to do the hit."

Greene nodded, still trying to take this all in.

"That's what Alpine said. He's the division detective."

"Alpine's a good cop," Greene said, finally finding his voice.

"I'm not saying Darnell isn't still a suspect. I've got him under twenty-four-hour surveillance, and we got in and miked his house. But I've got no grounds to arrest him. She was strangled. Not the kind of thing a hired gun would do. Too close. Too intimate."

Greene nodded. Kennicott was right. Every cop knew it was hard to strangle someone to death. You had to look them right in the eye. If Howard had hired a killer, you'd expect her to have been stabbed or shot. Choking homicides were textbook murders motivated by jealousy or anger. Personal rage.

"What other suspects do you have?" Greene asked.

Kennicott shrugged. "Some of the bad apples she prosecuted perhaps. We're checking up on all her major cases for the last five years. Looks like most of them are still in jail."

"Who else? I read in the papers last week that Wainwright, the movie guy, threatened her outside of court," Greene said. He and Jennifer had talked all about it last Monday morning. Courtroom pillow talk, she'd called it. She'd been smoking mad. Guy was an asshole, but would he go so far as murdering a Crown attorney?"

"Wainwright didn't show up in court today," Kennicott said. "Judge Norville issued a bench warrant this afternoon and we're looking for him everywhere."

Greene thought of seeing Raglan, neatly tucked into her bed. Her bruised neck evidence of an angry, intimate killing. But the candle left burning by her bed? Was it supposed to look like a movie set? It seemed a stretch.

"Anything else?"

"I've been looking into Raglan's family and background. Her oldest son, Aaron Darnell, just turned nineteen and he's still in high school. Kid's got a bad record. He's been in and out of trouble since he was thirteen. I checked with the cops at 55 Division. Apparently Aaron Darnell is a bit of a legend there. They said that he looks like a fourteen-year-old choirboy but don't be fooled. Lately he's got into some very serious stuff."

Jennifer had never told Greene this. He remembered once she'd mentioned that her oldest son was extremely bright and complained about how he'd bounced around from school to school. Her exact words had stuck in his brain: "Being 'gifted' is just another term for being disabled."

But he had no idea it was serious. Now that he thought of it, she'd insisted they wait until September before she finally left her husband because she said she needed to get Aaron settled in a new school.

Something else fell into place. The last time he was at a motel with her, Jennifer had asked him what he thought about a cop on the drug squad. Drugs were a federal matter. She was a provincial Crown and would never have reason to deal with the guy. He'd thought the question a bit strange.

"What kind of serious?" he asked Kennicott. "Drugs?"

"Big-time. He started as a graffiti artist, spray-painting everywhere. He caused a lot of serious damage and got arrested a few times for mischief. They kept letting him off if he paid restitution, so he'd sell drugs at school to pay the fines. Then, of course, he got kicked out of school. The cop I talked to this afternoon said he's turned into a major dealer. He's out on bail for the third time in twelve months. The parents, I mean Jennifer and Howard, had to put up twenty thousand bucks. And they've just put him in a special private school."

Jennifer, Greene thought, you had so many secrets. You carried so many burdens without complaint. Now he understood why it had been so hard for her to break away from her husband.

"Did you know Raglan was a cop before she went to law school?" Kennicott asked.

"What?" he said, probably sounding too surprised. He had no idea at all. At every turn he was learning things about her that he'd never known.

"Morality squad. Apparently she was really good."

The morality squad was a euphemistic term for the pretty young policewomen who posed as prostitutes in high-traffic residential areas plagued by hookers. They'd wait for johns to proposition them, then signal for backup and arrests. Greene could picture young Jennifer Raglan as a beautiful and tough cop, excellent at the job.

Okay Ari, quit stalling, he told himself. This was the moment. He had to tell Kennicott right now that he'd been in the motel room this morning. That he'd found her dead body.

But something made him pause again. The all-too-perfect setup. The squad car and the ambulance screaming past him on Kingston Road, how they'd arrived just at the time when he was supposed to be in the room.

That voice in the back of his head was telling him to be careful.

And Jennifer. He wanted to find out more about her. Needed to. Everything. Once he told Kennicott, he'd be totally sidelined.

"I can handle this," Kennicott said. "We need to keep our talks up here completely off the radar. Okay?"

Perhaps her husband, Howard, was right. The affair wasn't the important thing, Greene thought. He had to find the killer. That was all that mattered. Then again, what would it look like if he didn't tell Kennicott everything, right now?

"Ari?" Kennicott said.

Greene snapped his head up. Kennicott had never called Greene by his first name before. "Yes, what?"

"You okay?" Kennicott asked. "You look pale. I know you and Raglan did a lot of cases together. Maybe I'm asking too much for you to be involved in this."

Greene felt faint. He'd been thinking so intently, he'd hardly breathed. He had to decide. How could he deceive Daniel Kennicott like this? How could he let himself be cut out of investigating Jennifer's murder? And how much more was there about the woman he'd been in love with that he didn't know? He had to find out.

"We should meet here every day," he said.

Kennicott smiled. "That would be great. This is between you and me."

"On one condition," Greene said. "No secrets. You need to tell me everything."

"Why wouldn't I?" Kennicott said.

There are a thousand reasons why you shouldn't, Greene thought as he sat on the broken chair and felt the drying rack vibrate beneath his feet.

17

THE DISHES IN THE SINK HAD PILED UP FOR THREE DAYS. THIS IS WHAT USUALLY HAPPENED TO Amankwah during the weeks when he didn't have his two children. He got slovenly and depressed. And he threw himself into work more than ever.

He constantly calculated how long it would be until his daughter, Fatima, and his son, Abdul, would be back racing around his tiny apartment, causing havoc, spreading joy. He'd brought them to school this morning and their mother had picked them up there. This was the start of the longest, and saddest, gap in his access cycle and he wouldn't see them for nine days. Though he had to admit, with so much going on in the city right now, and this incredible story of Jennifer Raglan being murdered in a tacky motel out on Kingston Road, if he had to be alone, this was a good time for it.

There was no more dish soap left and he didn't have the energy to go back outside to buy any right now. Of course his ex-wife had a dishwasher in what used to be their home, but he'd been doing dishes in the sink his whole life.

Like many people who had grown up poor, Amankwah had had no sense of his family's poverty until he was a teenager. His parents left Ghana during a political coup in 1981, when he was six years old and his sister was ten. A lot of African immigrants to Toronto back then ended up living in high-rise apartments in Thorncliffe Park, a place always described in the press as a "densely populated, multicultural neighbourhood."

His father had been a newspaper editor back home. Amankwah's fondest early memories were of his dad reading the *Toronto Star* at the kitchen table of their two-bedroom apartment every morning before he went to the factory. He'd fold the paper to a page and leave a note on it telling him to read a certain story when he got home from school.

It was not until he won a scholarship to go to university in Ottawa that he met people his age who had expensive clothes, owned cars, and had no idea how to cook. When he got the job at the *Star* and his new wife, Claire, was hired as

the anchor on the morning breakfast TV show, overnight they had money coming in. They bought a downtown condo. Shopped at the hippest clothes stores.
Dined at the newest restaurants. Glossy magazines all wanted to do a feature
story about Toronto's sophisticated, media-savvy black couple. Invitations to big
charity parties poured in.

Then, after the children were born, Claire left him for a white TV sports-
caster and Amankwah crashed. His dream of becoming the newspaper's first
black foreign correspondent was in tatters. Replaced by his fear of getting fired
as his performance plummeted. Now he lived in this two-bedroom apartment
above a Chinese restaurant on Gerrard Street, about the size of the Scarborough
apartment he grew up in, and had to struggle every month to pay the rent and
support payments. For the first time in his life, he felt poor.

His apartment was hot, so he opened the front window. The sound of a
streetcar rumbling by mixed with the chatter of shoppers buying their fresh
vegetables from the grocery stores below, whose produce spilled out onto the
crowded sidewalk.

He was hungry, but he wanted to put in a good hour or two of work before
he went out to grab a bite to eat and get some dish soap. Tomorrow was an important day.

In early August, when Barclay Church had arrived as the paper's new editor,
he'd called a general meeting with all the reporters. A tall, skinny man with an
unruly tuft of red hair, the man dressed terribly and wore remarkably unfashion-
able glasses. Michelle Goates, the style reporter who was also the newsroom wit,
called him a cross between Woody Allen and John Cleese, with an accent you
could barely understand.

"Hello, hello, hello," he had said once everyone had assembled in the fourth-
floor cafeteria, the beautiful view of the lake behind him. "No doubt I must seem
like a strange bird to all of you, with my fucking thick northern English brogue."

A ripple of laughter slid around the room. "Fucking" had come out sounding like "fogging." *My fogging thick brogue.*

"I have the distinct advantage of knowing nowt about your city or any of
you lot. I plan to spend the next fortnight walking around, and then I'll chat
with each one of you in turn. But for now, I say we have some fun putting out
this ruddy paper."

And that was it. No big cheerleading session. No talk of some grand vision.
Strange.

Everyone assumed when Church said he was going to walk around, he meant he'd be lurking over their shoulders in the newsroom and fine-dining in trendy restaurants with the higher-ups.

Instead he completely disappeared. After a couple of days, reporters started sighting him on a streetcar, or walking by the lake, or browsing in some suburban shopping mall. One day, Amankwah was at the overcrowded and run-down courthouse in a strip mall in Scarborough, covering a preliminary inquiry into a shooting that had killed two innocent people at a street party, one of them a child. When he went to the washroom, there was Church, washing his hands in the dirty sink. An old camera was slung over his shoulder.

"Oh, hello," he said, as if they were fast friends.

"Hi," Amankwah said, stunned. "You out here to watch this shooting case?"

"Of course not," Church said. "Everyone else is fucking doing that. I'm taking pictures. I started out in the business as a photog. This place is a disaster. Imagine putting a courthouse in a strip mall in the middle of nowhere? Who in the world thought this is a good idea? Well, must be off. Ta-ra."

When Church came back from his two weeks of "walking around," he called everyone together again. "The only fucking promise I'm going to make," he said, to the group of now very intrigued reporters, "is that no meetings like this will last more than five minutes. Every ass-sitting, scumbag-sucking media pundit out there says newspapers are dying. Probably bloody right. Look, we've got the fifth-biggest city in North America here. There's got to be much more sex, drugs, and rock and roll going on, with a lovely dose of crime and corruption thrown in for some fun. If we're sinking anyways, let's at least kick in some windows."

Over the next few weeks, reporters talked about their "chats" with Church. He'd read each of their articles for the last few years, and wanted to know how to help them have more "fun." Even the most cynical, veteran reporters found themselves inspired.

Amankwah's turn was tomorrow afternoon. He'd been fretting about it for days. Worried that he hadn't landed a good story all summer. What new and exciting things could he offer up to fit Church's idea of fun?

Now he had the after-date story, with hockey players and call girls, and the hint of cops being involved. Add to this the Raglan motel murder. He'd have to come up with a good headline for that and call it in to the desk to impress Church.

Maybe CASE CLOSED ON PROSECUTOR. Or MOTEL MURDER MYSTERY. How about HEAD CROWN CAUGHT IN STRANGLEHOLD?

That's the ticket.

He couldn't wait until tomorrow when he could reboot his career. It had turned out to be a great Monday after all.

18

"DAD," GREENE SAID, LEANING ON THE RAKE HE WAS USING ON HIS FATHER'S LAWN, "SHE'S twenty-five years younger than you."

Greene's father was staring at the backside of his latest girlfriend, a larger-than-life Russian bombshell named Klavdiya, as she strutted up the concrete steps to his little bungalow. He snapped his head toward Ari. "Twenty-three and a half," he said. "And you won't let me drive at night. She drives at night."

It was a beautiful evening and all Greene could think was, Jennifer's dead. She's missing this gorgeous sunset. And everything else.

He bent down, grabbed a pile of weeds, grass clippings, and a few early falling leaves, and dumped them in the paper yard-waste bag by his side. "I bet she does," he said.

His mother had died two years earlier, after an extended descent into Alzheimer's, and since then Greene's father had been making up for lost time. First came a parade of women near his age, and almost his height. Armed with casseroles, they arrived at his front door, blush freshly applied to their cheeks, lips tight with determination. Then there were taller women, ten, maybe fifteen years younger. They showered him with tickets to the ballet, the symphony, and the theatre. And one, to Greene's utter amazement, even got his father to go to the opera.

Somehow, a few months ago, he'd discovered Russian woman. Were they really Jewish? Or just Jewish enough to get out of the old Soviet Union thirty-five years ago, grab a cup of coffee in Tel Aviv, then hightail it to North America. Klavdiya claimed to be in her early sixties. Although that fact, along with a host of half-truths she'd told his father, was shrouded in mystery.

None of it seemed to bother Yitzhak Greene, who clearly loved that the top of his bald head aligned perfectly with the top of Klavdiya's wide shoulders, giving him a front-row view of her pumped-up breasts.

Greene dumped a second pile of garden waste in the bag. "She can get rid of my bar mitzvah photos in the living room, but just don't let her take Mom's picture off the mantel," he said.

In the nine weeks since Klavdiya had appeared on the scene, she'd taken to renovating every aspect of his father's life, starting with ditching his decades-old wire-rim glasses for three new pairs from the three-for-one optical store her cousin ran on Bathurst Street. Next came new shirts and pants from her brother-in-law, a jobber down on Spadina who got everything wholesale.

Now she was starting in on his house, getting rid of the plastic geraniums in the kitchen window and the faded tablecloth in the dining room. Amazingly, she'd somehow managed to convince his dad to throw out the yellowed plastic cover on the living room sofa. For that, Greene would be eternally grateful, no matter what other havoc she ended up causing in his father's life.

"I heard about this murder of the lawyer?" his father said. "Didn't you do some cases with her?" He picked up a second rake from the lawn and began working beside Greene. The front yard had two trees near the house and a majestic red maple in the front, which they both liked the best. In the early fall its leaves turned bright scarlet, making the first ones to drop stand out on the lawn like scattered taillights on a near-deserted highway. Since he was a child, it had been a game between father and son to look for the most perfect one.

"We did a lot of things together," Greene said.

"Who's the detective on this?"

It always amazed Greene how knowledgeable his dad had become about the inner workings of the homicide squad.

"It's Daniel Kennicott's first case."

His father let out a low whistle. "You helping him on this?"

"Not officially."

"Of course."

"I just met with him at Brian's bakery."

"And what? Sound like the husband probably did it?"

"That's what we thought at first. But the man has an airtight alibi. Kennicott's still suspicious of him, though."

"He thinks the man hired someone to strangle his wife? Even in the camps, when someone was killed, it was never by hand. Always with a knife, or a brick."

"I know. It's hard to strangle someone to death. It's a very angry crime." Greene picked out a pristine, dark red leaf from the pile and handed it over.

"A good one," his father said, twirling the leaf by its stem. "And the man she was meeting in that motel?"

Greene pulled a second leaf from the pile. One of its corners was bent. He tossed it back.

His father examined the leaf in his hand, not saying anything. Greene knew him well enough to know that something was up.

"What's wrong?" he asked.

"Brian's bread. Don't bring me so much." His dad shrugged, and pointed the leaf toward his front door. "She eats gluten-free bread. I've even started."

Greene laughed. "She got you eating quinoa salad yet?"

"No. But porridge. First time I've eaten it since the Russians liberated us. An old Polish lady, wouldn't let me eat meat for three days. Only Cream of Wheat. Saved me. Some of my friends ate so much their stomachs exploded."

It was a story Greene had heard many times. His father, weighing seventy-three pounds, walking the streets alone and ragged, taken in by a woman who fed and bathed him.

"Okay, Dad. No more bagels. No more challah."

"Well, challah on Fridays."

Greene closed up his bag of leaves. "Don't let her move in yet."

"I might. I might not."

"Don't," Greene said with force. "Not now."

His father heard the tone in Greene's voice. He'd survived enough danger in his life to smell it miles away. He looked Ari in the eye, passed him back the perfect red leaf, picked up his rake, and started working. "What is it?" he asked.

Greene had checked out Klavdiya on the police database. She had a dated criminal record filled with fraud convictions, mostly bounced cheques. Her ex-husband was more of a problem. He was in jail for five years on an extortion charge and was getting out in a few months. There had been no need to tell his father about any of this. Until now.

"Klavdiya has a criminal record," Greene said. "If I get arrested, the only chance I'll have of getting bail is if I can stay with you. She can't be here."

For a near-imperceptible moment, the rake in his father's hand stopped moving. Then he kept going. He was a man who knew how to take a blow and not show it.

"Did you love her?" he asked at last.

"More, I think, than I knew."

"Have you told anyone else?"

"Just a lawyer," Greene said. "You remember Ted DiPaulo?"

"Not Kennicott?"

"I tried to tell Kennicott this afternoon," he said. "But he'd have to make me a witness. I'd be off the case. I need to find out who killed her."

"How much time do you have?"

"I don't know. Kennicott's smart. He's going to figure this out very soon."

"That's how much you loved her. That you are taking such a risk."

It wasn't a question, Greene realized. But a statement of fact.

"You know I hate the Poles," his father said. "But their vodka is the best. They make it with potatoes. You'll take a bottle for tonight."

There was a rattling sound at the front of the house. Greene looked up and saw Klavdiya struggling with the old screen door, the same one he had run in and out of since he was a little boy. At last she got it open.

"Stupid." She slammed it shut behind her. "Yitzee, we need to get rid of this."

We, Greene thought.

His father shrugged.

She strode across the porch and glared down at them. One of her high heels caught on the concrete steps and she grabbed the black railing to steady herself. "These stairs have to go too. They're awful."

"Don't worry, Ari, there's more to life than good tits," Greene's father hissed under his breath. He passed his rake to Greene and raised his voice to Klavdiya.

"They're my steps," he said. "I like them."

19

"TWO ORDERS OF PAD THAI," DETECTIVE ALPINE SAID AS HE CAME INTO THE LITTLE VIDEO room where Kennicott had been setting up the DVD player. "Chicken with yours. Mine's with shrimp."

"Thanks," Kennicott said, without looking up. His eyes were glued to the monitor in front of him that had just come to life. "I got this working."

Alpine looked over his shoulder.

Kennicott hadn't thought he was hungry, but as soon as he smelled the food he realized he was starving. His stomach started to churn.

One of Alpine's men had found that the Coffee Time doughnut shop two blocks west of the Maple Leaf Motel had four cameras. He'd seized the DVDs.

Kennicott pushed play on the remote. Four videos came on at the same time, each taking up a quarter of the screen. Camera One showed the entrance to the doughnut shop and the sidewalk and street beyond heading east. The other three cameras covered different locations inside. The counter on the bottom right-hand corner of the screen read 9:49:52. The images were jerky, like a cheap cartoon.

"There she is," Alpine said.

He pointed to Camera One. Clear as day, there was Jennifer Raglan dressed in running gear, walking toward the front door and moving quickly inside. Camera Three caught her heading straight for the washroom, as if she knew where it was. She wore the Lululemon sweatpants and Roots T-shirt they'd found under the bed in the motel room.

Kennicott took the carton of food, grabbed the chopsticks that were sticking out of the noodles, and started eating.

They watched in silence.

There were no cameras in the washroom. The time clicked by, one minute, two minutes. He tore through the noodles. Alpine had asked him if he wanted some soup as well. He'd said no, and now he regretted it.

"You get the feeling this wasn't her first time doing this." Alpine pulled out his notebook. "No one at Coffee Time remembered seeing her. Not surprising. You can see how crowded the place is. We checked every motel on the strip. Found five other owners who remembered a woman with red hair and sunglasses. They all said the same thing. She'd called them the week before, asked for room 8. Paid cash each time. Always for a Monday-morning rental."

"Got her on video at any of them?"

"No. None of them have cameras. She must have scouted them out, because most of the have-a-naps out there have them."

Kennicott dug out the last bit of noodles from the corner of the carton and pointed to the screen with his chopsticks. "She forgot about the cameras at the Coffee Time," he said. It had been three minutes now, and she still had not come out of the bathroom.

"The husband's alibi is solid?" Alpine asked.

"As a rock." Kennicott opened his notebook. "We've got him on CCTV at the Queen subway station at 8:23. Exactly what he told me. He said he rode around to Eglinton West and we have him getting off there at 8:45. The camera at Randy's Roti shop picks him up at 9:38, and Louisa, the woman who works there, remembers the white guy in a suit and tie who thought her beef patties were too spicy to eat for breakfast. We showed her his picture and she said it was probably him but white guys in suits mostly looked the same to her. He hangs around for a while and chats with people. Looks like he's enjoying himself. Leaves at 10:06."

"Guy was making sure we could trace his alibi," Alpine said.

"Perhaps." Kennicott crushed the carton and tossed it into the wastebasket in the corner.

Alpine reached into the plastic bag that he'd brought the food in and pulled out a bowl of soup. Then he brought out a second one. "You said you didn't want soup, but I knew you'd be hungry."

"Thanks." Kennicott could smell the fresh coriander and it made his mouth water. "The rest of his day is just as Darnell told me. We got him on the bus down to St. Clair, the streetcar across, and the librarian at the Deer Park Library, Anna Tharyan, remembered him being in that day. Says he comes in a few afternoons a week and reads magazines."

Up on the monitor, at 9:55:45, almost six minutes after Raglan had gone into the washroom, a woman of the same height came out wearing casual shoes and a nondescript blue dress. Her hair was red – the same colour as Raglan's wig – and she wore the same wraparound sunglasses they'd found in room 8. She carried a backpack. Same as the one in the motel room.

"She was determined that no would recognize her," Alpine said. "No doubt about that."

She walked over to the far wall, her back to Camera Two, and stopped. There was a long line up at the counter and the people obstructed the view. Only the top of her head was visible when someone shorter passed by.

"What's she up to?" Alpine asked.

"Don't know," Kennicott said. He stared at the grainy images as they went by.

"Here, you can expand it." Kennicott touched a button on the remote and the image took over the whole screen. The resolution was even grainier, but it was easier to see what was going on.

"Shit," Alpine said. "The people are in the way."

"Wait, there's a little boy coming up in line," Kennicott said. The kid moved forward and they caught a glimpse of Raglan. She had finished whatever she was doing, and walked off the screen toward the door.

"Damn," Alpine said.

"Wait, I saw something." Kennicott reduced the image and hit reverse until he got to the point where the boy in line was in front of her. He pressed another button and the images advanced frame by frame. "I saw something."

Like a badly animated cartoon, everyone moved in herky-jerky slow motion. The boy came in front of Raglan and for a moment they could see her. She turned from the wall just before a taller woman took the boy's place in line. Raglan moved toward the door and disappeared.

"Nothing," Alpine said.

"Wait." Kennicott reversed the video again until the moment Raglan moved away. He expanded the image to full screen.

"Look," he yelled, pointing at the wall. "Look."

"What?" Alpine asked.

"A pay phone. She was calling someone."

Alpine whistled. "She had her cell, but that could be traced."

"Who was she calling and why?" Kennicott asked.

"Has to be Mr. Monday Morning," Alpine said. "We can't trace a call from a pay phone. Ask any pimp or drug dealer. But if we find this guy, let's hope she called on his cell. Then we can match it to this call in a heartbeat."

The video went off pause automatically and started on its own again.

Camera One caught her outside again, walking quickly, swinging her back-pack back and forth. Kennicott imagined Raglan smiling. Happy. The camera tracked her for quite a distance. There was no one else on the narrow sidewalk.

Greene had taught him that as a homicide detective, you formed an intimate relationship with the deceased. You learned everything you could about her. Came to know and care for her. Kennicott was no longer a lawyer, but in many ways she was his client.

"I've seen enough," Alpine said.

Kennicott felt the same.

Before he switched off the screen, he took one final look at the last live im-ages of Jennifer Raglan as she headed unknowingly toward her terrible fate.

20

"HELLO, IT'S ALLIE HERE. MUMMY TOLD ME TO TELL ANYONE WHO CALLED THAT WE ARE AWAY on holiday," a young girl with a British accent said on the answering machine that had just picked up. *"Please do leave us a message at the beep. Bye-bye."*

Greene felt like an idiot. He also felt drunk. And stoned. And both at the same damn time.

The seconds ticked away in silence as he held the phone. He'd figured that one in the morning was seven o'clock in England. Or maybe six, he could never remember when it was five and when it was six hours' difference.

The silence on the line seemed overwhelming.

"Hello, Allie," he said at last, working very hard not to slur his words. "Tell your mommy that her old friend Ari just phoned from Canada."

He sounded so. So what? Stupid? Pathetic? Stoned and drunk?

"Beep," the machine said.

Damn, he'd forgotten to wait for it. Just hang up, he told himself.

"Allie, tell your mom her old friend Ari called from Canada," he managed to say in one breath. A slight improvement, perhaps, over his first unrecorded message.

What else to say? Allie's mother had been a professor at the University of Toronto a number of years earlier. Her husband then, also a professor, had been stabbed to death by a deranged student from his linguistics class. It had been Greene's case. A year after it was over, he'd hooked up with her and they'd lived together for a while, until she returned home, got married, and had her daughter, Alison. He'd seen the child grow up in the photos she sent him every December, but they hadn't spoken in years.

He closed his eyes. His living room was starting to spin. Quit while you're ahead, he thought, and hung up. He looked at the half-smoked joint on the plate in front of him. When he'd showed up at the bakery this afternoon, before

Kennicott arrived, Brian Silver had taken one look at him and said, "I don't know what the fuck is going on, but you look like total shit."

Silver had never gotten entirely beyond their last year or two of high school, when they'd spend most afternoons getting stoned in Greene's basement. "Be careful, this is really strong stuff," he had warned Greene, giving him a couple of joints. "Not like when we were kids."

He was right. It was powerful as hell. Especially on top of the half bottle of Polish vodka his father had given him, which Greene had already almost finished.

Pulling himself up, he stumbled to the washroom and braced himself, holding the sink. He ran the cold water and put his head under it. Boy, he'd love to vomit.

He lifted his head, dripping water all over the floor. He didn't care. He cupped his hands under the tap and drank cold water from them. Then he grabbed a towel, dried off his hair, and wrapped the towel around his neck.

Wait. He thought of another woman he knew. She lived in New York. It's Monday night, which was her deadline. She's probably long gone, but what the hell, leave another message. Just keep calling women and leaving messages. Shit.

Back in the living room he found his cell phone. Let's see. There it is. Cell, home, work.

He lay on the floor and tapped the work number.

"Kwon," she said a second later. The phone had hardly rung.

"Oh, Margaret, hi." Greene heard typing and the clatter of busy office in the background. He thought about hanging up.

"Ari, is that you?"

He swallowed hard but couldn't speak.

"Ari? Your name came up on my call display."

"Yeah. I didn't think you'd be there. I was going to leave message." Had he just said "leave message" instead of "leave a message"?

"Hang on," she said.

Her voice was muffled by her hand over the phone receiver. He picked up a few words. "Amazing . . . We need a picture . . . Fuck that, no way we're using a stock shot."

Kwon lived and worked in New York, where she was a story editor at *Faces*, a weekly celebrity gossip magazine. Last year she'd been in Toronto covering a high-profile case of his. They'd become friendly, but nothing more. She loved poking fun at him, and right now he just needed to hear a woman's voice.

"Ari Greene, Mr. Nice Guy," Kwon said, her voice now clear. "Amazing to hear from you. Any more good crime in Toronto?" She laughed.

"I remembered that Monday night is your deadline night, so, you know, I thought I'd give a quick call." His voice was higher than usual. And it felt like he was talking very slowly.

"You never forget a word," she said. "We're having a crazy night. How are you?"

"Yeah, I'm fine. Perfectly great."

"Ari, you don't sound right."

He breathed. Why did I do this? he thought. "Long day. I'll let you get back to your celebs."

"Wait," she said. "Don't hang up. I've got some great news to tell you."

She put her hand over the phone again. He was too tired to listen to the scraps of her conversation.

"No one knows this here yet," she whispered, coming back on the line. "I'm engaged."

"Wow," Greene said. "Wonderful."

"He's even a nice guy, can you believe it. All your fault, you know."

"Oh, why's that."

She laughed her big hearty laugh, which always seemed too loud for her slight body. "Fill in the blanks. I got to go. Keep in touch."

"Of course," he said, but she'd already hung up.

You're being pathetic, he thought, rolling over on the floor. He reached for the joint, lit it, and inhaled as deeply as he could. Held the smoke down. One, two three, four.

His lungs were searing. He blew it out and started to cough. Violently. He grabbed the bottle and swigged it back.

There was a sound. His phone was ringing.

"Ari Greene," he said very slowly. Who the hell would be calling so late?

"It's me," Margaret Kwon said.

"Oh," he said.

"You sounded so bad on the phone I checked the newswires for Toronto. I can't believe Jennifer Raglan was murdered."

"Tell me about it." He was definitely slurring his words now.

She sighed. "Ari, I know about you and Jennifer," she said.

"What?" he practically shouted. "What do you know?"

"Please," she said. "I'm a woman. I saw the way you two looked at each other in court."

"Shit," he said. "I shouldn't have called."

"Ari, I've never heard you sound like this."

"What's your fiancé's name?" He needed to change the subject.

"Anton. He's a Greek dentist. Couldn't be less like me if you tried. Thirty-eight, never married, and normal. My friends say in Manhattan that's an endangered species."

He lay back on the floor. He'd never see Jennifer again. How could this have happened? He felt the tears running down the sides of his cheeks. "You deserve him," he managed to say.

She must have sensed he was crying, because neither of them spoke for a long time.

"I know you loved her," she said at last.

"It's impossible to believe," he said.

Again they were silent.

"Ari, that night you drove me to Niagara Falls, and we sat together at your spot, where the water goes over the edge," she said.

He nodded. It was the only time they'd been out of the city together. A quiet, special moment between them.

"You knew, didn't you?" she asked.

He closed his eyes. "Yes but –"

"I know, bad timing. Now Jennifer's gone, and I'm getting married."

He was starting to fade out. "Be well, Margaret," he whispered. "Be happy."

He hung up, and a wave of exhaustion hit him so hard he knew he had no chance of getting off the carpet before he fell asleep.

PART
TWO

21

"HELLO, HELLO, HELLO. COME IN, COME IN," BARCLAY CHURCH SAID TO AWOTWE AMANKWAH, swinging around in his chair and popping up out of it, an oversize arm extending a huge hand in greeting.

Amankwah had not been in the editor-in-chief's office for a few years. The first thing he noticed was that Church had completely rearranged the furniture from the way his predecessor had it. He'd pushed the desk against a wall, so when he swivelled his chair he was right in front of whoever had come to see him. That meant employees no longer had to talk to their boss over the barrier of an imposing desk.

Amankwah had been warned by his colleagues that their meetings with Church had been unusual, to say the least. The guy was eccentric as hell. But everyone seemed to like him.

In just a few weeks he'd radically transformed the newspaper. Especially the front page. Church wanted the most sensational stories and he played them up big-time above the fold. This morning there was a photo of Oprah Winfrey and Tiger Woods, who were in town for the film festival and, along with other big-name celebrities, had attended some charity event at a local golf club yesterday morning. Beside it was the Jennifer Raglan murder story Amankwah had thrown together, complete with a smaller picture of the entrance to the ultratacky Maple Leaf Motel. The headline read: STRANGLEHOLD: CROWN ATTORNEY MOTEL MURDER MYSTERY. And to top it all off, below the fold, Amankwah had a second byline with an equally lurid headline: DEIRDRE, THE HOCKEY PLAYERS' AFTER DATE, IN THE PENALTY BOX.

Could there be a better moment to have his personal meeting with the paper's new editor?

"Let's get this straight, right from the ruddy beginning," Church said, a goofy grin on his face as they shook hands. "How the fuck am I supposed to pronounce your first name?"

Amankwah laughed. He'd been explaining this for a lifetime. "Start with *a* as in a reporter. *Wat* as in lightbulb and *way* as in that's the right way to pronounce my name. A lot of people simply call me Double A."

Church motioned Amankwah to a seat, sat down himself, wheeled his chair up close, took off his glasses, and cleaned them with his shirt. "I've got it. Start with *a* as in my editor's an arsehole, *wat* as in wot the hell does he want me to write about?, and *way* as in which way is the exit so I don't have to work for this twit? How'm I doing?"

"Not bad." Amankwah smiled.

Church slapped his hand hard across his knee, grabbed a thick file from his desk, and waved it at Amankwah. "We'll be on a first-name basis for sure. Awotwe," he said, pronouncing the name perfectly. "There isn't any room in my pea-size brain for your last name."

"No problem," Amankwah said.

Church bounded out of his chair and tossed his hands in the air like wings. "Awotwe, why don't you just take my seat? Do my job? Bloody hell, except for Queen Oprah and the Tiger, you own the front page. Fantastic, fantastic, fantastic stuff."

"It's been a good twenty-four hours," Amankwah said.

"Oh no. None of this boring Canadian modesty, please." He grabbed Amankwah by the shoulders. "Please, please, please. I mean it. Sit in my chair."

He pulled Amankwah over and sat him down.

"I bow down before talent," Church said.

Amankwah couldn't believe his eyes. The editor of the *Toronto Star*, the biggest newspaper in Canada, was down on his knees, throwing his arms up and down, like a devout Muslim at prayer.

He couldn't help himself, he started to laugh.

Church sat back on his haunches and clutched his hands to his heart. "Yes, at last" – he beamed – "we are having fun." He duckwalked on his knees over to his desk, reached up for the thick file, pulled it down, and waved it at Amankwah.

"I've read every article you've written for the paper since you joined. Shit, man, you were red-hot for the first six or seven years. Brilliant stuff. Then you went right in the crapper." At last he got up and sat down in the visitors' chair. "I looked at your personnel file. Bingo. No fucking wonder. Your wife left you for a boring white guy and suddenly your copy is as wet as a baby's nappy. Nobody's having any fun. That about right?"

"I – I guess so." Maybe this guy really was an asshole, Amankwah thought.

Church tossed the file on the floor and looked straight at him. "Mine left me for a Chinese chappie. Hong Kong money. Yachts. Country houses, horses and dogs, and all that hang-around-and-do-nothing rubbish. Creep was about five foot four and she's almost six foot. I went quite dotty. Even did a bit of a slasher."

Without ceremony, he rolled up his sleeve and showed Amankwah a number of deep scars on his left arm. "They do the counselling thing with you? Depression. Lithium. All that touchy-feely, voodoo, boo-hoo stuff? Must have, because the last two years you're filing ace stories again."

"Thanks," Amankwah said, breathless. "Part of the deal when I almost got fired was the counselling. But I didn't do the drugs."

"Good move. I tossed them after a month. Pills make you as boring as a roomful of newspaper executives. What's this nonsense about you doing night shifts in the radio room? That's no bloody fun."

Amankwah shrugged. "Support payments. I want to see my kids."

"Well, screw that. I told the publisher we're bumping you up to feature writer, that's a fifteen percent raise. Should have been done two years ago, so today you're getting a catch-up cheque for twenty thousand. That enough? I can't have my top talent doing the job of an intern at three in the morning."

Amankwah tried to stay calm. He wasn't even sure whether he nodded.

"Done." Church grabbed the front page of the paper from his desk. "Bloody good story, isn't it? Brilliant. Former head Crown attorney strangled to death in a sleazy motel." His eyes grew wide with excitement.

"Raglan was a very good lawyer."

"Even better. Front-page stuff for weeks."

"She has three teenage kids," Amankwah said.

"Yes, very tragic, absolutely horrific, our hearts go out blah, blah, blah. Anyone know who she was doing the horizontal dance with?"

Church's counselling clearly didn't include sensitivity training, Amankwah thought. "No clue."

"Well, mate, this is your story. Gold mine if I ever saw one." He flipped the paper over and stabbed a long finger at Amankwah's second story. "I love this 'Deirdre, the After Date' piece. Love, love, love it. What the hell is going on with the cops and the call girls?"

"Exactly what I want to find out," Amankwah said.

Church threw the paper on his desk and jumped up. He grabbed a phantom shovel and made exaggerated digging motions, flinging imaginary dirt everywhere. "Dig, Mr. Amankwah," he shouted. "Dig, dig, dig."

Mr. Amankwah. Church had pronounced his last name perfectly. *A* as in I'm *a* reporter. *Man* as in the Isle of Man. *Kwah* like the French word *quoi*. A . . . man . . . kwah.

Yes, he thought, watching Church flail away like a child at the beach with a new toy shovel. This was going to be fun.

22

EXCEPT FOR THE TWO HOURS OF SLEEP HE'D GRABBED ON ONE OF THE BEDS IN THE NAP room in the basement of police headquarters, Daniel Kennicott had spent every moment working on the case.

The autopsy had been performed after midnight. The only evidence they'd got from it was some fragments of black leather from under her fingernails. The leather most likely came from a pair of gloves. She'd probably tried to scratch her attacker, but he hadn't left any skin exposed. And under her right forefinger, a bit of paper and glue.

Then he and Alpine had meticulously combed through the records of every person Raglan had prosecuted for murder in the last five years. Three were gang-bangers, still in jail. One was an alcoholic who'd killed another alcoholic in a bar fight. He'd been deported back to Barbados. Another was a mother who had severe postpartum depression and killed her twin babies. She was still institutionalized. A man who'd murdered his wife after she found him sleeping with George, her personal trainer, had pled to manslaughter and was out on parole. He'd returned home to Niagara Falls, where he worked as a boat hand on *The Maid of the Mist*. When Raglan was killed, he'd been passing out rain slicks to tourists before they came on board.

It turned out that Seaton Wainwright, the film producer charged with fraud who'd threatened Jennifer Raglan in the courthouse last week, secretly had a Lithuanian passport. He used it to fly to Paris on the Sunday night, hours before the murder. Apparently he had a new Brazilian girlfriend there and no plans of coming back to Canada.

Finally there was a woman named Samantha Wyler, convicted two years earlier of stabbing her ex-husband to death in the kitchen of his suburban Toronto home the night before their divorce trial was set to begin. Raglan had won the trial, but a few weeks later Greene and Kennicott, who were both on the case, discovered that the husband's disabled brother was the killer just before he jumped off a bridge to his death. Wyler was released from jail.

Kennicott, determined to leave no stone unturned, wondered if it was possible the brother, who was in love with Wyler, had literally taken the fall for her. Perhaps she was an enraged, pathological killer, bent on revenge?

This morning he'd walked out of the building and used his cell to call Greene. He caught him on his car phone and told him about his idea.

"What do you think?"

"I don't think anything of it," Greene had replied, "until you find out if she has an alibi."

"And if she doesn't?"

"Why don't you find out, before you start worrying about the ifs," Greene said.

It had taken two phone calls to establish that yesterday Wyler had been up north in Cobalt, a small town six hours from Toronto where she was born and had gone back to live. She'd been teaching an adult reading class in the local library.

Some killer, Kennicott thought. He felt like an idiot and promised himself not to ask Greene any more stupid questions until he checked things out himself.

Right now all they had for suspects were Raglan's unknown lover and her husband, Howard Darnell, the man with the perfect alibi. Kennicott had put him under twenty-four-hour surveillance. Yesterday evening, on the live feed from their mikes inside the house, they'd heard one of the kids crying, all of them talking with their dad, phone conversations with friends offering condolences, a pizza being delivered. The oldest son, Aaron, even got in an argument with Howard because he wanted to go out. Classic family dynamics of shock and stress.

Kennicott felt horrible listening to it.

In the early hours of the morning, after he woke from his short nap, he collected the statements that the police officers on the scene had taken and put each one in a file, which he labelled by hand. It was the way he used to organize papers when he was a lawyer preparing for a big trial. He placed the files in a banker's box in the homicide-bureau boardroom and wrote RAGLAN HOMICIDE, ACCUSED UNKNOWN on the side with a thick black marker.

Alpine, who'd been tracking down all the officers' notes and compiling Zeilinski's identification photos, walked in.

"There's a new café north of Grenville," he said, carrying a coffee tray in one hand and a bag of goodies in the other. "Guy's Italian. Wouldn't sell me a latte. Said real Italians drink cappuccinos before noon, lattes in the afternoon, and espresso at night, to help them sleep. Go figure."

Kennicott eyed the cappuccino.

"I told him we had a long day ahead of us, so to expect me back a few times." Alpine put the tray down and opened the brown bag. A yeasty smell filled the room. "His mother bakes these every morning. They're still warm."

Kennicott reached for the coffee, trying not to grab it.

"An older lawyer named Lloyd Gramwell recruited me to the law firm where I used to work," he said, after his second long sip. "He hates technology. Says it makes us stop thinking. When I had an important case, he'd make me bring the file into his office and read every witness statement out loud. At first I thought it was a waste of time, but then I found it made me hear the story, which helped me to see it."

"Never done that before." Alpine tipped his paper cup at Kennicott. "Good coffee, eh?"

"Great. Thanks."

"Try a pastry," Alpine said.

Kennicott picked out a tiny, crusty croissant. It was delicious. "There are twenty-two witness statements," he said, reaching into the box nearest to him. "We'll take turns. I'll read one out loud, then you do the next."

"Okay." Alpine pulled out a pen and pad of paper. "You start. I'll take notes."

"No notes," Kennicott said. "That's another one of Gramwell's rules. No notes. Too distracting. Learn to listen."

They started with the statements from the people at the motel: the owner's, the translated versions of the Taiwanese girls', and the schoolteacher-turned drunk. Alpine picked up the transcript of the interview of the prostitute who worked in the room above the passageway.

"Question: Did you see anyone come in or out of the
courtyard this morning?"
"Answer: What time?"
"Question: Between ten and eleven?"
"Answer: One. A new client."
"Question: What did he look like?"

"Answer: The john? He looked like a john."

"Question: Come on, you can do better than that. Was he white, Asian, black? Tall or short, skinny or fat? You know the drill."

"Answer: White guy. Big belly. Probably couldn't see his own cock."

"Question: Facial hair?"

"Answer: Most of the time, I was on my knees. I wasn't exactly looking at his face."

"Question: Age?"

"Answer: Old enough that it took him a while to get hard."

"Question: Thanks for that. How long did this take?"

"Answer: Like I said, he wasn't exactly a smoking gun."

"Question: Where did he go after?"

"Answer: Out my door."

"Question: What kind of car?"

"Answer: No idea."

"Question: What time did he leave?"

"Answer: Like you said, between ten and eleven. Then I heard the sirens. Then you knocked on my door."

"Question: You see anyone else walk under the passage-way into the courtyard?"

"Answer: The ambulance and the cruiser."

"Question: What else can you tell me?"

"Answer: That I've got nothing else to say to the cops."

"Askari, the cop who interviewed her, says she slammed the door in his face." Alpine tossed the file on the table. "Lovely. Well, she's one witness we want to keep off the stand."

"Couldn't agree more," Kennicott said.

"So much for the Maple Leaf Motel," Alpine said.

By the time they were on their afternoon lattes, they'd read through all the statements of the employees at the Coffee Time doughnut shop, the people in the mall across the road – all of whom saw nothing – and the other motel owners on Kingston Road.

Kennicott intentionally left the interviews with the people in the strip mall next to the motel until the end. He thought they were his best hope. They were having their shots of espresso when they read through the statements. Seven store owners claimed they had seen nothing. Of the nine shoppers they found, four said they hadn't seen anything unusual and three refused to even give their names. Only one woman would talk to them at all.

"Your turn," Kennicott said, taking out the second-last file and handing it over. "Here's the woman who was in the Money Mart that morning. Cop found her shopping with her daughter at Kaks Hair Emporium."

"Annabel Sawney, DOB, May fifteenth, 1958," Alpine read.

```
"Question: Ms. Sawney. Where were you earlier this
morning?"
"Answer: When we first got to the plaza I went to
the Money Mart with Sadura, my daughter. She had a
sore throat, so I kept her home from school so she
wouldn't infect the other kids. I needed some cash
for the week because one of my customers was late
in paying me. I had my welfare stub, so I got a
three-hundred-dollar advance. You promised that this
wouldn't be reported. I didn't see a thing."
```

Alpine shrugged. "Hear no evil, see no evil," he said. "I told you what it's like in Scarborough."

"I'll read the last one." Kennicott opened the file. "I appreciate your patience. It was worth a try at least."

"It's the job," Alpine said. He didn't look happy.

"Sadura Sawney, ten years old," Kennicott said. "It's one page."

```
"Question: Sadura, were you with your mom earlier this
morning at the Money Mart?"
"Answer: Yeah. Mommy took me to the bank. I wanted to
get some red licorice and she said we could after she
got her money out."
"Question: What did you do at the bank?"
"Answer. Nothing. Just looked out the window."
```

Beside him, Kennicott felt Alpine edge forward on his seat.

```
"Question: Did you see anyone in the parking lot?"
"Answer: I don't know. Just cars."
"Question: Anything else. Anyone walking fast or run-
ning?"
"Answer: No. Just a man on a funny motorcycle. A lit-
tle one, like a scooter or something. And he was tall.
Wearing black boots."
"Question: Did you see what the man looked like?"
"Answer: No. He had on a helmet and gloves and every-
thing."
```

Kennicott looked at Alpine. They were both thinking the same thing. The killer had covered up his skin. The bits of leather under Raglan's fingernails.

```
"Question: Did you see where he went?"
"Answer: He drove off."
"Question: Which direction, did you see?"
"Answer: Yeah. Like up into the alley beside the Pizza
Nova."
```

Kennicott looked at Alpine. They knew where that alley led and were both thinking the same thing. Why wouldn't the killer escape by driving onto Kingston Road, the big, anonymous street right in front of him, instead of risking being seen on a side street?

He closed the file folder. "That's where the interview ends."

"Sounds like our man was driving a scooter," Alpine said. "There are thousands of them in the city."

"It's not much," Kennicott said. He put the file back in the banker's box and stacked their paper cups in a tower. "But at least it's more than we had when we started with those cappuccinos."

23

homeless men gathered on the north side of Queen Street, east of Sherbourne, in front of the Moss Park Discount Store. Huddled together, they sipped sugary cups of coffee from the Popeye's fast-food restaurant across the road while waiting for the three nearby men's shelters to open for dinner.

Many of the names and faces change daily, Ari Greene thought as he parked his Oldsmobile on the south side of Queen, between Rady Hair & Barber Salon and the Schnitzel Queen restaurant, but one man was usually there. Fraser Dent. He looked like a circus clown: bald on top, stringy hair down the sides, always wore a long jacket made of bits of cloth he'd sewn together. He never told anyone that the cloth came from his former life — each one lovingly cut from the expensive cotton shirts he used to wear to work when he was one of the city's top foreign-currency traders.

Dent was in his usual spot, two doors down from the corner, in front of Artatorture Tattoo Parlour, a few steps away from the crowd on the corner in front of the discount store.

This was prime real estate, where he could best catch the late-afternoon sun. But not quite as prime as the penthouse condo where he'd once lived. It overlooked the harbour and was a ten-minute walk to the bond-trading floor, where for fifteen years he logged ninety-hour weeks. That was before he started living inside a bottle. Then needles.

"Monsieur Detective," Dent said, his eyes coming to life when he spotted Greene. He was holding an extra-large cup of coffee and he raised it in a mock toast. "*Bonsoir*. Nice to see you, sir."

"It's been a while," Greene said. Dent's handshake was weak. He was thinner than usual. "How you doing?"

"Such a busy summer," Dent said. "I didn't get in even one round of golf and I never made it up to the cottage. Not even for a night."

Greene chuckled. "That sounds like your old life."

Dent smiled his remarkably childlike grin. "Funny thing is, that part of my life hasn't changed. I used to spend my whole summer working over there while my wife was up north with the kids," he said, pointing downtown to the high-rise towers in the distance. "Now I spend my summers on the street. Both ways, I never get to sit on a dock by the lake and listen to the loons. I thought I'd see you today."

"Why's that?" Greene asked.

Dent shook his head, sending his long hair flapping across his face. "Come on, Detective, I read the papers. Former head Crown strangled to death on a Monday morning out on the motel strip. Hubby's a meek and mild accountant type. If he did it, you'd expect him to jump off a bridge or walk into 55 Division in a bloodstained shirt."

"So?"

"So. You did a lot of trials with Raglan. She was tough. Put a lot of bad guys away. All sorts of people could have a grudge. I knew you'd be looking for me to see if I'd heard anything on the street. I'm a good researcher and I've done my homework." He looked over his shoulder. "I'll tell you about it when we're away from this crowd."

A few of the other men from the corner shuffled over. Greene recognized a number of them.

Greene pulled two twenty-dollar bills from his front pocket and turned to the closest man. "Coffee for all the guys." He handed the money over and jerked his head across the street toward Popeye's.

"Cool," the man said, waving the two bills in the air. "Thanks, Detective."

"Enjoy." Greene looked at Dent's cup. It was almost empty. "Come on, I'll get you a refill and a doughnut."

"No food," Dent said. "And I'm caffeined up. Let's walk."

"Good idea."

Greene guided him across Sherbourne, heading west in the direction of the office towers where Dent, who had taught himself Japanese in tenth grade, once routinely worked late to talk to the morning trading desk in Tokyo.

They walked in silence past the Moss Park Arena. A man in a suit and tie pulled his hockey bag out of the back of his Lexus SUV and rushed by another group of men from the shelters, who were lying on the overtrodden grass. A flock of pigeons scattered.

Greene had found Dent a few years ago, when he needed a smart, small-time criminal to go into the Don Jail and be the cell mate of a man accused of killing his wife. Since then they'd formed a friendship that benefitted both of them.

Dent spotted two dark-haired men on the south side of Queen, huddled in the doorway of the Anishnawbe Aboriginal Health Centre. He crossed over the street, gave them both cigarettes, took one out for himself, pulled out a lighter, and they all started puffing.

"Pals of yours?" Greene asked when he returned and they started walking again.

"It's my business to talk to people on the street." Dent sucked hard on his cigarette. "I'm going to deduct this whole pack. Call it corporate expenses."

"You look thin," Greene said.

Dent's main problem was alcohol. But every once in a while, he slipped into shooting up heroin. The previous year, Greene had found him half dead in a back alley two blocks from here and dragged him into rehab.

"I hit a bad patch for a while there," Dent said. "I've been clean for a month."

"Good," Greene said.

"You're one to talk, Detective," Dent said. "You look like shit. You want a smoke?"

"I quit in grade seven."

"You don't drink coffee either," Dent said. "Fuck, you're a piece of work."

They walked past the Dollarama discount store, a few pawnbrokers, an army-surplus shop, and a Persian and Oriental "rug gallery." Outside was a big white sign festooned with balloons trumpeting a 50-percent-off sale.

"You ever hear of a Persian rug that wasn't on sale?" Dent asked as they crossed Church Street and settled on the park bench where they always sat in front of the Metropolitan United Church. The downtown core was a few blocks away but this was Dent's personal boundary. He would never go a step closer to his former life.

He passed a cigarette to Greene and took one for himself, and put the pack back in his coat pocket.

Greene put the cigarette in his lips and Dent lifted his lighter. He was shaking. Greene held his hand firm and lit the cigarette. He took a deep drag. After the harsh dope last night, the tobacco felt smooth. He let it seep into his lungs and on from there into his bloodstream.

"What do you need?" Dent asked.

Greene watched a well-dressed young couple rush by. They carried matching briefcases and were both talking on their cell phones.

"You're probably right about the husband," he said. "But so far we've got nothing else."

"No leads on her boyfriend?"

Greene had expected this question. He knew how smart Dent was and that he preferred not to lie. "Might not be the boyfriend. One theory is that the killer got there first."

Dent blew out a stream of smoke. He didn't bother to turn his head away from Greene. "You want me to see if I can find anyone with an old grudge against her?"

"For a start."

"What else?"

"Her oldest son. I heard he had some problems. He was dealing a lot. Hard to think someone would take out his mother in revenge. But these are violent times."

"What's his name?"

"Aaron. Aaron Darnell. He's nineteen but I hear he looks much younger. Having a tough time getting through high school. Sounds like he's doing a victory lap or two."

"Yeah," Dent said. "He's the graffiti kid. Aaron 8, that's his tag. Whips around the east end on his bike. That the one?"

Greene nodded. Aaron 8, he thought. Raglan had rented room 8 at every motel. "How deep is he into it?"

Dent rolled up his sleeve and showed Greene some red marks on his skin. "A month ago he was a very reliable supplier."

Greene let out a low whistle. "That deep."

"Major league. High-stakes shit."

"Did anyone know his mother was a Crown?"

Dent, who rarely made eye contact, looked right at Greene. He had remarkably light blue eyes, and it was easy to imagine him as a fair-skinned, blond boy, the apple of his mother's eye until that Christmas morning in the Wellesley subway station when she stepped out in front of a southbound train.

"I figured it out. But you know me. I keep my mouth shut. Can't speak for anyone else."

"You heard anything about Raglan?"

"Back-in-the-day stuff," Dent said. "I already started asking around. Did you know she started out on the morality squad?"

"I heard."

"Sounds like she was a star performer. And a real looker. And some other shit."

"What kind of shit?"

"One day she just quit. Bye-bye birdie. Five years later she's back as a Crown attorney. Go figure." Dent stubbed out his cigarette and patted his jacket and found his pack. Greene took it from him, pulled out two more cigarettes. He lit one and passed it to Dent.

"Thanks, man," Dent said.

"Anything else about Jennifer?" Greene asked, her first name slipping out.

Dent gave him a long look. Nodded. "How many cases did you two do together?"

Greene turned away. Now he was the one not making eye contact. "A couple of murder trials," he said.

"A couple," Dent said.

Greene tried to picture it. Jennifer. Young, pretty, a small-town girl who wanted to make good in the Big Smoke. Eager to be a team player. What made her quit and become a prosecutor?

Greene used his first cigarette in four decades to light his second. "See what else you can find out, okay?"

"Will do, boss," Dent said, a big smile on his face. "I've got some ideas."

Greene pulled out a twenty-dollar bill and passed it to him. "I'd give you more, but I don't want it to go up your arm."

Dent held his hands up. Refusing the money, just as Ted DiPaulo had resisted taking his hundred-dollar bill. "No. Don't give me any cash. Now you can buy me a coffee."

Greene pointed at the Starbucks across the street. "You think you can handle a grande latte?"

"No, no." Dent shuddered. "We got to head east, back to Popeye's."

They walked again in silence.

Greene's mind was whirling. Jennifer. Every step of the way he was finding out new things about her. Why had she been so secretive about her past? He knew he had to keep going.

"Meet me here Saturday afternoon," Dent said. "I need a few days to see what ant colonies I can find under some rocks. I used to do that all summer long at my parents' cottage when I was a kid."

They were already back at Sherbourne Street. Greene didn't even remember crossing Church and Jarvis streets to get there.

"With your boss, Hap, about to run for mayor, you guys are going to want this cleaned up fast," Dent said.

"For sure." That wasn't the only reason, Greene thought.

Dent waved at a group of men on the other side of the street. "I only saw her once in court," he said. "But I remember her."

"You do?"

"It's hard to forget a beautiful woman like her, isn't it, Detective?"

24

THERE WERE FOUR ELEVATORS IN THE LOBBY OF THE APARTMENT BUILDING THAT WAS HOME to Annabel Sawney and her daughter, Sadura, who had both been at the Money Mart the morning of the murder. Three of them had faded "out of order" signs on them. Sawney lived on the ninth floor.

Daniel Kennicott hit the up button on the one elevator that was supposed to be working. There was no backlight to indicate that the signal had been received.

"Scarberia never disappoints," Alpine said. "We might as well walk up."

"Shit," Kennicott said.

"Sixty-eight percent of the people out here live in rental housing," Alpine said. "Most of it built in the sixties. You wonder why there's so much crime?"

Kennicott hammered the button again. "You sure we shouldn't have phoned first?" he asked Alpine.

"I'm telling you. People just won't talk to the cops. We were lucky to find them still at that strip mall. Your best chance is to try them at the door."

Kennicott hit the button again. "You're right, let's walk," he said. "Oh, wait."

He'd heard a rumbling sound and a few seconds later the old elevator door rattled open. Inside were at least ten people, half of them toting laundry baskets. There wasn't an inch of room, and no one was getting out.

The door clattered closed. He and Alpine headed for the stairwell. Graffiti riddled most of the walls on their way up, accompanied by dull scent of urine. Apartment 906 was halfway down the hall.

Kennicott knocked on the door and then both of them stood well back so Sawney could see them clearly through her keyhole. No one answered.

Alpine shrugged. "Scarborough. Twenty to one she's in there but won't answer the door."

Kennicott stepped forward and knocked harder. "Ms. Sawney," he said, raising his voice. "It's Daniel Kennicott from the Toronto Police. I was hoping we could speak to you for a few minutes."

After a few seconds, he heard the sound of footsteps, then of a chain lock being pulled back. The door opened slowly. A thin black woman with wild grey hair came out. She took a pair of reading glasses from her nose and smiled.

"I was going to call you folks today. I thought you might want talk to my daughter some more." She held out her hand. "Annabel Sawney."

Kennicott and Alpine introduced themselves.

"Why didn't you call first?" she asked.

Kennicott resisted the urge to glance at Alpine. "Ugh, we don't usually call," he said.

She laughed, a loud, infectious guffaw. "Especially in Scarborough. Figure no black woman will talk to the cops, don't you? Come on in."

"There's an exception to every rule," Alpine muttered to Kennicott.

A short hallway opened into a wide living room. In one corner a very old woman sat at a sewing machine, working away on a length of colourful cloth. In the other, a woman about Sawney's age was cutting out a pattern on a folding table. In the middle was an architect desk covered with designs and drawings. A girl was sitting on the floor, knitting what looked like a sweater. Racks of clothes were everywhere.

The girl looked up and immediately jumped to her feet. "Hi," she said, holding out her hand.

Kennicott smiled. Shook her hand. "You must be Sadura," he said.

"Yeah."

"Good. I'm Daniel Kennicott and this is Detective Alpine. We're police officers."

He looked at her mother and pointed to the galley kitchen behind the girl. "Can we go in there?"

"Why not?" Sawney said. "What can I get you to eat?"

"Thanks, we're fine," Kennicott said.

The space was small, and the four of them barely fit in. Sawney closed a set of white louvred doors behind them. There were two seats at the narrow table. Kennicott took one and motioned to the child to take the other.

"Sadura, do you know why we're here?" he asked.

"Uh-huh. Because of the day I was at the bank with Mommy."

"That's right. What school do you go to?"

"Maplewood. We took a community involvement course and this police-woman named Ms. Bailey told us how important it is to talk to the police."

"It is important," he said.

"I like to draw so my mommy said I should draw some pictures of the man I saw in the parking lot that day."

Kennicott looked up at Alpine. "That was very smart of your mom," he said.

"Back home Mommy was a doctor but then we had to leave because of the government."

"Are you going to be a doctor too?"

She shook her head hard. Her hair was braided in tight cornrows with different-coloured clips on the ends. They flapped back and forth across her smiling face, like a set of friendly flags. "No," she said. "I want to be the mayor so people in Scarborough can have parks and subways like downtown."

From the mouths of babes, Kennicott thought. "Where did you put the drawing?"

"In my room." She slid off the chair and scampered out of the kitchen.

"I think she'll make a good mayor," Kennicott said to Sawney when her daughter had left.

"I think she'd be a better prime minister. Or she might be an architect. Wait till you see how well she can draw."

"I got them," Sadura said, prancing back in. She put a beige folder on the table. On the outside she'd drawn her name with flowers and vines sprouting in all directions.

She opened it. "This is what he looked like when I first saw him. Just from behind."

It was a remarkably well-drawn picture of the back of a tall man with broad shoulders. He wore a leather jacket and gloves and a helmet.

Kennicott said to Sawney, "She's talented." He looked back at Sadura. "How old are you?"

"Nine and a half. Here's the next one."

This time the man, drawn from the back again, was holding his helmet in one hand and a cell phone in the other. In the background, she'd drawn an ambulance with its lights flashing.

"Did you see the ambulance?"

"Yep, then police car right behind it too. They went past really fast."

"Did the man use his phone?"

"No. I saw him take it out but then the ambulance and police cars went past and he shook his head and put it back in his pocket. Then he put on his helmet and drove away like he was in a hurry. I never saw his face."

Kennicott could see she had one more drawing.

"Did he ever turn around?" he asked. "Did you see his face?"

"No." She shook her head, cornrows flapping again.

This drawing showed the man from the front. He was sitting on a scooter with his helmet on and the visor down. He boots were lace-up.

"You notice anything else?"

"Yep. His pants. They were nice."

"What do you mean nice?"

"Good material. Like my mommy uses."

Kennicott smiled. "Anything else?"

"Well . . ." She became shy and started to giggle. She looked at her mother.

Kennicott looked at her mother too. "What is it?"

Sawney laughed. "Tell him," she said to his daughter.

Sadura gave her shoulders a big shrug, took her pencil, and pointed to the backside of the man in her second drawing. "He was white."

"Oh," Kennicott said. He caught Alpine's eye. "How could you tell, if he was wearing gloves and a helmet?"

She put her hand over her face. Embarrassed. "His bum," she said. "It wasn't roundy like a black man's bum. It was, you know, kind of flat like a white man's."

Her mother burst out laughing. Sadura took her hands away from her face, exposing a brilliant row of white teeth. Kennicott looked at Alpine. He was grinning too.

25

had been to every form of funeral ritual imaginable. Sikh cremations, Buddhist candle lightings, outdoor Muslim funeral prayers, Jewish shivas, Irish wakes, Catholic masses, and many "visitations" at local funeral homes.

He could understand the convenience and functionality of these places, but he found them creepy. The high-ceilinged, beige rooms with fake wainscotting and bland carpets. The ubiquitous piped-in music. The pastel landscape paintings. The overstuffed furniture. Worst of all was the perpetually unctuous staff.

A common feature of these visitations was a posterboard filled with pictures of the life lived. This afternoon, two days after Raglan's murder, there was a large crowd at the J. J. Patterson and Sons Funeral Home in Welland. Greene had slipped in unseen and was able to take his time looking at the photo tribute to Jennifer.

It began with baby pictures of her held by her mother on a blanket in a tiny backyard. Then shots of her as a toddler standing with her father, her brown hair in pigtails, beside the family station wagon. Photos of her waving a Canadian flag at tanker ships passing through the Welland Canal. She'd told Greene it was a mile from her house, and in the springtime, once the ice broke up on the Great Lakes, she'd ride her bike down there every day after school to watch the ships from all over the world. There were several graduation portraits: from high school, from university and law school. But the one that caught his attention was from police college. She looked radiant, happier in that picture than in any of the others.

Finally, Greene looked at a stylized wedding photo of a very young Jennifer and Howard, followed by pictures of her holding each of her three newborns, a series of Christmas snapshots of the growing family. At the bottom of the board were newspaper clippings of some of her high-profile cases.

"Detective Greene?" a voice said behind him. He turned to see Raglan's husband, Howard Darnell. The moment he'd been dreading.

Darnell was shorter than Greene had imagined he would be. And fitter too. Raglan had told Greene that when she left the marriage, her husband had been twenty-five pounds overweight and he had begun to exercise for the first time in years. It looked like he was still at it.

Greene pointed at one of the more recent family photos. "You must be Jennifer's husband."

"Howard Darnell." He put out his hand and Greene shook it. "I recognize you from some of the newspaper photos. Jennie told me many times how much she liked working with you. I know that you two did a lot of tough cases together."

"She was an excellent lawyer," Greene said. He remembered that, early on, he had once called Raglan "Jennie" and she'd gotten red with anger. "Don't ever call me by that name," she had said. "That's what everyone called me at home, and I can't stand it."

"Jennie was good at anything she put her mind to," Darnell said. "Anything."

The words could have sounded bitter, especially coming from a man who'd lost his job and was afraid to tell his wife about it. Then, after she was murdered, he had found out she'd been fooling around on him. But instead, Darnell sounded proud of her. Greene thought of what Kennicott had said about him – he seemed to be a man who loved his wife.

But he had to be wondering who his wife was meeting every Monday morning, Greene thought. By now he would have figured out that this was not just a onetime thing but had gone on for at least six weeks.

Greene played back in his mind the conversation he'd just had with Darnell. The first things out of someone's mouth often showed what they were really thinking. *Jennie told me many times how much she liked working with you. I know that you two did a lot of tough cases together.*

Was Darnell suspicious of him? Greene wondered. Or was he just being paranoid? He couldn't tell. But he knew for sure that Darnell would hate him one day if he ever found out.

"Detective?" Darnell said.

Greene realized he had drifted off. "It's very shocking. I can't imagine how it is for you. How are your children?"

Darnell pointed across the room. There was a tall young boy, awkward in an ill-fitting blue suit. Beside him stood a shorter boy, wearing black jeans and a T-shirt. To his side was a girl who looked like a young Jennifer.

"I think we're all in shock. Numb," Darnell said. "We were here at this same funeral home last winter for Jennie's mother. Who would believe we'd be back here now for her?"

A man in a cheap suit came up beside them. "Howard, I'm so sorry," he said.

Darnell turned. "Andrew. Been too long."

"Katherine couldn't be here. She's on a cruise with some of the girls from her church group. You remember. She was on the field hockey team with Jennie."

Darnell put his finger up to his friend and turned back to Greene. "Detective, if you don't mind, please say a word to my children. They know Jennie did those murder trials with you. It would mean a lot to them."

"Of course," Greene said.

Darnell went back to his old friend. "How's the store doing?" he asked. "That Walmart in St. Catharines couldn't have helped."

Greene took a final look at the photos of Jennifer, knowing he'd never see them again. He made himself walk away.

From a distance he glanced back and saw that Darnell was still talking to his old friend. The man was unbelievably polite. He had a smile fixed on his face, but he kept glancing over at his three kids.

Greene spotted Daniel Kennicott on the other side of the room, speaking to a handful of young Crown attorneys. He had the feeling Kennicott had been watching him. They met in the middle of the room.

"Sad," Kennicott said.

"Worst part of the job," Greene said.

"What do you think of the husband?"

Greene disliked the way some officers referred to the people they met during an investigation by their roles and not their names. New cops often did it because they thought it sounded important, just as interns in hospitals wear a stethoscope around their necks, or young lawyers tote the Criminal Code to court under their arm.

"'The husband?'" he said. "I think you mean Howard Darnell."

"Sorry." Kennicott frowned. "Point taken. What does your gut tell you about him?"

"That you're right. He loved his wife, he loves his kids, he's extraordinarily considerate of others. Hard to see him as a killer." Greene nodded toward the children, standing against a far wall. "If you arrest their father, you'd better be right, because their lives will go over the cliff."

"I know," Kennicott said. "Especially for the oldest one. I mean, Aaron."

A middle-aged couple approached the children. The tall boy in the suit smiled and shook their hands. His smaller brother looked away.

"He looks pretty okay," Greene said. "It's the one in the T-shirt I'd wonder about."

Kennicott snorted. "That's Aaron. His younger brother's about half a foot taller. Maybe that's part of the problem."

Greene stared at the short boy. "He's nineteen?"

"And looks about fourteen, just like I told you."

Greene kept staring at the boy, who, perhaps sensing his gaze, looked up at him and scowled. Don't take it personally, he told himself. The kid had been scowling at everyone.

"Darnell suggested I say hello to his kids," Greene said. "Maybe you can introduce me."

"Glad to," Kennicott said.

They walked over together.

The younger son, Barry, saw them approach and smiled. Aaron looked away. Corinne, the daughter, was talking to a friend

"This is Detective Greene," Kennicott said. "He worked on a few very large murder trials with your mom."

"We've heard about you," Barry said, shaking Greene's hand. "People keep telling us she was a good lawyer."

"She was very talented and very committed," Greene said.

Aaron, who wore a T-shirt that had the logo AARON 8 on both front and back in graffiti-style letters, turned his head. "Did you like working with her?" he asked in a snarky voice.

"Everyone did," Greene said.

"Thanks for coming," Barry said. Classic middle child, playing the role of the peacemaker, Greene thought. Compensating for his rude older brother.

"I'll see you guys tomorrow," Kennicott said. Clearly he'd established a good rapport with the family, which was impressive.

Greene had to get out of there. Away from the beige walls, the sickening music, the angry son, and the loving husband he'd betrayed.

"I've got to go," he said to Kennicott, probably too hastily, as they walked away.

"You okay?" Kennicott asked.

"Fine, just tired," Greene said.

Kennicott gave him a concerned look

Greene knew he wasn't a very good liar.

Out on the paved parking lot, the sun was hot. He steadied himself against the side of his car and closed his eyes. This all felt like a nightmare without end.

26

OVER THE YEARS AWOTWE AMANKWAH HAD NURTURED MANY SOURCES AMONG JUDGES, court reporters, clerks, registrars, Crown attorneys, and defence lawyers – anyone who could give him inside information about what was really going on in the courts. None was better than Nancy Parish, a defence lawyer he first met years ago, playing pickup hockey late at night at the outdoor rink in front of City Hall. It was the perfect place for them to get together, trade secrets, and then hit the ice, which they did a few times each winter.

When the ice was gone, one of the spots where they met was Ireland Park, a hard-to-find patch of green on the waterfront, tucked in behind the abandoned Canada Malting silos that the city now owned and had no idea what to do with. Five eerie statues of emaciated men and women, erected to commemorate the thousands of victims of the Irish potato famine who'd fled to the shores of the city back in 1847, were scattered about the grounds.

Amankwah was looking at the statue called *The Apprehensive Man*, reading the plaque at its base that described the outbreak of typhus among the Irish refugees. The city had built twelve fever sheds a few blocks from here, at King and John streets, and sent more than eight hundred immigrants there to die.

"So much for Toronto the Good," a female voice said behind him.

He turned and saw Parish. "In Africa, at least we send sick people across the river to die," he said.

"This city used to be a horrible place," she said. "My ancestors were on one of those death ships. When they got here, they were stuck in downtown ghettos. Weren't allowed in public parks in Protestant neighbourhoods."

"And when my parents came here, we were stuck in the burbs." He smiled. "Any luck?"

Amankwah had started to dig into the cops-and-prostitutes story. The day after the hockey-player trial collapsed, he'd tried to contact Deirdre "the After Date" Acton. But her website was down and every phone number he could find had been disconnected. He called Parish and they agreed to meet here at six. She knew a lot of cops, and she promised to get one of them to check for Acton's name on the police database.

Parish pulled a brown envelope out of the large purse slung over her shoulder. "Here's her record." She handed it to him.

"And?" he asked, opening it.

"It's about what you'd expect, up until two years ago. A few shoplifting charges. Two soliciting. One for giving a false name to the cops."

He looked at the printout. Acton had been fined a few times and two years earlier had spent thirty days in jail. Then nothing. "Looks like she cleaned up her act," he said.

"Don't be so sure," Parish said. "Look at the cases-withdrawn section on the second page.

Parish was right. In the last two years, Acton had been charged with soliciting four times, and four times the charges were dropped. "I guess she finally got a good defence lawyer." He chuckled.

Parish had a great sense of humour and often drew funny cartoons. But she wasn't smiling. "I've got something for you that could turn out to be important. You know I represent a lot of hookers."

"You have for years."

"They're always saying things like 'A cop made me give him a blow job to reduce the charges' or 'A cop took half my night's earnings and insisted on a hand job.'"

"We've all heard that before," he said.

"A few months ago, I represented a high-class prostitute who said the cops had put her up to charging a banker client with assault." She took a look around. A young couple was standing by another sculpture and an old woman with a shopping bag was feeding pigeons bits of white bread.

Parish took his arm and walked him over the edge of the park by the lake. "They arrested the poor guy and took him to the back of the station. Smacked him around a bit with a phone book so they wouldn't leave any bruises, then demanded five thousand dollars to yank the case. They charged her too, with soliciting. She said all she got was five hundred bucks for her trouble. And the cop who ran the whole thing demanded a blow job before she got paid and the soliciting charge was dropped. She said he likes to slap women around."

The island airport lay across the harbour and he watched a small commuter plane land. "Let me guess; you didn't believe her," he said.

"Not really at first. I'm a defence lawyer, we hear this kind of stuff all the time," she said. "Then yesterday morning, I'm in the lawyers' lounge at Old City Hall and I start talking to two other defence counsel about their hooker clients. Turns out they are complaining about the exact same thing. We compared notes. These women don't know each other. But they're telling the same story."

"Did their charges get dropped too?" he asked.

"Every time." She pointed to the printout in his hand. "Just like your Deirdre, the After Date."

This could really be something, Amankwah thought. "What are you going to do?" he asked.

"Canton Carmichael has been onto this for a while. He's been collecting information from defence lawyers about cop–hooker cases that are getting pulled."

Amankwah thought of Carmichael's behaviour at the trial. How self-assured he'd been. How it seemed he'd known that the Crown was going to withdraw the charge. And how frantic Kormos had been to get Fernandez to close the case down.

"Who are the cops involved?" he asked.

She shook her head. "Not yet, Awotwe," she said.

It was part of their understanding that at times there were limits on what they could disclose to each other, and it was important to respect them. Always.

He turned his back to the lake and scanned the park. The young couple and the old lady were gone. "What do you think's going on?"

She walked with him over to a sculpture of a desperate woman, prostrate on the ground. People had placed pennies along the base of the sculpture in an impromptu tribute.

"We're thinking maybe Internal Affairs is investigating," she said. "That they don't want to blow their own cover." She pulled two quarters out of her purse and placed them over the woman's eyes.

"Blind justice," he said.

"Let's hope not," she replied. "Canton's a really smart guy, why don't you go talk to him. I've already told him he can trust you."

"Thanks. But you didn't need to bother."

"Why not?"

"We went to the same high school and have been competing against each other our whole lives," he said. "Friendly competition, of course."

27

and the cars on the crowded highway were driving through a milky dusk. There was so much to say, and nothing to say, to Jo Summers, who was in the passenger seat beside him. She'd been crying for the half hour since they'd left the funeral home.

It had been two days since that horrible phone call, when he'd answered Raglan's cell and told Summers that her boss and friend had been murdered. It felt like a month ago. When he'd walked into the visitation room and seen her for the first time, he'd hugged her. Hard. She'd buried her face into his shoulder. "Oh, Daniel," she whispered. "It's so horrible."

"I know," he said.

"I'm so glad this is your case. I know you're smart. I know you'll do everything you can."

"Of course."

"Howard is a wreck. And her poor kids."

They'd let go of each other, but stayed close while talking to the other Crowns clustered in the far corner of the room. The old attraction between them, as complicated and unfulfilled as it had been, was an unspoken comfort they both needed.

"I'll take you home," he'd said when it was time to leave. And she hadn't objected.

Their night together a decade earlier at law school had been raw for both of them. Two years ago, when their paths intersected again, they kept missing each other. Mostly it was Kennicott's fault, because his ex-girlfriend, Andrea, a fashion model who'd become an international star, kept popping back into his life.

But that wasn't everything. There was a reserve about Jo that he couldn't get past. And he knew she'd probably say the same thing about him.

"What's the ferry schedule this evening?" he asked when they got close to the Toronto. Summers lived in a cottage on the Toronto Islands, and her life was ruled in no small part by the timetable of the boats that took her to and from the city. And also, Kennicott thought, gave her a good excuse to escape back into her own world.

She always carried a beeper with her that reminded her when it was time for her to leave to catch the last ferry back home. He saw she had it in her hand. He heard a click.

Her other hand reached out to his. "I turned my beeper off," she said. "I can't be alone tonight."

"I'm living by myself again," he said simply. A few months earlier she'd showed up at his place unannounced just when Andrea had returned for a few days.

"It's none of my business," she said.

He squeezed her hand. "I've got two bedrooms."

"Only two?"

"Very funny." He chuckled.

It was dark by the time they parked in the alley behind his place. They tip-toed together through his Italian landlord's vegetable garden. As soon as they were in the door of his second-floor flat, they fell into each other's arms. They kissed for a long time. Her hand reached around him, under his jacket. She pulled his shirt out and caressed the small of his back. He reached behind her neck and felt the softness of her skin.

She took his hand and led him to his bedroom, kicked off her shoes, pulled the sheets back, and lay down with her head on the pillow. He took his shoes off and lay beside her.

The blinds were not all the way down, and light drifted in from the streetlamp outside.

She turned to him and ran the back of her hand across his cheek. "Who was Jennifer having the affair with, do you have any idea?" she asked.

"No idea at all." He closed his eyes.

She pulled her hand back and nuzzled her head into his neck. He put his arm around her shoulder. "Whoever it is, the guy has to be your prime suspect."

"Of course. But she was incredibly careful in the way she covered her tracks." It seemed a bit extreme, he thought, for a woman who was having an affair.

"What's that make you think?"

He stroked her hair. "That it was someone who didn't want their identity known either."

"I miss her." She yawned again. Louder this time. "I haven't slept in two days." She curled her legs over his thighs. Her voice sounded sleepy.

He pulled the sheets over them.

"I've got to leave in a few hours," he said. "We're doing some surveillance. You can let yourself out. You don't need a key, both doors lock behind you."

"Who are you doing the surveillance on?"

He thought about it. She might be upset to know they were still suspicious of Raglan's husband. "I'll tell you if something comes of it," he said.

"Just hold me," she said. "That's what I need."

In seconds he felt her whole body go slack as she slid into sleep.

He lay still so as not to wake her, his eyes wide open. He stared at the ceiling as his mind raced. Wondering about Jo, about Howard Darnell, and about Jennifer Raglan. Who had she really been? And who had been her lover?

28

The late-night crowd that filled the banquet room at the Hilton Airport Hotel was chanting and clapping and whooping it up. On the balloon-filled stage a huge monitor was playing highlights from the career of the chief-of-police-turned-mayoralty-candidate in an endless loop. A big electronic timer, counting down the days to the election, hung under a long banner that read in big purple letters: HAP: TAKE BACK OUR CITY!

The room was so packed Greene could hardly move. He eased himself over to the a spot on wall near where a ramp led to the stage. Charlton had e-mailed him a few hours earlier and asked him to stand there.

"Mayor Hap! Mayor Hap! Mayor Hap! Mayor Hap!" people screamed in glee.

From the wings of the stage, a man with a shaved head, wearing a T-shirt that read HAP AIN'T PRETTY BUT HE'LL TAKE BACK OUR CITY, ran up to the microphone. The crowd burst out in laughter and applause.

"Ladies and gentlemen. My name is Roger Taylor. Most of you know me as the host of my TV show *O, O, Toronto*." He gave a self-deprecating chuckle. "You've heard of me. Right?"

"Yes!" the crowd shouted.

Greene smiled. He knew more about Taylor than his fawning fans did. The TV personality had been arrested three times as a "found in" at bawdy houses, a polite Canadian legal term for whorehouse. Each time he'd managed to wiggle out of the charges and keep the news out of the press. Very convenient, given that on the set of his highly rated show he sat at a desk on which photos of his blond wife and athletic kids were prominently displayed.

"Are you all as excited as I am?" he asked the crowd. "This is Hap's first big campaign rally!"

More wild cheering.

This was classic Charlton, Greene thought. Stage his first big event late at night to get maximum exposure on the morning newscasts. And instead of doing this in a downtown hotel the way every other candidate always did, do it out here in the burbs to underscore how unconventional his campaign was going to be, and how much support he had in the outlying areas.

"Ladies and gentlemen, what a great honour it is for me to introduce the great man who will soon transform our city. The man who will get the perverts and thugs off our streets. The man who will banish the bureaucratic waste at City Hall, clear the panhandlers and the litter from our streets, get rid of the graffiti that's spreading like weeds on steroids. The man who is going to take back our city!"

"Hap! Hap! Hap!" the audience began to chant.

"Okay, everyone, let's count down together," Taylor screamed. "Ten, nine, eight."

The crowd caught up to him and yelled in unison, "Seven, six, five, four, three, two, one."

"Here he is," Taylor shouted. "The next mayor of Toronto. Jumping Jack Hap. The chief. Hap Charlton!"

He pointed to a door a few steps past Greene. The Rolling Stones song "Jumping Jack Flash" blasted over the loudspeakers as the door swung open and a spotlight shone right on Charlton.

Greene smiled. Zachary Stone, the veteran *Toronto Sun* reporter, had given the ever-energetic Charlton the nickname decades ago and it had stuck. Now it seemed to be the perfect theme song for his campaign.

Charlton burst into the packed hall, bouncing up and down, clutching his big hands above his head like a prizefighter who has won the championship of the world.

The crowd began to jump up and down too. A group in front surged forward, but a phalanx of off-duty policemen held them back. The roar was louder than ever.

Greene kept his position and his back to the wall. With all the cheering and stomping, he could feel the floor vibrate through his shoes.

Charlton lowered his arms and began shaking hands with everyone on both sides of him. TV crews pushed supporters aside, holding their cameras aloft to capture their footage.

Charlton spotted Greene and reached for his hand. Greene shook it, but much to his surprise, Charlton pulled him closer to whisper in his ear.

"Ari, there's a little shithole bathroom in back of that room." He jerked his head toward the door he'd just exited. "Once I've done this fucking stupid speech and all the press crap, meet me there. We've got to talk."

"Sure," Greene said.

"About this Jennifer Raglan thing."

Despite the rising heat in the room, Greene felt a chill on the back of his neck. Before he could say a word, Charlton was swept back up in the crowd.

This was how Charlton always worked. The swearing and the bluster, the little secrets. Always wanted to let his inner circle know that despite the trappings of power, he was still one of them.

Greene watched him mount the stage. Despite his considerable bulk, the now-official candidate for mayor was still quick on his feet.

"Thank you, everyone, thank you." Charlton waved to the crowd as they cheered for about a minute, until he raised his hands like a preacher before his congregation, and they fell silent.

He flashed his toothiest smile. "You know, folks, for thirty-five years as a proud member of the Toronto Police Service, it's been my life's work to serve and protect the citizens of our great city."

Spontaneous applause erupted, but he silenced it with a quick wave of his hand.

Charlton wasn't really speaking to the crowd, but to the TV cameras. He was the master of a good clip to make the top of the newscast. "But I just couldn't sit by and watch the Toronto I love decline. That's why I'm running for mayor. To take back our city!"

The audience started chanting "Take it back, Hap!"

Charlton was loving the attention. Always had. Always would.

Greene had met him the first week he joined the force, twenty-five years earlier. Back then, it was unusual for a Jewish kid to want to be a police officer, and Greene was older than most of the other recruits. Charlton was his first staff sergeant and he saw something in the greenhorn. Became his mentor, his rabbi.

"Take back our litter-filled streets from the criminals who are terrorizing our neighbourhoods," Charlton said, pausing to let the roar of approval roll over him.

Charlton got Greene into the Major Crime Unit early in his career, then the undercover drug squad, then had him made a division detective. When Charlton became chief, he picked Greene for a secret assignment that took a year out Greene's life. When that was over, he sent Greene to Europe for another year to recover. When Greene came back to Toronto, he had his own office in the homicide squad.

"Take back our City Hall from the wasteful bureaucrats," Charlton said, sweeping the crowd along with him.

For years Greene had watched Charlton manipulate politicians and the press with a Svengali-like ease. Now, stepping into his first election campaign, he looked like a natural.

"Take back our parks. Our community centres. Our pride."

The Jennifer Raglan thing, Greene thought. *Thing*. In the long days since the murder, the ache of losing her, missing her, wanting her, had drilled a silent hole inside him.

"Take back all those extra taxes that have been piled on the citizens and the businesses of Toronto. I want *you* to take home more of *your* hard-earned money."

Greene knew why Charlton wanted to talk to him in the washroom. The chief loved to know every detail of any major crime investigation. What had happened with the wiretaps on the husband? Any other suspects? Who was Jennifer's secret lover?

But there was no way Charlton could have found out about his affair with Raglan. Was there?

"Best of all," Charlton said, his voice rising in a crescendo, "when I'm mayor, Toronto, the largest city in Canada, the most multicultural city in the world, will be ours once again. We are going to take it back and make it shine!"

This sent the crowd into rapturous applause. Charlton, who knew how to keep an audience panting for more, and how to make sure the press had enough time to file their stories, raised his hands again in triumph and headed off the stage.

29

SURVEILLANCE WORK WAS ONE OF THE MORE THANKLESS TASKS FOR ANY POLICE OFFICER. IT was like being a navigator in a long car race, Kennicott thought. There were lengthy stretches of boring nothing-to-do time, punctuated by urgent action. No one noticed if you did your job right, but if you made a mistake it left egg all over your face.

As the lead homicide detective, he didn't have to be sitting in this unmarked car, parked across from Howard Darnell's home, at ten minutes after midnight. But if he was going to be in charge of this investigation, he knew it was important for the other cops to see him putting in the hours. Besides, he wanted to do it.

Right now the moon was out, giving a soft light to the quiet street. The wind had died down to a breeze. There were no lights on in the Darnell home. Nor was there any noise inside. It was sad and uncomfortable listening in on Raglan's family and disconcerting to hear the children cry and their father try to console them. There was clearly friction between Darnell and Aaron. Earlier, as they were getting ready to drive to the funeral home in Welland, they'd had a huge fight when Aaron insisted on wearing a T-shirt and jeans. He was complaining about his new school, where he was already in trouble because he'd been late every morning except for the first day of classes. He said he hated the place and was threatening not to go back unless his father got him the new iPhone to replace his BlackBerry, which he claimed was "a piece of shit."

The judge who had issued the warrant, aware of this extreme invasion of privacy, insisted it had to be renewed every four days. Kennicott knew that if they didn't get something incriminating on tape soon, it would expire. Part of him hoped that would happen.

He lowered himself deeper in the driver's seat.

"Drago, you hear anything?" he asked, speaking quietly into the microphone that dangled from his right ear.

"Not a peep," said the sound technician in the delivery van parked at the top of the block. He was a Serbian guy named Slavko Dragic, who insisted that everyone call him Drago.

"I'll check with you in fifteen." Kennicott had set up a system of quick calls every quarter hour to make sure they were on top of things. It would also keep him alert. He was tired. The dull fatigue that comes from days and nights of getting short snatches of sleep, eating strange food at strange hours, and feeling the constant alertness of adrenaline coursing through his veins.

Last night, after Jo had fallen asleep on his chest, he had shut his eyes too and eventually drifted into a light sleep. Because he'd signed up for this shift, he'd set the alarm on his cell phone for eleven o'clock. He'd managed to grab it and turn it off before it woke her up. But he'd had to hurry.

In the kitchen he took the blue Pastis water pitcher that Andrea had brought him from Paris, and put it into a top cupboard out of sight, then he started writing Jo a note.

> *Very late*
> *Jo*
> *Had to get back to work on the case. Glad you stayed.*

He stopped. What to write next? *You're welcome at any time?* That sounded ridiculous. How about *Anytime you miss the last ferry there's a spare room?* That was worse. And *very late?* That seemed self-congratulatory.

He balled the paper up and stuffed it in his back pocket and tried again.

> *Jo*
> *Had to get back to work. Door is always open.*

Horrible. Clichéd. He ripped the page in half, then into quarters, and stuck them into the same back pocket.

He looked at the clock above the stove. Shit. It was 11:18. He had to be out the door in twelve minutes. And he needed to grab a shower.

> *Jo*
> *I put some fresh grounds in the espresso machine, help yourself.*
>
> *D.*

He yanked the handle off his machine, quickly rinsed out the old grounds, dried off the basket, and poured in fresh ones from the airtight jar he kept on the kitchen counter. He pulled out a drawer. Where was the tamper? Damn. Just use a spoon, he told himself. He grabbed a soup spoon and pushed down hard on the grounds, making a concave dent and spilling bits over the side. This is crazy, he thought as dug back into the drawer, trying not to be too loud. There it is. He grabbed the tamper, poured in more grounds, made sure he pushed them down firm and flat, flicked some specks off the rim, and shoved the handle back into position. He rushed to the shower, wishing he'd written a note that didn't sound so cold.

Too late now, Kennicott thought as he kept watch on Darnell's house. It was still dark. The street was quiet. He tried not to yawn.

A light came on in the front room on the second floor. The master bedroom.

"A light's on," he said into the microphone, sitting up. "Drago, what do you hear?"

Drago was parked too far away to see the house, so Kennicott was the eyes, Drago the ears.

"Feet on the floor," he said. "Wait. I hear footsteps. Someone's in the bathroom."

Kennicott watched the lighted curtain in front. Darnell probably had to pee. Most likely he'd be back in bed in a few seconds, and the light would go out again.

"Person is back in the original bedroom. Sounds like someone is getting dressed," Drago said.

"How can you tell?" Kennicott asked.

"I've been doing this a long time. Now someone's going downstairs. One set of footsteps. Pretty heavy-sounding. Wouldn't be a child."

"Light just came on on the ground floor," Kennicott said. "He's probably going to the kitchen to get something to eat or drink."

"I heard the light switch. Wait. What's that? Fridge opening. Closing. He's pouring something into a glass. Sitting down. Now nothing."

"Okay," Kennicott said. The mike wouldn't pick up the subtle sound of someone drinking.

"A faint sound. Something clicked. Scratching."

"What do you think it is?"

Drago was silent for a few seconds. Then he chuckled. "He's writing something at the kitchen table. I heard him tear a sheet of paper, like he was ripping it off a pad."

"You're good at this," Kennicott said.

"Thanks. Wait. A door opened and shut. Wait. Wait. Damn, now there's nothing."

"How could there be nothing?" Kennicott asked. In a few seconds he had his answer. Darnell was walking toward his garage and a light came on through the side window. They hadn't miked the garage, so there was no feed from inside. I won't make that mistake again, he told himself.

What was Darnell doing in there? Kennicott thought about how he'd got up in the middle of the night. Wrote something on the kitchen table. Was it a suicide note to the kids? It wouldn't take long for him asphyxiate himself sitting in the van with the windows open and the garage door closed.

Before Kennicott could get out of his car, he heard a loud rumble. The garage door opened. He could see Darnell silhouetted by the inside light bending down and lifting something very heavy then bringing it out to the driveway. It took Kennicott a few seconds to realize it was a canoe.

Darnell punched some numbers into the keypad by the garage door and it unfolded back into place. He went to the side of the canoe, bent deep down, slipped one hand under the near side, and reached for the far gunnel with the other. Using a confident rocking motion, he one-two-three hoisted it onto his shoulders in a swift move and started walking down the street. Kennicott sank lower in his seat as he passed, which was probably unnecessary since Darnell had a canoe over his head. As a boy, Kennicott and his older brother, Michael, had spent every summer at his parents' cottage. He knew a lot about canoes, and he could tell Darnell did too.

He waited until Darnell got well down the moonlit street before getting out of his car. It was almost comical to watch Darnell look left and right, and let the all-night Queen streetcar pass, before he portaged across the road. Kennicott started walking and called the officer in the unmarked squad car parked near the lake. He told him to come back to keep an eye on the house.

It was easy to follow the canoe, keeping to the shadows. Two blocks south of Queen, Darnell entered the bucolic park by the lake. Kennicott hid in a stand of tall bushes. The moonlight danced on the dark water.

Darnell crossed the boardwalk, lifted the canoe from his shoulders, and deposited it smoothly in the sand, the stern resting in the water. He stretched, looked up and down the empty beach, and then retraced his steps, walking past Kennicott's hiding place.

Where's he going? Kennicott wondered. Then he realized Darnell didn't have a paddle. He was going home to get one. Then what? Paddle out into the lake and jump in?

He called the second backup car that was around the corner. "Stand by out of sight." Then he called the one now stationed near the house. "Darnell's walking back home, I think he's going to get a paddle. Let him go. I'll grab him when he comes back here."

This was such a tragedy. Kennicott had no doubt now that in a few minutes, when he intercepted Darnell before he got in the canoe, the distraught husband and father would crumble and confess that he'd arranged to have his wife killed. And that now he was trying to end it all.

Kennicott would get Children's Aid to take care of the younger kids. Back at headquarters, he'd get kudos for solving his first homicide.

This meant he'd never find out who Raglan was having her affair with. Just as well. He didn't really care. All that mattered was that he was about to save Howard Darnell, the father of three children, from a watery grave.

30

went into the back room. A young woman in a silk suit was sitting on a beat-up old couch. She had a plastic Loblaws shopping bag on her lap.

"Hi," she said, standing. "I'm Dinah Renfrew, one of Mr. Charlton's campaign assistants."

In all the years he'd known the chief, Greene had never heard anyone refer to him as Mr. Charlton.

"You must be Mr. Greene," she said.

"Call me Ari."

"I was told you'd come in after the speech." She smiled. "I got this intern job yesterday. Mr. Charlton's ski chalet is next door to my parents'. I graduated from Queen's last spring and it's so hard to find anything."

The door flew open and Charlton burst in. He was followed closely by Clyde Newbridge, a short, fat cop whom Greene disliked intensely. The feeling was mutual.

Newbridge had joined the force a few years before Greene, and for many years their careers followed similar paths as they both worked their way through the ranks. But Newbridge was more of a careerist. He got involved in the police union and seemed to know everybody. Especially people in power. He showed up whenever there was a big event, hobnobbing with the top brass. Especially Hap Charlton.

Newbridge whipped the door shut. He glanced at Greene but didn't say anything. Neither did Greene.

"Hi, Dinah," Charlton said, giving Renfrew a friendly hug.

She gave him a shy embrace, stood back, and handed over the shopping bag. "I got what you asked for."

"Good work." He turned to Newbridge. "Clyde, Dinah's dad is waiting for her outside. Make sure you take her to him right now."

"I'll try to find him," Newbridge said.

Charlton's face flushed red with anger. "I said be sure you get Dinah to her father now. Understood. No fuckups this time."

"Okay, okay," Newbridge said, cowed into submission.

Although he'd never been a victim of it, Greene had seen Charlton's hair-trigger temper before. He could flare up at any moment. It was an effective way of keeping his troops off balance, and in line.

"And close that damn door and make sure it stays closed," Charlton said.

"I'll stay right in front of it," Newbridge said. He smirked at Greene and escorted Renfrew out.

Without saying another word, Charlton led Greene into a tiny washroom and closed the door behind them. *Shithole* was a pretty accurate description, Greene thought.

Charlton turned on the water. This was standard procedure for the chief, who forever feared being caught on a wiretap when he was skating close to the line. If not slipping over it.

The room had a small window to the outside. Charlton pushed it open and a rush of cold air flooded in. From the shopping bag he pulled out a package of small, plastic-tipped cigars, unwrapped it, jammed one between his teeth, reached back into the bag, took out some matches, lit up, and sucked hard.

Greene sniffed the sweet tobacco smell. He was tempted to ask Charlton for one. That would shock him, which was probably not a great idea,

"We got new poll this afternoon," Charlton said. "Now I'm ten points ahead of Forest. I'm going to kill her in the suburbs. If I can split the downtown vote, this is going to be a cakewalk."

"Still a long ways to go," Greene said.

"So long as nothing fucks up, I'm in like Flynn." He blew a narrow line of smoke out the window. "Look, Ari, I know how you felt about Raglan."

Greene held his breath.

"You two did a lot of cases together." Charlton took out a pack of mints and a small bottle of mouthwash and placed them on the rim of the sink. "And you thought she was the best prosecutor in the office, didn't you?"

"She was," Greene said.

Charlton sucked hard on the little cigar. "This thing is going to look bad on everyone."

It's not a thing. It's a murder, Greene wanted to say.

"If we're not careful, it could really fuck up my campaign. How close are we to an arrest?"

Greene shrugged. "It's Kennicott's case, so I'm staying out of it. I don't want to hover over his shoulder."

Charlton blew a perfect line of smoke out the window. "Give me a fucking break. Don't tell me you're not talking to him on the side?"

Greene turned the water tap up so it was louder. "Officially or unofficially?" he said.

They both laughed.

"Thank God you are doing it. Don't forget I was in homicide for eight years. Everyone needs advice. We practically invented 'don't ask, don't tell.' I'd be pissed if he wasn't using your brain."

"Kennicott's smart," Greene said.

"And a rookie. Smart means dick without experience. He needs resources behind him." Charlton took another drag. "Fuck, this cigar is just what I needed."

This was Charlton's way of asking without asking. Telling Greene what to do without telling him what to do. His message was clear. *I want to know what's going on. Stay close to this case, and I'll make sure Kennicott has all the backup he needs.*

"Husband's the prime, I assume," Charlton said, as a conversation starter.

For the next ten minutes, as the water ran, Greene related everything Kennicott had told him about the investigation, including how Darnell had a bulletproof alibi and that they had nothing to show he'd hired a killer. "Kennicott's parked outside his house tonight doing surveillance. He's keen."

Charlton puffed on his cigar while he listened. Nodded. "Husband might be innocent. No hired gun is going to strangle a woman to death," he said at last.

"Raglan put a lot of people in jail," Greene said.

Charlton shrugged. "I assume Kennicott's running down all the names."

"Most have the best alibi you can imagine. They were in custody."

"What about her lover boy?" Charlton asked. "Assuming that it was a boy? Never know anymore. Do we know who she was bopping?"

Do we know who he was bopping? How was Hap going to feel about me, his prize student, if he finds out I'm the one? Greene wondered.

"So far Kennicott's drawn a blank," he said, choosing his words carefully. At least it wasn't a lie.

"Keep me in the loop," Charlton said. "The sooner we get an arrest, the better." He took a final drag then stuck the end of the cigar under the running water. It hissed and sputtered until it went out. He tossed the butt out the window. "So much for taking back the litter from the streets." He chuckled.

All the years I've known Charlton, Greene thought, the guy was still an enigma.

Charlton unscrewed the top of the mouthwash, gargled hard, and spat into the sink. He tossed the bottle in the wastebasket, cracked open the mints, and ate a handful. "You've got twenty-five years as a cop, I've got thirty-five," he said. "There's only one thing we both know: Who the hell really knows anyone?"

He patted Greene on the shoulder. "I've got to give the print guys some better quotes before their editors bite their heads off. Stay five minutes until the coast is clear."

Greene heard the outside door open then close.

He slammed the top down on the toilet and thought about sitting on it. But instead, he gave the back wall a hard, swift kick.

31

"DO YOU SEE HIM?" KENNICOTT ASKED, SPEAKING THROUGH HIS HEADSET TO THE OFFICER parked near Darnell's house. He was certain Darnell would come back to the beach and he wanted to remain hidden. This was a good spot.

"He's walking up the street," the cop said.

"Where are you?" Kennicott asked.

"On foot. I'm across the street behind a big oak tree and my partner's in the cruiser at the end of the block. Wait. I see him walking up to his house now. He's going straight to the garage. He went in the side door."

"He'll probably be a minute or so." Kennicott looked at the moonlight dancing on the water. So much of Toronto was built to ignore that it was on Lake Ontario. When he was at law school and did volunteer work at the legal clinic, he had clients in suburban high-rises who didn't even know the city was on a lake.

There was a constant breeze, and the rhythmic lapping of the waves was soothing. A scent of guano hung in the air.

"He's been inside the garage for almost five minutes now," the officer outside Darnell's home said into Kennicott's earpiece.

"Hang on." Kennicott switched channels. "Do you hear anything in the house?" he asked Drago, the sound engineer.

"Squat."

It wasn't surprising that Darnell was taking his time. It was impossible for Kennicott to imagine what it must feel like to leave your home and your children, thinking you'd never see them again.

Thank God he'd been diligent about this surveillance. He switched back to the cop near the house. "Can you slip up beside the garage and peer in the window?"

"Too risky to walk up there. No trees or bushes for cover," the officer said. "Wait!"

"What?"

"The front garage door's opening. He's outside now. Carrying a green garbage bag."

"Does he have a paddle?"

"Yep, in his other hand. He's closing the door. Now he's walking back your way. And one more thing."

"What?"

"He's wearing a life jacket."

"A life jacket?"

"Looks like he's going for a paddle."

Kennicott had to think fast. He had no legal grounds to stop Darnell. If the man wasn't suicidal, there was no point. If he tried to talk to him, Darnell would know he was under surveillance and that would make him more cautious. And why would a man bent on killing himself wear a life jacket?

Soon he heard footsteps on the deserted street behind him. Seconds later Darnell walked past him, flicking on and off a little flashlight in his hand.

Move now, or wait? Kennicott had to decide.

Darnell went to the side of the canoe and placed the bag in the front. He secured the flashlight on top of it, a beacon facing out.

He's coming back to shore, Kennicott told himself. He didn't move from his hiding place.

Darnell was fast. He put his paddle across the gunnels and hopped into the canoe as he slid it into the water.

Kennicott was always amazed by how few people knew how to paddle a canoe. They'd sit too high up and hack away at the water on one side of the boat then the other.

Not Darnell. He knelt in the bow, facing the stern, and did the Indian J-stroke, the silent way of paddling used by advanced canoers. A few strong pulls and he was soundlessly out onto the water, the moon tracking him like a spotlight.

Kennicott walked out into the open and took his time approaching the shore. The sand beneath his feet was loose. He watched Darnell paddle in a perfect, straight line until he disappeared into the night.

He found a new hiding spot, at the side of a concession stand, and waited. It wasn't until almost two o'clock that he heard the subtle lapping of water against boat. Darnell jumped nimbly out onto the shore, pulled his canoe up, weaved the paddle in under the gunnels, and flipped it onto his shoulders.

Whatever had been in the garbage bag was now deep at the bottom of the lake. Far out.

There was one good thing about all this, Kennicott thought. Clearly Darnell had something to hide. Most likely he had just destroyed evidence of some kind, and his odd behaviour would be enough for Kennicott to get the judge to extend the search warrant.

Darnell portaged his canoe back up into the city, and Kennicott walked back down to the water's edge. The cop on the street reported that Darnell put the canoe back in the garage, entered the house, and turned the lights out, first on the ground floor, then on the second floor. Drago heard footsteps go up the stairs, then the click of a light switch.

The house was dark. Quiet.

A cloud drifted across the moon, darkening the already black water. Kennicott stood still. The wind blew lightly on his cheek, where Jo had touched him. He listened to the pebbles on the shore as the waves drew them back and flung them up the beach on their return.

PART
THREE

32

ago. He was sitting in his Oldsmobile across the street and a few doors down. Daniel Kennicott had told him about Darnell's strange behaviour the previous night, canoeing out into the lake to dispose of something in green garbage bag, and Greene had offered to take a shift on surveillance.

Every part of his body ached. Last night he had finally got to sleep, only to wake up, blinking in the darkness, bathed in sweat. He couldn't believe that Jennifer was gone. He was angry. Enraged that he had no idea who killed her. Or why.

He had somehow managed to get back to sleep, and had woken again in the dark, more lost than ever. This morning he'd gone to a coffee shop down the street from his house, ordered a double espresso, and downed it. Then had a second.

First cigarettes, now coffee, he thought, laughing at himself, better not let Kennicott see this suspicious behaviour.

He stared at the front door and imagined Jennifer coming through it every morning dressed for work. Except on their Mondays, when she'd be in her jogging outfit, the pack on her back, and a smile on her face.

Then, almost as if he'd willed it to happen, the door opened. Howard Darnell and his three kids walked out of the house. The younger two had on backpacks. Darnell kissed them both, and they walked off down the street. But Aaron stayed back and got into the van with his father.

Greene put his car in gear and followed them while he hit a preset number on his cell phone. Kennicott answered on the second ring.

"The two youngest kids just went off to school, but Darnell and Aaron are going for a drive. I'm going to follow them at a distance."

"I suspect he's still having a hard time getting Aaron to go to school. Maybe they're going shopping for that iPhone," Kennicott said.

"Where are you?" Greene asked.

"Home, for a change."

"Well, stand by," Greene said.

Darnell's van got to Queen Street and turned west, toward the city. After a few blocks he turned left toward Lakeshore Boulevard, the wide street that would take him downtown. But then he went up onto the Gardner Expressway, the highway that cut across the bottom of the city.

Greene called Kennicott. "He's not shopping, at least not downtown," he said.

"Where is he?"

"On the Gardner. We're passing the CN Tower right now."

"You want some backup?"

"I might. It's too tough to follow him alone on a highway. I'd be too easy to spot. How long will it take you to get on the road?" Greene asked.

"I'll be out the door in a minute. It'll take me about twenty to get down to the Gardner."

"Where's Alpine?" Greene asked.

"Up north, closing down his cottage. I told him to take the day off."

"Darnell's in the left lane. Looks like he's going for a drive," Greene said.

"What do you want me to do?" Kennicott asked.

"Bring sunglasses and a baseball cap so he won't recognize you if you get too close on the road."

"Good idea."

"Bring your portable siren so you can blast it if you need to catch up."

"It's in my glove compartment."

"And, Kennicott," Greene said.

"Yes."

"Just a hunch, but grab your passport."

33

black reporters in a newsroom of more than a hundred journalists. And when he went to court to cover cases, the proportion of black lawyers to white was about the same as it was back at the office. But in the years since, all that had changed. Now it was an everyday thing to see black prosecutors, black police officers, black judges, and most of all black lawyers.

At first, the young black lawyers had acted like any other rookie advocates, running from court to court, grabbing every legal-aid case they could find, scratching out a living. But soon some top legal talent had emerged, and Canton Carmichael was exhibit number one.

Always elegantly dressed, armed with a fine leather briefcase, the latest cell phone, and his initialed Cross pen, Carmichael had a brilliant legal mind and commanding presence in court. And, like a blues singer who had broken onto the mainstream charts, he'd busted out of the black-client, immigrant-client, legal-aid ghetto, and now represented some of the wealthiest white people in the city.

"Come on in, Double A," he said, greeting Amankwah at the door of his new, well-appointed office suite.

"Nice digs, Double C." Amankwah looked around the foyer at the polished marble floors and the oak wainscotting and let out a low whistle.

"Got to show the flash if you're going to get the cash," Carmichael said, a full-faced grin firmly in place as they walked down the corridor to his bright corner office.

"Looks like it's working," Amankwah said, taking a seat in one of the well-padded client chairs.

Carmichael sat behind his expansive glass-topped desk and dropped the grin. "I worked hard for this, man."

"I know," Amankwah said. "Nice win last week with the hockey player."

"Wasn't it? Thanks for the front-page coverage."

"You knew that bringing up her website about the cops was going to blow the case out of the water, didn't you?"

"Did I?"

For all his outward sophistication, Carmichael was at heart a survivor. Taken from his mother by Children's Aid when he was three years old, he'd grown up in foster and group homes all over the city. His was a rare CAS success story and he was proud of it. But also extremely cautious.

"You blindsided Fernandez with it on purpose, didn't you," Amankwah said.

"Why would I do that?"

"Because you know something else is going on. That Crowns have quietly been withdrawing all sorts of charges against hookers."

"Really, and what else do I know?"

"You know that a number of defence lawyers are getting the same complaint from their hooker clients about the cops shaking them down."

Carmichael curled his hands together and tapped his fingers, like a thoughtful judge teetering on the brink of a decision. He's studying me, Amankwah thought, holding his gaze.

"Awotwe. Remember when the two of us started in this game?" Carmichael said. "I was so keen, running out to the jails every night, giving my business cards to every fool I could find. And you were hustling like there was no tomorrow to get some ink in the paper."

"What else is going on with the cops, Canton?"

"I remember the first time you got a front-page story. That fool of an arts student who sent a fake bomb to City Hall to make a statement. I gave you the heads-up on that one."

"And I got you a ton of press. Yesterday Nancy Parish told me to come see you. You going to talk to me or are am I wasting my time?"

Carmichael tapped away.

Amankwah stood up. He had to force the issue. "Yes or no?"

"There's some heavy shit going on out there," Carmichael said, not moving.

"And . . ."

"Okay." Carmichael bolted out of his seat. "What I'm going to show you doesn't go anywhere until I give you the say-so. Agreed."

"Agreed."

"Let's go." He walked swiftly out of his office and over to a bank of elevators. One arrived seconds later.

"Where we going?" Amankwah asked when Carmichael pushed the button for B2.

"My storage locker. There is no record anywhere that this locker exists. A third party rents it for me. No key, combination lock."

"You afraid of a search warrant?"

Carmichael gave a loud guffaw. "Sometimes you're still that skinny little African kid, as innocent as baby's milk. If the cops are going to search my place, you think they're going to bother with a warrant?"

The elevator opened on B2. Carmichael let him through a maze of corridors. They both had to duck in places to make sure they didn't hit their heads on the heating ducts.

"Locker forty-two. Combination is twenty-two, thirty-two, twelve. You got that? Twenty-two, thirty-two, twelve."

"Why are you telling me this?"

"Because you never fucking know with the cops." This was the street-fighter Canton. "Look man. This is heavy shit."

Inside the locker there were stacks of banker's boxes, all neatly labelled. Carmichael pulled out one named *R. v. Whistle*. "Whistle as in whistle-blower." He laughed again.

He showed Amankwah letters from seven well-known Toronto defence lawyers. Attached to each was a statement by one of their clients. Amankwah took his time reading them. "All these women are telling essentially the same story," he said when he was done.

"Yes, and none of them know each other. And did you notice they are all older."

"With criminal records."

Carmichael snapped his fingers loud. "Exactly. Typical prostitute stuff. False name. Fail to appear. The kind of witnesses a good defence lawyer could rip to shreds. No credibility."

Unspoken, but clearly in his mind, Amankwah thought, was how Carmichael would treat these women in court if they ever testified against one of his clients.

"You think they were picked for that reason?"

Carmichael rolled his eyes. "Wake up, man. That's the cops' insurance policy. Everyone knows beat-up old hookers are useless witnesses. Half of them won't even show up on the trial date."

"How far up does this go?" Amankwah asked.

"That's the million-dollar question now, isn't it? In case you haven't noticed, the guy who was chief of police when all this was going down is now running for mayor."

"You think Charlton knew about this?"

"I think I told you this was heavy shit."

"Do you have copies of all this?"

"One set at home. I figure if the cops grab it, they will think it's the only one. There's a second set here, and a third set somewhere else. I'm not even going to tell you where it is. I'm still getting my ducks in a row, but I'll make my move soon. You'll be the first to know."

"Thanks," Amankwah said. "Have you done anything else with all this information?"

"Such as?"

"Analyzing it."

"No, man. I'm just a friggin' criminal lawyer. I can barely use a computer."

"I want you to lend me this copy," Amankwah said.

"What do you want it for? No way you can use this till I say so."

"Agreed," Amankwah said. "Let me put all this information on a spreadsheet and see if I can find a pattern."

"Okay," Carmichael said. "But don't make any copies. "

Carmichael put the box back in the stack under several others, walked Amankwah out of the storage room, and twirled the number dial on the lock, then walked him back through the maze to the elevator. "What's the locker number?" he asked as they waited for it to arrive.

"Forty-two."

"Combination."

"Twenty-two, thirty-two, twelve."

"Good," Carmichael said as the elevator dinged. "Don't forget it."

34

KENNICOTT WAS BLASTING DOWN THE HIGHWAY, TALKING ON HIS HEADSET TO ARI GREENE.
An hour earlier, he had been forty-five kilometres behind. Fortunately, Howard Darnell drove at the speed limit, so he hadn't needed the siren. Just some aggressive bobbing and weaving and at last Greene's sturdy old car came into view.

"I see you," he said. "Where's the van?"

"About ten car lengths up," Greene said. "I knew you were close, so I slipped back. It's thirty K to the next exit."

"Where do you want me to go?" Even though this was Kennicott's case, he couldn't help but defer to Greene.

"Cut ahead of him. I'll stay behind."

Kennicott got into the passing lane, pulled his baseball cap down low, and accelerated past Greene. "Where do you think he's going?"

"I thought he was heading back home to Welland," Greene said. "But he drove by the turnoff fifteen minutes ago, then I thought Niagara Falls."

"But we've just passed that exit too," Kennicott said.

"I know. Looks like he's on his way to Buffalo."

"Jesus."

"Don't worry," Greene said. "When Darnell hit the highway, I called someone I know at the border."

Greene has contacts everywhere, Kennicott thought. He spotted Darnell's van driving steadily in the right lane. "I see him," he said.

"Good."

Keeping his eyes straight ahead, he passed the van and cut in front. In his rearview mirror he could see Darnell in the driver's seat and Aaron in the passenger seat, looking out the window, white earbud wires sprouting from his ears. "Now he's behind me."

"Perfect. Stay there for a few minutes. I'm going to pass you. Wait another few kilometres then fall back behind him. When you get to customs, pick the lane farthest away from the van. The guards know what's going on. They'll hold up Darnell and time it so you get through right after he does."

"What about you?" Kennicott asked. In his side mirror he saw Greene's car coming up fast.

"I'm going to switch cars," Greene said. "I'll be in a brown SUV with Virginia plates. It's got an American flag on the back, so you can spot it easily. I'll get right behind him. You stay a few cars back. That way we'll have lots of flexibility."

In a few more minutes they hit the border. There were seven booths, with five or six cars lined up in front of each. Greene's car was in the lane on the far left. Darnell pulled his van into a middle lane. Kennicott went to the far right. The line moved quickly. He rolled his window down when it was his turn.

"Good morning, Detective Kennicott," the young female guard in the booth said before he could say a word. She had long brown hair and pretty freckles. She wore a headset.

"Thanks for your help." Kennicott opened his wallet and showed her his badge and passport.

She nodded, looking down at the screen in front of her. "Don't worry. Give me your passport so this looks like a normal check."

Kennicott passed it across.

She took it, but didn't look at it. "Roger," she said into her headset, nodding her head again. Her eyes were fixed on the monitor in front of her. "I'm to tell you Detective Greene has switched cars," she said.

"Good."

Her eyes were still on the monitor. "The subject vehicle has just entered booth number four."

"We really appreciate your cooperation," he said.

She finally looked at him. "It was easy. We held up his line until you were ready. Toronto's a beautiful city."

"It's got some good parts," he said.

"I like the clubs," she said. "We work shifts, so I get a lot of time off."

"Sounds like the life of a cop."

"On Saturday night I'm going with some friends to Riva Supper Lounge on College Street. They have a great DJ. You ever been there?"

"No, I don't think I have," he said. "I live around the corner."

"It's a lot of fun . . ."

She held up a finger. Someone was talking to her on her headset. "Roger," she said into her microphone, then looked back at the monitor.

"When questioned about the reason for his visit to America, the driver states he's taking his son across to buy him a new iPhone that's not available yet in Canada," she said, her voice returning to a bureaucratic tone.

"Right." What an idiot I am, he thought. On the wiretap in Darnell's home he'd heard Aaron argue with his father about staying in school, and the promise of a new iPhone if he didn't drop out.

He called Greene on his cell. "Darnell told customs he was taking his son shopping for a new iPhone."

"I heard that a minute ago," Greene said. "You told me the other night that he'd been bugging his dad about this."

Kennicott felt the adrenaline drain out of him. He wasn't pursuing a fleeing murder suspect in a homicide, but a grieving father taking his son shopping for electronics in Buffalo. Something that thousands of people in Toronto did all the time. "Should we bail?" he asked.

"No," came Greene's curt answer.

"The subject vehicle has been released," the border guard said. He saw her writing something before she handed him back his passport. Her teeth were a brilliant white.

"Thanks . . ."

"Rachel," she said.

"Thanks, Rachel."

"I put my cell number on a sticky note in your passport. Saturday night at the Riva."

In front of him, Darnell drove his van onto the adjoining expressway. Greene's SUV followed. He tipped his passport at Rachel and smiled, then, after a few cars had passed, he fell into line.

All three vehicles sped along the elevated highway that bisected the rusty hull of downtown Buffalo. Darnell was driving faster now.

In a few minutes Greene came back on the phone. "He's signalling to get off at the next exit. Look over to your right. Sorry if I took you on a wild-goose chase."

Kennicott peered out the passenger-side window and saw a massive electronics superstore down below, behind an enormous parking lot. A smattering of vehicles were parked near the store entrance, leaving a huge expanse of vacant pavement in front. "Perhaps you could get yourself an iPod, Detective," he said. "Do you have one?"

Greene laughed. "No. But my father's Russian girlfriend just bought the two of them a matching pair to celebrate their two-month anniversary."

"What should we do?" Kennicott asked as he followed Greene down the exit ramp. Ahead, Darnell's van was turning into the parking lot.

"Stay in our vehicles," Greene said. "Last thing we want is for him to spot us."

Darnell drove over to an open parking spot near the store.

"Let him go inside first," Greene said, turning into the lot.

"Sure," Kennicott said. He was right on Greene's tail.

Without warning, just before he pulled into the parking spot, Darnell swung sharply to the right and sped back across the lot. Two huge black SUVs, which had been parked in the second row, backed up, swerved, and took off after the van.

Greene slammed on his brakes.

Kennicott braked hard, almost ramming into him. "What's going on?" he yelled.

"Wait," Greene said.

Darnell headed for the exit, then veered to his right again and stopped at the edge of the lot. The two SUVs rushed up right behind and parked on either side, inches away. The van was sandwiched in.

"It's a carjacking," Kennicott said, rolling down his window. He reached for his gun. "Let's go."

"No," Greene said. "Wait."

"What else could it be?"

"Stay in your car," Greene said.

A tall blond man got out of the SUV on the passenger side of the van. He walked casually to the front of his vehicle and motioned for it to reverse. The car inched backward, just far enough to allow him to get closer to the van, but still blocking its passenger-side door. He looked at Aaron and gestured for him to wind down the window.

"Shouldn't we move in?" Kennicott asked.

"Absolutely not," Greene said.

"What's going on?"

"Wait."

The window on the passenger side of the van rolled down and Kennicott saw Aaron stick his head out. The blond man started talking to him.

The SUV on the driver's side backed up and Darnell got out. He moved out of the way and the SUV drove back into position, blocking the door again. A burly man exited the SUV, walked over to Darnell, and shook his hand.

"What's going on?" Kennicott asked. "Is Darnell part of this?"

"I've had a few cases where this has happened, but this is the first time I've seen it live. This is an intervention," Greene said. "They're taking Aaron away. Probably to a rehab program in some remote place. That's why the other kids aren't with him. Darnell used the iPhone to trick his son into crossing the border."

Kennicott saw the blond man signal for the big man to join him. When they were together, the blond man motioned for the SUV on his side to move back until there was enough room for the front passenger door to open.

The blond man opened the door. Aaron stepped out. He was wearing the T-shirt he'd worn to his mother's visitation, the one with AARON 8 painted across the front. The two men grabbed both his arms.

Aaron looked back at his father.

"Why are you doing this?" he yelled, loud enough that Kennicott could hear.

Darnell put his hands in the air in a gesture of hopelessness.

"This was Mom's idea, wasn't it?" he screamed.

Kennicott saw Darnell say something else and nod.

"I'll escape," Aaron screamed. "You'll see."

The two men manhandled him into the SUV.

"The way these things work is that they take the kid far out in the desert somewhere in the Southwest. He'll live in a tent for at least a year. Sometimes longer. He's going to learn to make fire with a flint. Tough, basic stuff. Then they'll slowly reintegrate him back into urban life."

"Sounds intense," Kennicott said.

"One counsellor for every two kids. These programs cost a fortune. Mostly it's kids sent by their super-rich parents."

The SUV with Aaron in it turned to leave. The other one followed right behind. In a few seconds both vehicles were gone. Darnell was left alone at the remote end of the near-empty lot. His defeated body slumped over the hood of his car.

"He's trying to save his son," Greene said.

Kennicott felt his throat constrict. "We have to find out," he said at last, "who killed that boy's mother."

35

"QUIET ON THE SET. QUIET ON THE SET," THE MAN IN THE HEADSET SAID, LOOKING OUT AT the audience in the TV studio.

Awotwe Amankwah reached for a glass of water on the table in front of him and took a silent sip of water. With all the front-page stories he was getting in the newspaper in the last few days, he was now being invited to do lots of TV appearances like this. To his left, the host of the show, Darren Rolland, stared into the camera, the pancake makeup thick on his broad forehead.

"Counting down, live in three, two, one." The man in the headset pointed at Rolland and the red light on the top of the camera lit up.

"Good evening, Toronto. My name is Darren Rolland, and welcome to the first televised debate between the two main contenders for the job of mayor of Toronto, Mayor Peggy Forest and the chief of police, Hap Charlton."

The man in the headset pointed at the camera on Rolland's left. He moved his head toward it nonchalantly, as if he were turning to talk to an old friend.

"Joining me tonight to question the two candidates is one of the leading journalists at the *Toronto Star*." He glanced down at his clipboard. "Awotwe Amankwah," he said slowly. "I hope I pronounced your name correctly."

"You got it just right," Amankwah said.

"Practice makes perfect," Rolland said. "Welcome to the show."

"Thanks for having me on, Darren." The show's producer had told Amankwah at least five times in the last half hour to be sure to look right at the telegenic host, never at the cameras. And always call him by his first name.

"Awotwe," Rolland said as if they were best friends, "you've been at the *Star* for a decade and a half, much of that as a court reporter. Crime, law, and order: They seem to be one of the major themes of this campaign so far. How do you see this shaping up?"

Before they went on air, Rolland had told Amankwah that he was going to ask this question. He was to make sure his answer was no more than fifteen seconds long.

"Ever since the so-called Timmie Murder, last year, when that little boy was felled by a stray bullet outside the Tim Hortons, crime has been on everyone's mind," he said.

Rolland splayed his hands out. "But you've been covering criminal trials for years," he said. "Surely you see a change. And not for the better."

"I've got an idea, Darren," Amankwah said. "Come to court with me and we'll watch a few trials together."

Rolland's eyes flickered for a moment with a this-is-my-show, don't-try-to-upstage-me look. Then he grinned and pointed a finger at Amankwah. "Watch out, I might just take you up on that." He circled his finger back toward the camera. "Time to get to the candidates and start this debate."

The two candidates were already in place, each standing behind a wood podium. Forest had on her standard campaign uniform: a dark dress, which she wore with a different scarf each day, prompting the *Toronto Sun* reporter Zach Stone to quip to his colleagues that, since Charlton had a stranglehold on this election, she had to protect her neck.

Instead of the blue blazer and open-collar shirt that he usually wore, Charlton had on a blue pin-striped suit, a white dress shirt buttoned up around his ample neck, and a red tie.

Rolland was the moderator, and he kept to a tight agenda. The first set of questions were about taxes, then the state of city parks and the candidate's stands on building more subways. Forest spoke in a nasal monotone that made everything she said sound excruciatingly boring.

In contrast, Charlton's delivery was passionate, dynamic. The man was a natural, and the audience, although told before the show that they could not chant or cheer in any way, greeted each of his answers with rousing applause.

"And now let's turn to the question that's dominating this campaign," Rolland said. "Crime. Awotwe, you're the expert, why don't you ask the first question on this topic?"

Without hesitating, Amankwah looked right at Charlton. "Chief Charlton, the *Toronto Star* has learned that tomorrow morning, eight distinguished defence lawyers will publicly release a letter outlining their concerns that in the last three years members of the Toronto Police Service were engaged in illegal activities with numerous prostitutes throughout this city. The allegations include sexual assault, extortion, and theft."

Rolland stiffened.

Amankwah had expected Charlton to look surprised. But he didn't.

"These allegations all pertain to the period when you were chief of police," Amankwah said. "Were you aware of them?"

Forest looked at Charlton, a spark in her eyes. At last, she seemed to be thinking, here was a chink in her opponent's armour.

Charlton undid his suit jacket, loosened his tie, and undid the top button of his shirt. "There, that feels better." He smiled and he shook his head, a sad look on his face.

"Awotwe, I'm so glad you asked me that question. Of course I've known about this for some time. In my forty years of policing, it's by far the most distressing thing I've encountered. But as the chief, sometimes you have to keep quiet about things until everything is in place. Your timing with this question is perfect. This evening, just before I walked into the studio, I issued a press release telling the citizens of Toronto that I've authorized a full and complete, no-holds-barred, departmental investigation into these allegations. More than five thousand four hundred brave men and women serve and protect the citizens of our city, put their lives on the line each and every day. And there's no way I'm going to let a handful of rotten apples destroy the best police force in this country."

Rolland put his hand over his mike, tilted his head toward Amankwah, and whispered, "Great stuff."

Forest's shoulders slumped. She looked like she'd sprung a leak in back. Thunderous applause broke out in the audience. Charlton beamed a self-satisfied grin.

But all Amankwah could think was that someone had tipped off the chief. He had seen this train was about to leave the station and had run hard to get out in front of it.

36

HOWARD DARNELL LOOKED LIKE A MAN WHO WAS BARELY HANGING ON, KENNICOTT thought. It was like watching someone slip into a pit in a slow and horrible descent.

At Darnell's suggestion, they'd arranged to get together early this evening at the local coffee shop in the Beach where they'd first met, instead of at police headquarters. It was a good idea, Kennicott thought, to go to a place where Darnell would feel comfortable, and at night the atmosphere in the café was relaxed. But from the pained look on his face as he walked in, Kennicott knew there was nothing he could do or say to give him much comfort.

"Good evening , Mr. Darnell," Kennicott said, standing up to greet him. He'd taken a seat in the back this time. More private.

"Evening, Detective." Darnell's skin was sallow. "I appreciate you coming down here tonight."

"Happy to be here," Kennicott said as they both sat. "How are the kids?" He wondered if Darnell would tell him about taking Aaron to Buffalo this morning.

Darnell put his face in his hands, and shook his head.

Kennicott willed himself to sit still. Watch. Listen. Wait. Don't move.

At last Darnell lifted his head. His eyes were red. "I probably should have told you this before." He spoke softly. "Aaron, my oldest son. He's been a mess for a long time. He was the main reason Jennifer came back after we split."

"What kind of a mess?"

"Drugs," Darnell said, louder. "It started with graffiti when he was thirteen. Then he got into dope and he started dealing. He was in way in over his head. Nothing we tried worked. Private schools. Counselling. Rehab programs. A few days ago I told him I was taking him to Buffalo to buy him the new iPhone. I had to get him across the border. Jennie set this up two months ago, and if we missed this date, it would have taken at least another two months, maybe more.

This morning I drove him down and he was seized in the parking lot of an electronics store and whisked away. It was horrible, but we had to do it. He's now somewhere in the desert in northern New Mexico, and he'll be there for at least a year."

We had to do it. Jennifer was still alive in Darnell's mind, Kennicott thought. He shook his head, feigning surprise. "A year?"

"Maybe longer. I know parents always say their kids are bright, but you have to understand that by the time Aaron was ten, he was building his own computers. He's off-the-chart gifted. But he's so unbelievably manipulative. He was destroying the whole family."

"What about your other two children?"

"I hated to do this at such a bad time, but I had no choice. They say they're upset he's gone, but I know they're also relieved."

"Did Jennifer know about this?"

Darnell squared his hands in front of him and put his chin on top. "This was all her doing. She found the program. Insisted we had to do it. We couldn't get funding, and it's incredibly expensive. He's our son. Secrecy was absolutely crucial. I couldn't tell anyone. Not even you. I hope you don't mind."

"Why should I mind?" Could anyone be more polite than Darnell? Kennicott wondered.

"There's another thing I didn't tell you."

"What?"

"Last night I got all of Aaron's drug stuff out of the house."

"What did you do?"

"I took all his dope, his scales, his water pipes. Everything. Put it all in a big green garbage bag. I was convinced you guys were going to get a warrant and search the house and then he would get arrested again. That would have been the worst. I know this sounds crazy, but I took my canoe out of the garage and portaged it down to the lake. I paddled way out and tossed the bag overboard."

"Really?" Kennicott said. "People do things like this when they're in grief. I love canoeing too. But I've never done it in the middle of the night."

Darnell laughed for the first time since Kennicott had met him. "You should try portaging a canoe through the city. I had to wait for the all-night streetcar to pass before I crossed Queen. I wonder what the driver thought."

Kennicott smiled. Was Darnell really so naive that he wouldn't think the police had been following him? Or was he a master manipulator who knew exactly what was going on and was offering up an explanation to throw him off track?

Darnell grew somber again. "I'm assuming you still have no news for me on the case," he said.

"Afraid not. I know it's frustrating," Kennicott said.

Darnell shook his head. "You still don't know who Jennie was with in that motel?"

"No."

Kennicott had breached this sensitive topic earlier. He'd asked Darnell if he could think of anyone his wife would be meeting like this. He made a point of not using the term "having an affair."

"I keep racking my brains," Darnell said. "I guess being a Crown, and seeing so many people mess up their lives, she'd got very good at keeping secrets from me."

They sat in silence. Darnell rubbed his eyes. "My old firm has offered me my job back," he said.

"That's good news."

"They're just trying to be charitable. I'm not going to take it. The kids need me around right now."

"Understandable. Maybe in a few months."

"It's time for me to do something else with my life. I'm thinking of opening up a fruit-and-vegetable shop down at this end of the Beach, if you can believe it. I hadn't turned on a computer since Jennie was murdered. But I took this afternoon to do some research and I couldn't help looking up the news on this case. One of the articles talked about you."

Kennicott had been wondering if Darnell would ever find out his background. Hap Charlton, who was the chief of police at the time he quit his law firm and became a cop, knew how to get publicity. The press had eaten up the story of the lawyer who turned cop after his brother was murdered, and it followed him around like a bad shadow.

"So you know what it's like to talk to a homicide detective who's investigating a murder in your family."

"Yes, and now I'm that detective."

"But you're also a victim. Your brother's murder is still not solved."

"That's right." Kennicott looked straight at Darnell. "Like you, I have to wait."

"The detective on your case was Ari Greene, wasn't it?" Darnell asked.

"He still is."

"I met him for the first time at the funeral home. He seems like a shy man."

"Greene's quiet."

"I remember his name because Jennie did a few murder trials with him."

"I was involved in some of those."

"Jennie talked about him a lot. I could tell she liked working with him."

Kennicott felt his heart rate speed up. His mind went back to the funeral home. Greene had looked so ill at ease. He was usually so calm but he'd been awkward when he met the kids. Then he'd left abruptly. And before that, the first time they'd met at the bakery he'd seemed upset. Totally out of character.

From the corner of his eye, he saw someone approach the table. It was Francis, the café regular, with a newspaper in both hands. "E-e-e-excuse me, Mr. Darnell," he said. "I found an article a-a-a-about the Vikings."

"Great, Francis," Darnell said. Endlessly patient.

Francis looked at Kennicott. "My name's Francis like Francis Tarkenton who played for the Minnesota V-V-V-Vikings and lost three S-S-S-Super Bowls."

"Nice to meet you." Kennicott shook his hand. But his mind was elsewhere. Something had tweaked in the back of his brain. *He was a white man. He was tall with big shoulders. His pants were made of a nice material.*

"I-I-I've got to clip the-e-e-ese articles," Francis said, before wandering off.

"Francis has been here every day since the café opened three years ago," Darnell said.

"It's nice the way people treat him," Kennicott said, distracted. This idea that had just come to him was so improbable. But . . .

"Everyone pitches in," Darnell said. "The Beach really is a community."

"In Welland, at the visitation, did you speak to him for very long?" he asked.

"To who?"

"Detective Greene."

"We chatted for a minute or two. He seemed uncomfortable being there. Then an old high-school friend came up to talk to me. I guess it's tough for you guys, losing someone you work so closely with and still having to deal with victim's families as professionals."

"Sometimes I think it's the most important thing we do," Kennicott said, thinking, *I remember his name because Jennie did a few murder trials with him. Talked about him a lot.*

He thought back to the last two murder trials he'd done with Greene. Raglan had prosecuted both of them. And both were during the time she had left Darnell.

It was unbelievable. It couldn't possibly be. And yet.

His mind went to something he had seen in Sadura's drawings of the man on the scooter. He had copies on his desk. Even though it was late, he had to get back to the office and take a closer look.

37

GREENE KNEW ALL THE VEHICLES THAT REGULARLY PARKED NEAR HIS HOUSE. THAT'S WHY the nondescript Toyota down the street from his front door caught his eye when he drove home at the end of a long day. He could see someone was in the driver's seat but not much more. He'd been wondering whether Kennicott suspected him and had put him under surveillance. But surely if he had, it would have been a hell of a lot less obvious.

He went inside, making a point of not staring at the car, and ate some Mexican food he'd picked up at a local restaurant while catching the end of Hap Charlton's debate with the mayor on TV. When he was done, he peeked out the front window. The car was still there.

To hell with it, he thought. He grabbed his car keys, walked quickly out the door, got into his Oldsmobile, and gunned it out of the driveway.

He tore past the Toyota and swung around the block, fast. But not so fast that the car couldn't follow him. It did. He cut through three or four streets, turning quickly. The car stayed close behind. At a T-intersection, he signaled left, then swung right and turned again at the next street, sure that whoever was following him wouldn't be able to keep up.

When he came back to the bottom of his block, he slammed his car into park, jumped out, and hid behind a big willow tree.

A few seconds later the Toyota drove up and parked behind his Olds, right under a streetlight. The driver's door opened and an elderly man wearing a suit and bow tie got out, an aged briefcase in one hand.

Without looking around, he walked to the front of the Olds and opened his case on the hood. Greene heard the click of a pen. The man wrote something on a small piece of paper and slipped it under the windshield. Then he walked straight back to his Toyota, started the car, and drove away.

Greene waited for about five minutes before checking his car. He found a business card, printed on simple white stock, tucked in under one of the windshield wipers. It read: ANTHONY CARPENTER, QC, LLB, AND CERTIFIED SPECIALIST IN ESTATES LAW, 500 DANFORTH AVENUE, TORONTO, ONTARIO, M4K 1P6.

He flipped it over. On the back a yellow sticky note was attached with a message in neat handwriting:

Mr. Greene, please come to my office at twelve noon tomorrow regarding my client, Ms. Jennifer Raglan, deceased. She suggested we should not communicate by means of telephone or electronic media. Please bring a one-hundred-dollar ($100.00) bill for the purpose of my retainer.

38

"WELCOME TO YOUR EARLY FRIDAY MORNING, DETECTIVE KENNICOTT," FRANCINE HUGHES said, giving him her usual greeting. The veteran receptionist at Homicide was the keeper of all administrative details for the squad, including the officers' schedules.

"And to yours," Kennicott replied. "Plans for the weekend?"

"Not really. Clean my apartment. Watch the telly."

Hughes was an older woman who, he'd long ago learned, was keen on knowing everyone else's private business but evasive about her own. He suspected she had few friends, and that was why in part she was so enthusiastic about her job.

"Hard to believe it's only been four days since the murder, isn't it?" he said, hovering near the edge of her desk while she opened the logbook and marked him as "in."

She looked up, her face sad. "Jennifer. I mean who would have thought such a terrible thing. And those poor children."

"By the time I started here, she'd stepped down as head Crown. Did she used to come by often?" he asked.

"More than the other head Crowns ever did. She was a very hard worker. But always had time for a chat. A few years ago when my mother was sick, she asked about her every time she was here."

"Detective Greene and I worked on two murder trials with her," he said. "Greene must have known her well."

"Very," she said. "He took two days off after she died. Can't say I blame him. He always tries to be the strong, silent type, but I could see how see how upset he was."

"It's hard to imagine Greene taking any days off," he said. "He's always in at work so early."

"That's Ari for you," she said, her eyes warming with affection. "I'm always telling him that he works too hard. Take some long weekends in the summer, for goodness' sake. A few weeks ago he told me he'd be coming in later on Mondays for a while and I said it's about time."

There were many facts in the case that Kennicott had been careful to not let anyone but Alpine and Greene know about. Probably the biggest one was that Raglan had booked into a motel on Kingston Road on each of the five Monday mornings before her murder.

"That's hard to believe," he said. "He always seems to be here when I get in in the mornings."

"Well, take a gander at the logbook." She turned it toward him, open to the charts for August and September.

They were easy to read. For the five Monday mornings before the murder, and on September 10, Greene hadn't come in to work until one in the afternoon.

"I was very happy for him," she said. "First time in years he's taken time off for himself."

"Really." His eyes were glued to the times on the chart. He could feel his hands starting to shake.

"A few days ago he told me his Monday-morning vacations were over and that next week he'd be back to his usual routine," she said. "To me, though, he still looks tired. I'm sure he misses Jennifer, just like we all do."

"I'm sure he does," he said, handing her back the logbook before it fell out of his hands.

39

THE LAW OFFICE OF ANTHONY CARPENTER WAS ON THE SECOND FLOOR ABOVE A GREEK REStaurant, accessed by a long, narrow staircase. A receptionist who introduced herself as Mrs. Stanopolis showed him straight into Carpenter's office, a highceilinged room with fake wood panelling that Greene thought had probably been installed in the 1960s, and a pine desk that appeared to be even older. As did the standing lamp in the corner, the battered steel filing cabinet beside it, and the high-backed leather chair where Carpenter sat. He wore a bow tie that was clipped on at a crooked angle and plastic-frame glasses with lenses as thick as a thumb.

"My apologies for being so circumspect yesterday," Carpenter said as Greene took a seat across from him. His desktop was empty. "But my client's instructions were very specific."

"Jennifer?" Greene said.

"Yes, Ms. Raglan. She told me to contact you on the evening of Thursday, September thirteenth, which I did last night, and to meet with you on the morning of Friday, September fourteenth, which I am doing now. But we can't discuss anything until I am retained. Did you bring the money as I requested?"

"I did." Greene took an envelope out of the thin leather briefcase he usually carried and passed it over.

Carpenter looked inside, fingered the hundred-dollar bill, closed the envelope, took out a pen, and wrote the date on the back. "Good," he said. He got up and pulled a file folder out of the top drawer of his ancient filing cabinet, put the envelope inside, put the folder away, pulled out another file folder, closed the drawer, and sat back down.

He smiled at Greene. "I believe in doing one task at a time. My desk is always clean."

"A good way to work," Greene said.

"Been doing this for forty-seven years," he said, opening the file. "I have here a prepared retainer agreement in duplicate. Please review the top copy and then sign both documents."

He handed Greene a ballpoint pen, his business card, and two sets of papers, each perfectly stapled in the left-hand corner. Greene read through the agreement, signed at the bottom of each copy, and passed them back.

Carpenter took a close look at his signature, put one copy in his file and the other in a large white envelope that had Greene's name typed on it. "This is for your records."

Greene put the envelope back in his briefcase.

"Now I need to go to my safe," Carpenter said. "Please wait here a moment." Without fanfare he left the room.

Greene looked around the sparse office. He tried to imagine Jennifer sitting in this same chair. Why, he wondered, would she pick a lawyer like Carpenter? And for what?

He got up, went to the window, and looked down on the busy street. He noticed a dark car pull up on the near sidewalk. He watched three men get out.

"Here you go," Carpenter said, returning to the room and sitting behind his desk.

Greene backed away from the window and sat across from him.

Carpenter was holding a sealed envelope, and he showed its back to Greene. "After it was sealed, Ms. Raglan and I both signed across the flap," he said. "My specific instructions are to deliver this to you and no one else on today's date."

He passed the envelope over, along with a long silver letter opener.

"Now, I am to leave you alone to read this for five minutes." Carpenter left the room again.

Greene looked at the signatures. He'd seen enough of Raglan's writing to know it was hers. He sliced open the envelope. Inside was one sheet of paper with a handwritten note.

SUNDAY NIGHT, Sept. 9

Ari, I'm writing to you tonight before I see you for our final motel rendezvous tomorrow. (I can't wait to see you, and I can't wait till we don't have to sneak around like this anymore!)

By the time you read this, I will have held my press conference and gone public with my terrible secret. I'll be bombarded and hounded by the press, so I'm going to lie low for a while. Once this blows over, I'll get in touch and we'll be together.

I picked Mr. Carpenter randomly so there would be no way for anyone to trace my contact with him, and through him my contact with you. I also made him promise he would never call or e-mail you.

Don't be angry that I didn't confide in you earlier. I couldn't. You had nothing to do with any of this, and this scandal is going to be so big that anyone close to it will be damaged. Give me points, at least, for keeping you out of it.

I always thought you'd wonder why I insisted on going to such extreme lengths to keep things between us secret. Well, after Thursday you will understand.

I know you will be shocked by what I was forced to do. The price of love is so very high. I had to save my son.

Always.

J.

He read the letter again and then turned the paper over. It was blank, as he knew it would be. Still, he'd been hoping there would be more words. More of her.

There was a quiet knock on the door. "I was instructed to inquire, after five minutes, if you required more time," Carpenter said, standing in the doorway.

"I'm done," Greene said. "I need a large blank envelope and some stamps."

Carpenter returned to his desk and opened a drawer. He produced an envelope and a roll of stamps. This guy must have won a ton of Boy Scout badges in his day, Greene thought.

"When did you meet with Ms. Raglan?" Greene asked.

"She came in early in the morning on the seventh, a Friday, and asked me specifically if we could meet that Sunday evening. I'd never met her before and she didn't have an appointment. She looked very distressed. We met on Sunday at four P.M. and I waived my usual weekend surcharge."

The price of love is so very high.

Greene wrote out an address on the large envelope. He looked at Carpenter's business card for the return address. He put Raglan's letter in the envelope, sealed it, put a stamp in the corner, and passed it over.

I had to save my son.

"Can you mix this in with all your regular mail and post it later today, please?" he asked.

"Consider it done," Carpenter said.

"Anything else?" Greene asked.

"Those are all of my instructions," Carpenter said.

Greene stood slowly. "Thank you, sir," he said.

They shook hands.

Two older women wearing white gloves were sitting in the lobby. The receptionist said a few words to them in Greek and they both smiled.

Greene made his way down the long staircase to the street.

The morning sun was out and it hit him in the eyes. His mind was reeling, so it took a moment for him to focus on the man standing right outside the door.

"Detective Greene," Daniel Kennicott said.

"Hello, Daniel."

Kennicott's face looked ashen. Two uniformed police officers moved in on either side of him. He knew them both. To his left was Arnold Lindsmore, a big lug of a man whom Greene had been friendly with since they were in police college together. To his right, Clyde Newbridge, Hap Charlton's nasty pal.

Good cop, bad cop, Greene thought. Nicely played, Daniel.

"Hi, Arnie," he said to Lindsmore.

"Hi, Ari." Lindsmore looked grim.

"Clyde," Greene said to Newbridge

"Ari," Newbridge replied, with a snarl.

Give me points, at least, for keeping you out of it.

Kennicott put his hand on Greene's shoulder and looked him straight in the eye.

Exactly how I taught him to do it, Greene thought as he heard the young man he'd mentored for five years, making him into a very good homicide detective, say, "Ari Greene, you are under arrest for the murder of Jennifer Raglan."

PART
FOUR

40

THE CN TOWER.

The second tallest freestanding structure in the world, and the first thing that came into view as Angela Kreitinger swung her old Toyota southbound on the Don Valley Parkway toward Toronto's downtown.

The CN Tower.

It had been the last thing she'd seen in the rearview mirror of the same Toyota six years earlier when she'd headed out of the city. Humiliated. Her life and career flip-flopped from promise to disaster.

Six years, and Kreitinger hadn't come back to Toronto once. She'd severed all ties with her friends, stopped reading the city's four newspapers, and had even avoided using the airport. Last winter, when she took her first beach vacation in a decade, she booked her flights out of Montreal and drove two extra hours each way. Happily.

On Wednesday, she'd got the call to return to Toronto to prosecute Detective Ari Greene. Her chance at redemption at last. She'd had the file, two full banker's boxes of evidence, couriered to her and had worked on it while packing up her life in Belleville, the town where she'd been marooned.

Her old vehicle must have muscle memory, she thought, because as her mind wandered over the rocky road of her past, it seemed to drive smoothly on its own down the DVP and through the city's empty, early-morning streets.

At every turn she spotted election signs. Hap Charlton's featured a photo of him with his two big fists clenched in front of his chest and the slogan VOTE HAP. TAKE OUR CITY BACK. She'd heard he was doing well in the polls, and he seemed to have more signs up than the current mayor, Peggy Forest.

She pulled into the parking lot north of the high court on University Avenue. It was before 7 A.M. and few cars were there. One had a vanity licence plate that she recognized: A F CROWN. Some things never change, she thought. Albert Fernandez was an ambitious young Crown attorney who, like Kreitinger, always got to work early and stayed late. A fellow workaholic. And a fellow true believer in early-bird parking.

She opened her car trunk. Careful of her bad back, she lifted the two boxes, marked *R. v. Ari Greene: First Degree Murder*, and roped them onto her old metal pull cart. It was the only thing she'd taken from the Toronto Crown's office when she'd left. It was creaky and one of its wheels wobbled, but she felt a loyalty to the contraption she'd used to carry files to and from court for almost twenty years.

The code for the side door entrance had changed in six years, and she had to fish around in her too-large purse to find the sticky note she'd written the new one down on. Inside the Crowns' office she inhaled the familiar smells of day-old pizza, stale coffee, and microwave popcorn, which seemed to have been stitched into the DNA of the place.

Fernandez, the only lawyer already in, was sitting at his desk in the head Crown's corner office. A picture of his beautiful Chilean wife holding a dark-haired baby was displayed prominently on the credenza behind the desk. Seven in the morning and he was impeccably dressed in a suit and silk tie.

"Hello, Ms. Kreitinger." He stood and extended his hand for a formal handshake.

"Albert, I think you can call me Angela. I was hoping that after all these years you'd loosened up a bit."

"Not yet." He smiled. "Welcome back."

"Thanks. Feels strange." She kicked the bottom box on her cart. "Looks like I jumped right back into the frying pan."

Fernandez's smile faded.

He was so well mannered and buttoned up that Kreitinger sometimes forgot that he'd come to Canada from Chile as a teenager. And although his English was excellent, he had no feel for nuance or slang. She had a hunch he'd never heard the expression "jumping from the frying pan into the fire."

"Everyone is in shock," he said. "First Jennifer is murdered. Then Detective Greene is charged."

"Thanks for giving me this opportunity," she said.

"We cleared out your old office for you," he said.

"Thanks, Albert."

Her cart seemed to have the same muscle memory as her car. It squeaked and rattled down the main corridor, turned left at the last hallway, and went down to the last room in the row. She'd always liked being at the end of the line.

Inside, the office was empty, except for the government-issue desk that had been there the day she'd started work here, a wood chair behind it and one in front. There was an institutional smell to the room. She could picture Esmeralda, the Portuguese cleaning woman she'd come to know over the years while working deep into evenings and over weekends, scrubbing hard to erase all traces of whoever had been in what she still thought of as her office.

All you get in the end is a box, she thought, looking at the blank walls.

After she'd finished university and her marriage had failed, she had packed up everything she owned, hauled it to a storage locker on College Street, and taken off. She'd spent a year hiking around the south island of New Zealand, travelling to distant parts of China that were barely opened to foreigners at the time, and fulfilled a lifelong dream by taking the Trans-Siberian Railway through all eleven time zones of what was then the Soviet Union.

She came back to Toronto in the middle of a steaming-hot summer. Opening her storage locker, she'd stared at the IKEA shelving units, three lamps that were even uglier than she remembered, a lumpy futon, two boring chairs, at least twenty pairs of shoes she would probably never wear again, boxes and boxes of books, and a coffee table she'd bought at a yard sale that desperately needed to be sanded down and refinished.

Her heart felt like she'd been walloped by a prizefighter's punch. This is it, she thought. After all I've travelled, all I've seen, all I've done. Everything I own in the world is in this box.

"Jo, do you know who's doing bail court this morning?" she heard a male voice say out in the hallway, steps from her office.

"I am," a woman replied.

The Crown attorneys were drifting into work. Kreitinger shut the door behind her, lifted the first evidence box, and plunked it on her ancient desk.

That endless ache in her heart was digging at her. The list of "I won't evers" played in her head like an old record stuck in a groove: I won't ever be a judge like my father wanted me to be – so much for *Your Honour Justice Kreitinger*; I won't ever be the successful politician that my mother had thought I would become – so much for *Prime Minister Kreitinger*; I won't ever get married again, have children, or be the kind of wonderful aunt to my brother's kids you see in the movies – so much for *Auntie Angie*. And when I retire, or get kicked out of here again, I won't even have a best friend I can travel with on package tours to the Valley of the Kings or the fjords of Norway.

I'm going to be nothing more, and nothing less, than a damn good prosecutor.

Everyone loved to talk about how Crowns never win or lose a case. Well, fuck that, she thought as she lifted the second box too quickly and felt a sharp pain in her lower right back.

Know this, Detective Ari Greene, she thought, dumping the box on her desk and reaching to massage her back, it doesn't matter that I never liked Jennifer fucking Raglan, or that you never liked me, because I'm going to get you convicted.

41

DANIEL KENNICOTT WAS SURPRISED THAT HE WAS NERVOUS. USUALLY HE WAS A CONFIDENT public speaker. It came from growing up as the younger child in an accomplished family. His father was a judge, his mother an investigative journalist, and his older brother, Michael, a top student. It meant that from a young age he'd had to hold his own at the family dinner table in debates about everything from politics to law to journalistic ethics to bass fishing.

As a lawyer, he'd had no trouble appearing in court before the toughest judges, arguing cases before the Court of Appeal, and even once before the Supreme Court.

But tonight's audience was a special group, and that's why he felt shaky.

There were twenty retired homicide detectives in the small banquet room. They got together every few months in this suburban Italian restaurant, to feast on pasta and veal and red wine. Over their after-dinner brandies they smoked cigars, and listened to young homicide detectives present their current murder cases.

Kennicott had heard about this legendary group, but this was the first time he'd been asked to attend. It was an honour, and a rare chance to get input from the top cops with years of experience in the field.

His turn didn't come until after 11 P.M. All of these men had worked closely with Ari Greene and Jennifer Raglan and so they'd saved his case till last. After everyone had pushed aside their tiramisu, he walked to the front table. He had their full attention.

"Thanks for inviting me," he said, opening the binder he'd used to organize the key documents. "I know this case has special meaning to all of us in Homicide."

He looked up and saw a number of people nod. Get right to it, Daniel, he told himself.

"At 10:39 on the morning of September tenth, police received a 911 call reporting a murder in room 8 at the Maple Leaf Motel out on Kingston Road. You all know the motel strip." Quick look back up. More heads nodded. "I arrived at 11:01 and was met by 43 Division's lead detective, Raymond Alpine. He informed me –"

There was a crash at the other end of the room. Kennicott looked up. The door had flown open and in walked Hap Charlton, who had officially announced he was running for mayor a few days earlier. He was accompanied by Clyde Newbridge, one of the cops who had helped Kennicott arrest Ari Greene.

All heads turned. Then everyone stood and applauded.

"Hap, Hap, Hap," someone chanted, and everyone joined it.

Newbridge dragged out a couple of seats for them near the front and sat in one of them. Charlton, still standing, took an exaggerated bow, then put his hands up to quiet everyone down. "Thanks, gents," he said. "Who's got a fucking cigar?"

Someone passed him a cigar and a lighter. Someone else poured him a glass of wine. He lit up, took a deep drag, let out a big cloud of smoke, and threw back most of the wine. "Ah, that's better. Don't let me interrupt. I came to hear about Ari's case. Off the record, or course."

All eyes turned back to Kennicott.

He walked them through the evidence step-by-step. Taking his time. Talked about the murder scene and showed them a blowup picture he'd brought of the kicked-in bathroom door. Then showed them the girl Sadura's drawing and pointed to the boots the driver of the scooter was wearing.

"You all recognize these," he said. "Same police boots everyone's worn for thirty years."

Everyone smiled.

He told them how he'd checked Greene's attendance at the squad's offices with Francine Hughes, whom they all knew very well. Then how he got Greene's cell-phone records and saw that Raglan had called him from the Coffee Time at 9:56:12, and finally the arrest.

He scanned the crowd. All eyes were on him. "Greene's bail hearing is set for Wednesday. Angela Kreitinger has been brought in to be the lead Crown. Judge is Norville. We think it's fifty-fifty she'll let him out. Questions?"

"How good a match is the footprint on the bathroom door to his boot?" one of the retired detectives asked.

"It's not bad, but no slam dunk," Kennicott said. "We're getting an expert opinion. I expect he'll say that it is, at best, possibly the same boot. It will be a good piece of circumstantial evidence, along with the girl's drawing. No more."

"No defensive wounds on Jennifer?" another man asked. "What about under her fingernails?"

Kennicott shook his head. "No skin. No hair. Nothing to get DNA. There was a bit of glue and paper under the nail on her right forefinger. She was probably taking a label off something. And bits of leather under a few others. If you look at the girl's drawing, it looks like he's wearing a leather coat and gloves. Even if she'd tried to scratch his arms, nothing would have stuck."

Someone else spoke up. "Rule number one in homicide is that the killer always leaves something behind. You telling us you don't have anything?"

Kennicott shook his head. "Not yet. Detective Zeilinski is the ident officer, and you all know how good she is. But we don't have a thing. Greene knew what he was doing. Gloves, boots, helmet, he'd totally sealed himself off."

"What about the scooter?" Hap Charlton asked. "Find it and you are half-way home, aren't you?"

"I've instituted a search in the area around Greene's house," Kennicott said.

"How big is your perimeter?" Charlton asked.

"Two kilometres," Kennicott said.

Charlton shook his head. "Make it five," he said.

Kennicott realized it wasn't a suggestion. It was an order.

42

PRISON VISITS AT THE METROPOLITAN TORONTO WEST DETENTION CENTRE TOOK PLACE IN a row of glassed-in booths, the prisoners on the inside, family, friends, and lawyers on the outside. Everyone sat on hard steel stools, and the only break in the separating glass was a wire grille atop a narrow ledge at elbow height. This meant both prisoner and visitor had to bend down to talk. It was awkward, especially for taller men, such as Ari Greene and his lawyer, Ted DiPaulo.

This was their last chance to prepare for his bail hearing, set for the following day. Greene was still getting used to his fate being in the hands of another person, even a talented lawyer such as DiPaulo. It reminded him of when he was fourteen. He'd shattered the femur of his left leg while playing football at school. In the ambulance he overheard the two attendants talk about amputation. He remembered watching the surgeon examine him in the emergency room before they put the gas mask over his face, thinking before he lost consciousness that this man will determine whether or not I lose my leg.

"I found out who the Crown is going to be," DiPaulo said, putting his briefcase by his side. Because Jennifer Raglan had been a local Crown attorney, an out-of-towner had to be brought in to prosecute the case to ensure there'd be no appearance of prejudice.

"Who is it?" Greene asked, looking at him through the thick glass, which was discoloured by a large greasy mark.

"Angela Kreitinger." DiPaulo frowned.

"Angie?" Greene said. "You're kidding."

"I'm not. The Argyle case was six years ago. They say she's cleaned up her act since she moved to Belleville."

Greene sat up. Rubbed his hands across his face.

The Argyle case had been one of his first homicides. Billy Argyle was a Bay Street tax lawyer who was found one summer evening after work in his red convertible, a bullet through his brain. Greene soon found out that his grieving widow, Verna, was having an affair with George, her handsome fitness instructor. It looked like an airtight case against the two of them.

DiPaulo was running the Crown's office back then, and he had picked Kreitinger to take the case. She was tough and competent. The kind of take-no-prisoners prosecutor defence lawyers hated to deal with, and a good choice. But, unknown to anyone, she had a serious drinking problem that she'd managed to hide for the decade and a half she'd been on the job.

The trial of the lovers pitted Kreitinger against two of the top criminal lawyers in the city, and she cratered under the pressure. On the morning of her key cross-examination of the widow, she didn't show up in court until 9:45. She was drunk.

DiPaulo was forced to take over the case at the last minute and adjourn the case for a day. He quickly discovered all sorts of errors had been made, including Kreitinger's failure to disclose a key receipt from a gas station across town that provided the fitness instructor with an alibi. The next morning George the personal trainer pled guilty to accessory after the fact to murder "by persons unknown" for a sentence of two years less a day. Verna walked out of the courtroom on the arm of her counsel, Canton Carmichael, and greeted the press in full victim mode.

"I'm grateful that justice has been done," she said, handkerchief to her eyes. "I certainly hope that, next time, the police do a better investigation before they jump to conclusions about innocent people like myself."

Greene was furious, and swore he'd never let a case of his go south like that again.

The fallout in the Crown's office had been swift. The attorney general wanted to fire Kreitinger, but the union jumped to her defence. After weeks of tense negotiations, she'd agreed to go to the States for six months of rehab, then when she came back to transfer to a job in a small-town Crown office.

"Has she been in Belleville all this time?" Greene asked, leaning back down to talk through the grate.

"Yeah. And apparently she's been clean. They stuck her in bail court for a few years, and she's slowly worked her way back up to major cases."

"It's ironic, you know," Greene said. "Kreitinger never liked Jennifer. She was always trying to compete with her."

"Now she gets another chance to prove herself," DiPaulo said. "She's going to fight your bail application to the death."

"Pedal to the metal, only gear Angie knows," Greene said.

"Kennicott will be on the stand, and I plan to poke some holes in his investigation," DiPaulo said. "It's going to be hard for you to see him testify against you."

"I'm fine with it," Greene said. But DiPaulo was right. It would be emotional, for both of them.

"Then your dad is going to testify. I'm going to propose twenty-four-hour house arrest at his home. It's the only chance we've got."

Greene winced. "Is there any chance for some wiggle room? Maybe an early curfew so I can get out and try to investigate?"

DiPaulo gave him a faint smile.

Greene laughed, as much at himself as with DiPaulo. "Okay, I get it. I'm starting to sound as unrealistic as everyone else in here, aren't I?"

"You're charged with the first-degree murder of Toronto's head Crown attorney. If I get you out and all you're allowed to do is sit in your room and go to the bathroom to take a piss, that will be a minor miracle."

Greene realized that DiPaulo was speaking to him the way he'd talk to any other client. That had been their deal when he'd agreed to take the case. Greene didn't want any special treatment.

"Got it," he said.

"Okay." DiPaulo pulled a black binder out of his briefcase and flipped through it until he came to the page he was looking for.

Greene was good at reading upside down – a trick he'd learned during many years in court, looking at people's notes from the other side of the table. He made out the heading: *Yitzhak Greene, Interview Notes.*

"We've talked about this every day," DiPaulo said, giving him a stern look. "The Crown can question your dad about every conversation you two had. It's all admissible evidence against you. I'm asking you for probably the tenth time, did you say anything to him that could possibly be incriminating? Last chance to tell me. Anything?"

Greene understood why DiPaulo was concerned, and he was smart to keep coming back to it. "As I've said. I told him what I told you in your office the day it happened. That when I walked into the motel room I found Jennifer dead. That I took off to find the person who was at the door. That I was going to tell Kennicott, but he told me not to come to the scene, and that later that day I decided not to tell him because if I did I'd be a witness and I'd be taken off the case. That I was determined to find the killer. That I knew the risk but felt I had to take it."

DiPaulo lifted his binder to read it, cutting off Greene's view of the pages. He had refused to show Greene his father's statement. He'd also made sure that after Greene's arrest, his father didn't visit or talk to Greene on the phone. This way it meant he could truthfully testify that he hadn't discussed any of his evidence with his son.

"You sure? I hate surprises," DiPaulo said. "We can't afford a misstep."

Greene closed his eyes and replayed the conversation with his father in his mind yet again. Perhaps it was the pressure of the upcoming bail hearing, or the frown on DiPaulo's face, but suddenly he remembered something.

"I just thought of this. I told my father I loved Jennifer, probably more than I realized until she was gone."

DiPaulo smiled.

For the first time in this grim visit, Greene could see that DiPaulo thought this was the type of heartfelt statement that could sway a judge.

DiPaulo took another look in his binder.

Greene trusted him. Admired his skill. But he had the feeling that his father had told DiPaulo something unexpected. Whatever it was, Greene could see DiPaulo wasn't going to share it with him. It was like the day after Greene had surgery to mend his broken leg. "Will I be able to play sports like football and basketball?" he'd asked the doctor who was reading the chart at the end of his bed. He'd taken off his glasses, looked at Greene, and shrugged. "We'll find out in a few days," was all he had said.

DiPaulo flipped to the next page in his binder. "An interesting character showed up at our office yesterday. Guy was bald on top with long stringy hair, and a jacket made from a million patches. You know who I'm talking about?"

Greene tensed. Fraser Dent had resurfaced.

"I have a lot of contacts on the street," Greene said. "Did he give you his name?"

"No. He said you'd know who he was. And to tell you this: 'It was already long gone.'"

Greene relaxed. DiPaulo was no fool. He could see the relief on Greene's face.

"Ari, we agreed I'd treat you like any of my other clients," DiPaulo said.

"One hundred percent."

"Every client holds something back, doesn't tell me everything I should know, and it can really hurt a case. I have a standard line: Tell me the truth, I can do wonders with the truth."

"Ted. She was dead when I got there."

"You've told me that already. But is there anything else?"

DiPaulo had a penetrating stare.

Greene thought about Jennifer's letter. About his last phone call with her. He couldn't tell DiPaulo about these things. Not yet. Maybe if he didn't get bail.

On the other hand, he didn't want DiPaulo to lose faith in him. He'd be foolish to hold back on this.

"Perhaps you were wondering what happened to the scooter," Greene said.

"I was waiting until after the bail hearing to ask you about it," DiPaulo said.

"Nothing to ask. I don't think it will ever be found."

DiPaulo smiled. "One less thing to worry about."

Their eyes met through the dirty glass. "Ted, do whatever you have to do to get me out," Greene said.

"If I do," DiPaulo said, "you better be ultracareful. You slip up one time on bail and that will be it. You'll be stuck in jail until your trial." He got off his stool and grabbed his briefcase. He looked relieved to be able to straighten up.

Greene stood slowly.

Suddenly DiPaulo pointed to the grille. They both bent back down to speak. "What is it?" Greene asked.

"I knew there was one more thing. Your father asked me to tell you that he's broken up with his girlfriend, Claudia."

"Her name was Klavdiya." Greene let out a hearty chuckle. "Did he find another Russian?"

DiPaulo laughed too. "No, he said you'd be glad to know he's back with Mrs. Greenglass. Said he missed her casseroles."

"That," Greene said, "sounds like my dad."

43

"DO YOU SWEAR TO TELL THE TRUTH, THE WHOLE TRUTH, AND NOTHING BUT THE TRUTH, so help you God?" the court registrar, Mr. Singh, said.

Kennicott stared straight into his eyes and grinned. They had met a few years earlier when Mr. Singh (as he always referred to himself), while delivering newspapers to a luxury condo, had come upon an apparent murder. It was Greene and Kennicott's case. They'd admired the man and were thrilled when he'd got this job.

Kennicott didn't want to look at the audience in the courtroom, which was packed to the gills with spectators and reporters. Nor at Judge Norville, who seemed to hover over his shoulder, peering down from her elevated seat. And certainly not over at the defence table, at the man who had been his mentor for such a long time. The defendant, Ari Greene.

He put his hand on the Bible. "I do so swear," he said. He watched Mr. Singh place the book back on the far corner of his well-ordered desk.

Angela Kreitinger stood up, moved over to the standing lectern by her table, lowered it to her height, put her binder on it, and took out a pen from her vest. "Detective Kennicott," she said. She was a short, rotund woman and her voice had such an edge to it that she seemed to be barking at him, not talking to him. "How long have you been a member of the Toronto Police Service?"

"Five years."

"What is your present rank?"

"Homicide detective." He could hear how listless his voice sounded.

"How long have you been at Homicide?"

"Four months."

"Do you know the accused?"

"Yes."

"Have you ever worked on any cases with him?"

"A few."

Kreitinger scowled. Clearly she wasn't happy with his staccato answers. She walked out from behind the lectern to face him and crossed her arms. "Detective, can you please tell us about the matters that bring you here to court today?"

This was a typical lazy Crown-attorney question for cops. It was code for *I haven't had time to read this file – or I haven't bothered to. Why don't you fill me in.* But he knew Kreitinger had read every word in the Ari Greene file at least a dozen times and there wasn't a lazy bone in her body. This was her way of saying, *Okay, Kennicott, you want to play the reluctant witness to protect your pal Greene, well, fuck you.*

He looked at her and she smirked back. "Detective, do you wish to refer to your notes to refresh your memory?" she asked.

"I don't need my notes." A surge of anger that he'd been keeping in check since the arrest coursed through his body. Greene had lied to him. Betrayed him. The magic of the courthouse, he thought. The place where raw emotions are laid bare.

"On June first, I became a member of the homicide squad, largely as a result of the work I'd done over the years for Detective Ari Greene."

"Mr. Greene, the accused?" Kreitinger asked.

She couldn't wait to strip Greene of his badge, call him "Mr." not "Detective," and the "accused" and not the "defendant," Kennicott thought.

"Yes," he said.

"And do you see that person in court today?"

Fuck you back, Kennicott thought. She was forcing him to look at Greene. He shifted his gaze. Greene was well dressed, as usual, but his skin was sallow and it looked as if he had lost weight. He tilted his head and met Kennicott's eyes.

The crowded courtroom was still. The silence felt heavy. He had no idea how long it took for him to say, "Yes. Detective Greene is the gentleman in the blue suit, seated at the defence table."

Kreitinger was no fool. As she'd known, looking at Greene broke the ice and the words flowed. Kennicott focused on a spot at the back of the courtroom and recounted every step he'd taken in the investigation. His mind was back in time, not here in the courtroom.

"We found out where her three kids were at school and made sure they were safe," he said after describing the murder scene. "The forensic officer, Brygida Zeilinski, gave me Ms. Raglan's cell phone and I called Detective Greene."

"What did you two talk about?" Kreitinger asked, snapping him back to reality and all the people looking at him.

"I told him not to come to the motel." Kennicott tried to resist looking at Greene, but like some magnetic pull, his gaze was drawn to him. Greene felt it, and looked back.

Kennicott broke off his stare and looked again at the far wall. "We agreed to meet later that afternoon. He suggested a bakery downtown that a friend of his owns. After that first meeting, I'd meet with Detective Greene every night and brief him on the progress I'd made that day. I was seeking his input."

"In other words, the accused was privy to all aspects of the investigation."

"He was. A hundred percent. I told him everything. He even helped out with surveillance."

"And what was your the main focus?"

"My number one priority was to find out the identity of the man Raglan had been meeting with every Monday morning. He was our prime suspect."

"In all that time, did the accused ever tell you, or even suggest to you, that he had a personal relationship with the deceased?"

"No, he did not. Never."

"And have you since learned that he was, in fact, romantically involved with Ms. Raglan?"

"I have."

"And who do you believe was this missing man?"

Kennicott closed his eyes. "Detective Greene."

A rumble went through the courtroom.

"The accused before the court?"

"Yes."

"The same man who mentored you and guided your career as a police officer, the man you were telling everything about this investigation?"

"Yes."

"So he lied to you," Kreitinger said.

"Objection!"

Kennicott looked over and saw Ted DiPaulo shoot to his feet. The defence lawyer was a powerful man and his voice rattled through the large courtroom. "There is not a stitch of proof before this court of my client saying one word of a lie."

"That's true," Kennicott said, jumping in before the judge and lawyers could argue the point. For days he'd played back in his mind, endlessly, every conversation he'd had with Greene. He realized how careful Greene had been with his words.

He resisted the urge to look at Greene again. "Detective Greene betrayed my trust. He misled me. He used me. But," Kennicott said, "he never in fact lied to me. Never."

44

GREENE HAD SPENT A GREAT MANY HOURS IN COURT, BUT HE'D NEVER BEFORE SAT AT THE defence-counsel table. Like everything else in his life right now, it felt strange, disjointed.

The first thing he noticed was that the jury box was farther away. The Crown was given the subtle advantage of having their counsel table beside the jurors and the witness box directly in front of them. Greene was accustomed to looking straight ahead at whoever was testifying, but now, from his seat behind the defence table, Kennicott sat to his right at a forty-five-degree angle, with Judge Norville in his sight line.

She didn't look pleased by the evidence she was hearing. He couldn't blame her. It sounded terrible. A senior homicide detective had run from the scene of the crime and then misled his colleague in a crucial murder investigation.

"How did you come to arrest Mr. Greene?" Kreitinger asked. Kennicott no longer looked uncomfortable on the stand.

"It took a few days to put it together," he said. "I met with Mr. Darnell, and he told me that he'd met Detective Greene at the visitation for his wife in Welland. He said his wife had done a number of cases with Greene and spoke of him often. And that Greene had seemed awkward talking to him at the funeral home."

"I see," Kreitinger said.

"I kept thinking about the mark on the bathroom door of the motel room," Kennicott said. "The door was dented right under the door handle. That is how we are trained to kick a door down at police college. Shortly after the murder, a young girl named Sadura Sawney saw a man get on his scooter and leave a nearby strip mall. She drew pictures of what she'd seen, and fortunately she's a very good artist. I took a close look at one drawing that showed the man's boots. They looked like the standard-issue type that all police officers wear. I have a copy of the drawing here."

Good detective work, Greene thought. He felt a strange pride, even though he was the fish Kennicott had snagged.

"Objection," DiPaulo said, jumping to his feet again.

Norville raised her eyebrows. "Yes, Mr. DiPaulo?"

"Your Honour, surely this is much too remote and prejudicial to go in as evidence at this hearing."

Norville frowned and turned to Kennicott. "Let me see it," she said.

He passed the drawing over and she looked at it carefully. Then lifted her eyes toward DiPaulo. "Have you seen this?"

"My friend Ms. Kreitinger showed it to me this morning."

"They sure look like police officer's boots to me."

"And that's my point, Your Honour. A drawing by a child that *looks like* something. What weight can it safely be given as evidence before a jury? Think of how prejudicial it would be."

"You make a very good point," she said.

"Thank you, Your Honour."

Greene kept his eyes on Norville. He could see she wasn't finished.

"Don't thank me yet," she said. "Yes, during a trial I'd be hesitant to allow this drawing into evidence. But before me at a bail hearing, it's simply a part of the narrative of how Detective Kennicott came to arrest your client. I give it no more or less weight than that. Crown counsel, please proceed."

As he sat down, DiPaulo tapped Greene on the shoulder and made a thumbs-up sign below the table. Greene understood why he was happy to lose his objection. He knew DiPaulo couldn't stop Norville from looking at the drawing during the bail hearing and didn't really care. He was feeling her out for the trial. If the jury saw a drawing done of him leaving the scene at 10:41, it would be devastating. Now he was confident that Norville would keep this evidence out.

Kreitinger cleared her throat. "What did you do after you took a close look at the boots in the drawing?" she asked Kennicott, getting him back on track with the story.

"I spoke to the receptionist at Homicide, Francine Hughes, about Greene's hours on the five Mondays before the murder. He hadn't come in to work until one P.M. on any those days. This was a complete break from his pattern for years of showing up first thing in the morning. And on the day of the murder, September tenth, same thing, He got to work at one."

A low murmur from the audience behind him told Greene the mood in the crowded courtroom had shifted. Norville looked down at him from her perch, and shook her head.

"Armed with all this information, I swore out a warrant to search Detective Green's house," Kennicott said. "We already had the boot mark from the bathroom door. We'd used an ultraviolet light to highlight and photograph it. While he was working at headquarters, we went into his house and found his boots in the back of the hall closet. We took them to the Centre of Forensic Science, where they made a mould and photographed that. Then we put the boot back, without him knowing."

"Did the two match?" Kreitinger asked.

"Objection," DiPaulo said, back on his feet. "Your Honour, Detective Kennicott is a very bright and impressive young police officer, but I'm not aware that he's an expert on boot-mark identification."

Norville nodded and gave Kreitinger a withering look. "Madam Crown, please."

DiPaulo sat down.

"I'll rephrase the question," Kreitinger said. "Do you have the results back from Forensic Science yet?" she asked Kennicott.

"No, but I have the photos of both."

"Let me see them," Norville said.

DiPaulo stood.

"You can sit down, Mr. DiPaulo," Norville said, before he could say a word. "It is on the record that no expert comparison has been made yet, but as you know, I'm perfectly entitled at this preliminary stage of the proceedings to view all the available evidence, without drawing a definitive conclusion."

"Actually, I was standing to say that I agree with Your Honour," DiPaulo said. "And I'm glad you clarified that for the record."

Greene knew this was nonsense. DiPaulo had wanted to object, but he was a master at knowing when he was about to lose an argument and making the best of it.

Norville gave him a wry grin. "Thank you for your assistance, Counsel."

"My pleasure," DiPaulo said, and sat back down.

Kennicott held up two enlarged photographs of the boot marks. Even from a distance, Greene could see they looked similar. As could everyone else in the courtroom.

Norville took the photos, studied them for a few seconds, and passed them to Mr. Singh. "Have these marked as Exhibit One."

"Detective Kennicott," Kreitinger said, "what other steps did you take before deciding to arrest the accused?"

"On the morning of the murder, indoor cameras at the Coffee Time dough-nut shop located close to the Maple Leaf Motel caught Ms. Raglan calling some-one from a pay phone. I subpoenaed Greene's cell-phone records and there was an incoming call lasting one minute and thirty-two seconds from the phone at Coffee Time."

"When was it received?"

"At 9:56:12 A.M. We triangulated the location of Mr. Greene's phone at the time he received the call."

"And where was the accused?" Kreitinger asked.

"At his house."

"And how long is the drive from the accused's home to the motel?"

"I instructed Detective Alpine, who is working with me on this case, to do the same drive last Monday, starting at exactly 9:58 A.M."

"How long did it take?"

"Twenty-three minutes. He arrived at 10:22 A.M."

"I understand there was an anonymous 911 call made reporting this murder. When was that received?"

"At 10:39."

Ted DiPaulo passed a folded over note to Greene. He opened it under the table. *Think of this as practice for the trial. It will feel much worse when the jury is staring at you.*

"I thought about putting Detective Greene under surveillance," Kennicott said. "He's an experienced detective, and I was sure he'd spot us if we got too close. When we took his boots, we installed listening devices in his home and also tapped his phone, but that didn't get us anything. We put a tracking device on his car, and two days later we followed him to a lawyer's office on the Dan-forth, a Mr. Anthony Carpenter. When he walked out I arrested him for first-degree murder."

Greene remembered how pale Kennicott had looked that day. He seemed even more tired today. Worn down by the work and by his mentor's betrayal. It made him a compelling witness.

45

Greene's bail hearing. This was a perfect perch for himself and his fellow court reporters. All morning, they'd sat riveted, watching Detective Kennicott on the stand wrestle with his emotions as Crown attorney Angel Kreitinger questioned him.

It was time for cross-examination. Ted DiPaulo, who was usually energetic and confident in court, didn't have his usual swagger this morning. He looked worried.

Amankwah wasn't surprised. Kennicott's open-wound sense of betrayal by Ari Greene permeated the courtroom like a foul odor. His emotions were unusually raw for a cop on the witness stand. He'd be tough to cross-examine.

"Congratulations, Detective Kennicott." DiPaulo walked slowly from behind his counsel table and stood in front of the witness box. "I understand you have recently joined the homicide squad."

That was a smart way to start, Amankwah thought, by highlighting Kennicott's inexperience.

"Thank you." Kennicott frowned.

"How long have you been on homicide?"

"Four months."

"And this was your —"

"Yes, it's my first murder case," Kennicott snapped. "And yes, Detective Greene helped me get the job."

"And for many years you trusted Detective Greene."

"Absolutely." Kennicott was looking straight at DiPaulo, yet his eyes seemed unfocused.

"But the events of the last few days have shaken that trust to the core, haven't they?"

"Yes, they have."

Amankwah could see what DiPaulo was doing. Tackling the elephant in the room. Everyone could see how much anger Kennicott felt toward Greene and it was best to get it out in the open.

"But Detective Greene has not given a statement to the police, has he?"

"No, he has not."

"He hasn't confessed to anything, has he?"

"No. He's chosen to remain silent. As is his right."

"You have no witnesses to this crime, do you?"

"Not to what actually happened. No."

"No video, no audiotape."

"Not at this time."

"So." DiPaulo took a step closer to Kennicott. "Without going into all of the evidence, chapter and verse, you'll agree with me that this is a circumstantial case, isn't it?"

"There's no direct evidence, if that's what you mean," Kennicott said.

"It's a circumstantial case, correct?" DiPaulo raised his voice for the first time.

"It's a circumstantial case, yes."

"And you understand the question here today at this bail hearing is not Detective Greene's guilt or innocence, but whether or not he is a good candidate for release on bail. Correct?"

"Correct."

This is what Amankwah admired about DiPaulo. He was keeping Kennicott on a tight leash by asking specific, leading questions to which yes or no were the only answers.

"And you know that Detective Greene has no criminal record."

"Of course."

"That he has never been arrested before."

"True."

"That he's never been investigated by the police for any crime."

"That's right."

"And putting aside the question of whether or not he committed this horrible act, you don't believe for one moment that, if he were released on bail, he'd be a threat to anyone, do you?"

Kennicott lifted his eyes and looked at the back wall. The place Amankwah noticed he had looked at earlier, when Kreitinger was examining him. "No, I don't," he said after a long pause.

"Nor do you have any doubt that Detective Greene would come to court if he were released on bail, do you?"

Kennicott bit down hard on his lower lip. "He'd come to court."

"And if one of the conditions of the bail was that he live under house arrest with his father, you believe he'd follow it to the letter of the law, don't you?"

Kennicott's gaze drifted to the defence table. "Ari loves his father," he said. Then looked away.

It was such a simple statement. *Ari loves his father.* It didn't answer the question, but that didn't matter. Kennicott's words had been sincere. And he had used his mentor's first name. Amankwah had covered hundreds of bail hearings, and knew they almost always hinged on one key piece of testimony that could turn a judge either way. This was it. Even the arresting officer, when pressed, knew that Greene would obey his bail.

"You made this arrest because you had reasonable grounds to believe that Detective Greene committed this crime, didn't you?" DiPaulo asked.

"That's the only reason I arrested him."

"But you don't know, for certain, that he is guilty."

"That's not for me to decide. He has the right to a fair trial," Kennicott said.

"But deep in your heart " – DiPaulo paused until Kennicott made eye contact with him – "you hope that Greene has an explanation for why he misled you. You hope you are wrong about this arrest, don't you? And you hope that he's innocent."

"Objection, Your Honour."

Angela Kreitinger was on her feet. She was a little firebrand, and she was hot. "My friend very well knows that the personal opinion of this witness is irrelevant," she shouted. "We all wish that people were innocent, but wishing is not evidence."

Norville peered over her glasses at DiPaulo, frown lines creasing her otherwise smooth skin. "Mr. DiPaulo?"

Amankwah saw what DiPaulo was doing. It was an improper question, but Kennicott looked frozen in thought. DiPaulo had hit his mark and planted a seed of doubt in the competing camp.

DiPaulo ducked his head a notch, as a gesture of faint apology to the judge. "Let me try this question instead. Detective, it's occurred to you that there might have been another reason why Detective Greene misled you in the early stages of this investigation, hasn't it?"

"Objection," Kreitinger said again. "Same thing, Kennicott's personal opinion."

"No." DiPaulo raised his powerful voice and it reverberated off the courtroom's wood-panelled walls.

Every lawyer had a different tool they used in court, and Amankwah had seen most of them. Some had charm. Others humour, their good looks, or their down-home demeanour. With DiPaulo it was all about his voice.

"Just a few minutes ago, Ms. Kreitinger spent a considerable amount of time with this witness establishing that, in her words, my client *deceived* him."

This was the Ted DiPaulo Amankwah was used to seeing. He was in full command of the courtroom.

"It was the cornerstone of her examination-in-chief. She is the one who opened this door. I'm entitled to walk right in and see what's inside."

Amankwah kept his eyes on Norville as she started to nod.

"Your Honour, the Crown is leaving you with the impression that Detective Greene's actions were deceptive for all the wrong reasons," DiPaulo said. "Surely I should have the chance to see if there's another explanation."

Norville stopped nodding. "Objection overruled," she said. "Keep going, Mr. DiPaulo."

He turned back to Kennicott. "Let's cut to the chase," he said. "Imagine that, in the early hours of this investigation, Detective Greene had told you that when he arrived at room 8 at the Maple Leaf Motel he found Jennifer Raglan strangled to death. If he'd told you that then, he would have been a key witness for the prosecution, correct?"

"Witness or suspect," Kennicott said.

"And if he was a witness," DiPaulo said, ignoring Kennicott's jab at Greene, "he couldn't take part in the investigative team, could he?"

Kennicott's expression brightened, and he sneaked a look at Greene. Clearly this had never occurred to him, Amankwah thought.

"That's right," Kennicott said. "If he was a witness to the crime, he couldn't investigate it."

"Imagine that he is an innocent man who wants, more than anything, to find the killer. Knowing Detective Greene as well as you do, can you see how he'd be prepared to do something so extreme as deceiving you because he was desperate to work on the case?"

"Objection again." Kreitinger was back on her feet. "Really, Your Honour, this is a bail hearing, not a jury address."

"She's got a point," Judge Norwell said. "Move on."

"Thank you, Your Honour," DiPaulo said, with a short bow. All politeness and contrition.

He looked back at the witness stand. "This is my last set of questions, Detective Kennicott. Take us back to the time you spoke to Detective Greene, minutes after you arrived on the scene. When you called him on his cell, he said he was about to call you, didn't he?"

"He did, but –"

"Yes or no, sir. Is that what Detective Greene said to you? 'I was about to call you'? Yes or no?"

"Yes. That's what he said."

"In fact he answered the phone on the first ring, didn't he?"

"I . . . I think so."

"And he told you that he was going to come right over to join you, didn't he?"

"He said he was close by."

"Answer the question." DiPaulo's voice was cranked another notch louder. He was looking straight at Norville. "Homicide detective Ari Greene offered to come over to the scene of the crime, didn't he?"

Kennicott's lips were tight. "Yes, he did."

Amankwah could feel the mood in the courtroom shift again, like a big ship listing from one side to the other. The portrait of Greene as a lying, deceptive murderer was being displaced by one of a man willing to risk all to find the true killer.

"Officer Kennicott, according to your notes, this call was made at 11:12 A.M. Please tell the court why Detective Greene didn't come right over to the crime scene, as he'd told you he wanted to."

Kennicott nodded.

"Do you want to see your notes?" DiPaulo asked. His voice was mellow now.

"No. I remember it very well. He didn't come over because of me. I told him to stay away. This was my first murder investigation, and I didn't want it to look like I needed my mentor to be there, to hold my hand."

That was the "aha" moment, Amankwah thought. DiPaulo had set this up right from the beginning of his cross-examination when he had congratulated Kennicott for his recent promotion to Homicide. He'd goaded the young officer into being defensive about the fact that this was his first murder investigation. And he'd used it to explain what minutes ago seemed unexplainable – why an experienced police officer such as Ari Greene had not rushed back to the scene of the crime.

"Thank you, Detective," DiPaulo said. "Those are my questions. Your Honour, I believe it is time for lunch."

"Good idea," Norville said, getting up from her chair.

The registrar jumped to his feet. "All rise," he shouted,

Everyone stood. As soon as Norville was out of the courtroom, a guard came forward and handcuffed Greene. Instead of looking upset, Greene turned to DiPaulo and smiled.

DiPaulo smiled back. Amankwah knew they had both felt it. The sweetness of the first step toward freedom.

46

ANGELA KREITINGER'S BACK WAS KILLING HER. HALFWAY THROUGH THE MORNING SESSION, the pain had started in the right base of her spine then radiated down her leg. She didn't want anyone to know about it, and she sure didn't need the distraction with the defence now calling evidence and Detective Greene's father about to take the stand.

She opened her binder and turned to a fresh page. On the top she wrote, *Yitzhak Greene, Father,* and underneath: *Key questions: 1. Have you ever been charged with a criminal offence? 2. What did your son tell you about his relationship with Jennifer Raglan and her murder?*

Ted DiPaulo stood.

Until today, she'd never seen him work as a defence lawyer. He'd done a good job this morning in his cross-examination of Kennicott, using the young cop to create some doubt about Greene's guilt. He'd also fixed in Judge Norville's mind the notion that, whether or not Ari Greene was guilty, there was little question that he'd obey any bail conditions. Kreitinger could see now that Greene was going to be released. And she didn't really care. Her focus was on the trial.

She knew DiPaulo had no choice but to put Greene's father on the stand. It was impossible for his client to get bail unless the judge heard from his surety. And this was going to give Kreitinger a golden opportunity to get key evidence down under oath.

"For its first and only witness, the defence calls Mr. Yitzhak Greene," DiPaulo said in that powerful voice of his.

Before coming into court after the lunch break, Kreitinger had caught a glimpse of Mr. Greene in the hallway. He was shorter than she'd pictured, but also stronger-looking. As a witness set to testify, he'd been excluded from court this morning. She had his police file on her desk, hidden under a pile of papers. She was ready.

He walked up to the witness box with surprising speed for someone in his eighties. He wore a well-tailored blue suit and a muted red tie. His shoes gleamed as if they'd been shined by a professional, which made sense since he'd run his own shoe repair shop for decades.

Judge Norville gave him a kindly smile. "Sir," she said, "I imagine you have never been in court before."

"I was once, in 1962. Two kids tried to steal from my shop and I stabbed one in the hand with my chisel."

Damn it, Kreitinger thought. She'd hoped he would try to bury this, because she'd planned to embarrass him with it on cross-examination. Forget that. She crossed out number one on her sheet of paper.

Norville looked taken aback by his frankness. "Oh, I'm sorry, sir . . ."

"Nothing to be sorry about. I stabbed the one who had the knife." He held up his own hand and pointed to the back of it with his finger. "Right here, when his hand was on the counter. He lied about it on the witness stand. Said he was unarmed. But then his partner told the truth, so they threw the case out. I wouldn't have stabbed him if he didn't have a knife."

"I'm sure not, sir."

"I would have punched him."

Kreitinger heard laughter behind her and couldn't resist smiling herself.

He's charming the skirt off Norville, she thought, and he hasn't even started to testify.

"I'm going to let the lawyers ask the rest of the questions," Norville said. "Would you like some water?"

"Water? Why not?" he said.

Kreitinger kept her eyes on him as DiPaulo led him through his evidence: Yitzhak Greene was born in a small town in Poland two hundred kilometres south of Warsaw. Four thousand residents. There were two thousand Jews and two thousand Catholics who'd lived there in peace for hundreds of years. On September 24, 1942, the Nazis came at night and rounded up all the Jews. He and his brother and one other man were the only ones who survived. After the war, he made his way to Canada with his new wife, whom he'd met in a displaced persons camp in southern Germany.

"I saw her at the meal station. She was beautiful. Neither of us had family left, and we got married three days later," he said.

A few people behind Kreitinger sighed.

"In 1948, finally, we came to Canada," he went on. "It was hard for my wife to get pregnant. Ari is our only child."

Norville looked transfixed by him. This little man with his polished shoes had the judge, and everyone else in the courtroom, eating out of his hand. Probably best not to even bother cross-examining him, Kreitinger thought.

Next, DiPaulo had him talk about opening his shoe repair shop downtown, working six days a week with his wife, Ari growing up above the store until they moved north to the little bungalow where he still lived. How his son had gone to the nearby high school, then the University of Toronto, then was a law student, but dropped out to become a cop, and now was in Homicide.

"The chief, Hap Charlton, he guided Ari through everything. They called him Ari's rabbi," he said. "We used to laugh at that. Then my wife got sick."

"Sick?" DiPaulo asked, as if he'd never heard a word of this before. He was the master at this – only asking questions to which he knew the answers, and playing them for all they were worth.

"Alzheimer's. She died two years ago."

Kreitinger hadn't made one note. Why bother? The man was going to be the best surety imaginable. Norville was going to let Ari Greene go live with his father. She circled her note number two. All she could do now was to try to tie him to a strict house arrest on his bail.

"If Her Honour chooses to release your son on bail, can he live with you?" DiPaulo asked.

"Of course. His mother wouldn't let me touch his room when he moved out."

This set off another chorus of laughter.

Norville smiled.

"Thank you, sir," DiPaulo said. "Those are my questions."

Kreitinger was surprised. DiPaulo was such a careful lawyer, why hadn't he covered off any conversations between father and son concerning Raglan's murder? He must be hiding something. Good.

Mr. Greene shrugged. "Okay," he said, and moved to step down.

"Oh, sorry, wait a moment," DiPaulo said. "The other lawyer here, Ms. Kreitinger, the Crown attorney, might have a few questions for you."

Kreitinger's back didn't hurt at all anymore. Yes, I've got a few questions, she thought. Being a smart Crown was like being a shark, probing for that soft underbelly. It was time to strike.

47

WATCHING HIS FATHER TESTIFY COULD HAVE BEEN ONE OF THE WORST EXPERIENCES IN Greene's life. But it wasn't. His father was being remarkably calm and self-assured. He had Judge Norville eating out of his hand. That was half the battle.

When DiPaulo finished his questions, Greene shifted his gaze to Angela Kreitinger. He'd been sneaking glimpses at her all through his father's testimony. The woman was tightly wound, and he could see her mounting frustration because his father was doing well on the stand.

"Do you think Kreitinger is going to cross-examine my dad?" Greene had asked DiPaulo down in the cells during the lunch break.

DiPaulo had smiled. "Angie? She can't help herself. Just watch."

Greene watched Kreitinger walk to the lectern. She seemed to be limping a bit. Her lips were tight with determination as she opened her binder.

"Mr. Greene, you told Mr. DiPaulo that if your son is released you'll make sure he follows each and every condition of his bail."

"Of course."

"Because you understand it is important to follow the law."

"Without law we have chaos."

Greene smiled. His father knew this better than anyone else in this courtroom.

"And when you took the stand, you took an oath to tell the truth, the whole truth, and nothing but the truth."

"I did. Why wouldn't I tell the truth?"

"The whole truth, that means everything."

"I understand."

"And you will do that today."

Kreitinger had done a good job of boxing in Greene's father, leaving him no wiggle room.

Smart lawyering, Greene thought. He glanced at DiPaulo, who winked back at him. Smiling.

"Ask me any question," Greene's father said. "I'll tell you everything."

Kreitinger flipped to a new page in her binder.

"Did your son tell you he was having an affair with the victim, Jennifer Raglan?" She put her chin out at Greene's father, as if to say, *There, bet you didn't expect this question.*

"Yes," he said. Calm.

"He did?" she asked. Surprised.

"The day of the murder, my son came to see me."

"And he told you about their affair?"

"Yes. Not the details. But he told me that he loved her."

A murmur went through the courtroom. Greene kept looking at his father.

"Did he say where he was the morning of the murder?"

"Yes. At the motel."

Someone in the audience gasped.

"He told you he was at the motel?" Kreitinger asked.

"And that she was dead when he got there. He took off chasing after someone who was outside but couldn't find the person. Then in the afternoon he met with Officer Kennicott, but didn't tell him he'd been in the motel."

Kreitinger pulled out a pen from her vest. "Let me be sure I understand this." She started to write in her binder.

It was an old Crown trick Greene had seen prosecutors use time and time again. Re-ask a question when you got a good answer, and make a show of writing it down, that way you underlined the importance of the evidence.

"He said he found Ms. Raglan dead. Correct?"

"Yes."

"But then he didn't tell the homicide officer on the case. Why did he say he did that?"

DiPaulo was right about Kreitinger, Greene thought. She couldn't help herself. Even if it meant breaking rule number one on cross-examination: Never ask a question to which you don't know the answer. Her open-ended question gave his father carte blanche to say whatever he liked.

"Ari said at first he rushed around the neighbourhood trying to find the husband. He was sure the man had killed his wife and was afraid he was suicidal.

Then he was about to go back to the motel, but Kennicott called and told him not to come and that they should speak later in the afternoon. He felt terrible not telling Kennicott right away. But when he thought about it, something about how the ambulance and police arrived so quickly didn't make sense. *I taught him my whole life to be careful. There's danger out there.* Plus, he knew if he told Kennicott he'd been in the motel, then he'd be a witness at the trial and couldn't work on the –"

"Thank you, Mr. Greene," Kreitinger said. It was clear from her face that she knew her question had been a mistake.

"Your Honour," DiPaulo said, instantly on his feet. "My friend asked an important question. Why is she cutting off the witness? Let's hear the whole answer."

"But, Your Honour," Kreitinger protested.

Norville held up her hand. "Mr. DiPaulo is right." She turned to the witness stand. Greene could see she was curious and wanted to hear more. "What else did your son say?"

"He said that, if he couldn't work on the case, how was he going to find the killer. Especially when they'd realized earlier in the day that the husband was probably innocent."

Kreitinger looked deflated. She started flipping the pages of her binder, as if desperate to find a better question. Greene almost felt sorry for her. If he'd been the officer in charge of this case, he would have sent her a note that said: *Sit down, do no more damage, we'll live to fight another day.*

DiPaulo's strategy had been brilliant, Greene thought. Sucker the Crown into cross-examining his father, and have him prepared to put in the whole of his defence.

He glanced at Kennicott. He looked stunned.

Kreitinger kept flipping pages. No one spoke.

"My son is not a murderer," his father said at last, without being asked.

"Oh," Kreitinger said. Her eyes flashed back up to the witness stand. Her nostrils flared in anger. "Let me understand this, Mr. Greene. Are you telling this court that you can tell whether someone is a killer?"

Very, very big mistake, Greene thought.

His father fixed her with a stare that Ari had seen only a few times in his life, on the rare occasions he spoke about the war.

"It was two in the morning the night the Nazis came to our village. They made every Jew go into the main square. One of the soldiers pulled my daughter, Hannah, away. She was four years old. My wife, Sarah, reached for her hand. The Nazi shot my wife in the face. My two daughters were exterminated at Treblinka and I spent eighteen months there before my escape. I've seen the eyes of killers and I know what they look like. My son is not a murderer."

Kreitinger flushed beet red. Her hand went to her lower back, as if she'd been stabbed there. She didn't seem to know what to do or say.

Everyone in the courtroom was in shock. No one more than Ari Greene.

"I haven't ever spoken about this before," his father said. "Not to my second wife. Not even to Ari."

Greene had never heard his father refer to his mother as "my second wife." He felt a part of him sinking. How had all this happened? Jennifer murdered. Like his father's first wife. Sarah. He'd never even heard her name before.

"Thank . . . thank you, Mr. Greene," Kreitinger finally said. She limped back to her counsel table as if she'd been injured.

No one else in the courtroom moved.

Greene looked over at DiPaulo. His eyes were fixed on the witness box.

"Mr. Greene, we all very much appreciate you coming to court today," Judge Norville said, filling the silence. "I have no doubt you will be an excellent surety. I will release your son to live with you, under very strict conditions."

"Why not?" his father said.

That seemed to say it all.

Greene watched as his father climbed down from the witness box and nodded at DiPaulo. DiPaulo smiled back.

Greene felt the penny drop. DiPaulo knew all along his father was going to say this and the powerful effect it would have. Especially on Judge Norville, who had herself lost a child. And on himself, hearing this for the first time. Norville would see the shocked look on his face as a mark of his father's sincerity. It was DiPaulo's trump card and he'd kept it hidden, even from his own client, to ensure the revelation had maximum power.

He remembered the sign in his office that DiPaulo had read to him the first time they'd met: *A trial was after all a savage and primitive battle for survival itself.*

48

"I SURE AS HELL GOT MY ASS HANDED TO ME TODAY, DIDN'T I?" KREITINGER SAID TO KENNICOTT the minute they were back in her office.

"Could have been worse," he said.

She laughed. "I don't see how."

Kreitinger knew that nobody liked to work for a loser. A criminal trial was like a prizefight, with many tough rounds. Some you win, and some, like today, you lose badly. It was important to take defeat in stride, laugh it off, rally the troops, and move on.

"You didn't really think Norville would keep him in jail, did you?" Kennicott asked.

He was remarkably self-assured for such a young man, Kreitinger thought. But she could see that having to testify against Ari Greene had shaken him. DiPaulo had done a good job with him as a witness and had got him to question Greene's guilt.

"No, I didn't, and frankly it doesn't bother me that he's out," she said. "What's more important is that we now know the theory of the defence. That Greene came upon Raglan when she was already dead, and raced off to chase a phantom killer. Sounds like a movie, doesn't it?"

"Far-fetched," Kennicott said. He didn't sound convinced.

There was a knock on the door.

Kennicott opened it and Jo Summers marched in. She had to be close to six feet tall and had the kind of high cheekbones you see in models on the covers of fashion magazines. Then there was her beautiful blond hair that she wore tied up with a dark wooden clip. Her face was flushed and angry. "Can you believe that?" she said.

"What?" Kreitinger asked. "That Norville gave him bail?"

"No. I don't give a shit about that. But his story? Greene's a homicide detective. He walks into the motel room, sees Jennifer strangled to death, and then he doesn't tell anyone? Unbelievable. Un-fucking-believable."

"One thing is true," Kennicott said. "When I called him he said he wanted to come and meet me at the scene and I told him not to."

"Screw that," Summers said. "He could have gone back to the department and told anyone he'd been there, for God's sake."

"True."

"And when you met him that afternoon, he didn't tell you a bloody thing, did he?" she demanded.

"You're right," Kennicott conceded. "He used me."

Kreitinger was impressed. Summers was a crackerjack cross-examiner.

"Guy's a liar. He broke up Jennifer's marriage. He's saying there was someone else at the door who took off? That's a laugh. Who was it, a one-armed man?" She looked at Kreitinger. "You're the prosecutor, what do you think?"

Kreitinger's first thought was that she needed a junior lawyer on this case. Summers was smart and passionate. Pretty too. That never hurt in front of a jury. She'd be perfect.

"In most trials we never know in advance what the accused's story will be or even if he will testify. But now we know that if his father testifies, we get in the evidence that Greene and Raglan were having an affair, that he was there that morning, and that he took off."

"It's perfect," Summer said.

"Not really," Kreitinger said. "Because then the father can give his whole defence. How Greene thought there was someone outside the door and how he took off to try to find the killer. Why he misled Daniel because he wanted to investigate who killed the woman he loved."

Summers rolled her eyes. "It is such total bullshit."

"The problem is the jury will love the father. And then Greene won't have to testify."

Summers nodded. "You're right."

"We won't tell the defence this, but DiPaulo will probably figure it out. Still, we'll subpoena the father to make it look like we're going to call him. And you never know."

"I've already got him on my list," Kennicott said.

"We can't get distracted. We have to figure out how to prove this circumstantial case without the father. How do we put Greene with Jennifer and in that motel room?" Kreitinger said. She made a fist and smacked her open palm. "We have to force him into the box. Make him testify."

Summers grinned. "I can't wait to see you cross him. You'll nail him."

"One day at time. This case is going to be a battle." Kreitinger turned to Summers. "I need a junior lawyer who's prepared to put in the hours to help me with this case. It's going to be tough slogging. You interested, Jo?"

Summers beamed. "There's nothing in the world that I'd like more. Daniel, are you on board?"

It was the question that Kreitinger had wanted to ask him since they left court. She'd read his body language on the witness stand. Sensed his torn emotions. He was having second thoughts about Greene's guilt. A jury would pick up on this in a flash.

He straightened his back. "Jo. I arrested him, didn't I?"

This is interesting, Kreitinger thought. They were both young, both good-looking. And, as far as she knew, both single. They'd called each other "Daniel" and "Jo." What was that all about?

"Okay, team." She pulled the top evidence box off her trusty old cart and dumped it back on her desk. "Time to get to work."

49

"DAD, LET ME DRIVE," GREENE SAID AS THEY WALKED TOWARD HIS FATHER'S DODGE, PARKED underneath the courthouse in the lot reserved for judges. Ernest Sapiano, the shift supervisor from the jail cells, was with them. He'd arranged for Greene's father to park down here so they could drive out this way and avoid the press, who were hovering around all the usual courthouse exits.

"You're not too tired?" his father asked.

"Not at all," Greene said. "This good officer has treated me very well today."

"Thank you, sir," his dad said.

"My pleasure," Sapiano said. "Your son is a gentleman. Drive up to the gate, I'll put my card in, and you're out of here. I suggest you gun it."

It felt good to Greene to be behind the wheel of a car, just as it had felt good ten minutes earlier when the handcuffs were taken off. He zipped up the ramp and headed north on Centre Street. In his rearview mirror he saw a few TV cameramen facing in the wrong direction. A reporter heard his car, turned, and pointed at it.

"We've been spotted," he said.

"So, let them look," his father said.

"I bet there will be a bunch of camera crews at your house."

"Who cares?"

They drove in silence for a long time.

Greene had been in jail for only four days, but in that short time the city had changed. Summer had turned to autumn. There was a chill in the air. People in the street were no longer wearing shorts and sandals. And with the election officially on, campaign signs had sprouted on almost every street. Again and again they passed Hap Charlton's garish sign, with the photo of him, his sleeves rolled up, showcasing his powerful forearms.

"Looks like your old boss is going to be mayor," his father said when they got about halfway to his house.

"That's what Hap's always wanted," Greene said. "You never told me your first wife's name."

Sarah, he thought. Sarah. He didn't dare say the name out loud.

"I never wanted to tell you that story."

"I know."

"Your lawyer is a very smart man."

"He is."

"You told me you were in love with this woman who was murdered," his father said.

"I'm discovering that I was in love with someone I didn't really know," Greene said.

"What's unusual about that?" his father asked.

They drove in silence again until Greene got to his father's street. It was packed with TV trucks waiting by the curb. Cameras flashed as he passed the crowd of reporters and steered into the driveway. He put the car in park and turned to his father. "I'm going to walk you to the door. You go inside. I'll talk to them."

"What are you going to say?"

"Nothing. They don't care what I say. They want a photo. Much better that I do it head-on than look like I'm trying to hide. I'll make sure you are kept out of this."

"Okay."

"How's Mrs. Greenglass?" he asked.

"I hope you like casseroles."

He walked his father up the concrete steps to his house and waited while he unlocked the front door. As he was about to walk back down, his father grabbed his arm. "Ari, time to start thinking how you can get out of this mess."

"It all still seems unreal."

"It's very real. And don't be foolish. Just because you found out some surprises about a woman doesn't mean you weren't in love with her. You knew who she was and she'd want you to take care of yourself."

Before he could respond, his father let go of his hand and disappeared inside the house. Greene's whole body felt lighter, as if a second pair of handcuffs had been removed.

He walked over to the reporters, who were waiting at the edge of the property. They jostled around him, some stepping on the grass. Cameras and microphones were jammed unnaturally close to his face. The *click, click, click* sound of the cameras was like crickets. But louder and more annoying.

He shook his head and pointed to the feet of the reporters on the lawn. "We need some ground rules, folks," he said. "No one on my father's property. And no one says anything about his address. And no funny stuff, like saying it's in the Bathurst and Lawrence area. And no pictures of him or the front of his house. Judge Norville slapped a publication ban on the bail hearing. Simple. You play ball and I'll play ball. Agreed?"

The people on the grass stepped back to the curb. A few of them looked at each other and nodded.

"Agreed," Awotwe Amankwah said. He was one of the few reporters Greene trusted.

"I'll make a statement, then you'll all leave. Deal?"

"Deal," Amankwah said, without consulting his peers.

"Okay. You've got your picture of me. Here's my statement: 'I am grateful to Justice Norville for releasing me on bail. I look forward to the opportunity to defend myself on these charges.'"

He turned and started to walk back to the house.

"Detective Greene, how does it feel to be arrested by Detective Kennicott, the officer you trained?" someone shouted. "Detective, what was your relationship with Jennifer Raglan?" another voice said. "Are you going to testify at your trial?" a third asked. Then someone yelled, "If you get off, are you still going to work on Kennicott's brother's unsolved murder?"

That last question almost made him stop in his tracks. He longed to talk to Kennicott. Apologize. Tell him that this would only make him more determined to find his brother's killer.

Instead, he waved without looking back. Their clamour died down as he climbed the front steps. Like well-trained pets, none of them had dared step onto his father's property.

Sarah, he thought again. He pulled hard on the sticky screen door he'd opened several times a day for most of his life, and headed inside the home he grew up in.

50

THERE HAD BEEN MANY TIMES IN HER LIFE WHEN KREITINGER HAD WISHED SHE'D BEEN A MAN. And now, inside a stall in the women's washroom at the Crown's office, pissing into a bottle, was one of them.

It was part of the deal she had agreed to when she took on this case. She had to go to the Canterbury Clinic twice a week to get her urine tested. Canterbury was a no-nonsense drug-and-alcohol rehab place, different from any of the other rehabs she'd been to. It wasn't fancy. The people were friendly. They called you by your first name. No bureaucracy. No bullshit. And Marshall McGregor, the director, was no fool. Twice-a-week testing wasn't enough to stop a smart drinker, who could get the alcohol out of her system in twenty-four hours, and he knew it.

At their first meeting, she and McGregor had sat for an hour in cheap plastic chairs on a skinny little rooftop patio. It had taken him about ten minutes to tell her his life story as he chain-smoked no-name cigarettes he'd bought in Chinatown. A farm boy from Wisconsin, he'd been blessed with a great pitching arm and "too much brainpower to keep me on a tractor." A baseball scholarship landed him at Cornell right in the midst of the Vietnam War. "Then my Nixon number came up, forty-one, which was ironic since Eddie Matthews was my favourite player when I was a boy." In 1969, he crossed the border as a draft dodger, got married, had two kids, realized he was gay, and hid it for ten years with booze.

"When my wife kicked me out, I did every self-destructive thing in the book for five years, got into rehab, thought, 'Hey, I'd be good at this,' went back to school, and graduated with honours. I worked for ten years at big, fancy clinics for rich people and couldn't stand all the bullshit bureaucracy. Now I have this."

Kreitinger was a big Blue Jays fan and they talked baseball and literature and politics. Everything but addiction. When she got up to leave, he gave her a big hug. "I have to warn you, Angel, I'll pop up when you least expect it with a bottle for you to do a little pee-pee in. The big bad government is going to cover the costs of my keeping an eye on you. Even my cab fares."

Sure enough, there he'd been, sitting in the waiting room this afternoon when she left the office. What luck. After one of the worst days in court in her life.

"Rough job you have, huh, Angel?" he'd said, standing and giving her a hug.

"That's why they invented tomorrow," she'd said, hugging him back.

"Come on, my dear, do your little tinkle" – he'd waved a brown paper bag at her – "then I'm taking you to the game. Those Republican Yankees are in town, and I love to hate them."

The clinic had bottles with broad rims, which made the task of giving a urine sample a little less humiliating. She loosened her bladder and felt the jar grow warm in her hand. She finished, put the top on tight, washed her hands twice, put the bottle back in the paper bag, and headed outside.

It wasn't alcohol that was a problem for her anymore. It was the little blue pills, Percocets, that she'd started taking two years earlier to relieve the pain in her twisted back. It had all started innocently enough. Her car was rear-ended in the Walmart parking lot, and she thought all that she'd suffered was a mild case of whiplash.

But it turned out she had a bad curvature in her spine, made worse by her being overweight and doing no exercise. A week after she was hit, she ended up one night in the emergency department, writhing in pain. She was given a little blue pill, and half an hour later, her body felt the sweet glow it had craved for the whole six years she'd been on the wagon.

She was worried about Marshall McGregor. He was street-smart and wise to addicts' tricks. He took her paper bag and put it into his knapsack. "It's a beautiful night and the dome is open. A client of mine's a lawyer with seats right behind third base. We can jeer at A-Rod and Jeter and eat candy popcorn."

It sounded a thousand times better than going home alone to the one-bedroom apartment-hotel suite she was renting month to month. Until she knew whether she would be able to stay in Toronto, her whole life was in storage. Again.

"It'll be a lovely walk," he said once they'd passed through the security doors and were outside. "Besides, it'll be good for your back."

"You read my file, didn't you," she said.

"Every word of it, my dear. And remember. My instructions are to keep you off the booze and report back that you're not drinking." He linked his arm with hers. "As for keeping you off the Percs, that's between you and me."

"Thanks," she whispered, and squeezed his arm, trying not to cling to him.

51

talk-show host in the city would rant and rave about a police officer charged with murder being given bail. As a result, she'd locked Greene down with strict conditions.

Essentially he was under house arrest. He wasn't allowed to leave his father's home "except for medical appointments, visits to his lawyer, or for religious purposes." He couldn't "associate with any person known to him to have a criminal record" and he had to "keep the peace and be of good behaviour."

He'd been in his father's house for only two days, and already he was going stir-crazy. Some leaves had fallen and he'd raked the square front lawn within an inch of its life. For years he'd taken out all his meals from all sorts of different restaurants throughout the city, and now he was having to teach himself to cook all over again. His father had become an avid CNN watcher, and the endless loop of overexcited news was on all day long.

He'd already made about twenty pots of tea, started and tossed away five paperbacks, cleaned up the basement, and made list after list of things he'd like to do to investigate Jennifer's murder, if only he wasn't locked down like this.

Sleep was a real problem. He couldn't get to sleep, and when he did, he couldn't stay asleep because he kept replaying each step in his relationship with Jennifer. Seeing everything from a different angle and feeling like a fool. How could he have been so naive? So unaware of what was really going on?

And an unexpected and unwelcome emotion was creeping in: anger. It was ridiculous, but still that's how he felt. Mad at her for not being honest with him. For using him. For not turning to him for help. If he'd known what was going on, maybe he could have saved her, but now she was gone and he was stuck in this prison of a world, without her.

Tonight, even though he hadn't gone to synagogue in years, he was going to go to Friday-night services with his father. Anything to get outside, and out of his head, for a few hours.

He was putting on his suit when there was a knock on the front door. It better not be a reporter, he thought as he went to answer it. He yanked the door open to find Arnold Lindsmore, one of the cops who'd helped Daniel Kennicott arrest him, standing there. His considerable frame took up much of the small concrete porch.

"Arnie," Greene said to the officer he'd known since police college. "What are you doing here?"

"You're under house arrest, Ari. Remember?"

"You checking up on me? Here I am."

"Looks like you're going out."

"With my dad. To synagogue. For religious purposes."

They both laughed.

"Trust me, I don't usually spend my Friday nights with a bunch of old Jewish men," Greene said.

"Sounds like a hot date to me."

"I've got to get out of here."

"Me, I don't blame you. I'd be going nuts stuck inside."

"I'm having a lot of fun. There's still an old tabletop hockey in the basement I got when I was a kid. Now I'm learning to play it against myself. I take a shot, get up, go to the other side, take another shot, go back again."

"Boy, that sounds exciting."

"A thrill a minute. You want a cup of coffee?"

"Sure." Lindsmore lumbered in. He saw Greene's father and his face lit up. "Hello, Mr. Greene. We met once, years ago, when Ari and I graduated police college. I was a lot thinner then."

"And I was taller," Greene's dad said. "I only make Sanka, not that fancy stuff. And Ari doesn't drink coffee."

"I know," Lindsmore said.

Greene's father looked closely at Lindsmore. "You two go on in the living room. I'll bring the coffee."

No one could read people as well as his father, Greene thought. They could both tell Lindsmore had something to say to Greene in private.

They sat on the old sofa. Greene said a silent thank-you once again to his father's ex-girlfriend Klavdiya for getting him to throw out the decades-old plastic cover.

"How come you're the one doing this checkup?" Greene asked. "Usually it's some rookie cop who runs around knocking on doors."

"It was Kennicott's idea."

"Kennicott?"

"He thought you might be a little lonely."

"My dad and I are playing gim rummy for two or three hours a day. What else could a guy want?"

"Seriously, he thought you might need some help."

"Help? With what?"

Lindsmore leaned closer. The fat in his stomach rippled over his waistband as he bent forward. "Help you figure out who the fuck killed Jennifer."

PART
FIVE

52

DANIEL KENNICOTT BENT DOWN TO LACE UP HIS OLD RUNNING SHOES. HE WAS ON THE SIDE-walk a block north of Jennifer Raglan and Howard Darnell's house, about to follow Raglan's footsteps on the last morning of her life. Run a few miles in her shoes, so to speak. He checked his watch. It was 8:30, the time he'd estimated she would have left home on her jog to the Maple Leaf Motel.

It had been a long time since Kennicott had run any substantial distance and his old running shoes were worn down at the heel. A decade earlier, when he was in law school, he was so bored that he'd spent hours training for and running in marathons. But during his five years as a lawyer, and another five as a cop, he'd had neither the time nor the inclination to keep at it. If he started getting serious about running again, he'd need a new pair of shoes, he thought as he started up the hill, heading north.

It took him about ten minutes to jog up through the hilly, leafy residential neighbourhood. By the time he hit Kingston Road, he could feel the strain in his calf muscles and he was sweating. Heading east, everything gradually changed from upscale residential to tacky commercial strips and the four-lane street became a six-lane thoroughfare divided by a concrete barrier. The blocks grew longer. The traffic went faster. And a cold wind bore down on him, chilling his skin.

He was the only one running. There was no street life and no place he could see where on a Monday morning two weeks ago someone would likely have noticed a female jogger with a backpack.

By the time he got to the Coffee Time, where Raglan had been caught on video, he was getting a second wind. Inside, he saw the phone where she'd called Greene, and checked his watch. It was 9:39, ten minutes before she had arrived here. He bought a coffee and waited. At exactly 9:58:33 he walked out, just as she had done.

This part of the strip was even uglier with the sudden profusion of cheap motels. The names were as colourful as the places were tacky: the Lido, the Grand, the Park, the Manor, the Americana.

He walked by the strip mall where Greene had parked his scooter. He saw the Money Mart, where young Sadura had seen the back of a tall man with a white man's bum. Hap Charlton's rugby-team poster was still up. Where someone had originally spray-painted HAP IS A HAZARD, the word "hazard" had been spray-painted over, except the H had been left, followed by the capital letters ERO.

He checked his watch when he got to the Maple Leaf Motel and it was 10:02:41. It had taken four minutes to walk here from the doughnut shop.

He stopped in front of the courtyard. There was no one around. He walked over to the office. It was closed, the same handwritten sign still up saying the owner wasn't there from 9 to 11 A.M.

Back at the entrance to the courtyard, he closed his eyes and tried to envision Raglan, dressed in her wig and sunglasses, happily swinging her backpack, walking through the entranceway to room 8. Why always room 8? Then Ari Greene drives up in his scooter. Parks in the strip mall and comes through here too.

"Psst. Hey, mister," a throaty whisper called out from somewhere nearby.

He opened his eyes, looked around. He couldn't see anyone.

"No. Here." It was a female voice. "Look up, would you?"

A dirty sheer curtain hung in the room above the entranceway. Behind it he could just make out a woman with long hair and thick lips.

"You interested?" she asked.

Oh, Kennicott thought, this must be Hilda Reynolds. The prostitute in the window who had been uncooperative when she spoke to the police. No surprise there.

"How much?" he asked.

She looked around to check no one else was around before she answered. "Depends on what you want. Stairs are on your left."

"Give me a range." He pointed down the street. "There are lots of other motels."

"Shit. Okay. Twenty for this." She pumped her hand up and down quickly. "Fifty for a blow. More for the rest."

"Thanks. I've got a better idea, Hilda. Come down and let me buy you breakfast."

"Fuck," she said.

"You don't want me to pull out my badge."

"Shit, I knew I shouldn't have –"

"Relax. Let me buy you a meal. I'm here about a homicide. Talk to me for half an hour and then you can go back to work."

53

A CADILLAC PULLED INTO GREENE'S FATHER'S DRIVEWAY AND BRIAN SILVER GOT OUT, A PAPER bag in his arms. Greene had witnessed this scene hundreds of times when he was growing up: Brian coming over early in the morning to hang out and always bringing a ridiculous amount of food from the bakery.

"Dad, answer the door," he called out.

His father put down the sports section he was reading. "Unbelievable. Every team in Toronto is getting worse. The Blue Jays never win. The Leafs still don't have a goalie and the Raptors are a bunch of kids."

"You'll be pleasantly surprised when you see who is here."

His father went to the front hall. "Oh, Brian," he said, opening the door. "Good to see you."

"How are you, Mr. Greene? Long time. I brought you guys a few things."

"Wonderful. How's your father?"

"Pretending to be retired, but still coming in all the time to tell me what I'm doing wrong."

"Good. That's his job."

Greene came into the hallway, nodded at Silver, and took the bag from him.

"I'll unpack it," Greene's father said.

"Dad, I got it," Greene said.

Silver patted the bottom of the bag. "Mr. Greene, let Ari do some work. Let's go down to your basement to watch the highlights of last night's game, like old times. The Leafs won."

"So what? It was only an exhibition game. They don't even have a goalie, and for sure they're going to stink this year. Now all these players have concussions. I get a headache just watching them."

Silver laughed, put his long arm around his shoulders, and guided him out of the kitchen.

Greene waited until he heard them walk down the stairs before he pulled a loaf of challah, one of rye, and a half-dozen bagels wrapped in a plastic out of the paper bag. He peered into the bottom and found what he was looking for.

Jennifer's letter.

He had mailed it to Silver from Anthony Carpenter's office, before he was arrested.

He went into his bedroom, shut the door behind him, sat on his bed, and read Jennifer's letter again.

> *Ari, I'm writing to you tonight before I see you for our final motel rendezvous tomorrow. (I can't wait to see you, and I can't wait till we don't have to sneak around like this anymore!)*
>
> *By the time you read this, I will have already held my press conference and told the world my terrible secret. The fallout will be devastating.*

What terrible secret? Who had killed her to prevent her from going public with it?

> *Don't be angry that I didn't confide in you. I couldn't. You had nothing to do with any of this, and this scandal is going to be so big that anyone close to it will be damaged. Give me points, at least, for keeping you out of it.*
>
> *I always thought you'd wonder why I insisted on going to such extreme lengths to keep things between us secret. Well, after Thursday you will know.*

After Thursday you will know, he thought. Know what?

> *The price of love is so very high. I had to save my son.*

Her son. That had to be Aaron. Howard Darnell had taken him to Buffalo on Thursday. They had arranged this well in advance. Jennifer's plan was to wait until her husband got Aaron across the border that morning before revealing her secret.

The more he learned about her the less he understood.

He pulled the thick world atlas off his bookshelf. He'd been given it for his bar mitzvah and soon afterward had cut out a rectangle where, as a teenager, he'd hidden his *Playboy* magazines. It was not the world's most original hiding place, but it would do.

He put the letter inside, closed the book, and put it back on the shelf. Then he headed downstairs to be with his father and his best friend and watch the highlights of a hockey game that didn't count for a thing.

54

IT WAS ALMOST 9 A.M. AND ANGELA KREITINGER WAS NOT SURPRISED THAT JO SUMMERS wasn't in yet. Summers was the daughter of a judge and must have grown up with a silver spoon in her mouth. She was probably slumming it in the Crown's office for a few years before moving on to a special appointment on some board or commission. Why do anything more than work civil-servant hours?

Looks like I'll have to give her my usual lecture, Kreitinger thought: *You're my junior, and this is a murder trial, not a shoplifting case. Be prepared to work.*

There was a confident rap on her door.

"Come in," Kreitinger said.

"Hi." Summers pulled the door open and strode in. Like she owns the place, Kreitinger thought. Why not? She was tall, gorgeous, and rich.

"I didn't want to bug you until nine," Summers said. "I figured early mornings are your private time."

Give me a fucking break, Kreitinger thought. "I get in at seven every morning. The first thing we need to do is steal an empty office, where we can lay everything out and shut the door."

"I already found one," Summer said.

"You did?"

"I called Albert Fernandez on Sunday and talked him into letting us use his now that he's camping out in the head Crown's office."

"Good work." Well, at least Summers has some initiative, Kreitinger thought. She pointed to a stack of banker's boxes against the wall. What had began as two cardboard boxes before the bail hearing had ballooned to four as more witnesses were interviewed, case law was prepared, forensic reports arrived, and officers' notes were copied and collated. "Let's haul these over there."

"Great," Summers said.

Little Miss Enthusiasm. Wonder how she'll feel after I really put her to work?

Kreitinger thought. She loaded up her old pull cart with two boxes. "We'll come back for the other two," she said.

"I'll take them." Summers lifted both boxes easily and marched down the hall.

The confidence of youth, Kreitinger thought.

Fernandez's office had been transformed. His desk had been shoved against the back wall. Two long tables had been brought in and lined up against the sidewalls. There was a large flip chart on an easel with what looked like a new set of coloured markers. Neatly positioned at the end of one of the tables was a stapler, a three-hole punch, a labelling machine, a stack of sticky notes in different sizes and colours, a fresh box of pens, a fresh roll of tape in a tape dispenser. Lined up beside all this were two large black binders with the words *Summers Trial Binder* and *Kreitinger Trial Binder* on printed labels running down the spine.

"Who did all this?" Kreitinger asked.

"I was here yesterday scrounging this stuff up," Summers said. "This morning I got Calvin, the custodian, to lend me his moving cart. I figured with these tables we could spread out, get everything organized. Then we still have our own offices to go back to when we need to work. Anything else you can think of?"

Fuck me, what an asshole I am, Kreitinger thought. "No, this is a good start," she said.

Two new file folders were on the desk to her right, one red, one blue. Summers put her box down and handed Kreitinger the red one.

"I made these up for both of us. You're red. Hope you don't mind. I like blue."

"Red is fine." Kreitinger opened the folder. "What's here?"

"First is a preliminary to-do list with civilian witness interviews I think you'll want me to set up and legal issues for me to research. Then there's a chart of all the police witnesses and what we can expect them to say. I've also included a summary of all the forensic evidence."

Kreitinger took a few minutes to go through everything. She tossed the file back on the table, uncapped a black marker, and wrote in capital letters on the flip chart: DAY ONE: OUR THREE BIGGEST PROBLEMS.

She turned back to Summers. "What you've done is great, and I appreciate the effort. Every day we're going to come in here and each of us will write our top three problems on a new page. We'll compare notes, then prioritize."

"Good idea. I think mine would be —"

"No, stop." Kreitinger put her hand up. "You need to learn to really think. Work on this tonight and come in tomorrow morning with your three choices. We've got a lot to do for this murder trial. I'm going to teach you how to win."

55

"I'VE GOT ONE GOOD PIECE OF NEWS FOR YOU," TED DIPAULO SAID TO ARI GREENE.

They were sitting in DiPaulo's boardroom, eating Silverstein bagels that Greene had brought for their lunch. DiPaulo's partner, Nancy Parish, had joined them and was pinning up a chart on the far wall.

"What's that?"

"We've got you an extremely early trial date. Monday, December third," DiPaulo said.

"You're kidding," Greene said.

"Pays to buy the trial coordinator a nice bottle of red wine every Christmas. Bunch of cases collapsed and I grabbed it."

"Is it enough time?"

"You don't want to live under house arrest for a year, do you?"

"Absolutely not. Just ask my dad."

"Time's our enemy, Ari," DiPaulo said. "Who knows what evidence they might find, what witnesses might come forward."

"The O. J. Simpson defence," Greene said.

"That's right. Get the trial done before they discover your seven-hundred-dollar Bruno Magli shoes."

"In your dreams. A shoemaker's son always goes barefoot."

Everyone laughed.

"How do you feel about testifying at the trial?" DiPaulo asked, turning serious.

"Torn," Greene said.

"That's a typical reaction."

"I'm not afraid of being cross-examined, and, believe me, a big part of me wants to get up there and talk."

"But?"

"But," Greene said.

He hadn't told DiPaulo about Jennifer's letter. Or their plan to be together. He knew it would sound foolish to tell his lawyer he was hesitant to testify because he didn't want to hurt Howard Darnell any more by saying publicly that his dead wife was about to leave him. There was still time.

"I've seen enough people cross-examined to know that there's always a big risk in testifying. Even if you're innocent," Greene said. "On the other hand, how can we possibly win unless I take the stand and explain what happened?"

"That's the wrong way to look at it," DiPaulo said. "The better question is, How can the Crown prove the case if you don't testify? That's why Nancy and I did this."

Parish had used six different-coloured pushpins to put up the chart. Each pin was also a different shape. When I was a kid, Greene thought, pins were all the same shape and all grey. Everything changes.

The chart was easy to read. There were four columns: *FACT: to be proved; PROOF: how to prove it; PROBLEMS: with the proof; SOLUTIONS.*

"When I was a Crown, I did this for every big trial," DiPaulo said. "It helps you see the whole case. I still do it as a defence lawyer. I pretend I'm the prosecutor and look at everything from their point of view. Know your enemy."

Greene moved to a closer chair and studied the chart, starting with entry number one.

FACT	PROOF	PROBLEMS	SOLUTIONS
Greene and Raglan knew each other.	Work they did together on recent murder trials.	None	Kennicott testifies to it from his personal experience and knowledge or Alpine proves this through police records.

"First one is straightforward," Greene said.

"Look at number two," DiPaulo said. "You start to see how complicated this can get for the Crown."

FACT	PROOF	PROBLEMS	SOLUTIONS
Greene and Raglan were having an affair.	a. Circumstantial evidence: Both took Monday mornings off for six weeks. The phone call from the Coffee Time to Greene's cell phone. The boot mark comes close to putting Greene in the motel room. Description by Sadura Sawney of a "white guy" with wide shoulders fits Greene, though pretty generic. Drawing of his boots bad evidence, crucial to keep it out. Conclusion: very strong circumstantial case. b. Direct evidence: Testimony of Yitzhak Greene that Ari said he loved her.	a. Circumstantial case is strong. But is it enough for proof beyond a reasonable doubt? Probably, but not a lock. b. Direct evidence: Yitzhak Greene's evidence is definitive. But if the Crown calls him to the stand, this allows us to put in Ari Greene's whole defence, without having to call him to testify.	a. Find more evidence, such as witnesses or the scooter. Or find other proof— e-mails, texts, diary entry, friend who was confided in, other? b. Call Yitzhak Greene as a witness only as a last resort.

"Do you see what Ted has done?" Parish said. "By calling your dad at the bail hearing and letting the Crown hear his evidence, he's presented them with a huge dilemma."

Greene grinned. "I get it. If my dad's a Crown witness, you can cross-examine him about everything I told him about finding Jennifer dead and why I ran out. He says it for me and I don't have to testify."

"Exactly." DiPaulo stood up, excited.

"And," Parish said, "Ted says your father is one of the best witnesses he's ever seen."

"The jury will love him," DiPaulo added.

This was Ted at his best, Greene thought. Energized.

"Look down the whole chart. How do they prove you were in the motel room? It's still a problem for them."

He turned to Parish. "Pull out the footprint file," he said.

She fished a file folder out of one of the boxes and handed it to him. He opened it for Greene to see.

"They have the tread from the place where you kicked in the bathroom door. Their expert took it off its hinges and brought it to the lab. She used standard black fingerprint powder to come up with an impression. Here take a look, it's pretty good."

Greene looked at the image. The black-and-white image of the treads looked like a gigantic fingerprint, bracketed by a ruler on two sides.

"According to her report, she could tell it's a standard Vibram sole and that it was made by a right boot," DiPaulo said. "She then compared it to the right boot they found in the front hall of your house after you were arrested."

"How good is the comparison?" Greene asked.

"We got lucky," DiPaulo said. "The best she can say is that it's a *possible* match. Doesn't help the Crown that much. What else? How do they prove you ran away? Bigger problem. How do they prove you loved her, and perhaps had motive to kill her? Remember, except for the inconclusive boot mark, there's no DNA, no prints, nothing. Whoever the killer was, he sure knew what he was doing."

Greene sat back in his chair. "And I was wearing the gloves, the helmet."

"Exactly," Parish said, excited too. "If they don't call your dad, they can't prove beyond a reasonable doubt you were ever in the motel room. Case over."

"Let's not get ahead of ourselves," DiPaulo said. "Evidence you read on the page always feels different than when you hear and see it in court."

"What would you do if you were the Crown?" Greene asked. He looked at DiPaulo. Parish did too.

DiPaulo went up to the chart and studied it. He was not a man who liked long silences. But he was unusually still. Deep in thought. "I'd do everything I could to make you take the stand," he said after what seemed a very long time.

"Meaning you wouldn't call my father?"

"Meaning I'd pile up enough evidence against you that you simply have to testify."

56

HILDA REYNOLDS HAD HIGH CHEEKBONES, A SLENDER NOSE, AND FULL LIPS. IT WAS EASY TO
see that if she took care of herself, if she lost fifteen pounds, if she cut and styled
her too-long frizzy hair, she'd be attractive. Instead, Kennicott thought, she
looked like central casting for a burned-out prostitute near the end of her run.

He introduced himself and reached out to shake her hand.

She looked at his hand as if it were a foreign object. Then gave it a weak
shake.

"Where do you want to eat?" Her voice was a deep rasp, almost masculine. "I
got to be back before ten-thirty."

"That's no problem." If he wanted her to cooperate, Kennicott thought,
it would do no good to make her miss her next appointment. "Wherever you
want," he said.

"Not the fucking Peking." She glanced to her right. The Peking Restaurant
was steps away in the strip mall.

Kennicott pointed across Kingston Road. "What about that buffet restaurant."

She frowned. "The Sisters? That's no surprise. You cops like it there."

"I've never heard of the place."

"Yeah, right," she said. Not convinced.

"I'm not from Scarborough."

"Welcome to heaven on earth."

They walked to the traffic lights in silence and waited a long time for a green.
The sign on the faded blue awning outside the Sisters boasted that they'd been
in business since 1957, and it looked as if they hadn't updated the decor in at
least thirty years. Well-worn red carpeting, fake brick interior, cracked ceiling,
the only thing that looked new were the brown square bars on the windows, in
a wide enough pattern that they looked like mullions, not protection. The $9.99
buffet was set out on a series of long tables with steam trays of scrambled eggs,

bacon, sausages, pancakes and French toast, and dishes of bread, muffins, cold pasta salads, and the like.

Reynolds stacked up every inch of her plate. Kennicott got a coffee.

They slid into one of the booths farthest from the window.

"You only get one plate for the ten bucks," she said. "It's bottomless coffee but they make a big deal if you try to share the food."

"Don't worry, I'm not hungry," he said. "I'm running."

She slurped her coffee, then stabbed a sausage with her fork and chewed on it. Next came two pieces of bacon. Then she piled a mound of dry-looking scrambled eggs on top of a pancake, poured syrup over it, cut off a corner, and stuck it in her mouth.

Kennicott looked around. The restaurant was almost empty. No one was monitoring whether they shared the food. He let her eat for a few more minutes before he said, "I want to talk to you about September tenth, the Monday morning of the murder in room 8."

She had cut up the French toast into squares and was about to attack it. Instead she sat back and downed the rest of her coffee. "Look, I made my statement. There's nothing else to say. Some bitch from the Crown's office called me on the weekend to try to set up a meeting and I told her to subpoena me if she wants to drag me to court. I'm too busy."

She held up her empty cup and peered out of the booth. "Where's the fucking waitress."

"I'm sure they'll make you come to court," he said.

"You want to buy me breakfast, fine. I talked to David, my lawyer, when this crap happened. He says I don't have to say shit unless I'm on the witness stand."

"That's true."

"So what? You going to bust me for soliciting to make me talk? What are they going to give me? A week in the West? CAS already has my girls, what else can they do to me?"

"I told you I'm not going to arrest you. I'm going to buy you breakfast."

"So?"

"So, what are you afraid of?"

Reynolds leaned farther out of the booth and waved her arm. "There's the bitch with the coffee," she said.

A stout older woman in a light pink uniform came over. She frowned at

Reynolds, and shot Kennicott a suspicious look as she poured a fresh cup of coffee.

"You got more cream?" Reynolds asked.

"Lots." The waitress reached into her half apron and tossed a handful of creamers on the table. She turned to Kennicott. He put his hand over his cup. "No thanks." he said. She shrugged and was gone.

"Cunt hates me," Reynolds said.

"She wasn't very friendly to me either," he said.

"Why should she be?" Reynolds said. "She figures you're another trick. And you're easy to spot as a cop. She's seen enough cops in here to know."

"Know what?"

"Cops. Tricks. You fill in the blanks."

"Some cops? That who you're afraid of?"

She took a sip of coffee and slammed the cup down. "Holy shit. This is burning hot. She did that on purpose. I hate this fucking place."

That was twice she'd avoided answering his question, Kennicott thought. Whatever was scaring her, he wasn't going to get it out of her. Maybe she'd find talking about her statement easier.

"Hilda, you told the police officer who interviewed you on the morning of September tenth that when the murder happened you were with a fat, older guy you'd never seen before."

"Or since." She stabbed a square of French toast, swirled it around in the syrup, and ate it.

"Can you describe him?"

"I have to admit, they have real good French toast," she said.

"I'm serious."

"I don't want to talk about it."

"I guess we should go, then," he said.

She looked at her half-eaten French toast.

"What was he wearing?" Kennicott knew the best thing to do was to keep asking questions.

"Clothes, before he took his pants off." She chuckled at that and plunged her fork into another square, and again coated it with syrup.

"You sit in that window and watch the street all morning. Tell me, how did this fat guy get to the motel?"

She ate a few more pieces, then sat back and poured a long line of sugar into her coffee. She opened four of the creamers and tipped them in too. "That should cool down this black mud," she said.

"Did he jog up, like me? Or ride a bike?" he asked.

She laughed. "Very funny. He was a big piece of blubber. Just like Newman."

"Newman?"

"Don't you watch *Seinfeld*?"

"Come on, Hilda. What was he driving?"

She took a deep breath and sipped her coffee carefully. She looked scared.

He kept his eyes on her.

"Okay, fuck it," she said. "He wasn't driving. I saw him get out of a van."

"A van?"

"Yeah, a white van."

"Can you describe it?"

"It was white. Like he was."

"Any name or writing on the side?"

She shook her head. "It was white as my ass, that was all I saw. He got dropped off at the entrance. He knew I'd be in the window."

"Really, how'd he know that?"

"You're a pretty young copper. Don't you know the strip?"

"No, I don't."

She looked directly at him for the first time. Squinted. Pulled herself forward, hovered over her plate, and whispered, "He was a fucking cop."

Don't react, stay calm, Kennicott told himself. "Did he tell you that?"

She rolled her eyes. "Yeah, right. Give me a break. Sure he gave me his rank and badge number too. Man, you're naive."

"How do you know he was a cop?" he asked.

"How do you know he was a cop?" she mocked him. "I can smell it. That's how. I can just tell."

So much for your credibility in court, Hilda, Kennicott thought. "You were wrong about me a few minutes ago," he said, pointing across the street at the motel.

"Everyone messes up sometime. Besides, you're prettier than most."

"Where did the van park out front?"

"Park? You crazy. He got dropped off like they all do. What do you think, they're going to come in their squad cars?" She pushed her plate away. "That bitch isn't looking, why don't you have this last piece? I'm full."

"No thanks."

"What time is it?"

Kennicott checked his watch. "Ten-twenty."

"Let's get out of this dump. I can't be late."

"One more question. Where did it go after he was dropped off?"

"What?"

"The van."

She smiled for the first time. Her teeth were badly stained. "You know, you're smart. That's the one weird thing."

"Weird in what way?"

"Instead of driving back onto Kingston Road, like everyone else, this one drove right under my place and into the courtyard."

"Did you see it drive out again?"

"No. Like I said in my statement, I was down on my knees."

"Did you see where your customer went after?"

She frowned. "Okay, I told the cop who came to the door that he took off in a blue car. That was bullshit. Truth is I didn't look out the window after I'd turned the trick."

"Why not?"

"Because I don't want to get involved with bullcrap like this."

57

in the boardroom of their law firm. They'd been here for hours, meticulously going through every witness statement, all the police officers' notes, the autopsy and other forensic reports, and a large binder filled with photos of the motel room and surrounding area. The air in the room felt stale, accentuated by the smell of the remaining slices of the pizza that had been delivered twenty minutes earlier.

"This will not be fun for you to watch," DiPaulo said. He motioned to Parish, who pushed a button on the remote she was holding. A video started on a screen in the corner of the room.

Greene watched in silence as Jennifer came into view on the camera outside the Coffee Time. She went inside and cameras there showed her going into the washroom, coming out a few minutes later wearing her wig and sunglasses, making the phone call to him, and then walking out the door.

"Please turn it off," he asked Parish, after they'd watched Jennifer take a few steps outside.

The screen went blank. No one spoke.

"It's never fun seeing a video like that," DiPaulo said at last. "But it had to be done. I don't want you to react to it at all in court when Kreitinger plays it in front of the jury."

Greene nodded. He wasn't ready to speak.

"Let's get to the bottom line here," DiPaulo said, between bites of pizza.

Greene nodded again.

Despite being shut in this room all afternoon, DiPaulo showed no signs of slowing down. He opened a can of Coke, making a loud pop. "Assume the worst. Let's say that Kreitinger can prove you were having an affair with Raglan for at least the last six weeks, that she can put you in the motel room on the morning of September tenth, that she convinces the jury you ran away from the scene, then misled Kennicott and used him to try to influence the investigation."

"Sums up the Crown's case against me, doesn't it," Greene said.

DiPaulo slugged back the Coke and seemed to drink half of it in one gulp. "Here's my problem. Once the jury hears that you were in that room and you took off, all they're going to think is: He's a homicide detective, for God's sake. Why the hell did he take off if he didn't kill her?"

"But I didn't kill her. That's the truth."

"I don't care if it's true or not." DiPaulo grabbed another piece of pizza. "The point is it doesn't sound true. It doesn't sound believable."

Greene looked at Parish. She looked as tired as he felt. "Sorry, Ari," she said. "Ted's right."

Greene stood and stretched. "So what do we do?"

DiPaulo took a bite of pizza, then threw the rest in the box and snapped the lid shut.

"Enough of this shit," he said. "Ari, listen, and sorry to be blunt, but this is not a charity fund-raiser that we're going to. It's a blood sport. And right at this moment, the Crown has all the facts on their side. What I need is some fucking facts that refute their story."

"Such as?" Greene asked.

All day Greene had watched DiPaulo take meticulous notes on a long pad of lined yellow paper. At some point he realized that DiPaulo had a second pad he wrote on occasionally. DiPaulo pulled that one out.

"Time," he said, waving the pad in Greene's direction. "Time."

"Time?" Greene asked.

"People can say anything they want in court. But no one can bend time. I've been taking notes on this pad of every indication we have of when things happened that morning. If we can prove, and I mean prove objectively, factually, irrefutably, that Raglan was dead by the time you got to room 8 at the Maple Leaf Motel, then maybe at last we have something other than your word for what happened."

He turned to Parish. She perked right up.

"Nancy, put up a new piece of Bristol board. We're going to make a minute-by-minute chronology. Write three headings: 'Time,' 'Person,' and 'Event.'" He pulled the pizza box back toward him, opened it, and retrieved his slice.

"Here's what I have." DiPaulo looked at his pad of paper. "Eight A.M. Howard Darnell leaves home saying he's going to work. About 8:15 the three kids leave for school. Assume Raglan starts on her run about 8:30. We know from the cop's notes it's fifteen kilometres to the Coffee Time and she gets there at 9:49:52. At 9:56:12, she makes the phone call to Ari's cell, which shows up on Ari's invoice. They talk for a minute and thirty-two seconds."

DiPaulo put his pad down. "Ari, that puts you at your house at 9:57 A.M. A few minutes after ten she's in the room. At 10:39 someone makes a 911 call. You tell us you arrived at 10:41 and found her dead. At 10:44 the cavalry arrives: cop cars and the ambulance."

"Wait," Parish said, rummaging through one of the sets of files and pulling out a piece of artwork. "Sadura Sawney, her drawings. Look. There's Ari from behind, about to call on his cell phone. But check out the background. The ambulance is rushing past at the same time."

"I hadn't notice that," Greene said. "That puts me there at 10:44. I was in and out of that room in less than five minutes," Greene said. "Felt like a lifetime."

Parish stood back and looked at her chart. "In that approximately thirty-seven minutes between Raglan arriving in the room and the 911 call, she's killed."

"In his notes," DiPaulo said, "Alpine shows he did a test drive from your house to the Maple Leaf Motel leaving at 9:58. Took him twenty-three minutes."

"That puts Ari arriving at 10:21. Eighteen minutes before the 911 call," Parish said.

"It's tight, but they're going to say that was all the time he needed to kill her," DiPaulo said. "Ari, tell me how can I get rid of those seventeen minutes and we're home free."

Greene shook his head. "I parked the scooter about ten minutes' walk from my house. On a normal day, it took me about twenty minutes to get to the motel strip. This motel was a bit farther than most of them. Twenty-three minutes sounds right. But that day the traffic on Kingston Road was terrible. Obviously on a scooter there's no radio and I couldn't get a traffic report. I really didn't think much of it. What else can I tell you?"

DiPaulo frowned. "You didn't stop anywhere for gas? Go to a florist that has a video camera and buy her some roses?"

"I wish," Greene said.

DiPaulo strode up to the Bristol board and studied it. He took out a red marker and circled 10:41. "It only works, Ari, if we can prove you went into that room at 10:41. Two minutes after the 911 call. Right there. That is the fucking fact we need to prove."

He turned to Parish. "Nancy, check with that media monitoring firm we use. Get the tape of the morning radio and TV traffic reports. The local traffic cops' notes. Hourly weather report. Maybe there was a hailstorm farther up the road or a Martian landing we don't know about."

He looked back at Greene. "The one thing I know for sure is that there is never a *Perry Mason* moment when someone stands up in court and says, 'I did it!' or runs in from the hallway and says, 'Detective Greene is innocent, I saw the murder and it was Colonel Mustard, with a candlestick, in the library.'"

They all laughed. DiPaulo was good at defusing tension with humour.

DiPaulo turned serious. "Ari. Anything else you can think of?"

"I know I got there at 10:41. I hate being late and I know I checked my watch before I walked into the room."

"You're sure it was 10:41."

"One hundred percent."

"And no jury in the world is going to believe that, unless we come up with some solid proof. Why don't you stop thinking like a defendant, or like a man who's lost the love of his life, and start thinking like a detective?" DiPaulo spread his arms. "Look at all of this. Four boxes of evidence. What am I missing? Be a homicide cop."

Greene felt he'd been slapped hard across the face. Twenty-five years of his life were on the line and he was drawing a blank.

And then it came to him.

Of course.

If things don't work in one direction, look at them the other way.

"Ted, you're right," he said.

"About what?" DiPaulo said.

"I haven't been thinking like a cop."

"Meaning?"

"Meaning, I can't believe I didn't see this before." He reached into his wallet, took out fifty dollars, and slapped the bills on the table.

"Here take this," he said to DiPaulo.

"What for?"

"We need to rent room 8 at the Maple Leaf Motel."

58

FOR YEARS AWOTWE AMANKWAH HAD BEEN AMUSED BY THE LEVEL OF CORRUPTION IN STO-ries that made the headlines in Canada. Coming from a country, and a continent, where bribery, nepotism, electoral fraud, to say nothing of rape, murder, and continual warfare, were as ingrained into the culture as the monsoons in rainy season, he found it hard to get too worked up about what passed for scandals here: government-hired consultants who had lattes and muffins, protesters at the G8 summit in Toronto who had to go half a day without their vegan meals, and, imagine this one, a federal cabinet minister on a foreign trip to London who spent sixteen bucks for a glass of orange juice. Soon after this stunning revelation, she'd resigned.

Last spring, when Barclay Church had arrived at the *Star*, determined to find dirt in squeaky-clean Toronto, reporters in the newsroom had rolled their eyes. "Dig, dig, dig" was his mantra. And to everyone's surprise, soon there were front-page stories with screaming headlines about filthy restaurants that had been badly inspected, private schools where kids bought good grades, public-school repair bills that were as inflated as the Pentagon's budget, and aquatic theme parks that abused their cuddly dolphins.

Church had breathed life into the newsroom, but no one had cracked anything as big as a major police corruption scandal. A story like that could make Amankwah's career.

For the last week he had been busy doing his own version of the Big Dig. It took him a couple of days to enter all the information from Carmichael's files in an Excel spreadsheet, and even longer to figure out what it all meant. But, like a jigsaw puzzle, the pieces eventually started to fit together.

Two years earlier, in anticipation of the G8 summit that was going to bring the world leaders to Toronto, the police had put together a number of three-officer units to clean up the streets. Their main task was to make sure no problems occurred between prostitutes and politicians while the whole world was watching Toronto.

Amankwah noticed that the names of three cops kept coming up in case after case. Then he realized they were working together in the same unit. Through persistent access-to-information requests, he was able to profile them.

Colin Kimber, a twelve-year veteran, had faced internal disciplinary hearings three times and had two reprimands on his record. Plus a female colleague had filed a sexual harassment complaint against him that she later withdrew.

George Noguchi had been on the force for twenty-one years, much of his early years on the holdup squad, and was still there when it was investigated for "alleged" violent interrogation techniques. Five years earlier he'd been charged with assault by the Special Investigations Unit for stopping and beating up a black man who was walking home from work. The guy wore baggy jeans and a do-rag on his head. Noguchi thought he was a teenager, but in fact he was a thirty-six-year-old nurse. It was a high-profile case. Noguchi was acquitted, but the judge made it clear he was not impressed with the officer's testimony, even though he was not quite persuaded of his guilt beyond a reasonable doubt.

The man who'd put this ragged group together, nicknamed "Trio," was its leader, Clyde Newbridge. A big, fat, intimidating cop, Amankwah had often seen him swagger through the halls of the Old City Hall courthouse. Newbridge had been on the force for thirty years. No official complaint had ever been filed against him, and he'd never been subject to any disciplinary hearings. But his reputation was that he was "old school," meaning he was not afraid to lay on the lumber if need be to force a confession. He certainly was a curious choice for such a sensitive job. This looked like his reward for sucking up to Charlton for all those years.

Amankwah dug deeper. He got the court records of the other special units working at the same time. Most of them had pretty good conviction rates, ranging from 40 to 60 percent. On average, 20 percent of their cases were withdrawn. But with Trio, an amazing 84 percent of their cases had been tossed out. The contrast was startling.

He focused on Newbridge. And that's where he hit a wall. Every access-to-information request was either denied or so redacted it was useless. All he could find was a meager biographical sketch. A high-school graduate, he'd joined the force when he was nineteen. Spent his career moving from division to division, doing a bit of everything. Knew everyone. Divorced twice, both ex-wives alleging mental cruelty. Pretty standard stuff for a veteran Toronto cop.

But Amankwah knew it was only the tip of the iceberg. Newbridge was a big player in the combative police union and a buddy of Hap Charlton. Always popping up at the chief's side at important events. And these days a constant figure on the campaign trail.

But how to find out more? Amankwah needed to get someone to talk to him, and that's why he was standing on University Avenue at 6:45 A.M., watching the parking lot to the north of the courthouse. He had finished reading the lead story in the newspaper about how Hap Charlton was pulling way ahead in the polls when he saw Albert Fernandez drive his car into the lot.

He waited until the young Crown attorney collected his briefcase from his trunk before approaching. This was going to be tricky. Unlike defence lawyers, many of whom were very adept at dealing with the media, most Crown attorneys were very bad at it and simply chose to avoid all contact.

"Good morning, Mr. Fernandez," Amankwah said when he was a few steps away.

"Hello," Fernandez said, surprised, his eyes wary. "What brings such a well-known newspaper reporter here this early in the morning?" He tried to smile but it was obvious he was nervous. He glanced at the envelope in Amankwah's hand.

"There's something I'd like to chat with you about privately," Amankwah said. "I have a hunch you have a pretty good idea what I'm interested in."

Fernandez looked around the near-empty lot. "We both know that the ministry advises us to not talk to the media."

"I'm only looking for background. You have my word, I'd never quote you without your express permission."

Fernandez checked his watch. He bit his lip.

Amankwah could read the emotions on his face. Fernandez was a good lawyer and played by the rules. If he found out about some rogue cops, he wouldn't turn a blind eye. On the other hand, ever since Charlton had made a show of calling for an investigation into allegations of police corruption, all the Crowns were under a strict gag order.

"I appreciate your being discreet," Fernandez said. "But this isn't a good time – or place, for that matter."

Amankwah handed him the sealed envelope. "I did a spreadsheet of all the charges involving prostitutes that have been withdrawn in the last three years. The rest of this is the court papers that I used for my research. One group of officers stands out like a sore thumb."

Fernandez stared at the envelope, not moving to take it.

They locked eyes.

"Trio," Amankwah said.

Fernandez's face flushed and his arm twitched. He wouldn't make a good poker player, Amankwah thought.

"Take it, Albert," Amankwah said.

Fernandez grabbed the envelope and slipped it into his briefcase.

"I need to know where to look next," Amankwah said.

Fernandez's eyes travelled around the parking lot. "Ten minutes," he said. "Now, before other Crowns arrive."

Traffic in the city was starting to pick up. Fernandez led him quickly up Centre Street for two blocks and down an alley beside the University of Toronto Dentistry Faculty building. Behind a big tree, there was an old wood bench that faced north, tucked out of view of the street. Fernandez opened the envelope and took a fast look at Amankwah's chart. Then he scanned the court papers.

"You can check all the court documents," Amankwah said, "but I know I got it right."

Fernandez ignored him. There were sixty-eight sets of charges, and he kept flipping back and forth through them. Obviously he was looking for something specific.

"I don't want to keep this," he said at last, putting the papers back in the envelope and handing it to Amankwah.

"Didn't you understand the chart?" Amankwah asked. "This Trio unit kept arresting people and almost all the charges were thrown out."

"I'm well aware of this," Fernandez said.

"You are?"

"Yes."

Amankwah smacked the envelope on his knee. "Then the only reasonable explanation has to be that they were shaking prostitutes and johns down. Arresting them then getting payoffs or favours to yank the charges. Don't you see that?"

"You know I'm limited in what I can tell you," Fernandez said.

"Okay," Amankwah said. "Explain this, then. How could this go on without anyone in the Crown's office being aware of it?"

Fernandez stood up. "I've got to get to the office," he said. "They made me the temporary head Crown."

"I heard. Congratulations," Amankwah said, standing up with him. "But you didn't answer my question."

"I understood it. The answer's right in your hand," Fernandez said. "You were only looking at the cops involved. Why don't you go back and see who the Crown was who was pulling all these charges."

"The Crown?"

"It's all in the documents," Fernandez said. He walked off before Amankwah could say another word.

Amankwah sat back down on the bench and pulled out the papers. Fernandez was right. He had been focusing on the arresting officers. It had never occurred to him to check which Crown attorney was in court each time. He flipped to the first case. Then the second, the third. He stared at the pages in disbelief. But he kept going through all sixty-eight of them.

There it was. Every charge had been withdrawn by Jennifer Raglan.

59

AT PRECISELY 7:30 A.M. KREITINGER HEARD A KNOCK ON HER OFFICE DOOR. "COME IN," SHE said.

"Morning," Jo Summer said.

Kreitinger had told her she wanted to start early and so here was Little Miss Keener, right on time.

"I'm not sucking up or anything," Summers said, "but I brought you a Starbucks coffee. Albert said you take it black."

Kreitinger reached for the cup. It was steaming hot. "Sounds like sucking up to me," she said.

"Yeah. Okay. Guilty as charged." Summers smiled. "I've got my top three problems for our case. It was hard to narrow it down to three."

"It should be." Kreitinger pulled out the little green stick that covered the opening in the lid. The coffee smelled very good. "Let's go to our war room and see what you've got," she said, jamming the stick back in place.

The hallways were empty. They passed a few Crown attorneys in their offices, heads down in final preparations for the day's battle in court.

"Here are my choices," Summers said, when they entered Fernandez's former office. On the flip chart she'd already written out her three points.

1. Can we prove Greene was in room 8 without calling his father as a witness?
2. What proof do we have of Greene's motive?
3. If Greene testifies that Jennifer was dead when he arrived, how do we counter that?

Kreitinger put her coffee down and rummaged through the markers, found a red one, crossed out number three, and said, "That's not something tangible we can deal with right now."

"Okay, I see that." Summers nodded, her bound-up blond hair bouncing above her head.

Kreitinger renumbered "1" as "2" and "2" as "3" and drew a line from the top of the page to the blank space below and wrote a big "1?" She capped the marker and reached for her coffee, pulled out the stick, tossed it in the garbage, and took a generous sip.

"A trial is not only about facts," she said. "It's about perception, nuance, emotion, theatre. You missed our biggest problem. And it has nothing to do with the facts."

"I don't get it," Summer said, looking perplexed.

Kreitinger smacked the marker into her open palm. "What's the jury going to think of your friend Jennifer Raglan?"

"I think they'll respect all the work she did as a Crown. Feel terrible for her children. And feel sorry for her husband."

"What else?"

"They're not going to be too impressed that she was having this sleazy affair with Greene behind her husband's back."

"No, they're not," Kreitinger said. She smacked the marker into her palm again. "Here's an even tougher question. What will they think of Greene?"

"That he was a cold-blooded killer, I hope."

"Don't hope. Answer the question. What are they going to think of accused murderer, homicide detective Ari Greene?" She pointed the marker at the new number three on the chart: *What proof do we have of Greene's motive?* "Especially if his father testifies, or Greene himself takes the stand, and tells the jury Raglan was already dead when he got to room 8 in the Maple Leaf Motel, and that he didn't tell anyone right away because he was in shock and grief. And most of all, that he loved Jennifer so damn much that he was willing to risk everything to find the real killer."

Summers slapped the table. "Come on. You don't think the jury will believe that fairy tale, do you?"

She sounded defensive. Angry. This was good, Kreitinger thought. She was showing some emotion.

"I don't know what the jury will believe," she said. "That's the whole point. We have to be sure there is absolutely no doubt in their mind that all of us on the prosecution team are one hundred percent convinced Ari Greene is the killer."

"But we are convinced," Summers protested. "Totally."

"Who is 'we'?" Kreitinger asked.

"You and me, of course."

"Exactly." Kreitinger uncapped the marker and wrote "1" beside *Daniel Kennicott*. She capped the marker and tossed it into the holding tray. "He's the officer in charge of this case. You saw him at the bail hearing. We both know he's not sure that Greene is guilty. And trust me, one thing I know about juries. They can smell doubt a million miles away."

Summers's eyes widened. "I know. It was obvious."

Kreitinger opened the top box on her cart and passed some stapled papers over to Summers.

"What's this?" Summers asked.

"Yesterday, Kennicott did some more investigating. Remember Hilda Reynolds?"

"The prostitute at the motel who wouldn't talk."

"Very good. Kennicott interviewed her. It's a bunch of crap about cops and hookers. These people are all the same. I'm sure she read about all this stuff in the papers, and I'll bet she smelled a great lawsuit. I've already couriered a copy over to the defence counsel."

Summers was reading fast. "She says a van drove into the courtyard."

Kreitinger threw up her hands in frustration. "Exactly my point. It's a total red herring and gift from heaven for the other side. I'm sure DiPaulo is salivating reading this nonsense and dreaming up alternative-suspect theories."

"What's this going to do to our case?" Summers asked.

"Confuse the hell out of it if we're not careful. We have think this through. No way I'm putting this hooker on the stand. And now I can't put Kennicott up there either."

"But if you don't call Daniel as a witness, how do we get in the evidence of how Greene misled him?"

He's still "Daniel" to you, Kreitinger thought.

"It's what I said at the very beginning. We need to get Greene into the box. If I call Kennicott, on cross-examination the defence will get all this crap about there being a mysterious van that went into the courtyard and claim there's another suspect running around out there that we somehow missed. This kind of smoke screen could fuck up our whole case."

She underlined the word "Kennicott" in red. "I'm telling you," she said. "Our own OIC is our number one problem."

"Shit," Summers said, throwing the papers on the table. "You're right."

60

"WITH ALL DUE RESPECT TO YOUR FATHER'S SANKA," LINDSMORE SAID TO GREENE AS HE walked up to the front door of Greene's father's house, "I went to Timmies and bought my own double-double."

Lindsmore was in uniform. A thin briefcase, with *Toronto Police Service* stencilled on the side, was tucked under one of his thick arms. In his other hand he held a large cup of coffee and a Tim Hortons paper bag. Greene knew the bag would contain at least one doughnut.

"My dad won't mind. No one has drunk his coffee since my mother died. Even his new girlfriends can't stand it," Greene said, giving the screen door an extra shove to get it open.

"Besides," Lindsmore said, "it's Roll Up The Rim."

Roll Up The Rim was a hugely popular contest run by the ubiquitous coffee-and-doughnut-shop chain, in which potential prizes could be found under the rims on their decorated paper cups.

"Maybe you won a car," Greene said.

"No, that would be my ex-wife," Lindsmore said. "With my luck, I'd be happy with a free coffee."

"My father's still asleep," Greene said. "Let's go downstairs."

The basement had hardly changed since he was a teenager. In one corner an old sofa and two chairs faced a television. In the middle of the room a large table was stacked with boxes. Greene's father had taken a keen interest in the still-unsolved murder of Daniel Kennicott's brother, and Ari had made him a copy of everything in the file. Usually the table was strewn with open papers, but over the weekend Greene had made his father clean it up.

In the far corner was a plastic bridge table flanked by two stacking chairs. On top sat a tabletop hockey game, which had been in this same spot since Greene got it as a Chanukah present when he was eleven years old.

Lindsmore sat at the big table, took his paper coffee cup, pulled off the plastic lid, took a sip, and bit into the lip of the cup with his bottom teeth. He took a second sip and rolled up the edge of the rim higher with his thick thumbs.

"'Sorry, try again,'" he said, reading the contest message underneath. He laughed. "Story of my life."

Greene laughed too. "At least you're persistent."

Lindsmore put his briefcase on the table.

Greene looked it. "You find anything?" he asked.

"We have a lot to talk about."

The previous Friday, when Lindsmore had come over to the house for the first time and offered his assistance, Greene had been wary. "Why did Kennicott send you?" he'd asked when they'd sat down in the living room.

"I think young Daniel is torn, so I'm his insurance policy," Lindsmore had said. "He figures if you and me come up with the killer, he's done his job. And if we can't, he'll see you in court."

Lindsmore opened the paper bag. "First things first. Honey glazed or maple?" He brought out two doughnuts and napkins.

"Honey glazed," Greene said.

"Good," Lindsmore said. "Me, I like maple."

Greene broke his doughnut down the middle and ate half. The other half he left on the napkin.

Lindsmore was a slow eater. After a final bite and a last sip of his coffee, he unzipped his briefcase and brought out some papers.

"I looked up Raglan's son on CPIC like you asked me to." Lindsmore shook his head as he passed a copy of the same papers to Greene. "And did some asking around. Kid's a piece of work."

It was a three-page printout of Aaron Darnell's criminal record.

"Starts when he's fifteen years old, for God's sake," Lindsmore said. "Graffiti. He's charged three times in eighteen months."

Greene was scanning through the pages with a practised eye. This must have driven Jennifer crazy, he thought. "Look at these fines he's paying. Two thousand dollars' restitution. Four thousand, then this last one, eight. A ton of money."

"Kept him out of jail," Lindsmore said.

"Seems like a lot for some spray painting."

Lindsmore snorted. "You've been in Homicide too long. Charlton is right about this graffiti problem. That's why it's working in his election campaign. You don't see it so much downtown, but in the suburbs, *whew*. Last few years it has gotten totally out of hand. It's not only defacing garage doors or the bottoms of bridges and tunnels, but the whole sides of privately owned buildings."

"Aaron 8," Greene said.

"What?"

"I heard that was his tag. His signature."

Lindsmore gave him a sideways look. "That's right. What else do you know about this kid?"

"He was into drugs, pretty big-time."

"Turn over the page, you'll see all the drug stuff. Probably where he got the money to pay for the fines. I talked to some of the cops in 43 Division. They said he looks about fourteen. Rides around everywhere on a bike he built himself. Real smart. Parents kept putting him in gifted classes, then private schools, and he kept getting booted out."

"And now?"

"They say he's disappeared. No one knows where he is," Lindsmore said. "You going to eat the other half of that doughnut?"

"It's all yours."

Lindsmore didn't hesitate to grab it.

"Cops said Aaron was always very polite. Never let on that his mother was a Crown. But he was a big-time dealer. Trouble was, he wasn't keeping up with his payments to his main supplier. Some bad actor from Scarborough."

"Not good."

"Gets worse. The week before Jennifer was murdered, someone took a shot at him. Missed. Must've been just a warning. People saw the shooter run, a witness put Aaron as the target, but he clammed right up, of course. Serious shit. Cops told me that any day now they're expecting to find his body in a Dumpster."

Greene could see it. Aaron, the brilliant, out-of-control older son. He understood why Jennifer and Howard were desperate to get him out of the country and into rehab.

I had to save my son.

"Why do I have this feeling, Ari, that you know where this kid is?"

Greene smiled. "He's down in the American Southwest, in one of those remote rehab places in the middle of nowhere."

"At least he's alive," Lindsmore said. "I found your street guy in the clown suit."

This had been the second thing Greene had asked Lindsmore to do. "Fraser Dent?"

Lindsmore nodded.

"What did he say?"

"That's he's got something for you."

"What?" Greene asked, a little too quickly.

"He wouldn't tell me what. He wants to see you in person." Lindsmore looked Greene straight in the eye. "Ari, he can't come here."

"Of course not. When does he want to meet me?"

"He said midnight tonight." Lindsmore stood up. "Look, I can't know anything about this."

"Understood." Greene stood up with him.

"You screw up your bail, you're totally fucked."

"I know," Greene said.

Lindsmore reached out and shook Greene's hand. "He said meet him at midnight in the usual spot across from Popeye's. But, Ari, be fucking careful."

61

DANIEL KENNICOTT WALKED DOWN THE ALLEY SOUTH FROM KING STREET WEST, LOOKING for the place where Jo Summers had told him to meet her to talk about the case. The sides of the buildings on both sides were covered with graffiti art, much of it very beautiful. He was almost at Wellington Street when he saw the sandwich-board sign for Spin Toronto. Descending into the basement, he walked up to the steel reception desk.

"Hi there," said a young woman wearing a Spin Toronto T-shirt that featured a pair of crossed Ping-Pong racquets. "You here to play?"

"Yes." He looked beyond her and saw a huge room filled with Ping-Pong tables and players volleying back and forth. "I'm here to see a friend, Jo Summers."

"Oh, Jo," the woman said. "She mentioned someone was coming. She reserved a private table in the Beijing Room. Turn left and keep going past the bar, you can't miss it.

Although it was in a basement, the place was high ceilinged and well lit. Music boomed from every corner, punctuated by the *pop, pop, pop* of Ping-Pong balls being hit back and forth across the tables.

A young man with big circle earrings in his earlobes, also wearing a Spin Toronto T-shirt, was skirting around with a large net, scooping up balls from the floor and depositing them into baskets by the players' sides.

Ping-Pong heaven, Kennicott thought. He'd grown up playing with his brother, Michael, in the basement of their summer cottage, where they spent at least half the time retrieving errant balls.

At the doorway of the Beijing Room he stopped. Summers's back was to him. Her long hair was tied up in her usual wooden clip. She held the racquet with the handle between her thumb and forefinger, the way they did in China and was volleying with a rail-thin young Asian woman who was focused on the ball. They grunted as they played, trading slam for slam.

At last Summers put away a soft spin shot. Her opponent smiled. They both bowed and said some words in Chinese.

Kennicott remembered that Summers had told him she spoke fluent Chinese. Her father, a successful lawyer before he became judge, had insisted she and her brother grow up downtown, and she'd been the only non-Chinese girl in her kindergarten class.

Her opponent spotted Kennicott at the door and nodded toward him. Summers turned.

"Oh, hi, Daniel. You're a bit early. Lin and I are finishing up."

"Don't let me interfere."

"It's okay," Lin said. She spoke without a trace of an accent. She gave him her racquet on the way out the door. "Jo's dished out enough punishment for me today. I haven't beaten her since grade five. Good luck."

"Looks like you're a regular here," Kennicott said. He went to the other side of the table, took a ball, and hit it over the net.

"I come to blow off stream. You play?" She hit him a low ball back.

"Not since my brother and I were kids." He returned it, but he knew it was way too high. He took a step back, expecting a slam.

"It will come back to you." She undercut the ball softly and it barely made it over the net, the spin turning it hard to his left.

"We'll see." He lunged and just got his racquet under the ball, sending it even higher.

Instead of slamming it, she tapped it sideways. It hit and bounced off the far edge of the table.

He looked up from his compromised position. "Your point," he said.

She laughed, then hit him another ball. "Let's rally to warm you up," she said.

"Fine by me," he said, hitting the ball back into the middle of her side. "What was it you wanted to talk about?"

"You," she said.

"Me?" They were up to six rallies.

"You and Greene."

They were up to ten rallies, the ball flying faster and faster.

"What about me and Greene?"

"He's playing you," she said. "Don't you see it?"

"Give me a break." He hit the ball as hard as he could.

"No, you give me a break." She returned it with a backhand slam. "You looked like you were part of the defence team when you testified at the bail hearing."

He got to the ball at the last possible moment and hit it high up in the air again.

This time she showed no mercy and hit a vicious forehand slam that he had no chance of returning.

He threw his racquet on the table.

"You made your point, so to speak," he said. "You happy?"

"No." She aimed her racquet at him. "I think you should get off the case."

"What?"

"How can you be part of the prosecution if you have doubts that Greene is guilty?"

Kennicott heard a *pop* as he came around the table. He looked down. "Fuck," he said. He'd stepped on a ball. He kicked it under the table. "Who the hell do you think you are? You just got on this case. I'm the one who figured this out and made the arrest."

"Well, whoopee. You take the stand and a jury is going to see in a second that you are all tangled up about this. I know he was your mentor, Daniel, but he strangled Jennifer to death. He broke up her family. He lied to you too. Don't you see it?"

"What I see is that we have a strong case. In my world, I let the jury decide on guilt or innocence."

"Strong? Well then, why are you deliberately trying to weaken it?"

"What are you talking about?"

"The hooker you interviewed. Of course she's going to say that some cop was her trick when this happened. How convenient for her. Next thing you know, her lawyer will be signing up with Carmichael and all those other defence lawyers whining about police brutality." She raised her voice. "You watch. Any day now she'll be on the front page of the *Star* with her half-a-million-dollar lawsuit."

"I'm a cop, in case you hadn't noticed," he growled. "I investigate. Collect evidence. That's my job."

"No." Her white skin was turning red with anger. "You still think you're a lawyer. And all you're doing is muddying the waters."

He felt his face flush. Suddenly the room was too hot. He started to walk past her to the door.

"Where you going?" She moved in front of him and shut the door.

"Back to the office to get some work done. Move out of the way," he said.

"We need to talk things out."

"There's nothing else to say."

"Greene's a cold-blooded killer," she said. "He strangled Jennifer with his hands."

"Oh, really. How can you be so convinced?"

"I can see it in his eyes."

He grabbed her by the shoulder and made her look at him. "Jo, I can't believe you just said that. What's happened to you? Two days working with Angela Kreitinger and you've become Attila the Prosecutor."

She jutted out her jaw. "Get your hands off me," she hissed.

He released her. They glared at each other. "What's really going on here?" he asked. "Is this somehow about us?"

"Us?" she exclaimed. "Us? There's no fucking 'us,' unless you include your international model girlfriend."

A torrent of anger rolled through him. He felt blood surge through to his fingertips. "How about all the unmarried lawyers in your old Bay Street law firm you're dating."

He hadn't heard anything about her personal life. He was making it up on the fly.

"Ha!" she snarled. "Who said they're all unmarried?"

Sweat beaded on his forehead. His breathing was sharp. It had been years since he'd been this furious.

"If Greene's such a great detective," she said, "why hasn't he solved your brother's murder yet? Ever think about that?"

A wash of calm broke over him. His fury died. Every part of him felt cold.

He reached around her for the door handle, careful not to make contact. "I think about it every day. Maybe you should think about upholding Jennifer's legacy as a fair-minded Crown."

"Fuck you, Daniel." She smacked him hard on the shoulder with her racquet.

He stared down at the spot where she'd hit him and then back at her. "Really looking forward to working with you on this case." He turned his back and walked through the door.

He thought about slamming it behind him, but decided not to give her the satisfaction.

62

"ARI, ONLY FOR YOU WOULD I BE DRIVING A BREAD TRUCK AGAIN," BRIAN SILVER SAID OVER his shoulder as he pulled his delivery truck out of Greene's father's driveway.

Greene was squatting in the back between racks of fresh bread. "When I get out of this mess, Hap Charlton will give me tickets to the see the Raptors," he said. "You can take your son."

Silver had a fifteen-year-old boy with severe learning disabilities, who was obsessed with Toronto's basketball team.

"Deal," Silver said.

"Don't speed, whatever you do. The last thing we want is to get stopped."

"I'm driving like a Boy Scout."

The ride was bumpy, and Greene rolled with the sway of the truck. He couldn't see out the front window, but it was late and he could tell there was no traffic. He closed his eyes and let the time pass. Even hiding in the back of a truck with bad shocks felt better than being cooped up in his father's house.

"Heading down Jarvis," Silver said after a while. "Queen is the next block."

Greene moved up and crouched behind the passenger seat. "Make a left at the light and keep going till just past Sherbourne. He should be across the street on the north side."

Silver turned and Greene had to hold on to the seat back to keep his balance. Silver steered the truck into the curb lane and stopped. Greene sneaked a look out the driver's window. There was no one there. He checked his watch. It was exactly midnight.

"Where is this guy?" Silver asked.

"I don't know," Greene said.

Silver put on his flashers. "Get down, Ari," he hissed.

Out the front window Greene saw a patrol car approach from the east and glide past.

"I better look busy," Silver said. He got out, opened the back door, put three loaves of bread in a paper bag, and closed the door.

Greene rose up enough to look out the front window and watch Silver drop the bread in Popeye's doorway.

He heard a sound and ducked.

The passenger door opened and Fraser Dent climbed in. He was wearing his usual patchwork jacket, and his stringy hair was longer than ever.

"Evening, Monsieur Detective," he said with a chuckle.

"Thanks for doing this," Greene said.

Silver came back and opened the driver's door. "Hi, Brian Silver," he said to Dent, reaching out to shake his hand as if they were old friends.

"Call me Fraser," Dent said, grasping his hand.

"This truck's heading back to the lot," Silver said. "Fraser, you better get back there with your pal. Help yourself to a loaf."

"My pleasure," Dent said, slipping into the back. "This is like being in a paddy wagon, but with free food and no handcuffs."

Silver did a U-turn and drove through the downtown at a steady pace. Soon they were parked in the bakery's lot, surrounded by other delivery trucks.

"Ari, I'll be back in an hour," Silver said as he got out.

Greene moved into the driver's seat. Dent sat beside him in the passenger seat and tore open the wrapper on a loaf of white bread. He pulled out two slices and offered one to Greene.

"No thanks," Greene said.

Dent took a bite then opened a pack of cigarettes and held it out to Greene.

"No thanks again," Greene said.

"Don't tell me you quit already." Dent shook his head. "Take one, Detective. You might need it."

Greene took a cigarette and Dent lit it for him. It tasted foul. "What did you find out?"

"Why Raglan quit being a cop." Dent wolfed down a second slice of bread and lit up his own cigarette, tossed the match out the window, and took a few puffs.

Dent often took his time when he had something special to say and Greene had learned it was best not to rush him. The windows were open and the cool night air felt refreshing.

"I read in the paper that her husband called her Jennie," Dent said at last.

"That's right. Everyone in her hometown did. She hated the name."

"It jogged something in my memory," Dent said. "When I was an up-and-coming trader, I spent a year working in Tokyo back in 1985. I remember there was a story on the local news about Toronto, which when you are living over there is very weird. There was this Japanese judge at Old City Hall. Guy was a Second World War hero, fought in Germany. He used to give the cops a hard time on the witness stand. Started tossing out their cases."

"When was this?"

"September first, 1985. I went to the reference library and figured out the whole story. I'm still a good researcher when it counts. Before you joined the force, Raglan was a young recruit on the morality squad. I've asked some of the old guys. They say she was a star performer. Sounds like she was a real looker. Shit like that."

Greene pulled hard on the cigarette. It felt like everything in his life was off-kilter.

"Jennie was picked for the job," Dent said. "Went into the old fart's chambers all dolled up like a hooker up on charges. Offered to do him a little personal favour if he could help her out. Sucker fell for it. Yanked down his pants right under his robes. She called in backup and he was busted. It was all over the papers right across the country. The States too. Like I said, it made the news in Japan. Two days later, the war-hero judge jumps off a bridge. Had a wife and two kids, like I used to have."

How much more am I going to find out about Jennifer that I never knew? Greene wondered. He could imagine how horrified she must have been when she heard the judge had killed himself. "That's when she quit the force?" he asked.

"Very next day, I heard, back in the mid-1980s," Dent said. "Want to guess who her partner was on the assignment?"

"No idea."

"Newbridge."

"Clyde Newbridge?" Greene's head started to throb. "He was one of the cops who arrested me with Kennicott."

"The very same asshole. Hap Charlton's fat attack dog. You didn't know about any of this stuff?"

"No," Greene said. He tossed the cigarette butt out the window.

"Everyone's got secrets, Detective. You of all people should know that." Dent reached behind him and grabbed another loaf. "Got to go."

"Thanks," Greene said.

"Anytime. Take these, you're the guy on the bubble this time." Dent tossed the rest of his pack of cigarettes in Greene's lap, opened the door, and disappeared.

Greene looked at his watch. It was only 12:30. Silver wouldn't be back for half an hour. Greene hadn't brought his cell phone. He didn't want to leave a cyber-trail of his movements when he was flagrantly breaching his bail. And he couldn't risk walking on the street.

He stepped outside and leaned against the truck. He looked south at the lights on the CN Tower, flicking high above the city in the night sky. He lit another cigarette, inhaled, and blew out the smoke in an awkward white puff.

He smelled something familiar. Smoke. Not from his own cigarette, but a heavier scent. It took him a moment to place it, and as his memory clicked in he heard a voice he knew very well.

"Being on bail's driven you to smoking," Hap Charlton said, walking out of the darkness and waving a tipped cigarillo.

Greene wasn't surprised to see him. Charlton loved making an entrance when he was least expected. It was his way of letting you know he had his fingers on the pulse of everything. He'd probably had him followed all the way downtown. They hadn't spoken since Greene's arrest, and he knew Charlton had to be itching to pick his brain.

Greene put his hands together and stretched out his arms. "You got handcuffs?" he asked.

Charlton laughed. "Ari, you're a lousy smoker." He stood beside Greene with his back to the truck, took a puff of his little cigar, and exhaled a perfect line of smoke.

"I quit in junior high," Greene said. "Cold turkey."

Charlton smiled. "How's your dad?"

"Having me around is cramping his style. How's the campaign?"

"To tell you the truth, the poll numbers are so good we're trying to play them down."

"Jennifer getting killed didn't hurt, did it?" Charlton was blatantly using

Raglan's murder to ratchet up his tough-on-crime campaign, and clearly it had worked.

Charlton shrugged. "Politics is politics. If you're not in it to win, there's no point in running. The murder happened. Bad timing for my opponent, so we take advantage of it. Like Obama with that storm. Hey, shit happens, but I've never thrown you under the bus."

The news media had tried to make a big deal out of the fact that one of Charlton's top homicide detectives had been charged with murder. He had stated unequivocally that Greene was innocent until proven otherwise and had publicly pledged to have no involvement at all in the investigation or the trial.

Greene banged the side of the bread truck. "I thought I'd done a pretty good job of covering my tracks while I breached my bail," he said.

"Not bad. But you forgot, I've known Lindsmore for twenty-five years."

Greene nodded. Of course, Charlton would figure out the Lindsmore connection, and Lindsmore, although he was a good guy, would have no choice but to spill the beans.

"So Lindsmore's been telling you what I've been telling him," Greene said.

"Which is basically fuck-all," Charlton said. "Except that you didn't kill Jennifer. This Fraser Dent guy you were just talking to. I looked him up. He's been one of your sources for a while."

Greene waved his cigarette pack at the high-rise towers that filled the city core. "He used to work in one of those offices. Made more money in a month than you and me make combined in a year."

"And now he's stealing loaves from a bread truck," Hap said.

They smoked in silence.

"The condemned man has his last cigarette," Greene said.

"Fool for love is more like it," Charlton said.

"You talked to Kennicott?"

"Hey, I made a campaign pledge to stay out of it."

"That's why I'm asking."

Charlton laughed. "I'm glad to see you haven't lost your sense of humour. The answer is no, I haven't."

"Let me guess. He's too wet behind the ears. Easier to talk to me like this."

"Something like that."

A thought occurred to Greene. "Did you have Lindsmore wired?"

"Like I said, you didn't say shit to him anyways," Charlton said with a shrug, tacitly, but not explicitly, confirming that Lindsmore had been wired and he'd heard the tapes.

This didn't surprise Greene either. It was Charlton's style. But he wouldn't have been able to wire the bread van or Fraser Dent and he was probably dying to know what Greene was up to.

"So you know I asked Lindsmore to find Dent, and that I asked Dent to find out more about the time when Jennifer was a cop. Detective Work 101: Get to know your victim," Greene said.

"What did Dent tell you?" Charlton asked,

"Not much. She worked morality for a few years. Some of the old guys remember her being very pretty. Quit and went to law school."

"Did he say why she quit?" Charlton asked. Anxious for an answer.

Who was Jennifer Raglan? Greene wondered. He didn't know anymore. He didn't really know anything. That sense of caution, which had been gnawing at him since the morning of the murder, was back.

"No, Dent had no idea." Greene tossed his cigarette on the concrete and ground it out. "Looks like it's a mystery that died with her."

PART
SIX

63

NOTHING LIKE A COURTROOM AT TEN O'CLOCK ON A MONDAY MORNING WHEN A BIG trial was about to begin, Angela Kreitinger thought as she watched the twelve members of the jury file in. Every seat in the courtroom was filled, the front rows by the press, except for the one directly behind her chair, which was set aside for Howard Darnell and his three children. He sat there, alone.

When the jurors were seated and settled in their chairs, Mr. Singh rose. He adjusted his robes and looked up at Judge Norville. "Your Honour," he said, "all twelve members of the jury are present."

"Thank you, Mr. Registrar," Norville said. "Before we start these proceedings, as I suspect everyone in this courtroom is aware, today our new mayor, Hap Charlton, is being sworn into office. Court will rise at four, instead of our usual four-thirty time. That way I and many of my colleagues can attend the ceremony."

While the rest of us go back to the office and work all night, Kreitinger thought.

Norville smiled at her. "Madam Crown, please proceed."

"Thank you, Your Honour." Kreitinger walked to the lectern between her table and the jury box and placed the court binder that Jo Summers had prepared on it. The only thing the jurors knew about Ari Greene was his name, what he looked like, and that he was charged with first-degree murder. Most wouldn't even know who the victim was. Since the Crown always addressed the jury first, this was her chance to draw the picture of him that she wanted them to see.

Opening addresses were tricky. Some overeager Crowns started their case by throwing out a laundry list of every fact they thought they could prove. Often all this did was confuse and overwhelm the jury. Even worse, if during the trial they fell short of their mark, when the defence made its closing argument, they'd pounce on every unproven detail, no matter how minute.

Other Crowns, fearful of overreaching, were too cautious. They watered down their remarks to the point where their advocacy had no passion, leaving the jury unmoved, not engaged.

Kreitinger believed the key was to tell a story. Find the theme that ran through the case and drive it home.

"Ladies and gentlemen of the jury," she said, looking up from her binder. "This trial is about a man who murdered his lover, because she was about to end their affair."

She paused to let it sink in.

"The accused man is right there with his two lawyers." She glanced over at Greene, who was sitting between Ted DiPaulo and his partner, Nancy Parish.

"His name is Ari Greene. He is a police officer. A twenty-five-year veteran of the Toronto Police Service and a homicide detective for the last five years. All very impressive for sure. But whether he is a homicide detective, a bank president, a gold-medal athlete, or a sanitary worker who collects garbage every day doesn't matter to the Crown. And I know it won't matter to you. In this courtroom he is one person: the accused. And what he's accused of is the most heinous crime in the criminal code: first-degree murder. "

A few of the jurors nodded. Good. Time to get to the bad part of the story right away. Lay it out there.

"The victim was a woman named Jennifer Raglan. Her full title was Crown Attorney Jennifer Raglan. That's right. She used to do the same job I'm doing. For years she stood right here, at this very lectern, speaking to jurors like yourselves. But it doesn't matter what her job was. What matters is this: She was a woman who was viciously murdered by her lover, the accused." No more using Greene's name. Until the trial was over, as many times as she could fit it in, Kreitinger was going to call him the accused. And work in the most compelling verb of all, "murdered," as often as possible.

One of the jurors who had nodded, a well-dressed, middle-aged woman who had listed her job as arts administrator, flicked her gaze toward the defence table, then quickly back to Kreitinger.

"'Lover' might sound like an old-fashioned word to you, and perhaps it is," she said. "But the facts are not in dispute. As you will soon hear, Jennifer was married to Howard, her high-school sweetheart from Welland, the small town where they both grew up. Mr. Darnell is in court today."

She turned slowly and looked at Darnell, seated alone behind her, flanked by empty seats in the packed room, then back at the jury. She focused on the arts administrator. The woman looked like the kind of take-charge juror she wanted to get on her side right away.

"Howard and Jennifer have three children, Aaron, Barry, and Corinne, and you'll be glad to know they are not here. I do not intend to call them as witnesses."

She wanted the jurors to feel good about a prosecutor who would spare the children. The arts administrator looked back at Kreitinger and practically mouthed the words *thank you*.

Time to deliver the dirt. Kreitinger left the lectern and her binder and walked to the far end of the jury box. Twelve sets of eyes followed her.

"It probably won't shock you to hear that like many couples, especially, it seems, when they marry young and are busy raising their families, Howard and Jennifer's marriage was not perfect. They had problems."

She bridged her hands in front of her. A few of the women jurors sneaked looks at her fingers. She knew they'd want to check whether she wore a wedding ring. She was sending them a message: *No, I'm not married, but yes, I get it.*

"Two years ago, Jennifer even left the marriage. She moved out on her own for a few months. These things happen, we all know that. But then Jennie, as Howard and all her high-school friends called her, went back home."

She intentionally referred to Darnell and Raglan by their first names. Plain small-town folks. A good marriage, with a few little rocky parts. All destroyed by this murder.

Back at the lectern, she flipped the page in her binder. She'd typed out this part in a large font size to make it easy to read.

It was crucial that the jury believe one hundred percent that Greene had been present at the scene of the crime. She still hadn't decided whether to put his father on the witness stand to prove this. Probably not. She'd subpoenaed him, and he was sitting in a waiting room outside.

In case she didn't call him, and in case Greene never testified, she needed the jury to fill in the blanks.

"For six weeks in August and September, Jennifer lied to Howard," she said, half reading, half talking to the jury. "She had become interested in long-distance running, and for six consecutive Monday mornings she'd told him she was going for a training run. She'd told her colleagues that she couldn't come in those mornings as well. But it was a lie. Instead, she would jog from her home in the Beach, and go to a different motel room along Kingston Road. She wore a disguise when she arrived. Paid cash. Brought with her music to play and candles to burn."

All of these were facts Kreitinger was going to prove by calling the motel owners as witnesses, playing the video from the Coffee Time, showing the photos of the motel room. Here is where it got tricky.

"On those same six Monday mornings, the accused, who for years came to work bright and early every day, didn't show up until one o'clock in the afternoon."

To prove this she had Francine Hughes and the meticulous attendance records she kept for the homicide squad.

"Monday, September tenth, was the last day that the two of them were going to meet this way. Why? Because she was scheduled to start a three-month fraud trial on the next Monday, right in this courthouse."

A few jurors sneaked looks again at Greene, then snapped their eyes back to her. The arts administrator didn't bother. She was listening to every word.

"Her six-week tryst was about to finish. Some men could have understood that. Why a married woman with three children would end things. But not the accused. Because on that Monday morning, less than three months ago, he murdered her."

Although in law, the Crown was not required to prove motive, Kreitinger had learned from years of prosecuting people that for juries, motive was everything. It was important that they understand the how and the when and where of a serious crime. But, to get them to convict, you had to convince them of the why.

She flipped a page over in her binder, making a loud snapping sound, telegraphing to the jury that she was going to say no more on the subject. That she didn't have to. That they got the message.

"Sadly, as part of this prosecution, I'm going to be forced to show you some very disturbing photographs." She wasn't using her notes anymore. And she had chosen the word "sadly" very deliberately to make it sound as if it were all Greene's fault they were even having a trial. A real man would take his licks and plead guilty, wouldn't he?

"You will see that Jennifer was killed in a most vicious and angry way. Not by a gun at some distance. Not by a knife that did the dirty work. She was strangled to death. Her killer had his hands on her throat. Stared into her eyes. Squeezed the life out of her. It's terrible to even say these words. Never mind contemplate the act. The pain. The sheer horror. But yes, that's what the accused did. He strangled her. First-degree murder."

At last she turned toward Greene and glared at him. Some Crowns liked to point at an accused, but it wasn't necessary.

Greene was experienced enough to know not to look away. He took a deep breath, then broke eye contact and looked straight ahead.

She spun back to the jury. "He killed Jennifer with his own hands, before she had the chance to go back home to her family."

The last line had only come to her this morning on her third cup of coffee. As soon as she heard it in her head, she knew it was a zinger. The stunning silence in court told her she'd hit her mark.

Bull's-eye.

64

GREENE FELT A GENTLE TAP ON HIS THIGH. HE LOOKED DOWN. IT TOOK HIM A MOMENT TO realize that DiPaulo was passing him a note.

He bought it up to the table on the side farthest from the jury and read it.

DiPaulo had written: *Great fucking opening.*

Well, that sure makes me feel better, Greene thought. He picked up his pen and wrote, *But what do you* really *think?* and passed it back.

DiPaulo glanced down at it and smirked.

Greene took the note back and wrote: *I thought she'd make a big deal about how I "deceived" Kennicott.*

DiPaulo shook his head and wrote quickly. *She's afraid to call Kennicott because then I'll cross-examine him on the new alternative-suspect evidence of the prostitute. She's betting I'll put you on the stand, then she can hammer you on cross.*

Greene folded the paper over and steadied his hands on the table. He felt something touch his left fingers. Nancy Parish's skin was soft. She mouthed the words: *Hang in.*

Judge Norville smiled at Kreitinger. "Thank you, Madam Crown." She looked at the jury. "Ladies and gentlemen, the defence has the option of making an opening address to you now, or later in the proceedings, or even, if it chooses, not at all. Mr. Greene's lawyer, Mr. DiPaulo, has informed me that he will not make an opening statement at this time."

Last night, when the were doing their final preparations for today, Greene and DiPaulo had spent a lot of time debating this. With so much up in the air with witnesses, they'd agreed it was best to wait. It kept their options open, which could be crucial later in the trial. But the price they paid for their silence was that initially the jury would hear only the worst version of everything.

Norville turned back to Kreitinger. "Madam Crown, your first witness, please."

This is it, Greene thought.

For the last week, Kreitinger and DiPaulo had been playing a cat-and-mouse game about which witnesses would testify. She had provided him with a long list of names, but refused to say which ones she would call or in what order.

"Kreitinger is playing hardball," DiPaulo had explained to Greene. "Unless I tell her whether or not you are going to testify, she's going to keep us in the dark about who she's going to call and when."

"What did you tell her?" Greene had asked.

"No deal."

Greene watched Kreitinger bend down and talk to Jo Summers, her junior lawyer on the case. They both nodded. She straightened back up.

"The Crown calls as its first witness," she said, "Officer Brygida Zeilinski."

Parish squeezed Greene's hand.

DiPaulo looked at him. "Be warned," he whispered, "when the jury sees those photographs, they are going to hate you."

65

THERE WERE THREE SEATS AT THE CROWN'S TABLE. AS THE LEAD COUNSEL, KREITINGER SAT closest to the jury. Jo Summers was in the middle, and Daniel Kennicott was farthest away from the jurors and closest to the defence.

Since their fight at the Ping-Pong place in September, Kennicott and Summers had been cold and clinical with each other. They made a point of never being alone. When they worked together, they talked only about the case. She avoided making eye contact with him.

He had tried to convince himself that he was too busy to care because as the officer in charge of the case he had a full plate. The OIC had to make certain the witnesses were in court, to arrange all the exhibits in order, to have at his fingertips any statements, reports, or other pieces of evidence the Crown attorneys might need, and to ensure that the defence was given copies of everything.

What was even tougher was having to sit in court and watch the proceedings unfold. He kept going over and over in his mind every detail of the case. He was still trying to sort out his feelings of betrayal by Greene, and then there was the aching question he couldn't answer: Was Greene was guilty or innocent?

The ident officer, Zeilinski, walked up to the witness stand, carrying a large briefcase. She perched it on the wood railing by her side as she was sworn in. Then she reached in, removed a pair of reading glasses on a chain that she strung around her neck, a green police notebook, and a thick white binder. She placed the glasses on her nose, put the briefcase on the floor, and smiled at Kreitinger.

"Yes, am ready now," she said in her charming Polish accent.

She was like an experienced civil servant taking her place at her desk and setting up for a day's work, Kennicott thought. He glanced at the jurors and saw a few of them were smiling at her.

Kreitinger moved back to the lectern while Zeilinski was sworn as a witness.

"Officer Zeilinski," Kreitinger said, "you have been a member of the Toronto

Police Service for twenty-one years and a forensic officer for the last seven. Correct?"

"Yes, is correct," Zeilinski said.

Kreitinger looked down at her notes, and Kennicott saw Zeilinski glance over at Greene and smile. A few of the jurors also noticed.

"To begin," Kreitinger said, looking up, "you know the accused."

"Yes. Of course. Detective Greene. Many, many years. We do many, many cases together."

"But the accused didn't work on this case with you."

"On this case, no."

"And did the fact that you knew the accused, that you had worked with him, did that in any way affect your investigation?"

"No, I treat Detective Greene case like every other one."

Zeilinski's binder was filled with photographs from the crime scene. All morning Kreitinger had her patiently explain each picture, passing them one at a time to the jurors, then to the defence, who had a binder of the same photos open on their table, and finally to Mr. Singh, who marked each one as an exhibit before he passed them to the judge.

Kennicott knew that the most effective thing he could do during the trial was to keep his head down and make meticulous notes. The jury would see the OIC hard at work and dispassionate. It was boring and in many ways useless work. After all, every word was being taken down by the court reporter and would be available in transcript.

Still, it kept him grounded. He wrote page after page of Zeilinki's testimony. *Can you identify this photograph? Is exhibit number 1G, is showing candles on dresser. Six, all blown out. This photograph? Is exhibit number 1M, is showing clothes of deceased found under bed. Is exhibit number 1PP, is showing face of deceased. Is exhibit number 1QQ, is showing bruises on neck.*

The pictures became increasingly graphic. Zeilinski narrated, and Kreitinger paraded them around the court in a ceaseless carousel.

"And finally," Kreitinger said, spying the courtroom clock. It was almost 11:30. "This last photograph. Can you identify it?"

"Yes. Is exhibit number 1WW. Is boot mark on door of bathroom."

Kreitinger took the picture and did her tour of the jury, defence, and the registrar, then returned to her lectern.

"For the record, Officer Zeilinski, where is this boot mark in relation to the door handle?"

Zeilinski looked a bit taken aback at being asked a question that wasn't "Can you identify this photograph?" After a moment she replied: "Is below door handle."

"You were a police officer on general patrol for fourteen years before becoming an identification officer."

"Yes, is true."

"And one of the things you learned to do was to kick in doors. Correct?"

"Is correct."

The jurors, and even Judge Norville, who'd been numbed by the relentless rounds of photographs, were all now paying close attention.

"And in your experience and training as a police officer, where is the best place to kick a door if one wants to open it quickly?"

Zeilinski, who had never hesitated in her testimony all through the morning, faltered. Kennicott saw her steal another glance at Greene.

"Is in same spot as exhibit 1WW," she said, at last.

"Under the door handle?"

"Yes, under handle."

"And why is that, Officer Zeilinski?"

Kennicott looked over his last page of notes. Kreitinger had kept referring to Zeilinski as "Officer," driving home the fact that she, like Greene, was a cop.

"Because, is close to lock. Break lock, door open fast."

Kreitinger gave her a subtle smile. "Thank you, Officer. Those are my questions."

Norville looked at the clock then at Kreitinger with an inquisitive look.

"Your Honour, I see that it's eleven-thirty," Kreitinger said. "Perhaps this is the appropriate time for the morning coffee break."

Norville broke out into a big smile. "Excellent suggestion," she said.

66

"THE CROWN CALLS DETECTIVE RAYMOND ALPINE," KREITINGER SAID FROM HER PLACE AT THE lectern when everyone was back in court after the break.

Greene watched Alpine walk to the witness box, his back straight. He was the kind of confident, no-nonsense police witness Crowns and juries loved.

After he was sworn, Alpine adjusted his seat, placed his police notebook on the front ledge of the witness stand, and smiled at the jury. Taking his time, he looked over at Kreitinger as casually as a company president sitting down in a boardroom for his weekly staff meeting.

Greene had known Alpine in the casual way senior officers got to know each other in a police force as large as Toronto's. A decade earlier they'd worked out of the same division downtown for a year or two. Alpine had never made it all the way to Homicide, and Greene's sense of the man was that it didn't matter to him.

After having Alpine run through his impressive work history as a cop, Kreitinger got down to business.

"Detective, before I ask you about the events of September tenth, what, if anything, did you discover about the movements of the victim, Ms. Raglan, on the five Monday mornings before that date?"

"We interviewed the owners of all of the motels along Kingston Road and discovered that, on those five Mondays, Ms. Raglan had rented rooms at five different motels," he said. "Each time she reserved room 8. Each time she paid cash. Each time she wore the wig and sunglasses that we found under her bed at the Maple Leaf Motel."

"Didn't she have to work those days?" Kreitinger asked.

"No, she had specifically requested to have those Monday mornings off. She'd told the people at work and her family that she was preparing to run in a marathon and needed the time for training."

"And the accused?" Kreitinger pointed at Greene.

She's not at all shy about it, he thought, feeling the eyes of the jury following her finger.

"Did you discover anything about his work schedule during the same time period?"

"I did. For the last five years, he's always arrived at work early on Monday mornings. The only exception was those six weeks."

"When did he show up on those Mondays?"

"At one o'clock in the afternoon, including on September tenth."

DiPaulo had been right. Even though Greene had read the disclosure many times, hearing it out loud in court made it sound much worse.

Alpine described the 911 call, received at 10:39, how he had rushed to the scene, entered room 8, saw the dead woman, and deployed his men to search for suspects and witnesses.

Kreitinger walked up to Mr. Singh and had him take two pictures out of Officer Zeilinski's photo binder.

"Detective, I'm showing to you Exhibits 1N and 1XX. Do you recognize these pictures?" she asked.

"I do," he said. "Exhibit 1N is a photo of the boot mark found on the door to the bathroom in room 8. And Exhibit 1XX is a photo of the treads of a boot found in the accused's home."

"I understand this boot was seized temporarily as a result of a search warrant," she said. "And that this was done before his arrest and without his knowledge."

"Yes. I had the identification officer prepare a comparison chart of the two exhibits."

Kreitinger went back to the Crown's table and Summers passed up a board to her. "This it?" she asked him.

Two photographs were mounted side by side on the board, showing both sets of tread marks. The jurors craned their necks to look.

"It is," he said. "The mark on the door is on the left, the actual boot print is on the right."

"We'll call a footwear expert later for his professional opinion on how similar these are," Kreitinger said as she slowly paraded the photos in front of the jury box. "But right now I want to show these to the jurors."

Greene knew this was pure theatre. Even though the expert would say only that the treads were "probably" the same, Kreitinger was driving home to the jury a none-too-subtle message: Use your common sense, you can see for your-self that it's obvious Greene had been in the room.

Kreitinger returned again to the Crown table and Summers handed her a large paper bag. She took it to Alpine and opened it for him to look inside.

He nodded. "Yes," he said, pulling out a black, right-foot boot. "This is the boot we seized from the accused's home after his arrest. We used it to make the impression seen in the second photograph on the board you just showed me."

"I see," Kreitinger said as she walked the boot in front of the jury. "And, De-tective, did you recognize this type of boot?"

"I did. It's the standard uniform boot issued to every member of the Toronto Police Service."

She took the boot and the bag over to the registrar, had them mark it as an-other exhibit, and retreated behind the lectern.

Well done, Angie, Greene thought. In a circumstantial case, any piece of physical evidence bolstered the case. Helped fill in the gaps.

"About the accused's home," Kreitinger said. "Do you know if any other adults were living there at the time of your search?"

"It appeared from the limited number of clothes that we found that only one person lived there. Only one of the two bedrooms seemed to be used. Very little food was in the refrigerator and freezer. I did a record check of the address for any driver's licences, residential phones, taxes, and water and electricity bills as well as the electoral roll. Each time only one name came up. The same name was on all the mail I found."

"And what name was that?" Kreitinger asked, with a self-satisfied grin.

"Ari Greene."

"Thank you," Kreitinger said.

Greene realized that this was about a lot more than matching his boots to the mark on the bathroom door. Kreitinger had used this whole scenario to portray him as a loner. The kind of love-starved, jealous, possessive man who would snap and kill a woman who was trying to end their affair.

67

IN RECENT YEARS, AMANKWAH HAD FOUND IT INCREASINGLY DIFFICULT TO GET AN INTER-view with the families of murder victims during a trial. It used to be that they would walk in and out of court with everyone else, eat in the same cafeteria, hang out in the hall on breaks. Once the proceedings were under way, Amankwah would start by saying a polite hello in the hallway, and then perhaps make a comment about the food while in the lunch line with them, and after a few weeks they'd start to talk to him. First chitchat, but eventually he'd get a full interview, which he'd hold off publishing – it was called embargoing a story in the trade – until the trial had ended.

But now families were protected by an army of Victim Witness people, who escorted them to and from court, where they sat in specially reserved seats, sat beside them during the proceedings, provided them with a private room where they went during breaks and where they ate their meals. Like first-class passengers with their own boarding lounge and their own flight attendants, they travelled in a protective cocoon.

Amankwah didn't begrudge them their privacy, but he missed the casual intimacy of the old system. And often, he found, the families really did want to talk.

Every once in a while, there was someone who rejected this blanket coverage, and to his surprise Howard Darnell was one of them. All last week, while the pretrial motions were being held and the jury was being selected, he had come to court on his own, sat by himself, waited patiently in the hallway during breaks in the proceedings, and went out of the courthouse alone during lunch breaks.

Amankwah had watched him from a distance. Last Wednesday, he had timed it so that they got in the elevator at the same time.

"Hi," he'd said, when the doors closed.

"Hello," Darnell said.

They travelled in silence. Before they landed on the main floor Amankwah spoke. "No secrets. I'm a reporter for the *Star*, covering the trial," he said.

"I know who you are," Darnell said. "I've read your stories for many years."

The elevator stopped, the doors opened, and Darnell insisted that Amankwah exit first.

At the end of the day last Thursday, Amankwah had made sure he left the courtroom at the same time as Darnell. They rode down in the elevator again. When the doors opened, Darnell said, "Good night, Mr. Amankwah," before he walked away.

On Friday, court finished early. Amankwah caught up to Darnell in the hall. His heart was pounding, like a teenager asking a girl out on a first date. "I don't want to intrude," he said, "but do you have time for a cup of coffee?"

Darnell smiled. "Please, call me Howard," he said. "Sorry, I can't today, I've got to go pick up the kids."

This morning, when he came into court, Amankwah made a point of sitting in the press seat closest to Darnell. They'd exchanged glances and smiled at each other.

It was lunchtime, and his gang of journalists was debating where to eat. Kirt Bishop from the *Globe* wanted dim sum on Dundas, Zach Stone from the *Sun* wanted Italian on Bay, and Kristen Thatcher from the *Post* voted for sushi on Queen.

"I'm going to beg off today, guys," Amankwah told them.

"Oh, now that you're a, quote unquote, political commentator, you can't be seen hanging out with us lowly, ink-stained wretches," Bishop said, clapping a hand on Amankwah's shoulder.

They all laughed and the three reporters went off for sushi.

Amankwah had been eyeing Darnell, who he sensed was deliberately lingering nearby. They got in the elevator at the same time yet again.

"Tough morning," Amankwah said when the doors closed.

Darnell pushed the button to the main floor. "Would you like to go for that cup of coffee?" he asked.

"Sure, let's leave by the north door. Not many people use it," Amankwah said.

Snow had been forecast. It hadn't yet arrived, but it was cold outside. They both buttoned up their overcoats. "Jennie used to tell me most Crowns were afraid to talk to reporters," Darnell said, moving at a quick clip. "She thought it was a mistake."

"Your wife was a very good lawyer."

"That's what everyone tells me. Look, I don't really want to go for coffee. Let's walk, if you don't mind."

"Sure," Amankwah said.

They headed up to Dundas Street, then west, and soon they were in the midst of Chinatown.

"I'm a mathematician. You're going to have to explain to me this on-the-record and off-the-record stuff you journalists use," he said.

"It's simple," Amankwah said. "You tell me something. If you say it's off the record, then it's our secret. If you don't, I can print it."

"So the onus is on me to be clear about things."

"That's right. You can also embargo a story with me."

"Meaning, we talk about something now, and I say you can use it, but not until after the trial is over?"

"Exactly."

They were already at Spadina Avenue. It was surprising how far you could go in a short time if you headed in one direction, Amankwah thought. They crossed the wide street and Darnell kept going. In two blocks he turned north, and soon they were in the midst of Kensington Market, the city's old outdoor market district, filled with a dizzying array of shops selling cheese, bread, nuts, meat, and fruits and vegetables; a jumble of eclectic vintage-clothing stores; tons of restaurants with foods from all over the globe. Every immigrant group that had come to the city had passed through here and left its mark. Every spare wall was filled with colourful graffiti.

Darnell stopped in the middle of the street. Reggae was playing from a music store that also sold rugs from Nepal. The smell of fresh bread drifted from another. Tortillas were frying at Mexican restaurant with its windows open despite the cold.

"Look at this place, isn't it fantastic?" he said, a smile on his face for the first time since Amankwah had met him. He checked his watch. "It took us fifteen minutes to walk here."

"We used to shop here all the time when my family first arrived from Ghana, but I haven't been here for years," Amankwah said.

"Okay, this is off the record, for now at least. Jennie and I moved to Toronto when we were both so young. I started at an actuarial firm and I worked all the time. She was a cop, and then became a lawyer. We bought our house out in the Beach. Then we had kids. I was sheltered. I'd never seen much of the city. Imagine, I'd never been here, Kensington Market, until this summer, after I was fired. She was lying to me about her affair. Well, I never told her I'd lost my job. I spent six weeks walking all over Toronto. I couldn't believe what I'd missed."

Amankwah looked closely at Darnell. Was the man crazy? Still in shock? He could never have predicted a conversation like this.

"I've come here every day since the trial began," Darnell said. "I don't have much of an appetite these days. I get an apple at that fruit stand over there. Can I buy you one?"

"Sure, but why don't you let the *Toronto Star* pay?"

"No," he said firmly. "Because we're still off the record. You have children, Mr. Amankwah?"

"Six-year-old daughter and four-year-old son. I'm divorced. I only get to see them every other weekend and Wednesday nights."

"I'm sorry to hear that."

"I could say you get used to it, but that would be a lie."

Darnell shook his head. "You know, sometimes I think if this hadn't happened, we probably would have ended up getting divorced. And then, how often would I see my kids?"

"I know it's such a clichéd question, but how are they doing?" Amankwah asked.

They were at the fruit stand on the corner. Darnell bought a pair of bright red McIntosh apples and handed one to Amankwah.

"The younger two are going to be okay, I think. As okay as you can be. It's my oldest son I'm worried about."

"Anything I can do to help?"

"I don't think so," Darnell said. "But make sure this is off the record. Aaron is an out-of-control graffiti artist who has a serious drug problem. I tricked him to get him across the border and put him in a rehab program down in a remote location in New Mexico. He was supposed to be there for at least a year. But he's too smart for them. They went into town last week and he escaped."

"Where do you think he's gone?" Amankwah asked.

"Oh, he's back here in the city."

"How'd he manage that?"

Darnell shook his head. "That's Aaron. As much as we can tell, he met some girl, talked her into letting him use her phone to text a friend in Toronto who wired him some money. He either hitchhiked or took a bus. Or both. Got to the border, and even though he didn't have a passport, he's a Canadian citizen and an adult. He talked them into letting him in without notifying me."

"How do you know he's here?"

Darnell took another bite of his apple. "Yesterday he sent me an e-mail from an Internet café. Said, 'Dad, I'm back. I'm safe. Don't look for me.' And last night I checked the garage, and his bicycle was gone."

"Where could he be?"

Darnell chuckled. "Your kids are young. Wait till they're teenagers. Aaron's done this before. He can couch-surf for months and he's impossible to find."

"Why don't you tell the police?"

Darnell took a final bite of the apple and tossed the core in a garbage bin. "This is still off the record. Aaron's had more than enough problems with the police. The cops at 43 Division were glad to see him go and I don't want to tip them off that their least-favourite graffiti artist is back in town."

68

GREENE OFTEN STAYED UP FOR FORTY-EIGHT HOURS STRAIGHT, OR MORE, DURING THE FIRST days of a homicide investigation and usually didn't feel tired at all. But by three o'clock on the first day of his own trial, he was more exhausted than he'd ever been in his life.

And he knew the worst was yet to come.

"Detective, I want to play you the video from the Coffee Time doughnut shop, the one located down the street from the Maple Leaf Motel," Kreitinger said to Alpine, who'd been on the stand all afternoon.

During the lunch break, Jo Summers had set up a screen and positioned it so that everyone could see it. Now she picked up a remote, Kreitinger nodded at her, and the four-part video began to play.

DiPaulo had repeatedly told Greene never to look at the jury, but he couldn't stop himself from stealing a glance at their faces. These people only knew Jennifer from the still photos of her dead body. Now they would see her moving. Alive.

The jurors watched intently as Alpine described for them what they were seeing on the screen: Jennifer coming into the Coffee Time in her running gear, slipping into the washroom, coming out in her new clothes wearing the wig and sunglasses, going to the pay phone.

When Jennifer headed toward the front door, Alpine nodded at Summers. She hit a button on the remote and the one-quarter image filled the screen.

No one spoke as Jennifer walked briskly along the empty sidewalk, swinging her backpack. It was like the final scene in a movie you never want to end, Greene thought.

"Could you pause it here for a moment please," Kreitinger said.

The image of Jennifer froze.

All Greene could think of was that she looked beautiful and happy and was about to die. He felt ill. He wanted to cry. He wanted to scream in rage and frustration.

He heard one of the jurors sob, but he didn't dare look over again.

"Officer, the pay phone we saw Ms. Raglan using," Kreitinger said. "Were you able to find out who she was calling?"

Greene couldn't stop staring at the screen. Summers had paused it at a perfect point. Jennifer's body seemed to be in full motion. This was how Kreitinger had staged it, for maximum emotional impact.

"Yes, we were," Alpine said. "Before we arrested the defendant, we obtained a search warrant for his cell-phone records."

"Excuse me," Judge Norville said.

Kreitinger looked up. "Yes, Your Honour?"

Norville pointed at the video screen. "Do we really need to have this on any longer?"

As if on cue, the video started up again on its own and within seconds Jennifer walked into the void. The street was empty.

"Of course not, Your Honour," Kreitinger said, acting as if this was some oversight. She nodded at Summers, who immediately hit the remote and the screen went blank.

They'll be high-fiving themselves about this back in the Crown's office after court, Greene thought. A criminal trial was theatre, and they'd put on a show-stopper.

Kreitinger focused her attention back on Alpine.

"Detective, you were telling the jury about the defendant's cell-phone records. What were you able to find?"

Alpine opened his notebook to a page he'd folded over to mark it.

Greene knew that a veteran cop such as Alpine didn't need to refer to his notes. He'd have all the numbers burned into his brain. But it was a good prop. It made his testimony more authoritative.

"A call was received on the defendant's cell phone that originated from this phone at the Coffee Time at 9:56:12 on September tenth. It lasted for one minute and thirty-two seconds. We triangulated the location of the cell phone at the time the call was received."

"What does 'triangulate' mean?" Kreitinger asked.

Alpine turned to the jury. "All cell-phone calls in Toronto are located between three towers. By a method known as triangulating, we can track which cell tower received the strongest signal, and by comparing it with the strength of the signal received by two nearby towers we can get an exact location of where the incoming call was received."

"And where was the accused's phone located when it received the call the victim made from the pay phone at the Coffee Time on Kingston Road?"

"At the accused's residence."

"The same place where you found Exhibit Two, the boots?"

"Yes, the same location."

"And, Detective, it's a bit hard to read up on the screen, but can you please tell the jury the time indicated on Exhibit Three, the tapes from Coffee Time, when we see Ms. Raglan pick up the receiver of the pay phone."

"9:56:12," Alpine said.

"The exact same time to the second."

"The exact same time."

Greene didn't dare look at the clock on the wall above the jury. He pulled back the cuff on his left wrist and checked his watch. It was 3:50. Ten minutes to go until court ended.

From her position at the lectern Kreitinger motioned to Summers, who reached down for a board that she took over to her. Greene couldn't see what was on it.

Kreitinger walked back to the witness box. "Detective Alpine, this is a scale map of Toronto, which I have had enlarged and mounted." She showed it to him, turned it toward Judge Norville, and then the jury.

"As you can see, I've marked the location of the Maple Leaf Motel and the Coffee Time on Kingston Road with yellow arrows and labelled them. Are these accurate?"

Alpine studied the map, pretending he'd never seen it before. "That's right," he said.

These last ten minutes are going to seem like an hour, Greene thought. He could see what Kreitinger was going to do. It was like being buried alive.

"I have more of these arrow sticky notes in my pocket," Kreitinger said, pulling them out of her vest pocket. "Could you please place one on the location of Detective Greene's residence, where he received that phone call."

Alpine took the first label and placed it pointing at Greene's house.

"Thank you. Do you the know how long it would take to drive from the accused's house to the Maple Leaf Motel?"

"I tested it myself," Alpine said, referring to his police notebook again. "On Monday morning, September 24, at 9:58 A.M. I left the accused's residence and drove at the legal speed limit."

"How long did it take?" she asked.

He traced his route along the map. This was very shrewd. Often lawyers would talk about streets assuming the jury knew the locations they were referring to. But with twelve jurors in such a large city, it was impossible to know if they were familiar with these roads and neighbourhoods.

"Twenty-seven and a half minutes. I parked in the nearby strip mall and walked into the courtyard of the motel. I arrived at the door of room 8 at 10:23:08."

"And remind me please, what time was the initial 911 call received?"

As if she needed any reminder, Greene thought.

"10:39:12," he said, without looking at his notebook, but at the jury instead. Sixteen minutes and four seconds later."

Kreitinger plodded back to her lectern, her footsteps the only sound in the big courtroom.

"Excuse me, Madam Crown," Judge Norville said. "I see it is almost four."

Thank God, Greene thought.

Kreitinger smiled at Norville. "Thank you, Your Honour. I have one more brief set of questions for the detective. I know it's been a very long day, and that Your Honour has an important commitment at City Hall, but if I could complete it, then my friend Mr. DiPaulo can start his cross-examination first thing in the morning."

"Shit," Greene heard DiPaulo mutter. My sentiments exactly, Greene thought.

Norville gave an exaggerated frown. "Okay, be quick."

"Detective, you told us about checking the records on the accused's cell phone, and how you can triangulate the position of a cell phone when a call is received. Were any other phone calls received on his cell phone that morning?"

"Only one. At 11:12."

"And who was that from?"

Alpine pointed to the Crown counsel table right in front of him. "Detective Daniel Kennicott, the officer in charge of this case. He made the call from the Maple Leaf Motel."

"And please, put a last arrow on the spot where the accused was located when he received the call from his fellow police officer."

"Right here," Alpine said, placing the arrow on a side street behind the motel. "Once I got these cell-phone records, I went back to the motel and walked to the spot. It only took me three and a half minutes."

"The accused is a homicide detective," Kreitinger said, "isn't he?"

"Correct."

"Was he a part of this murder investigation?"

"No."

"Had you or anyone else on the police force notified him of the murder?"

"No."

"Or the indentity of the victim?"

"No."

"Was there any reason tied to this investigation why he should have been so near to the Maple Leaf Motel that morning?"

"No official reason."

"Thank you, Detective Alpine," she said.

And with that last piece of evidence, Greene realized, Angela Kreitinger had just pushed him into the witness box.

69

back felt as if it was about to go into spasm. But she wasn't going to break. I did it, she thought. I did it.

Judge Norville looked at the courtroom clock and scowled. It was 4:38. "Ladies and gentlemen of the jury, court will resume at ten tomorrow morning," she said.

The jurors stood up, then bunched up at the exit as they waited awkwardly in line to leave. Much like airline passengers trying to get off a plane.

"Counsel, anything we need to discuss?" Norville asked the moment the last juror was out of the courtroom and the oak door had closed behind them.

DiPaulo stood. "Thank you, no, Your Honour," he said.

Kreitinger could hardly get to her feet. She half stood. "No," was all she was able to say.

Norville nodded at Mr. Singh, seated below her. He rose to his feet in his usual dignified way and announced, "Court stands adjourned until ten o'clock tomorrow morning."

Norville raced off the bench.

Behind her, Kreitinger heard the courtroom fill with noise. A hand touched her shoulder.

"Incredible," Jo Summers said. "You were amazing."

Kreitinger smiled. She didn't want to talk. She wanted everyone to leave so she could savour the moment by herself. She took a deep breath. "I'm going to wait for the court to clear," she said.

"Sure," Summers said. "Can I get you anything? A coffee? A Coke? Sandwich?"

Kool-Aid, Kreitinger thought to herself. Jo, you've drunk the Crown Kool-Aid. She poured herself some water from the silver jug on the table and took a small sip. "No. But thanks. You were a great help."

"I've made a list of potential witnesses for tomorrow. I'll go back and pull out all the files. Lay everything out for you."

Already the hubbub behind them had begun to subside. DiPaulo and the defence team had left. Soon there would be blessed quiet. "Perfect," Kreitinger said between gritted teeth.

"You weren't watching the jury, but I was," Summers said. "I'm telling you, it was incredible. When you showed Jennifer in that video, did you know that one of the female jurors started to cry?"

"I didn't." It was a lie, but Kreitinger had to end the conversation. Her back felt as if a huge hand were squeezing the life out of it. She looked at Summers and her enthusiastic, smiling face and wanted to smack her. God, I'm an asshole, she thought.

"Okay, see you back at the ranch," Summers said.

Back at the fucking ranch? Kreitinger said to herself. What is this? Some rich kids' summer camp? It was a totally unfair thought, Kreitinger knew. *Just leave, Pretty Ms. Perfect. Just leave.* She put one of her hands under the table and dug her nails into her palm until it hurt.

Summers seemed to take a hundred years to pack up her files, but at last Kreitinger was left alone. With her unclenched hand she reached into her vest pocket and took out four little pills. She slipped them onto her tongue and drank them down with the blessed glass of water.

The relief would take some time to arrive, but at least it was on its way. Soon thousands of receptors in her body would open their welcoming arms to the familiar soma of the drug. The heat would spread out across her skin in a luscious, warm wave.

She unfurled her tightened hand. It felt like she could breathe again. She smiled. Of course she'd kept an eye on the jurors. One had cried. Two others had sniffled. A number of them had looked at Greene with a look of total disgust.

Today was the result of six years of re-creating herself. She'd reined in all the excesses of the old Angela and distilled her performance down to a perfect pitch.

She closed her eyes.

I'm back, she thought. I'm back. And it felt good. So, so damn good.

70

GREENE LEANED HIS HEAD BACK IN A COMFORTABLE LOUNGE CHAIR IN THE BARRISTERS' lounge and looked out the floor-to-ceiling windows onto City Hall Square. DiPaulo sat beside him, equally prone. The top button to his court shirt was undone and his starched white tabs were in his hand.

"I don't think I've ever been this tired," Greene said.

"Welcome to the defence side of the courtroom," DiPaulo said. "The opening day of a trial always feels endless. Especially when you don't make an opening statement. It's like travelling for the first time on a road in the dark. Seems to go on forever."

"Tell me this gets easier," Greene said.

"The only good news is that Monday is over. There are only four more days in court this week."

Greene rubbed his eyes. He yawned.

"Nancy's gone to get your father," DiPaulo said.

"I saw him during the lunch break. He's having a great time. Talking to everyone," Greene said.

"Glad that someone had a good day," DiPaulo said.

"Was it as bad as I thought it was?" Greene asked.

"It was worse," DiPaulo said. "I always knew that if Angela could control herself, she'd be a top lawyer. What she did in there was masterful."

"She's forcing me to testify, isn't she? The boots. The video from Coffee Time. My cell phone putting me around the corner after the murder."

"Let's say it's close," DiPaulo said.

"She's not going to call my dad, is she?"

"Highly doubt it. She subpoenaed him to try to catch us off guard. That's no-holds-barred Angela."

Greene closed his eyes. Somehow, foolishly, until today nothing about the trouble he was in had felt real. Despite all he'd been through – being charged with murder, going to jail, the bail hearing, the long days of house arrest – he hadn't really believed he could be convicted and go to jail for twenty-five years. Denial runs deep, he realized. But seeing those jurors, the disgust and anger in their eyes directed right at him, had changed everything. For the first time he was afraid.

"They hated me today," he said. With a great effort he hauled himself to his feet. Blood rushed from his head and he felt dizzy. He steadied himself on a chair in front of him.

"Ari, are you all right?" DiPaulo asked.

"Yeah, Ted. Never better."

He went to the coffeemaker, got two coffees, came back, and sat on the couch. "I started drinking coffee," he said.

"That's progress," DiPaulo said.

"And I sold my big old car."

DiPaulo laughed. "I guess you don't have to be a married guy to have a midlife crisis."

Greene took a sip. The coffee tasted bitter. "What are you going to ask Alpine in cross-examination tomorrow?"

"No idea," DiPaulo said.

Greene looked at him. He couldn't tell if DiPaulo was joking.

"I've spent the last threee months working flat out on this case and going over every detail," DiPaulo said. "When I'm in court, I have to let it happen."

"I don't entirely believe you," Greene said.

"You shouldn't. I'm going to ask Alpine about some things we've never discussed. Watch carefully and please make sure you don't react at all."

"You going to give me a hint?" Greene asked.

"No. You'll have to trust me. And don't be so hard on yourself. You did well today in very trying circumstances."

Greene got back up and walked over to the big windows. People down below were scurrying across the square, clutching their coats closed around their necks. The remaining light of the day was flat and bleak. Low-hanging black clouds had moved in, like prison guards at the gate, incarcerating the city in the oncoming darkness.

71

DESPITE THEIR BEST EFFORTS OVER THE PAST COUPLE OF MONTHS TO AVOID BEING ALONE together, tonight Kennicott and Summers had ended up by themselves in the Crown's office. Kreitinger had only stayed for an hour after court, before saying she was going with a friend to watch the Toronto Raptors play the Chicago Bulls. She said watching the basketball game would help her relax before another big day in court. Alpine had joined them for take-out sushi and had helped them interview a few of the witnesses set to go tomorrow before being called back to division to investigate a home invasion.

They worked in silence. Kennicott was standing by one of the long tables, packing up the evidence boxes to take to court. Summers stood with her back to him, going through a box of folders, pulling files for a legal memo she had to write tonight.

"How do you feel about the case?" he asked at last.

"More convinced than ever that Greene is guilty," she said, without turning around. "But you still don't think he is, do you?"

"All I care about is making sure everything is ready," he said. He tried to imagine how Summers would react if she ever found out that he'd sent Lindsmore to help Greene. She'd probably never talk to him again.

She jammed a folder back into a full box and looked at him. "I have to admit, you've done a good job, Daniel."

"Thanks. But I always wonder what I've overlooked."

"I can't think of anything," she said.

"You've done very good work too." He put the last file into the box he was working on. "I can see Kreitinger is impressed."

"She's a hard-ass, but she cares."

A chime sounded. She reached into her purse, found her cell phone, and turned it off.

"Time for Cinderella to go home?" he said.

She shook her head. "No, I'm staying late. I've got too much to do."

He wasn't sure what to say. Was this a chance to thaw the cold war between them or was he misreading her?

"I'm done," he said. "I have to be in early to line up the witnesses."

She turned back to the table, sat down, and started reading through a photocopy of a case.

He closed the box and put it on neatly on top of the stack in the corner.

"Jo," he said.

"What?" she answered, without looking up.

He took in a big breath. "It's going to sound stupid, I know. But if you're stuck in the city, I do have a second bedroom."

"It sounds extremely stupid." Her back was still to him. "I've got a lot to do. This memo has to be on Angela's desk at seven o'clock tomorrow morning."

"Okay," he said.

He picked up his jacket, walked to the door, and looked back. Her head was down, reading, and she was twirling an errant strand of hair.

"Jo," he said.

"Daniel, please leave," she said, without lifting her head.

He turned to the door, opened it, and closed it softly behind him.

72

GREENE HAD DRUNK A CUP OF COFFEE THIS MORNING BEFORE COURT WHILE HE READ THE newspaper reports about Hap Charlton's inaguration as mayor yesterday, his broad face beaming as the gold chain of office was draped around his neck. Charlton had promptly declared this coming Saturday a "War on Graffiti" day and promised to go the Scarborough Civic Centre to power-wash some walls himself.

Now Greene was back in court and the coffee was churning in his stomach. The jury door opened and he tried to make eye contact with each of the jurors as they took their assigned seats. DiPaulo had instructed him to do this at the beginning and end of the day so they wouldn't feel he was afraid to look at them. But to be careful not to stare. He felt awkward, looking quickly at those who glanced at him and not looking too hard at those who did not.

"Mr. DiPaulo," Judge Norville said after everyone was in place, "your witness."

DiPaulo strode out from behind the long counsel table, leaned against it, and folded his arms.

"How are you this morning?" he asked Alpine, who was back on the witness stand.

"I'm fine, Ted, I mean Mr. DiPaulo," Alpine said.

DiPaulo opened his hands magnanimously. "Detective, we've known each other for many years, haven't we?"

"Yes, sir. We have."

"I used to be a Crown attorney, like my friend Ms. Kreitinger. And you were the officer in charge of many of cases I did, just as Detective Kennicott is the officer in charge today."

"We did lots of trials together," Alpine said.

"You've known my client even longer than you've known me."

"Ari and I have been on the force for a long time. We worked the same division years ago."

"You always respected his work."

"I did." Alpine said.

"And you knew Ms. Raglan."

"Very well. We did many trials together too."

It was as if DiPaulo was having a normal conversation with an old friend. He strolled across the floor and stopped in front of Alpine, blocking his view of Kreitinger. He smiled at the jury. He had no notes. He nestled his elbow into the palm of his hand and cupped his chin. "This whole thing is tough for you, isn't it?" he asked.

Alpine seemed taken aback. "Tough? What do you mean?"

"I mean everything." DiPaulo put his arms out in front of him and walked up to the witness box. For a second Greene thought he was about to give Alpine a bear hug. "Your friend Jennifer Raglan is horribly murdered in a seedy motel. Then a trusted colleague of yours is arrested for first-degree murder. Tough, this is real tough, isn't it?"

Alpine looked relieved. "It is difficult," he admitted. "But I'm treating it the same as I would any other case."

"As you should," DiPaulo said, turning to the jury and letting his voice out like an engine revving up to full speed. "Detective Greene never asked for special treatment, did he?"

"No."

"And he hasn't been given any, has he?"

"Not at all."

Greene realized that DiPaulo was talking about the elephant in the room. Everyone knew this was no ordinary case, and hearing it said out loud was like releasing the pressure from an overblown tire.

"The Maple Leaf Motel had no video camera, did it?" DiPaulo said, his voice taking on a more let's-get-back-to-business tone.

Alpine shook his head. "No."

"This boot mark we heard so much about yesterday, you have no idea exactly when it was made, do you?"

"Exactly when? No, I can't give you a precise time."

"It looked pretty recent, didn't it?" DiPaulo said. "But you agree, even if it was done that morning, the impression could have been made before or after the murder. Correct?"

Alpine took his time answering. He knew from the bail hearing just how important this point was for Greene's defence.

"There's no way to know," he said.

DiPaulo grinned. He went over to the registrar's desk. "Mr. Registrar," he said, "I can never remember exhibit numbers, but can you please pass me that map the good detective put all those yellow arrows on yesterday."

Mr. Singh smiled, warmed by the limelight of DiPaulo's attention. He passed it over.

"Detective, I noticed yesterday when you traced out the route you took a few weeks ago, on that Monday morning . . . You started here, at Detective Greene's house, in midtown Toronto, drove south and east through the city until you hooked up with Kingston Road. Correct?"

"Yes."

"Fortunately, I'm the father of a seventeen-year-old young lady." DiPaulo gave Alpine a big grin. "So last night she showed me how to use Google Maps. You ever use that?"

"Many times. My teenage son showed me how."

This got a laugh from the jury, a smile from Judge Norville, and titters from the audience.

"Well, Google Maps showed that the fastest way to get out there was to go north on the Don Valley Parkway, east on Highway 401 to Morningside, and then down to Kingston Road. Takes about twenty-one minutes." As he spoke DiPaulo traced out the route with his finger.

Alpine stared at the map. He nodded. "Technically it's the fastest route, but not early in the morning."

"Why not?"

"Rush hour. The parkway is usually jammed, both directions. You know how bad traffic is."

DiPaulo went back to the defence table and Nancy Parish handed him a white file folder. On the outside in bold black letters Greene saw the words *Tuesday Morning Drive – DVP – 51 minutes*. DiPaulo held the file to his chest and returned to his spot in front of the witness box.

With his back to the Crown, he opened the file halfway so that the jurors could read the words Greene had just seen, but Norville and Kreitinger could not. "My partner, Ms. Parish, and I have looked carefully through your notes for the rest of the week," he said to Alpine. "On Tuesday you tried going up the Don Valley Parkway, didn't you?"

"I did," Alpine conceded. "It took a lot longer."

"Fifty-one minutes sound about right?"

"It does."

Greene saw a few jurors read the back of the file and then nod along with Alpine.

"So the route you told us about yesterday, along Kingston Road, was the only one that could fit the time frame you had for Detective Greene, wasn't it?"

"I chose the route that I thought someone would take at that time of day."

DiPaulo snapped the file shut and brought it back to his chest. He shot Alpine a fierce look, all his goodhearted folksiness gone in an instant. "I want an answer to my question, Detective. Any other route, and he would have got there too late to commit this terrible murder. You chose the only route that Detective Ari Greene could possibly have taken to fit the time frame. Didn't you?"

Alpine looked chastened. "I did."

DiPaulo stabbed the map. "You work out of 43 Division, which is east of the Maple Leaf Motel. Isn't it?"

"Yes."

"On September tenth, when you went to the Maple Leaf Motel, you drove down Kingston Road from the east, not up it from the west, the way you did on your test drive."

"That's right."

"So you don't know what the traffic was like heading east out of the city on the morning of September tenth, do you?"

"Not that day, no. But in the morning, traffic is usually much heavier going into the city than coming out."

"It usually is, isn't it?" DiPaulo grinned. He was back to his warmhearted self. He tapped the map again. "Farther down here on Kingston Road, west of the Maple Leaf Motel, there's the Scarborough Golf Club on the north side."

"That's right," Alpine said, looking more relaxed.

"Ever play there?" DiPaulo asked.

Alpine grinned. "A few rounds."

"Lovely course, isn't it?"

"It's very nice."

"At this point Kingston Road is six lanes wide, with a concrete divide down the middle. Practically a highway."

"That's right."

"So, if, say, Detective Greene was driving east on Kingston Road, and there was a traffic jam before the left turn onto Scarborough Golf Club Road . . . well, then he would have been stuck, wouldn't he?"

For the first time since he'd been cross-examined, Alpine glanced at the Crown's table. "It's a theoretical question," he said.

Angela Kreitinger rose to her feet. "Your Honour, the witness is right. He's been asked to speculate."

Judge Norville frowned and looked at DiPaulo. "Counsel?" she asked.

DiPaulo smiled. He went back to the counsel desk and put the file in his hands down on the desk. Nancy Parish handed him a red file folder with *Alpine Police Record* written on the cover. He turned back to the judge. "Your Honour, I'm not asking this good officer to speculate about ridiculous things such as, is the moon made of cheese, or will Jennifer Aniston ever get married," he said. A few jurors laughed.

He opened the file as he continued to speak. "I have here Detective Alpine's complete work history as a police officer. In his career, he has worked in the Scarborough traffic unit for seven years. He's investigated, by my count, more than thirty fatal or near-fatal car accidents, six of them on this same stretch of Kingston Road."

He handed the file back to Parish and she handed him another one. It was titled *Kingston Road Traffic Reports for Last Two Years*. "As well, I have summary of the last two years of traffic reports for Kingston Road at morning rush hour. There are forty-three instances of what are termed 'significant delays' on this stretch of road during that time."

Greene could see that DiPaulo had suckered Kreitinger again. Because of her objection, he'd had the opportunity to make his well-rehearsed speech in front of the jury.

"Can I assume you'll be entering all of this information into the record at some point during this trial?" Norville asked.

"It will be the first thing I do, as soon as I call my defence. They'll be made exhibits for the jurors to have during their deliberations."

Norville nodded. "Proceed."

"It's true," Alpine said, without waiting for DiPaulo to re-ask the question.

"If a vehicle gets stuck in traffic at that point, there's no way to get off. All you can do is wait."

DiPaulo shifted his gaze to the jury, calmly handed the map back to the registrar, and returned to his table.

Greene saw Jo Summers open her binder of disclosure notes and begin to flip through it. Kreitinger shot out her hand to stop her, but not before a few jurors noticed.

"Last few questions," DiPaulo said, pouring himself a glass of water and turning back to the witness stand. "The week of September tenth, that was when the Toronto Film Festival was on, wasn't it?"

"I think so."

"It's always the first week after Labour Day, isn't it?"

"It is."

"Most police officers I know have worked overtime shifts at the festival. Have you ever done that?"

"Sure."

"For about ten days, the city is packed with movie stars, isn't it?"

"Happens every year."

"And this year, did you hear that Oprah Winfrey was here?"

A jolt of recognition flashed across Alpine's eyes. Everyone in the court could tell DiPaulo had jogged his memory.

"She was," he said, his voice suddenly tight. "I remember there was a big breakfast event at a golf course with her and Tiger Woods for disadvantaged kids."

"And you remember it was sponsored by the Armitage Foundation, because their son Ralph Armitage used to be a Crown attorney, don't you."

"Yes. They do something for poor kids every year."

"Do you remember where it was held?"

He frowned. "At the Scarborough Golf Club."

"Do you remember what day that was?"

"No," Alpine said.

"It wouldn't shock you if I told you the event was held on Monday, September tenth, at ten in the morning, would it?" DiPaulo said. "And that the whole of Kingston Road was blocked off in both directions."

"I'd have to look it up," Alpine said.

"There will be no need, Detective. We already have," DiPaulo said. He tossed the file back on his table and walked around it. "Those are my questions, Your Honour," he said, and sat down.

This was the evidence DiPaulo had warned Greene would be a surprise to him. And it was perfect, Greene thought. Now everyone in the whole courtroom knew his defence was that he could not possibly have driven to the motel in time to commit the murder. There was only one problem. Greene had never told DiPaulo where he had been on Kingston Road when the traffic had delayed him. And DiPaulo had made a point of not asking.

73

THIS MUST BE WHAT IT IS LIKE TO HAVE A FRONT-ROW SEAT AT THE FINALS AT WIMBLEDON, Amankwah thought as he watched Kreitinger and DiPaulo duke it out in court.

Both lawyers were at the top of their game and the battle lines were clearly drawn. Kreitinger had spent the rest of Tuesday putting a string of witnesses on the stand. The 911 operator who took the original call, the police officers who knocked on doors in the motel and the surrounding neighbourhood, and the owner of the Maple Leaf Motel, who described a woman wearing Raglan's disguise, the sunglasses and red hair, coming in and paying for the room the day before. In cash.

On Wednesday, Kreitinger followed up with the owners of the five other motels on Kingston Road. Each one described similar encounters with the red-haired woman in sunglasses who insisted on paying cash and only wanted room 8. Next came the homicide squad's receptionist, a very organized woman with a British accent. She showed her chart that detailed how Greene had come in late six Mondays in a row. Fortunately for the defence, Judge Norville had disallowed the girl's drawing of a man wearing what looked like police officer's boots. Kreitinger finished the day with the footwear expert, who had told the court that the print on the bathroom door was a possible but not definitive match with Greene's right boot.

Now it was Thursday morning and the coroner, Dr. Fassen, a thin woman with a lilting Trinidadian voice, was the first witness on the stand. From her usual place behind the lectern, Kreitinger had Fassen go through the evidence from the autopsy and her conclusion, which, to no one's surprise, was that the cause of death was manual strangulation.

"Can you please tell the jury what actually happens when someone is strangled to death?" Kreitinger asked.

Faasen swiveled in her chair and faced the jury. "The neck is vulnerable to injury because it doesn't have any bones to protect it. Strangulation causes death when extreme pressure is placed on the airways. The victim first experiences pain, followed by anxiety as he or she tries to breathe. This is a terrifying feeling, known as air hunger, as the lungs desperately search for air. When enough force is applied to impair respiration, the victim will typically lose consciousness within ten to fifteen seconds. It could take another four or five minutes until the heart stops and they are clinically dead."

The gruesomeness of what the doctor said was in strange contrast to the lilting accent in which she spoke.

"And how much force needed to be applied?" Kreitinger asked.

"It's estimated that as little as two-point-five kilograms of force can be fatal. It depends on the relative strength of the parties."

"In other words, Doctor, the stronger the assailant, the more likely he is to able to strangle someone to death?"

Kreitinger looked at the defence table. The implication of what she was saying was obvious. Greene was a tall man, with broad shoulders and big hands, who was clearly capable of choking Jennifer Raglan to death.

"Yes, a stronger assailant can kill more easily. Quicker as well," Fassen said.

Kreitinger quietly closed her binder and walked to her seat.

DiPaulo took his time rising to cross-examine.

What was there left to ask? Amankwah wondered.

DiPaulo stayed behind his counsel table. "Dr. Fassen, you will agree with me that in this case, it is impossible to fix an exact time of death."

"That's correct."

"The act of strangulation can take as little as ten, even eight seconds, or as long as a few minutes. Correct?"

"As I said, it depends on how strong the parties are. But you are right. It can be very swift or take some time."

"After the person is unconscious, the actual death does not happen right away, does it?" DiPaulo asked.

"That's right. It can take a few minutes for the brain to cease to function, and in time the heart stops."

Amankwah had seen many defence lawyers be much too deferential in their cross-examination of medical experts, but DiPaulo was treating this doctor as he would any other witness. Controlling his cross-examination of her and making it seem as if he were as much an expert as she was.

He walked from behind his counsel table. "For the killer to come into the room, commit the murder, make sure the victim is dead, place her neatly on the bed under the covers, as she was found in this case, could all take eight to ten minutes. You agree with that, don't you?"

"Yes," she said, "that sounds about right."

"We know from the Crown's evidence in this case that the deceased arrived at the motel at approximately 10:02 A.M. and that the 911 call was received by the police at 10:38 A.M. In other words the murder had to happen at some point in time during those thirty-six minutes."

"So I understand."

DiPaulo smiled. "Doctor, as a result of your expert examination, you'll agree with me there is absolutely no way to know if that eight to ten minutes started right at 10:02 or began as late as 10:30. Is there?"

"None at all."

"To be absolutely clear. If, on the morning of September tenth, the killer entered room 8 of the Maple Leaf Motel at 10:02 A.M., he could have killed Jennifer Raglan, put her in the bed, covered her up, and been out of there by 10:10. That's right, isn't it?"

"Yes, it is."

DiPaulo turned his eyes to the jury and took his time looking at every face. Many of them acknowledged him with I-get-it nods.

Zach Stone, sitting beside Amankwah, whispered, "No way Greene could have done it if Raglan was killed at 10:02."

"Exactly," Amankwah whispered back.

"No further questions, Doctor," DiPaulo said. He returned to his seat, put his arm on Greene's shoulder, and slowly sat down.

During the morning recess, Stone and Amankwah speculated about which witness Kreitinger would call to the stand next. There seemed to be only three people left. Ari Greene's father, who at the bail hearing had testified that Greene had admitted to him he'd been in motel room that morning. Daniel Kennicott, the OIC, who would tell the jury all about how Greene had deceived him. And, of course, Howard Darnell, grieving husband, but also someone who had to be a suspect in the jury's mind, given what his wife had been up to.

As soon as everyone was seated in court, Kreitinger stood. For the first time since the trial began, she didn't go to the lectern.

"The Crown's next witness is Mr. Howard Darnell." She turned around and smiled at him. Dressed in a blue blazer, grey flannel pants, and a white shirt, he walked slowly to the witness box. He took the Bible and was sworn. He still wore his wedding ring. His hand was shaking.

A man alone, was all Amankwah could think. A powerful witness for the prosecution.

"Mr. Darnell," Kreitinger said, starting right in. "You were Jennifer Raglan's husband."

"Jennie and I were married for twenty-three years."

"And the father of her three children."

"Aaron, Barry, and Corinne."

His answers were as lifeless as his demeanour.

"Sir, I have to ask you this. Did you kill your wife?"

"Of course not," he said.

This is going to be quite something, Amankwah thought. Better settle in for an amazing day in court. He took his notebook out and began writing.

"Where were you on the morning of September tenth?"

"I had lost my job in the summer and, when I look back on it, I realize I must have been very depressed. I hadn't even told Jennie. I was going to tell her that day. In the morning I got dressed and pretended to go to work but instead I rode the subway and walked around the west end of the city all day."

"Thank you, sir, those are my questions," Kreitinger said. Without hesitation she sat down.

What just happened? Amankwah had never seen a key witness in a major trial like this be asked so few questions.

Norville was totally caught off guard. She took a deep breath. Looked at the clock. It was only 10:45.

"Mr. DiPaulo," she said, trying to act for the jury as if nothing unusual had happened.

"He's going to ask Norville for a few minutes," Stone whispered. "Try to figure out what to ask."

Instead, DiPaulo pushed his chair back and walked out from behind his counsel table. He went to the jury box, turned, and looked squarely at Darnell.

"Sir," he said. His voice was softer than normal. "You loved your wife."

Darnell took a deep breath. The whole courtroom waited for him to exhale.

"Very much," he struggled to say. It was as if someone had ripped the scab off a deep wound.

What do you ask after that? Amankwah wondered.

"That's my only question," DiPaulo said. "Thank you, sir."

Amankwah stared at his notebook. Not even half a line of notes. He looked at his watch. It was 10:47. Unbelievable.

Norville looked totally bewildered. "You are free to step down," she said to Darnell.

He looked dazed and relieved as he left the witness box.

"'Not with a bang but a whimper,'" Stone whispered. "Who's she calling next?

Kreitinger stood. Once again she didn't go to the lectern.

"That, Your Honour, is the case for the Crown."

Norville's eyebrows shot up so far it was comical. Amankwah looked at Di-Paulo. He was nodding, as if he'd expected this.

"Mr. DiPaulo, are you prepared to call your defence?" Norville asked, sur-prise still registering on her face. "We've had a long week already, and I'd cer-tainly understand if you wished to take a day to consider your options."

Norville had a hopeful look on her face. She probably wanted to get away for a long weekend at her cottage up north.

"Thank you very much, Your Honour," he said.

"Fine. Then we'll adjourn until Monday at –"

"But it won't be necessary," DiPaulo said.

Norville's shoulders sagged.

"The defence will be ready to go first thing tomorrow morning," he said.

"Tomorrow morning at ten, then," Norville said, not even trying to smile.

74

DIPAULO HAD CLEARED EVERYTHING OFF HIS DESK, AND TO GREENE IT LOOKED STRANGELY naked, like a table in an expensive restaurant with the silver cutlery and linen tablecloth removed. DiPaulo himself, despite being in court for three and a half straight days, looked as alert as ever. They were both relieved to be back at the office for the afternoon, and happy to have the time to prepare for tomorrow.

"You never asked me where I was on Kingston Road when I hit bad traffic," Greene said, taking a seat across from him.

"I know that," DiPaulo said, grinning from ear to ear. "And I'm not asking you now. I want you to think about it for a while."

They both knew that if Greene got on the stand and said he'd been caught up in the traffic in front of the Scarborough Golf Club Road because of the Oprah and Tiger Woods event, the case against him would be in tatters. It offered the perfect explanation for how he had arrived too late to have killed Jennifer.

Of course, if he hadn't been there, then everything was still on the line.

The problem for DiPaulo was that, as an officer of the court, he couldn't knowingly present false evidence at the trial. That's why he had never directly asked Greene the question. He was avoiding an answer he didn't want to hear and virtually inviting Greene to get on the stand and testify that his scooter was caught in the Oprah traffic jam. In effect, he was saying to Greene: *If I'm right about this, great. If not, well, you decide what you want to say under oath. With twenty-five years in jail on the line, if you decided to tell a little white lie, so be it.*

DiPaulo pulled out his cell phone. "My daughter gave me this iPhone for my birthday last year," he said. "She put all these apps and other junk on it. I still don't even know how to use most of them. But the one I love is called 'Clock.' Look, you tap here and there are four things. World Clock, which is perfect for me. I've been dating an air hostess who works for Air France. If I want to call her, in a second I can find out what the time is wherever she happens to be.

Alarm, which I use every morning. Timer, perfect for my workouts. But the one I like the most is this one: Stopwatch."

He put the phone on the desk between them.

"You know, Ari, defence lawyers call it peeling back the onion. You get a case, there are so many facts, and you work and you work and you work. But every time, no matter how hard I try, there's always one simple and obvious thing that I've overlooked. And often it's something that my own client hasn't told me."

Greene watched DiPaulo's fingers caress the rounded corners of the phone.

"Time estimates are the most difficult thing for people in court. Witnesses are constantly saying, 'I watched such-and-such happen for five minutes.' You know what I do on cross-examination now? I take this out and say, 'You're sure it was five minutes?' They always say yes. Then I show them this, and have them push the button. The seconds start to click off, then I take it with me and sit down. I say, 'Okay, close your eyes, play back in your mind what happened, and open them when you're done.'"

Greene had a pretty sure he knew what DiPaulo was after. He reached out his hand and DiPaulo put the phone in it.

"It works every single time in court," DiPaulo said. "People can't stand the pressure of the silence. Usually in less than half of the time they've said, they open their eyes and say that's how long it took. I push the stop button and show it to them and the jury."

Greene held the phone up so they could both see it. "You want me to replay the phone call I had with Jennifer in my mind, don't you?"

"Good guess."

Greene touched the start button and handed the phone back to DiPaulo. Then he closed his eyes. He heard the conversation. It was easy. Her every word had been running in a loop in his brain since the horrible moment he had found her dead.

Ari, Howard texted me this morning and wanted to meet up. I told him I couldn't because I was running. I'm so glad this is almost over. One more week. I can't wait to be with you.

He heard her voice. And her last words to him: *I'll see you soon, my love. Don't be late.*

"Okay," he said, opening his eyes.

DiPaulo touched the screen and looked at Greene. "Thirty seconds short." He turned the phone around. It read 1:02.

They stared at each other.

"Kreitinger made a big mistake in her opening address to the jury, didn't she?"

"How so?" Greene asked. It was foolish. They both knew he was playing dumb.

"She put all her eggs in the motive basket. You were the spurned lover. Jennifer was ending things. Going back to work on Monday mornings. Back to her family."

"And?"

"I looked at your cell-phone records for the other five Mondays. She never called you on any of them. She was super careful. I think she called you that morning to tell you about her husband's text, how she'd lied to him and said she was jogging that morning, and I bet how she told you she was looking forward to ending all your secrecy and finally being together. If she was about to end your relationship, she wouldn't have risked calling you that morning."

"Anything else?"

"You were arrested walking out of a lawyer's office in the east end. The only reason in the world I can think of why you were there is that she must have hired him. I looked up Anthony Carpenter in the Law Society registry. His practice is restricted to two things, estates and family law. She went there because she'd finally decided she wanted a divorce."

"You'd be a good detective, Ted," Greene said. His body was full of nervous energy. He stood up and started to pace. "How did you figure it out?"

"The champagne was the giveaway. A woman who's going to end a relationship with a man doesn't bring champagne to celebrate that it's over. It was meant to be a celebratory bottle, wasn't it?"

"Sounds foolish, doesn't it?"

"Love is always foolish. But a man who is going to see a woman he loves, a woman who is about to leave her husband and family for him, has no motive to kill her. Instead he's got every reason in the world to do incredibly stupid things, such as take off from the scene to try to find the killer, and to hide the fact he was there from the police. Especially if he happens to be a homicide detective."

Greene sat back down. "Does this make my story 'sound true, sound believable'?"

"Very. But only if you get on that witness stand and tell it to the jury. But you don't want to testify because you don't want to hurt Darnell."

Greene started to laugh. "All this time I've thought that Kreitinger was trying to force me to testify. But it was you, wasn't it?"

"I had to wait you out. A modern jury needs to see you step in that witness box, put your hand on that Bible, and tell them that you are innocent."

"I know you're right. But I hate the thought of Darnell sitting right in front of me in court. Saying it to his face. And for his kids to hear that their mother was about to leave their father for me."

"Get over it. Going to jail for twenty-five years for a murder you didn't commit to spare someone's feelings is downright stupid," DiPaulo said. "And besides, I hate to lose."

75

KENNICOTT WORKED LATE SO THAT, AT LAST, HE'D HAVE SOME TIME OFF THIS WEEKEND. RA-chel, the border guard in Buffalo, had texted him that she was going to be in town again to go dancing at the Riva Lounge on Saturday night. What the hell, he deserved it.

It was almost ten o'clock when he walked out of the courthouse into the cold night. A smattering of snowflakes drifted down, hurled about by a strong wind. None of the trees on University Avenue, the widest boulevard in the city, had any leaves left on them, and a couple of work crews in cherry pickers were stringing up Christmas decorations. None of them was lit yet.

The fresh air felt good. He decided to walk and made his way through a series of side streets. Most of the houses had lights on inside. People were in their homes, sitting, talking, being together.

He was extremely tired and yet also keyed up. He probably wouldn't be able to sleep. But he didn't care. For a change he wanted to spend the night at home, instead of at work.

This is what you always wanted, Daniel, he thought as he passed block after block of houses. You worked for years to make it to the homicide squad. And this is your reward. You blew any relationship you might have had with a woman you care for, you arrested the man who took you under his wing for a murder he might not have committed, and you are no closer than you ever were to finding out who killed your brother.

As his favourite law professor used to say about a case when the bad guy won, "Nice work if you can get it."

He walked up Clinton to College Street, near his home. Here, in Little Italy, Christmas had come early. Decorations were hung high across the street, flood-ing the sidewalks with light. Shop windows were all aglow, the sidewalks packed with people and the restaurants filled with diners.

Almost two years ago, on a December night like this, he'd run into Jo Summers at this very spot, right across from the Café Diplomatico, a place where they'd often met for coffee. She had been going out for dinner with a well-dressed, handsome man, and Kennicott had assumed they were dating. Turned out he was her stepbrother, and six months later he had been murdered.

He could picture Jo, turning and smiling at him as they'd crossed the street. He'd better get that image out of his mind.

A few steps north on Clinton Street, he was glad to be in near darkness again. The block and a half walk to his place was quiet. Peaceful.

He was surprised to see a big car, parked half on the sidewalk in front of the house. As he got closer he recognized the vehicle. A Cadillac with the distinctive licence plate HAP on the back.

The driver's door opened and Hap Charlton got out. He had glass jar of tomato sauce in one hand. "Good evening, Detective," he said, as if this were something that happened every night. He held out his meaty hand.

"Hello, Mr. Mayor," Kennicott said, shaking hands.

"Fuck that Mr. Mayor crap. How you doing, Daniel?"

"Fine, sir."

"Hap, call me Hap. I've officially been mayor for three days. Always wanted this job, and already I miss being a cop. Crazy, isn't it?"

Kennicott smiled. He knew that when Charlton was the chief he also always wanted to know what was going on in big cases. Clearly that hadn't changed.

"Your landlord, Mr. Federico, he's quite a gardener." Charlton held up the jar. "He showed me his cellar with his tomato crusher, his canning machine, his stack of mason jars. Quite an operation. He insisted on giving me one. He says you work too hard."

"He's a good landlord."

"Sounds like you're a good tenant."

Stop being an idiot, Kennicott told himself. Charlton hadn't come to here to talk about making tomato sauce. He's here for information.

"Crown closed its case this afternoon," he said.

"So I heard. How does it look?"

"Hard to tell. DiPaulo's theory is that the murder happened close to ten, when Jennifer first got to the motel room. Greene's defence is going to be that he got stuck in traffic and didn't get there until after she was dead. You remember during the film festival, when Oprah and Tiger Woods had that Armitage Foundation event out at the Scarborough Golf Club?"

Charlton twisted the jar in his large hands. "Oh yeah. I'd forgotten about that."

"Well, DiPaulo showed the jury how it bunged up traffic farther down Kingston Road that morning. Raglan called Greene from a Coffee Time near the motel just before ten. From Greene's cell records we've got him at his house at the same time. I had Detective Alpine test-drive from Greene's place to the murder scene. On a regular Monday morning it took him about twenty-three minutes. That means the earliest he could arrive was about 10:23, and the 911 call goes in at 10:39. It's just enough time for him to do the murder. But now DiPaulo's got Greene stuck in traffic, so it pushes back his arrival time. We know from what his father said at the bail hearing that Greene's going to say she was dead when he got there."

Charlton tossed the jar from hand to hand, like a cop with a baton. "I see."

"The time before Greene arrives is a blank. DiPaulo established through the pathologist that the murder could have happened in the first twenty-three minutes, when Greene couldn't have possibly been there."

Charlton stopped fiddling with the jar. "Is there any evidence of someone else going into the room then?" he asked.

"No. Nothing."

Charlton smiled. "DiPaulo's a very smart lawyer."

"We also know from the bail hearing that Greene's going to say he saw someone run away from the scene. That's why he took off and didn't call in the murder."

"Any evidence of that?" Charlton asked, tapping the tin top of the mason jar.

"No. Nothing again."

Charlton put a hand on Kennicott's shoulder. "You look tired."

"One more day to go this week."

"Strange, isn't it," Charlton said. "You worked with Ari for, what, six years. I've known him for twenty-five. He's been my top homicide cop for years. And neither of us can talk to him. In a few days, if he's acquitted, things will probably go back to normal. If he's convicted, I guess we'll never speak to him again."

"I guess so."

Charlton opened the door to his car. "By the way, I had Lindsmore wired when you sent him to check up on Greene."

"You did?" How did Charlton know about Lindsmore?

"Sorry I didn't tell you. Turned out there was no need."

"What did Greene say?" Kennicott asked. Charlton had gone around his back to do the wiretap. But he should have known. The chief was famous for poking his nose into everything.

"Nothing that helps your case. Ari said he was innocent and determined to find the killer."

"Maybe it's true," Kennicott said.

"Or maybe he realized he was being wired and tried to throw us off track," Charlton said. "With Ari you never know. Good night, Daniel."

"Good night, Hap," Kennicott said.

Charlton tossed him the jar of sauce and jumped into his car. For such a big man he was surprisingly nimble.

It occurred to Kennicott that Charlton had made it a campaign issue that he'd drive his own car instead of using a limousine and a driver because of the independence it gave him. He still wanted to know everyone's business.

I better get used to it, Kennicott thought as he walked up the stairs to his flat. And I better get to sleep so I'm in shape for Saturday night with Rachel at the Riva.

76

She had hoped to catch him off guard by finishing her case quickly. But she could see as he walked over to the jury, no notes in his hands, that he was ready. All she could do was watch his opening to the jury and hope that she'd at least get her answer to the big question in her mind and, she was sure, in the mind of the jury as well: Is Ari Greene going to testify?

"Good morning," DiPaulo said with a warm smile. He didn't bother addressing them with the tried-and-true ladies-and-gentlemen-of-the-jury opening that almost everyone else used.

"You've all seen enough courtroom dramas on TV and the movies to know what a lawyer's opening address is supposed to sound like. You probably expect me tell you how important and vital a role you are playing in the justice system and thank you profusely for doing your civic duty. Wax eloquent about the presumption of innocence and tell you over and over again how my client has the absolute right to remain silent. And I'm supposed to speak in solemn tones about the heavy, heavy burden of truth on the Crown to prove its case against my client beyond a reasonable doubt."

Kreitinger saw a few jurors smile.

DiPaulo shrugged. "Well, be prepared to be disappointed. I'm going to spare you all that mumbo jumbo."

DiPaulo had put the jurors at ease, Kreitinger thought. They like him. They'll never like me. But that's not my style. This isn't a popularity contest. Still.

"Life is never as simple as it seems, is it?" He looked at the jurors one at a time. A number of them nodded. "Clearly, for Jennifer Raglan, by the morning of September tenth, it had become very complicated. Hadn't it?"

He walked right up to the railing of the jury box. Put his hands softly down on it and shook his head.

"Why?" he asked. "Because she was loved by two men. Yes. Two good men. Both loved her."

Kreitinger thought back to DiPaulo's gentle cross-examination of Howard Darnell.

Mr. Darnell, you loved your wife.

Very much.

That's my only question. Thank you, sir.

He'd set this up right from the start, she realized. The jury was totally with him.

"Howard Darnell didn't kill his wife of twenty-three years, the mother of his three children. Of course not. He loved her. And Ari Greene didn't kill Jennifer Raglan either.

"Ari Greene loved her too. And that's exactly what he's going to tell you when he takes the stand right here in this court."

He walked over to the witness box, put his hand on the high front ledge, and rubbed it back and forth, comfortably, like a chauffeur getting ready to open the back door of a limousine for a special guest.

"You all know the law. Ari Greene has the absolute right to remain silent. He doesn't have to testify. But of course he will."

Well, that settles that, Kreitinger thought. She'd been up night after night preparing for this cross-examination and had a binder filled with her questions and notes.

"He's going to tell you that he loved Jennifer Raglan. That on the morning of September tenth, thanks to a traffic jam on Kingston Road, he didn't get to room number eight at the Maple Leaf Motel until 10:41. And what happened next was the worst thing that ever happened in his life. Worse than getting arrested. Worse than having to endure this trial. Worse than being publicly exposed for his human failings. Worse than having to see the pain he caused to Mr. Darnell, and his and Jennifer's three children."

DiPaulo's voice rose steadily as he spoke. Kreitinger looked up at Judge Norville. She was staring at DiPaulo, as captivated as the twelve jurors.

"He found her dead. Horribly murdered. Who did this terrible crime? We still don't know. But what we do know, and we know it with absolute certainty, is that Ari Greene loved Jennifer Raglan. Is that Ari Greene did not kill her."

DiPaulo looked at the jurors again, one at a time, went back to his chair, and sat down.

The courtroom was still.

Here we go, Kreitinger told herself. This was going to be the battle of her legal career.

Judge Norville leaned forward. "Mr. DiPaulo," she said. "The first defence witness, please."

77

THERE WAS VERY LITTLE ABOUT BEING A LAWYER THAT KENNICOTT MISSED, NOT THE TEDIUM of the paperwork, the politics of a big law firm, the constant pressure to docket for time, and the difficult, demanding clients. But whenever he was in court and watched a top lawyer at work, it planted a seed of doubt about his impetuous decision to quit the law and become a cop. And it helped him justify his decision to keep paying his annual legal dues.

Watching Ted DiPaulo at work this morning was one such moment. After his powerful opening to the jury, he'd seamlessly led evidence to bolster the key point of his case: that Greene could not possibly have committed the murder because he couldn't have got there early enough.

He started by calling as his first witness Matthew Arban, a technician from a media monitoring firm, who played a tape of a TV reporter broadcasting from Kingston Road at 10 A.M. on September 10. There was a huge traffic jam behind her, caused by the Oprah–Tiger Woods event. Arban also had the audio of the helicopter traffic report from one of the local radio stations, which he played to the otherwise silent courtroom.

Next DiPaulo had a retired traffic cop take the stand. He testified that a vehicle caught behind this mess would be delayed "a minimum of twenty minutes."

Who was he going to call next? Kennicott wondered when he came into court after the morning recess. DiPaulo was up at the front of the court, chatting to Mr. Singh, still looking relaxed.

Clearly he was saving Ari Greene until the end. Would it be the prostitute, Hilda Reynolds? She could introduce the idea that there was an alternative suspect still out there. He thought not. She'd be a terrible witness, and would make the defence look like it was grasping at straws.

Greene's father?

The defence was not allowed to lead an exculpatory statement by the accused, so he couldn't get on the stand and say: *Ari told me he didn't do it.* No, he was only good for the defence as a Crown witness.

"Good afternoon, Mr. DiPaulo," Judge Norville said when everyone was seated. "Your next witness."

"The defence calls Detective Daniel Kennicott."

Kennicott was shocked. He couldn't move.

He felt his whole body jolt. Jo Summers looked him right in the eye for the first time in months, even though they were sitting side by side. Angela Kreitinger swung her head around. She looked stunned.

"Detective?" Judge Norville said. She looked surprised as well.

Kennicott straightened his neck, put his pen down, and walked to the witness box. As he was being sworn he kept wondering why DiPaulo was putting him on the stand. What was he missing here?

"Good morning, Detective," DiPaulo said once Mr. Singh had sat down.

"Morning," Kennicott said. Try to smile, he told himself. Don't let the jury see how confused you are.

"I want to take you right back to room 8 at the Maple Leaf Motel on the morning of September tenth."

"Fine."

DiPaulo went to the registrar, who handed him a cardboard box. He strode right back to the witness box. DiPaulo had dropped the aw-shucks-I'm-never-good-with-things-like-exhibits persona he'd used earlier in the week. Kennicott realized he'd organized everything during the break. He was loaded for bear.

"I have here a number of exhibits that were put in evidence as part of the Crown's case." DiPaulo reached into the box and pulled out the six candles, the iPod and dock, the wig, the backpack, the sunglasses, the champagne bottle, and two plastic wineglasses.

What is he doing? Kennicott wondered.

"These are all items seized from room 8 at the Maple Leaf Motel, correct?" DiPaulo asked. His eyes were fixed on Kennicott.

"Yes," Kennicott said. But there was something missing. What was it?

DiPaulo put the box to the side, reached into the backpack, and pulled out two pillowcases.

"And these two pillowcases as well. They were found like this, inside Ms. Raglan's backpack. Weren't they?"

Kennicott stared at the pillowcases. He couldn't even blink. His mouth was dry. He was such an idiot. How could he not have seen this?

He looked at Ari Greene. This had his fingers all over it.

He's still my mentor, Kennicott realized. And he's just taught me a very big lesson.

78

You have nothing to be ashamed of Daniel, Greene thought. I didn't see this for the longest time either.

It was 3 P.M..

DiPaulo had had Kennicott on the stand for a few hours, going through every detail of the investigation of room 8. Also, as at the bail hearing, he got Kennicott to admit he'd told Greene not to come to the scene. And DiPaulo didn't shy away from what happened afterwards: that the two detectives had met at the bakery, that Greene had never told Kennicott about his affair with Raglan or that he'd been in the motel room that morning.

Kreitinger tried to make some headway on cross-examination, but DiPaulo had put everything on the table and there wasn't much left for her to ask.

"Your next witness, please?" Judge Norville said, glancing at the clock.

"The defence calls Ms. Nancy Parish," he said

Kreitinger bounced to her feet. "Your Honour, Ms. Parish is part of the defence team. How can she be a witness at this trial?"

Judge Norville shrugged. "Mr. DiPaulo?"

"Your Honour, Ms. Parish is going to testify to the results of an examination she undertook as part of the defence. This is no different than if, for example, Detective Kennicott, sitting right here at the Crown table, was called as witness. There's nothing improper about it at all."

"Proceed for now," Norville said.

Parish walked to the witness stand, carrying a familiar-looking backpack, identical to the one Raglan had used that morning. Greene saw that a few of the jurors were nodding. They got it.

"Ms. Parish," DiPaulo asked, once she was sworn as a witness, "I understand last week you rented a motel room. Why don't tell us about it."

"Last Friday, before the trial began, I rented room 8 at the Maple Leaf

Motel. I brought with me six candles, a half bottle of champagne, two new plastic wineglasses, an iPod and dock, and two pillowcases. All of these items were the same as the ones found there on September tenth. I brought them all in this backpack, which is the same size and brand that Ms. Raglan used that morning. I also put in it the same pair of running shoes and gear that she was carrying."

As she spoke, Parish pulled each item from the backpack.

"I also brought a tape measure, a thermometer, a timer, and a camera," she said.

"Tell us what you did when you got to the room," DiPaulo asked.

"I started at exactly ten in the morning. First thing I did was set up the iPod and began playing the same Oscar Peterson song that was playing on Ms. Raglan's iPod that was seized in evidence. Then I went down the hall and filled one of the motel's ice buckets with ice. I brought it back, put the ice in the sink, poured cold water on it, and put the bottle of champagne in it."

"After that?"

"I set up the candles the way they'd been set up that morning and lit each one."

"And then?"

"I took my clothes off, except a one-piece bathing suit I was wearing underneath, and put everything under the bed."

"What about the two pillowcases?"

"I left them in the backpack where they were found."

"Why did you do that?"

"They were made of very good cotton. Much nicer than the ones supplied by the motel. I photographed the ones that were on the pillows when I arrived and compared them with the ones in the crime-scene pictures."

"And?" DiPaulo asked.

"They appeared to be the same. Here."

She had copies of both photos mounted on a small board. DiPaulo paraded it slowly in front of the jury, showed it to Kreitinger and her team, and then handed it back to the registrar to show the judge before marking it as an exhibit.

"As you can see," Parish said, "both sets have the same pink frill."

"Did you check the label to see what material they were made of?"

"They were sixty percent polyester, forty percent cotton."

"And the ones in Ms. Raglan's knapsack?"

"One hundred percent cotton. A heavy weave."

"And why did you leave them in the backpack?"

"I assumed that Ms. Raglan had intended to put them on, but that something had interrupted her."

Such a simple thing but it was the key to whole case. Thank you, Jennifer, Greene thought, for caring about the little details. The small things that really matter. His dad was right. He did know her after all.

"And the music was still playing?" DiPaulo asked.

"It was. This all took me five minutes and thirty-two seconds to set up everything."

"What did you do next?"

"The two plastic wineglasses had price tags on them." She turned to the glasses on the ledge.

"I sat down on the bed and began to pick the tags off," Parish said.

"Why did you do this?" DiPaulo asked.

She started to pick away at the edges of the first label. "In the autopsy report bits of glue and white paper were found under Ms. Raglan's fingernails. As well, we independently tested the plastic glasses that were found in the motel and discovered traces of glue in squares the size of a small label like these ones."

Greene let himself look at the jurors. They were fixated on Parish's fingernails as she picked the second glass clean.

"How long did this take?"

"A little more than a minute and a half. I put the glasses beside the candles on the chest of drawers, as they were found at the scene, and sat back on the bed. It was exactly 10:07:15."

"What did you do next?"

"I sat on the bed and didn't move until 10:15:33."

"Why 10:15:33?"

And thank you too, Oscar Peterson, Greene thought.

"When the police arrived the iPod was not playing. It had been paused at fifteen minutes and thirty-three seconds in. The recording was "Canadiana Suite" and it is thirty-three minutes and thirty seconds long."

"And after that, you say you didn't move for eight minutes and eighteen seconds?"

"That's right. Didn't move."

"Let's see how long that actually is," DiPaulo said. He walked back to his counsel table and leaned against it. "I have a timer right here on my iPhone. I'll start it right now."

The courtroom was silent. DiPaulo, a man constantly in motion, didn't flinch. Silence in such a large space, filled with people, was powerful. As the seconds, then minutes rolled by Greene could feel the tension rise. The words of the coroner, Dr. Fassen, played back in his mind. He hung his head. Every person in the courtroom could imagine the horror of these minutes and seconds of Jennifer Raglan's life.

After about five minutes, he heard someone in the first row start to weep. He didn't dare turn. Didn't have to. Howard Darnell was crying.

So was Greene.

At what point, he wondered, did Raglan realize she was going to die? At what point had his dad known that Sarah would be killed? At what point did Kennicott's brother, Michael, know that his life was about to end?

"That's eight minutes and eighteen seconds," DiPaulo said at long last.

There was a collective intake of breath.

"Ms. Parish," DiPaulo said. "What did you do next?"

"I stood up and paused the iPod, then blew out all the candles, except the one by the bed."

DiPaulo continued with his questions. Everything lined up. Parish had used her tape measure and the four candles had burned down to almost the same level as the ones taken from the scene. The one by the bedside she had let burn until 11:05, the time that Kennicott and Zeilinski had entered the room and blown it out. It was a match as well. Same for the picture of the ice in the sink. She photographed the amount of ice in the water after the eight minutes and eighteen seconds had passed, and then again at the time Kennicott and Zeilinski arrived. The temperature was within one degree of what Zeilinski had recorded. And the two pictures of the half bottle of champagne resting in the icy water were similar.

"Thank you, Ms. Parish, those are my questions," DiPaulo said as the clock in the courtroom neared 4:30.

Judge Norville looked expectantly over at Kreitinger. "Does the Crown have any questions?"

"No questions," Kreitinger said.

There was nothing for her say. DiPaulo had all but proved that Raglan had been murdered soon after she'd arrived in the room, and well before Greene could have got there.

"Well then," Norville said, clearly relieved that she wasn't going to have to lose one minute of her precious weekend. "Court is adjourned until Monday morning. Ten A.M. sharp." She practically flew off the bench.

PART
SEVEN

79

after night he woke up in the dark, his body bathed in sweat, and stumbled down to the basement to play the DVD again. And again. And again.

Jennifer.

He had this cruel need to see her alive, moving. Even if it was only the grainy Coffee Time video. Anything to erase from his memory the last image he had of her, horribly strangled to death in that disgusting motel room.

This morning it had been light outside when he awoke. He looked at the old clock radio on the side table. It was 8:35. Amazing. He'd actually managed to sleep through the night. Baby steps, he thought as he ripped off his soaking T-shirt, and like an addict who needed another fix, went downstairs and clicked on the DVD yet again.

Today he had an idea of how he might wean himself off this habit. He fast-forwarded through Jennifer coming into the doughnut shop, going to the washroom, coming out in her disguise, and going to the wall phone to make her last phone call to him. The last time he'd heard her voice. *I'll see you soon, my love. Don't be late.*

What would have happened if I'd gotten there earlier? he asked himself for the thousandth time. Could he have saved her?

He slowed the video to play as he came to the part where she walked outdoors. Her back came into view. At least he couldn't see her face. That was progress.

He looked at her walking. Swinging her backpack. How many times had he watched her stroll out of view along the bleak, deserted sidewalk? Then turning off the DVD when she was out of the frame.

But this morning, he paused it at the last image of her in view. This is enough, he told himself. One more second and she's gone. Ari, she's gone.

He put the remote down and lay back on the couch. This way madness lies, he thought. He rubbed his face hard and closed his eyes. Tried not to see her. He forced himself to think of the trial. How well everything had gone in court yesterday. How close this other nightmare in his life was to being over. Still, he had yet to testify. Be cross-examined. It all made him feel tired.

He heard the disc start up on its own. He made himself count slowly to ten before he opened his eyes. How bleak it must be to live out there in Scarborough, he thought, looking at the cracked, unused sidewalk, the treeless street, and the cars and trucks whizzing past.

He reached for the remote. Where had it gone? He patted around the cushions on the couch and finally found it. He took one last look and was about to turn off the DVD when he saw it come on the screen.

He bolted upright and watched transfixed as it came completely into view.

He hit the pause button and stared.

"I don't believe it," he said out loud, even though he was alone.

He reversed to the last image of Jennifer, hit play, and watched until it the moment it first came into view. He wrote down the time: 10:01:15.

Then he tore back upstairs to his bedroom. He needed to find his phone. He needed to call Kennicott.

80

"DADDY, CAN WE WATCH TV?"

"What?" Awotwe Amankwah said. He was so tired.

"At Mommy's house we watch TV every morning," It was his four-year-old son, Abdul.

Amankwah's head was pounding. He'd been up until three o'clock, filing his story on the Ari Greene trial and working on his big retrospective piece about Jennifer Raglan. Barclay Church wanted it ready for the day the jury reached its verdict, which, thanks to how quickly things had gone this week in court, could be a heck of lot sooner than anyone had expected.

Fatima, his six-year-old daughter, climbed on the bed and tried to pry his eyes open. "Why can't we watch TV at breakfast in your house?" she asked. "We don't have day care or school today."

Coffee, Amankwah thought. He needed coffee, and Tylenol. "Kids, please," he said. "Let Daddy get up."

"I found the clicker," Abdul said.

"Put it on," Fatima said.

Amankwah flung his arm out to grab his son's hand, but Abdul was too fast. There was a thump across the room, and his old TV clicked on.

"You rascal, you." Amankwah grabbed Abdul's other hand and started to tickle him under the arm.

"Stop, stop, Daddy." He giggled. "Fatima, take it." He held the remote aloft in his free hand.

Fatima grabbed it and jumped away from them on the bed. The screen had come on now and there was a close-up of a reporter, who looked like he was standing in front of the skating rink at City Hall.

At the bottom of the screen the words *Breaking News* crept across in a red banner.

"Yuck, news," Abdul said.

"Police say that this message must have been spray-painted in the middle of the night," the reporter said.

Amankwah let go of Abdul's arm and sat up.

The camera swung to the side to show the message painted across the ice surface in graffiti-style letters: HAP IS A MURDERER.

"A spokesman for newly elected Mayor Charlton says this outrageous . . ."

Amankwah heard a click. A garishly coloured spaceship flew across the screen.

"Fatima, give me that clicker," Amankwah said. Fully awake.

"No, we want cartoons," she said.

"Cartoons, cartoons," Abdul chanted.

They started running around the room singing together: "Cartoons, cartoons, cartoons."

"Okay, okay," Amankwah said. "You can watch cartoons in a minute, but this is Daddy's business. Give me the clicker right now."

"Can we eat our cereal in front of the TV too? Mommy lets us," Fatima said.

"Just today, but I need that clicker right now."

She surrendered it.

"Go get your cereal." Amankwah frantically switched back to the news channel.

Clyde Newbridge was speaking at the other end of the square at what looked like a hastily prepared news conference. His face was red with anger.

"Could there be a better example of why Hap Charlton was elected mayor?" Newbridge said. "This is exactly the type of criminal behaviour he is determined to wipe out."

"We have heard reports that similar messages have been spray-painted in landmarks all around Toronto," one of the reporters said.

"Art? This isn't art, it's vandalism. Plain and simple," Newbridge retorted.

"Does the mayor have any comment?" another reporter asked.

"Yes. This is garbage. To say nothing of outrageous slander and falsehood."

"Do the police have any idea of who is doing this?" a third reporter asked.

"No comment," Newbridge growled.

The reporters' questions continued as a voice-over, while a series of still photos came up on the screen. Picture after picture of the same graffiti message on Toronto landmarks: the CN Tower, the Eaton Centre, the Rogers Centre, the

Air Canada Centre, the Royal Ontario Museum, the Scarborough Civic Centre, the Hockey Hall of Fame.

Every message had a tag at the bottom: AARON 8.

Jennifer Raglan's son had come back with a vengeance, Amankwah thought, staring at the screen in disbelief.

"Daddy, you only have regular Cheerios, not Honey Nut," Fatima said, rushing back in.

He hugged his daughter. "At Daddy's house, you get to put on your own honey."

"Oh," she said, "that's a good idea."

He kissed her on the top of her head before she scurried away.

He reached for his home phone and looked around for his cell.

81

KENNICOTT'S CELL PHONE RANG WITH A SPECIAL RING TONE HE HADN'T HEARD FOR months because he'd programmed it exclusively for calls from Ari Greene. He stared at it in disbelief. What the hell was Greene doing phoning him in the middle of the trial? On a Saturday morning no less, when he was half awake.

He let it ring three times. He could think of a million reasons to ignore it. Let it go to voice mail.

On the fifth ring he answered it. "Ari. Why in the world are you calling me?"

"Daniel, if you never speak to me again in your life after today, I'll understand completely. But right now you have to do something."

"Have to?" Kennicott felt the same anger toward Greene he'd felt when he'd testified at the bail hearing. Except now there was no reason to hold back. "You have the nerve after the way you deceived me, you used me, you made a fool of me, to tell me what I have to do?"

"I can't argue with you. Do you have the DVD?"

"Fuck you."

"From the Coffee Time."

"You think I didn't know what DVD you're talking about?"

"Daniel, I'll give you back your brother's file. I'll resign from Homicide. I'll do anything you want. Just look at the end of the DVD. Go to thirty-two seconds after Jennifer disappears from sight."

"You called me this early on a Saturday morning in the middle of your trial to tell me to watch the video of an empty sidewalk?"

"If it stayed empty, I wouldn't be calling you," Greene said. "Until they fire me, I'm still a cop."

Kennicott looked across his bedroom at the TV screen. The DVD was already loaded. He'd been watching it last night.

"You are too dedicated not to have brought a copy home with you," Greene said.

"Okay," Kennicott said. "I've got it on. What are you telling me to do again?"

"Look at Camera Four, the outdoor one. Fast-forward to 10:01:12. Then pause it."

Kennicott didn't say a word as he hit the button and watched the images fly past. But he could feel the anger in him ebb.

"I'm there, the street's empty," he said. "What's the point?"

"Go slow for the next three seconds."

Kennicott hit the button.

Bit by bit, he saw a front bicycle tire come into view, then the whole bike, and the rider, who was walking beside it. He was wearing a familiar-looking T-shirt. Thanks to the bright spray-painted colours, it was easy to read what was written there: AARON 8.

82

AMANKWAH HAD BOTH PHONES GOING, HIS HOME AND HIS CELL, TEXTING AND E-MAILING. He had to get hold of his sister to take the kids. He had to contact Howard Darnell to tell him what Aaron was up to. He had to get hold of Barclay Church, who'd made it clear many times that if a big story hit, he wanted to be in the loop. And he had to find Nancy Parish. For sure she and Ted DiPaulo and Ari Greene would want to know about this.

His sister was a software engineer and thankfully lived with her BlackBerry attached at the hip. She got his text right away. She was pissed off, but on her way over.

Barclay Church answered his cell phone on the first ring. Either the man never slept, or he had no life, or both.

"Mr. Double A. What a spectacular morning. We so seldom get blue skies like this in England. Looks like our new mayor has angered a local artist," he said. "Tut tut."

"You saw the news."

"The news never stops. That's why we're all addicted to it."

Amankwah quickly told Church how he'd made contact with Darnell during the trial and gained his trust. How his older son, Aaron, had been shipped down to New Mexico for drug rehab but had escaped and got back to Toronto a few days ago. That his son's name was Aaron and his tag was Aaron 8.

"The plot thickens," Church said. "Excellent work."

"This is for your ears only. I promised Darnell I wouldn't print a word without his permission."

"That promise has to be rock solid. You and me and no one else." All of Church's usual flowery sarcasm had disappeared. He's a pro, Amankwah thought.

"In fact I don't think you should have told me," Church said.

"Normally I wouldn't," Amankwah said. "But my gut tells me this whole thing is going to blow up. The case against Greene fell apart in court yesterday. The mayor's got his first big event planned for this morning at the Scarborough Civic Centre. He's going to be power-washing away graffiti."

"Yes, at eleven so he can make the noon news," Church said. "I want you to be there."

"Okay, but send another writer and a photographer."

"Done. We pay you for your instincts."

Next Amankwah called Nancy Parish. There was no answer at her home. He called her cell. She sounded very tired when she answered.

"Awotwe?" she asked. "Why are you calling so early?"

"Only would do it in an emergency. I think you should turn on your TV."

"Well, wait a second."

He heard the sound of sheets ruffling, then footsteps, then a door shut. "Awotwe," she whispered. "What's this all about?"

"Nancy, I feel terrible calling you like this."

"As you probably guessed, I'm not exactly at home."

"Someone's been spray-painting 'Hap Is a Murderer' all over the city."

"What?"

"The tag is Aaron 8. It's Aaron Darnell."

"Wow. I thought he was in the States."

"You didn't hear this from me," he said. "But the kid escaped from his southwestern boot camp a few days ago and is back in the city."

"I've got to call Ted. Thanks, Awotwe."

Next he called Howard Darnell.

"Aaron has emerged," he said.

"I know. My daughter told me already. It's all over the social media. What should I do?"

"Sit tight, and keep your kids home."

"That's what I planned to do. Call me the minute you have news."

"Of course."

Just as Amankwah hung up, his cell phone rang. He took one look at the display and answered it immediately.

"Hello," he said. "What can I do for you, Detective Greene?"

83

GREENE HAD BEEN IN THE *TORONTO STAR* OFFICES A FEW TIMES YEARS AGO, WHEN HE WAS dating a sports reporter who eventually moved to San Diego. The building was located at 1 Yonge Street, at the base of the longest road in the world, as a sign on the outside of the building proclaimed. Amankwah was waiting for them just inside the front door. This early on a Saturday morning, the sidewalks were empty.

"Thanks for coming down on such short notice," Greene said. He'd called Amankwah and told him about what he'd seen at the end of the Coffee Time video. "We really appreciate it."

Amankwah shook hands with Greene and Daniel Kennicott, who stood beside him.

"Not a problem."

"I doubt you expected to see the two of us together when you woke up this morning," Greene said.

Amankwah grinned. "Nor did I expect to see that Aaron Darnell had spray-painted 'Hap's a Murderer' across half the city."

"He must have ridden his bike all through the night. When you think about it, probably the best way for him to get in and out of places fast."

"We have to be fast. I need to get up to Charlton's event at the Scarborough Civic Centre. This story is going viral."

Amankwah signed Greene and Kennicott in at the front desk and in a few minutes they were in the archives room in the basement.

"What was the date you wanted?" Amankwah asked as he went into the stacks of old newspapers.

"September second, 1985," Greene said.

"Here it is," Amankwah said a few minutes later. "It's a front-page story written by Zach Stone. Guy's been around forever."

Greene held his breath as he looked at the headline: JUDGE CHARGED WITH IN-DECENCIES, COMMITS SUICIDE.

"Indecencies," Amankwah said, chuckling. "The *Star* wouldn't be so discreet today."

Greene's eyes were fixed on the story. *Disgraced provincial court judge Jack Nakamura, recently charged with propositioning a police officer in his chambers whom he mistook as a prostitute, has jumped to his death off the Bloor Street Viaduct.*

Amankwah and Kennicott read it over his shoulder.

The story described how Jennie Raglan, an attractive young police officer on the morality squad, had been the police officer involved. Her partner had stayed outside the door in case something happened, and had entered on a prearranged signal and arrested the judge. Her partner's name was Clyde Newbridge. The officer in charge of the case was Hap Charlton.

"Jumping Hap," Amankwah said.

"What?" Greene asked.

"That's Zach Stone's nickname for Charlton. I always thought it was because Hap's such a restless guy. Now I know better."

"Jumping Hap, Jumping Jack," Greene said. "It was his idea."

"And Newbridge was in on it too," Kennicott said. "To think I had him help me arrest you."

Greene kept reading.

"'This was all a police setup,' Nakamura's son Oscar told reporters from the steps of the family home. 'My father wasn't afraid to stand up to the police, and that's why they targeted him. It's a disgrace.'

"'It is understandable that the family would be upset,' Detective Hap Charlton said, when asked about the family allegations. 'But nothing could be further from the truth.'"

Greene put the newspaper down. "Charlton targeted Nakamura because he was the only judge at Old City Hall who had the guts to call the cops liars. This was back when the holdup squad was regularly beating confessions out of prisoners. Whacking them with phone books so they wouldn't leave any marks."

"And Raglan was the bait?" Kennicott said. "But why is this all coming back now, after so long?"

"Because Aaron was in trouble and Hap knew it," Greene said. "Hap had a problem with Newbridge. His and his two buddies were out of control, beating up pimps, extorting prostitutes for sex. No way Hap could win the election if that became public or if the old story came out of how he drove a judge to suicide. Especially a former war hero."

Kennicott nodded. "And Newbridge was coming unglued, because Carmichael and his gang of defence lawyers kept collecting more and more incriminating evidence from their clients. It looks like Raglan was in on this too."

Amankwah looked at Greene. "I'm sorry, Ari, but she was. I'm working on a story about her that's going to come out at the end of the trial and there's some shocking news in it."

"What?" Greene asked.

"Raglan was the one who withdrew all of the charges against Newbridge and his Trio gang."

I know you will be shocked by what I was forced to do. It felt to Greene as if someone had at last pulled a curtain away from a window, letting light into a dark room.

"You sure Jennifer was doing that?"

"I put all the allegations into a chart, and there it was, clear as day. Raglan pulled eighty-three charges for the three Trio cops."

The price of love is so very high.

"Why did she do it?" Kennicott asked.

"We don't know," Amankwah said. "That's going to be my headline: 'The Mystery Died with Her.'"

"No, it didn't," Greene said.

"What to you mean?" Amankwah asked.

Greene pulled Jennifer's letter from his coat pocket and showed it to them. As they read it, he explained to Kennicott how the lawyer on the Danforth, Anthony Carpenter, gave it to him the day he was arrested.

"We searched you," Kennicott said. "Where did you hide it?"

"I didn't. I saw you and Lindsmore and Newbridge on the street, so I had Carpenter mail it to a friend."

"Good thing you did," Amankwah said. "Otherwise Newbridge would have seen this, and told Hap."

"Raglan was planning to go public on the Thursday," Kennicott said when he finished the letter. "That was the day we followed Darnell when he drove Aaron to Buffalo. He told me the next day that the date had been arranged two months in advance."

"Jennifer was waiting for Aaron to be safely away before she told the world that Charlton was using her son to blackmail her into withdrawing the charges against Newbridge and the two other cops." Greene looked Kennicott right in the eyes. "For Hap, killing Jennifer was the only way to keep the lid on it. He found out about our affair, and I was easy to frame."

"Even if he knew about you and Jennifer, how would Hap have known she was about to go public?" Amankwah asked.

Greene and Kennicott looked at each other knowingly.

"Hap has his finger in every pie," Greene said. "Maybe he found out about Aaron going to the States. Maybe some reporter got wind of Jennifer wanting to call a press conference. Maybe he bugged her phone or her house or both. One night I snuck out on my bail to investigate something, and who shows up out of nowhere? Hap."

Kennicott nodded. "I was coming home from work last night, and Hap was waiting for me in front of my house. And now that I think about it, he was shaking me down for information about Aaron."

"That's Hap," Greene said. "We'll probably never find out how he knew, but I'm sure he did."

"Amazing," Amankwah said. "What a story."

"So Aaron is spray-painting 'Hap Is a Murderer' all over town," Kennicott said to Greene, "because he was the witness you caught a glimpse of running out of the courtyard. He took off on his bike before you could find him.

"Aaron must have figured out about Jennifer and me and was following his mother. But Charlton got there first and Aaron saw her being murdered."

"Do you actually plan to arrest the mayor?" Amankwah asked.

Kennicott looked at Greene. "We need to talk to one more witness."

What was he thinking? Greene wondered.

Kennicott turned to Amankwah. "Can you get me recent photos of Charlton and Newbridge. We need to hurry if we're going to make it to the Scarborough Town Centre by eleven."

Smart Daniel, Greene thought, realizing what he had in mind. Very smart indeed.

84

KENNICOTT SLOWED HIS CAR AS THE TRAFFIC UP AHEAD CAME TO A STOP. HE LOOKED OVER at Greene. The irony wasn't lost on either of them, he thought. Here they were, at 10:20 in the morning heading east on Kingston Road, stuck in a traffic jam.

They were on the part of the street where it opened up to six lanes, three in each direction, with very few exits. Almost exactly at the point, half a kilometre west of Scarborough Golf Club Road, that Ted DiPaulo had pointed out to the jury.

Kennicott looked over at Greene. "This look familiar?"

Greene met his eyes, then surveyed the traffic in front of them more closely. "Get into the left lane. That red light up there is Markham Road. It's your last chance to get off before you get totally stuck. Turn left and keep going north to Lawrence, then go east again."

Kennicott put on his blinker and nudged his way into the left-turn lane. "If you weren't caught in traffic the way DiPaulo suggested to the jury yesterday, what were you going to say on the stand on Monday?" he asked.

"Are you asking me if I would have perjured myself about a minor point, such as where I happened to be on this road when traffic jammed up, in order to ensure I was acquitted of a murder I didn't commit?"

"I think it's a valid question." Kennicott made the turn.

"Theoretically, if I was only slowed down by the traffic but not stuck, and managed to find an alternative route," Greene said, "how would I account for being ten minutes late?"

"That's what I'm wondering." Kennicott accelerated up the side road.

"Of course, if I'd parked my scooter away from my house. Say a ten-minute walk or so."

Damn, Kennicott thought. Charlton had been right. He should have done a larger perimeter search right from the start.

"I wish you'd told me this on September tenth," Kennicott said.

"I don't have any excuse," Greene replied. "She was dead when I got there, Daniel. What DiPaulo said in his opening to the jury was true. It was the worst moment of my life."

They drove in silence. Greene hadn't answered his original question about what he would have said in court. Perhaps he didn't know himself.

"Did you know Charlton had Lindsmore wired when he was at my dad's house," Greene said when they were close to the motel.

Kennicott nodded. "He showed up at my house the other night and told me. He kept asking about whether we'd found a witness."

"He was getting nervous. One night a few weeks ago I snuck out on my bail to talk to a source. He followed me, and now that I think of it, he was trying to shake me down for information too."

The Maple Leaf Motel came into view.

"Let's hope she's here," Greene said when the car came to a stop.

"She should be. She has a john who has a regular ten-thirty appointment."

Kennicott had the photos they'd copied at the *Star* with him in a large envelope. A few cars were parked in front of the motel. Business must pick up on the weekends, he thought. He walked to the archway and looked up at the apartment over it. The same dirty sheer curtains covered the window, which was open. The wind off the lake was cold.

"Hilda," he called out.

No one came to the window.

"Hilda," he said again. "It's Officer Kennicott. This is important."

"Shit," a female voice said from inside.

"Hilda, we're going to come up there."

"Ten minutes, okay."

"Hilda, tell your client to go sit in the hall. Lock the door behind you and come down. This will only take a few minutes, I promise."

He heard a scuffling noise, then the sound of a door slamming. Moments later there were footsteps on the stairwell to their side. The door opened and a short, bald man rushed out, avoiding eye contact. He ran to the edge of the lot and jumped in his car.

The door opened again, and Hilda Reynolds stood holding it open. She wore sweatpants and an oversize T-shirt and was smoking a cigarette.

"You've got great timing," she said. "At least I make them give me the money first."

"This is Ari Greene," Kennicott said. "He's a homicide detective too."

"I saw the news," she said, making no move to come outside. "He's the one charged with this murder."

"I am," Greene said. "We can come inside or we can talk here if you like."

"I don't like anything, but there's no way I'm going to be seen with you two in public. And hurry up, it's almost ten-thirty."

She shoved the door open and they both went into the stairwell. The concrete floor was littered with empty potato-chip bags and pop bottles. There was a strong smell of antiseptic.

"I've got a photo," Kennicott said without waiting. He pulled out a recent picture of Clyde Newbridge. "Do you recognize this man?"

She looked at it, turned her head, and blew smoke away from them.

"I told you I was on my knees most of the time."

"Hilda, this is serious."

"I'm not going to be no witness," she said.

"We got the licence plate of that john who just took off," Kennicott said. "You really don't want me to go there and neither do I."

"Okay." She stabbed at the photo. "That was him. He's even fatter than Newman."

"Anything else you can tell me about him?"

"He smoked one of those cheap cigars, the ones with the white tip on it. Smelled gross."

Kennicott glanced over at Greene. "Look at these two pictures." He showed photos he'd picked up at the homicide bureau on his way down to the *Star* to meet Greene and Amankwah.

She pointed to the first one. "It's a kid and a bicycle. Is this some kind of joke?"

"It's no joke at all. Did you see him on this bike? We think he might be in serious danger."

She yanked her cigarette out of her mouth and stomped on it. "Yeah. I saw the kid with the tag painted all over his T-shirt. He was on a bike."

"What about the woman in this second photo?"

"I saw her too, the day she got strangled. Whistling away to herself. Acting like she was a movie star with her sunglasses and that red wig."

Kennicott saw Greene stare at Reynolds, transfixed. He knew what Greene was thinking. Except for her killer, this prostitute was the last person to see Jennifer alive.

"Who came to the motel first?" Kennicott asked.

"She did. Swinging her backpack like she was walking down Hollywood Boulevard. Kid came a few minutes later. I had no idea he was following her or anything. The parking lot inside is good concrete. A lot of them go in with their bikes and skateboards and do tricks. Drives Alistair, the owner, nuts."

Kennicott showed her the photo of Newbridge again. "When did he show up?"

"About five minutes later, after the kid. Maybe less than five."

"Then he comes up to your room."

"Yep, then like I told you last time, when we're done he gets into that white van and takes off."

"Can you remember anything else about the van?"

She shrugged. "I could tell the driver was smoking a cigar too, by the big puff of smoke out his window."

"Do you know approximately what time that was?" Greene asked, jumping in. Kennicott couldn't blame him. This was going to put Hap at the scene of the crime.

"I know exactly when he left my room: 10:25."

"Before your regular ten-thirty appointment," Kennicott said.

She started to laugh. "It's not a john at ten-thirty, stupid."

"Who is it, then?" Kennicott asked.

"*Seinfeld* reruns. I watch them every day." She was giggling now, almost like a child. "I never miss one. I finished off the fat bastard and had him out the door so I had time to make my microwave popcorn, light up a fresh smoke, and watch."

Kennicott shook his head. "Did you look out the window again?" he asked her.

"Yeah, about ten minutes later."

"Why?"

"I mute the sound during the commercials. Stupid me, I went to the window to see if there was anyone waiting for me."

"Did you see anyone else go into the courtyard?" Greene asked.

She looked at him closely. "A few seconds later. Tall guy with broad shoulders, all dressed up in motorcycle gear, including the helmet."

"Where was he coming from?" Greene asked.

"The strip mall next door, he parked near the Money Mart."

"Where did he go?" Greene asked.

She flicked her thumb to the side, pointing toward the courtyard. Like a hitchhiker trying to get a ride.

"What about the kid on the bike?" Kennicott asked. "You see him again?"

"Yeah. I saw him on his bike riding away real fast. Then the guy in the helmet came running out. Then the ambulance and cop cars showed up."

"You see anything else after that?" Kennicott asked.

"Yeah. I went back to watching TV. It was the soup Nazi episode. One of my favourites."

85

Kennicott swung the car around and roared out onto Kingston Road. He lifted his handset for his radio.

Greene grabbed his wrist. "What are you doing?" he said.

"Calling it in. I want to get some backup."

"Backup? I still don't think you see what's happening. They tried to frame me. Now they'll try to put it on Aaron. If they don't kill him first."

Kennicott took his hand from the radio. "And Newbridge is going to be listening." He put his hand back on the wheel.

"We have to get there," Greene said.

"How can you be so sure Aaron will be there?"

"Why do you think he sprayed 'Hap Is a Murderer' graffiti all over the city? He's calling Hap's bluff."

Kennicott was a good driver. He zipped through traffic. "Maybe I owe you an apology too," he said after a few minutes.

"You don't owe me anything," Greene said. "I was proud of you, even if I was the one who got snared."

"I should have thought of those candles and the Oscar Peterson tape. And the pillowcases."

They were approaching the civic centre. Media trucks were all over the place.

"Don't eat yourself up over it. I didn't see it for the longest time," Greene said. "Throw the car up on the grass and let's run."

Kennicott hopped the curb and in seconds they were parked. "Jennifer was brave, wasn't she?" he said just before they got out of the car.

Those were the words, Greene realized, he was longing to hear. "She was very brave," he said.

86

THIS HAD TURNED INTO A PERFECT MEDIA STORM, AMANKWAH THOUGHT AS HE LOOKED UP from the crowded main-floor atrium of the Scarborough Civic Centre. Five stories of circular balconies were packed with spectators looking down on the stage that had been set up for Hap Charlton to make his first appearance as mayor.

On what would normally be a quiet Saturday morning for news, the dramatic story of a graffiti artist spray-painting up Toronto, accusing the city's newly elected mayor of murder, was everywhere. As if that weren't enough, to highlight Charlton's antigraffiti campaign, a garage door covered with ugly spray-painted designs had been brought in and placed at the back of the stage. Two members of his rugby team were holding it up, and behind them four others were hoisting a gigantic sheet of plastic. Another sheet protected the floor. A power washer was in front of it, and soon Charlton was going to come out and use the gunlike nozzle to clean it off.

Put it all together, and you had a news tsunami.

Amankwah had rushed up here after his meeting at the *Star* with Greene and Kennicott and snagged a spot near the front. TV cameras and reporters were everywhere. Two raised platforms had been put up near the back of the main floor with microphones for citizens to ask questions.

Charlton's support people had already warned the press that the new mayor wasn't going to talk to them about the incendiary "Hap Is a Murderer" tags that had been discovered overnight. Instead he planned to have a "direct dialogue with the people of Toronto."

The rest of Hap's rugby team was in the front row, leading the crowd in a new chant: "Hap is our mayor. Hap is our mayor." Everywhere hc looked in the audience, Amankwah could see police officers walking through the crowd, their progress impeded by the crush of people.

The back door behind the stage opened and Charlton strode in, his arms raised above his head in his now-familiar Rocky-style entrance. He wore a sweat-shirt, jeans, and gloves. A pair of work goggles were perched on his head.

He went right up to the microphone at the front of the stage.

For a moment he was silent. Amankwah could see he was scanning the crowd. Looking for someone.

"Welcome, Toronto," he said. "Today in my first public appearance since my election on Monday. By now you've all heard about the latest graffiti garbage that has littered our city this morning. That's exactly why you elected me. This has got to stop, starting right now."

There was a roar of approval from the crowd.

"Hap is our mayor. Hap is our mayor," the rugby players bleated, like a chorus of sheep, and everyone soon joined in.

Charlton moved over to the power washer and picked up the long hose. He swung it back and forth, quieting the crowd. His eyes still alert, looking.

"It's time to clean up our city." He pulled the goggles over his eyes. An aide rushed up behind him and started up the pressure washer. It made a loud rattling sound.

"Give me some juice," Charlton yelled as he aimed the water spray at the offending paint.

The rugby players started yelling "Hap, Hap, Hap" above the noise and soon the whole hall was chanting along.

Charlton sprayed off a few letters from the door, a rather token effort, Amankwah thought, before he signalled for his aide to turn the machine off. The water stopped. So did the noise. He strode back to the microphone, holding the nozzle in his hand like a gunslinger who'd just won a shoot-out at the O.K. Corral.

"Don't let anyone tell you that's art," he said. "It's garbage."

The audience cheered even louder.

"And we're going to get rid of all if it. Brick by brick."

Amankwah could see he was scanning the crowd again.

"We all hear too much from the media," he said, "so today I want to talk to you, the real people of Toronto. I see folks are already lined up at the two wireless microphones we have set up. Fire away your questions."

"The fence at the dog park in our neighbourhood has been broken for six months," a woman with a cane said. "Who do I call to get it fixed?"

Charlton pointed to himself. "Call me."

The hall erupted in applause.

"I'm not kidding. Give one of my aides your number and we'll take care of it Monday morning."

For twenty minutes he answered questions about cracked sidewalks, front pad parking, noise bylaws. But Amankwah could see he looked uneasy, constantly scanning the room.

Suddenly he pointed the hose at a young man wearing a hoodie, who was near one of the microphones.

"There he is," Charlton shouted.

Amankwah saw Clyde Newbridge, Charlton's fat partner in crime, push his way through the crowd to get to the young man. The man jumped to the front of the other people in line and grabbed the wireless microphone. He flung back his hood.

"Hap Charlton killed my mother, Jennifer Raglan," Aaron Darnell shouted. His voice rang out, silencing the huge hall. "I was there. I saw it. I have the proof."

"Get him, stop him," Charlton yelled.

Amankwah saw Newbridge tossing people aside, like a bowing ball scattering pins.

Darnell jumped off the edge of the platform and disappeared into the crowd, clutching the mike.

"She was in room 8 of the Maple Leaf Motel. I was there. I saw him strangle her," his voice soaring to the upper levels.

Newbridge was stomping his way toward him.

Charlton's face turned crimson. His eyes flashed in anger. He barrelled down from the stage, dragging the pressure washer behind him.

"Form a block," he shouted at his rugby players in the front row. They turned toward the crowd, shoulder to shoulder, and started advancing like infantry.

"Out of my way," Charlton yelled at the people in front of him. He pulled the trigger and sprayed them, opening a gap for his gang.

"I saw Hap Charlton drive away in a white van. Detective Greene came after. He's innocent," Darnell's voice said. "I was scared and I ran."

People were rushing to get out of the way. Amankwah saw the top of Darnell's hoodie, burrowing through bodies like a frightened animal. Newbridge was gaining on him.

"I didn't know who the man in the room was when he killed her," Aaron said, his voice soaring. "I was away during the election. But I just got back and saw Hap's face all over the city. It was him. He's a murderer."

Another police officer, even larger than Newbridge, jumped in the fat cop's way. Then, seemingly out of nowhere, Daniel Kennicott and Ari Greene appeared, and stood in front of Aaron.

Amankwah looked back at Charlton. He'd got to the end of the power-washer cord and had dropped the nozzle. His rugby players had scattered. He tried to push his way through the crowd but a group of men grabbed him and wrestled him to the ground.

TV cameramen and photographers shoved their way through to capture the moment. Amankwah recognized the man with a camera who got there first. It was Barclay Church, beaming from ear to ear.

PART
EIGHT

87

IT WAS HARD FOR ANGELA KREITINGER TO BELIEVE THAT SHE'D BEEN BACK IN TORONTO FOR only eight weeks. It felt like a year since she'd spotted the CN Tower on her early-morning drive into the city. Today was a very different Monday morning. After the wild events of the weekend her case against Ari Greene had gone south. Where does that leave me? she wondered. It was a good thing that she was on a weekly lease at her hotel apartment.

"All rise," the friendly court registrar said, walking into court before Judge Norville, who rushed up to her raised seat with what seemed like an extra spring in her step.

The courtroom was packed with reporters. Even some of the American networks had picked up on the story of the chief-of-police-turned-mayor who had been charged with first-degree murder.

Last night Kreitinger had called Ted DiPaulo and told him what she was going to do today.

"You are a formidable opponent," he'd said. "Don't hang your head, Angie, you did a very good job. No one should blame you that in the end it was the wrong guy."

"Thanks, Ted," she'd replied. "Means a lot coming from you."

Then she'd called Howard Darnell.

"I understand," he'd said.

"How is Aaron?" she'd asked.

"He's pretty shaken up. But we're all glad he's safe and that he's home."

Norville took her glasses off and peered down at Kreitinger. "Madam Crown, given recent events, is there any need for me to bring in the jury?"

Kreitinger took her time rising from her seat. My fucking back, she thought, resisting the urge to reach behind her and rub it.

Her day had started at seven in the head Crown's office, where she had met with Albert Fernandez, Jo Summers, and Daniel Kennicott. Kennicott, to his credit, hadn't gloated and made no mention of his doubt about Greene's guilt. Summers looked stunned. Her emotions had been whipsawed, from her grief at the murder, to her anger at Greene and her absolute belief in his guilt, to shock at this sudden turn of events. Fernandez was his usual, cool professional self. Together they had worked out the exact wording of what Kreitinger would say in court.

"Thank you, Your Honour. I ask you to wait to bring in the jury until I have made a statement." She plodded to the lectern with a pad of paper in one hand and a glass of water, which Summers passed to her, in the other. What was about to happen was a show trial for the media and for the court record. She cleared her throat and started to read.

"Your Honour, in the last forty-eight hours information relevant to this case, which was not previously known to the police or the Crown attorney's office, has come to light. As a result, the Crown has done a thorough review of all of the new evidence now available, all of which, I want to emphasize, was immediately shared with defence counsel."

She took a long drink. Her throat was dry. Strange to feel nervous at this moment, when the trial was about to end and when all she had to do was read a few more words on a page. But that's how she felt.

"Last evening, once the Crown had decided how it wished to proceed in this matter, I spoke to defence counsel and conveyed to him what the Crown's office would do in this court today. I wish to emphasize that there is no question in my mind, and this opinion is shared by senior members of the Crown's office, that Detective Daniel Kennicott was fully justified in his arrest of the defendant."

In Fernandez's office they'd discussed how to refer to Greene in the statement. Summers still wanted to call him the accused, but Kreitinger, to everyone's surprise, insisted on calling him the defendant.

"As well, I again wish to emphasize that before this new information came to light, the Crown had every reason to prosecute this case in the manner in which it did."

She paused. Looked at the glass of water, but decided not to drink any more. Next sip was going to be with a pill, or three, she thought.

She looked down at the final paragraph. The power of words always amazed her. How strange it was going to be to have it all come to an end when she read these last two sentences.

"In all of the circumstances," she said, "the Crown has concluded that there is no reasonable prospect of conviction in this case and it is no longer in the public interest to continue this prosecution. Therefore I ask that the charge of first-degree murder against Detective Ari Greene is withdrawn."

She'd made one change herself after the meeting this morning. From "the defendant" to "Detective Ari Greene."

She walked to her seat. No one in the courtroom seemed to breathe. A fresh stab of pain hit her back but she was determined to ignore it.

Ted DiPaulo stood. Beside him Greene sat with his hands over his eyes.

"Your Honour," DiPaulo said, "I wish to thank my friend. She has acted in the finest tradition of the Crown's office. On behalf of my client, he is glad his ordeal is over. And he has asked me to convey to the family of Ms. Raglan his most sincere regrets for their terrible loss."

To Kreitinger, things seemed to move as if everyone was on autopilot. Norville asked Mr. Singh to bring the jury back in. They took their seats, she thanked them for their service to the community and dismissed them. They filed out.

"I want to thank both counsel for the professional way in which they handled a most difficult case," Norville said, and then was gone.

The courtroom erupted in noise but Kreitinger couldn't really hear any of it. Jo Summers gave her a hug. Kennicott shook her hand.

Albert Fernandez, who'd been sitting in the front row, came over.

"I hope you haven't packed up your apartment," he said, smiling. "I just spoke to the ministry. All your tests are clean. We want you to stay and prosecute Newbridge and Charlton."

Behind her, people were quickly leaving the courtroom. Soon it would be empty, the way she liked it most. "Can I get the rest of the day off?" she asked.

"I think we can handle that," he said. "See you tomorrow at seven."

88

ARI GREENE FELT NUMB AND TIRED AND RELIEVED AND ANGRY AND EXPOSED AND ALL HE wanted to do was go back at last to his own house.

Before they had walked into court this morning, DiPaulo and Parish had suggested a complicated way they could sneak out of the building and avoid the media. He'd thanked them, but he wanted to get it over with right away. Otherwise they would hound him for days.

Still, he wasn't going to hurry. The reporters could wait. He wanted to sit and take this all in.

At the Crown counsel table, he saw Albert Fernandez and a few of his fellow prosecutors huddle around Angela Kreitinger and Jo Summers, shaking their hands and patting them on the back.

Daniel Kennicott stood back from them. He looked over at Greene and smiled. Greene smiled back.

A warm hand wrapped around Greene's fingers. "Congratulations, Ari," Parish said.

DiPaulo clamped a hand on his shoulder. "Absolutely. How do you feel?"

"About five hundred emotions at once," Greene said.

"That's how it always is with my clients. People win a big case and the world expects them to be ecstatic. But it's an emotional roller coaster. Relief, of course. But your emotions will be all over the map for the next few days."

"You're probably right," Greene said. "I really don't know how to thank the two of you."

"Thank yourself," DiPaulo said. "You solved the case."

"Once a detective, always a detective."

"Even after all this?" Parish asked.

Greene shrugged. "I've heard the top brass can't decide if they want to hold a discipline hearing and suspend me for a year for dereliction of duty or make me the new chief."

"Which would you prefer?" she asked.

"Tough call."

Everyone smiled.

Greene looked at Kennicott. He was thinking of going over to talk to him, but now Kennicott was talking to Jo Summers.

"Let's all go for lunch and celebrate," DiPaulo said, packing up his briefcase.

Greene pointed to the back of the courtroom, where his father looked like he was having the time of his life talking to Arnold Lindsmore and Fraser Dent, his two new best friends. "I have to take a rain check, Ted. I've got a date with those characters."

"Dinner?"

Greene shook his head. "Last night after I got the final word they were pulling the charge, I booked a flight to London. I'm going to see an old friend. I need to get out of here for a while."

"Smart move," DiPaulo said.

He hugged both his lawyers.

The courtroom was emptying out. He saw Awotwe Amankwah, who had been sitting with his fellow reporters, approach.

They shook hands.

"Congratulations," Amankwah said.

"Not the kind of victory I wanted," Greene said.

Amankwah looked around, to make sure they were alone. "I've killed the Jennifer Raglan story. My editor's not happy with me, but he understands. I think everyone's been through enough."

"Maybe her secret did die with her after all," Greene said.

"Feels like how it should be."

"I'll give you a quote for the record."

"I didn't come to get a quote."

"I know," Greene said. "But here it is. 'May she rest in peace.'"

89

NO GOOD DEED GOES UNPUNISHED, DANIEL KENNICOTT THOUGHT. JENNIFER RAGLAN'S HO-micide was still his file. Now that the trial of Ari Greene had collapsed, he had to get back to work on the case against Hap Charlton and Clyde Newbridge.

At the other end of the counsel table a group of Crown attorneys had surrounded Angela Kreitinger and Jo Summers.

Kennicott had only brought his trial binder with him to court. He put it in his briefcase. He felt like an outsider at a party. It was time to go.

He took one last look at Summers. She turned her head and broke away from the crowd. He wasn't sure what to do, so he put out his hand. She took it. It felt strange to shake hands with her, but what else could he do?

"You're the hero of the day," she said,

"No one's counting," he replied.

"Can we talk outside for a minute?"

"Sure. Then I have to get back to the office."

"It's only a few blocks, why don't I walk with you."

They left the courtroom through the barristers' entrance and exited the building through the north door, where there was no press.

He squinted into the early December sun, low and strong against the sky.

They walked in silence up Centre Street. A block north of Dundas, she directed him down an alley beside the Dentistry Faculty and they sat on a deserted wood bench. No one was around. She looked at him.

"I'm moving to Vancouver," she said.

"Oh," he said. Thinking how dumb that sounded.

"I got a Crown's job. Three-year contract. They love that I speak Chinese."

"I'm sure they do."

"I'm not going alone, Daniel. There's a lawyer from the firm where I used to work. We've been friends for years and, well, about a month ago it just happened. He's getting a transfer. Going to be heading up the Vancouver firm's litigation department."

Kennicott didn't know where to look. He thought back to the night last week when he'd offered her a place to stay in his spare room if she missed her ferry. He felt like an idiot all over again. "I'm happy for you," he said.

"You met him once. Remember a few years ago, when I ran into you at that Chinese restaurant on Spadina? The Valentine's Day Singles Night? His name is Roger Humphries."

"There were a lot of people there." He shrugged.

"You sat beside him at dinner."

He remembered Humphries now. A fat guy. Friendly as hell.

"That's right," she said, reading his eyes. "The fat guy. Everyone is a bit shocked. Roger said he'd go on a diet and I said don't bother."

He was desperately trying to think of something to say that didn't sound trite or foolish. "Your father's going to miss you."

"I know. But the sailing out there is amazing. He's already talking about coming in the spring. Someone at the club has a contact who will rent him a great boat."

"When do you leave?"

"Now that this case is over, next week."

She was sitting close to him. Their shoulders touching. The park bench was in the shade, and his hands were cold.

"You selling your place on the island?" he asked.

She reached behind her head and took out the hair clip that she always wore. Her hair tumbled across her face. She looked straight at him.

Had he ever noticed that hint of green at the edge of her blue eyes?

"I'm renting it out."

It felt like slow motion. She brought her head closer, her hair cascading around his face. Her lips to his ear. "I had to do this, Daniel," she whispered. "I was drowning."

He was about to speak, but she put her finger to his lips. "Don't say a word and don't you dare be sad. We both know there'll be someone else for you. *Cherchez la femme, mon amour.*"

She took her finger from his lips, and kissed him.

90

that he'd meet them in the front foyer in few minutes. There was one person Greene wanted to talk to, and he was still sitting in the courtroom.

Greene walked over and sat beside Howard Darnell.

Darnell didn't move.

"How's Aaron?" Greene asked.

"Home," Darnell said. "I think he's going to stay this time."

"Good," Greene said.

"You saved his life on Saturday," Darnell said.

"That was only one day," Greene said. "You and Jennie are the ones who saved him."

They sat in silence. The journalists had all left the court. Greene had seen Daniel Kennicott and Jo Summers leave a few minutes earlier, and now he watched Kreitinger shake hands with Ted DiPaulo. Then all the lawyers from both sides filed out together.

"Are they going to arrest Aaron for the graffiti?" Darnell asked when they were by themselves.

"No. I took care of that last night."

"Small mercies."

"He's going to have to testify at Charlton's trial," Greene said. "It won't be easy for him."

"I know. Angela Kreitinger has recommended a new drug counsellor. The fellow sounds smart and down-to-earth. Who knows, maybe it will work."

"Hope so."

After another long silence, Darnell said, "I have to tell you something. I did steal that thirty thousand dollars from my firm."

"I know," Greene said.

"You do?"

"In the early days of the investigation, when you were still a suspect, I had Kennicott pull all of your financial records. Jennie's too. I saw thirty thousand go in and out of your account in the middle of June. I checked the fees of that place in New Mexico where you sent Aaron. They require a nonrefundable thirty-thousand-dollar deposit ninety days in advance."

Darnell didn't move. "She always said you were a good detective. What did Kennicott say?"

"I didn't tell him. Or anyone else. Why would I?"

"Because I'm a thief?"

"You're a father. You had to save your son."

The guards at the back door had left now. The courtroom was empty except for Mr. Singh, who was responsible for locking up. He had his head down, busying himself at his desk. Not wanting to rush them.

Greene stood up.

"I have to ask you one last question," Darnell said, standing too.

"Of course," Greene said.

"Why would Jennie bring champagne if this was going to be your last time together?"

"It was my idea," Greene said. "A final toast."

Darnell nodded. "Now the bottle's sitting somewhere in an evidence box. Which I guess will be its final resting place."

He picked up his overcoat, slung it over his arm, and walked out of the courtroom without looking back.

Greene looked at the chairs behind the Crown's counsel table, where he'd sat so many times with Jennifer.

He walked to the front of the court.

"What's on the docket tomorrow, Mr. Singh?" he asked.

"Lots." He looked up from his well-ordered desk and gave Greene a pleasant smile. "There's never any shortage of crime, is there, Detective?"

ACKNOWLEDGMENTS

When I was an English student at the University of Toronto, I had a special professor named J. Edward Chamberlin (whose new book, *Island: How Islands Transform the World,* will be out by the time you read this). A quiet, thoughtful man, he was loath to criticize anyone.

In my final year, I dashed off an essay on John Keats the night before it was due. I can still see myself a few days later walking into his book-filled office. He gave me his usual warm smile, then his face turned grave. "Bobby, I've given you an A," he said, "but this is the last time. Writing comes too easily to you. You must work harder."

There was nothing I could say. I'd been caught out. He was right. They were words that drove me like no others.

After I graduated I didn't see him again for many years. Then one Halloween night, I was taking my oldest son out trick-or-treating in our new neighbourhood. We knocked on a door and to my amazement Professor Chamberlain answered it. I mumbled an awkward hello then dashed with my son off his front porch. For years I made a point of avoiding his street.

In 2009, when my first novel was published, I worked up the nerve to knock on his door again. Sure enough, he'd moved to Vancouver. I found his e-mail address and wrote:

Professor Chamberlain:

I was a student of yours back in the 1970s and have always looked forward to the time when I could present to you a book that I was able to get published. Fortunately that day arrived and my first novel, Old City Hall, *has recently been published in nine languages.*

I'd love a chance to meet you again after all these years and give you a copy. It would mean so much to me.

10

25

The same day he wrote back:

Dear Bobby (if I remember rightly . . . or maybe you are now a more stately Robert, as befits a distinguished author! If so excuse the old handle),

It is so good to hear from you with such splendid news. Congratulations. This is a real achievement. I'm very much looking forward to reading Old City Hall. *Good on you.*

Later that year he was in Toronto. We met for coffee and I brought my faded Keats essay with me, his red-marked comments still there on the front page. When I showed it to him and told him how much his words and teaching had meant to me, tears came to both of our eyes.

Now Professor Chamberlin insists that I call him Ted. I'm still getting used to it.

Which leads me to thank those who have helped me with this novel. (Please note: feel free to skip this paragraph as it is filled with names that will mean nothing to you.) Matthew Arbeid, Paul Barker, David Basskin, George Chaker, Alison Clarke, Carey Diamond, Natalka Falcomer, Ash Farrelly, Joseph Frankel, Bonnie Freedman, Elizabeth Fisher, Dr. Marc Gelman, Edward Greenspan, Anneliese Grosfeld, Gary Grill, Kevin Hanson, Angela Hughes, David Israelson, Amy Jacobson, Christina Jennings, Jake Jesin, Nicola Jowett, Justine Keyserlingk, Tom Klatt, Denise Kask, Marvin Kurz, Corinne LaBalme, Julie Lacey, Michael Levine, James Levine, Howard Lichtman, Kathy McDonald, Douglas Preston, Jim Rankin, Michelle Sheppard, Alvin Shidlowski, Victoria Skurnick, Patty Winsa.

A special nod to Travis West, my online guru, for redoing my webpage. (You can check it out at robertrotenberg.com and sign up as a subscriber. Don't worry, I only send out short and funny updates a few times a year and *no one* gets your e-mail address but me.)

Plus a shout-out (wouldn't you love to know who came up with that phrase?) to Dinah Forbes, my extraordinary new editor.

And of course to my wife, Vaune Davis; my children; and all those close to me. On to book five.

Toronto
December 2012